THE IRISH ORPHAN'S SECRET

RACHEL WESSON

Storm

This is a work of fiction. Names, characters, businesses, places, events and incidents are either the products of the author's imagination or used in a fictitious manner. Any resemblance to actual persons, living or dead, or actual events is purely coincidental.

Copyright © Rachel Wesson, 2026

The moral right of the author has been asserted.

All rights reserved. No part of this book may be reproduced or used in any manner without the prior written permission of the copyright owner. This prohibition includes, but is not limited to, any reproduction or use for the purpose of training artificial intelligence technologies or systems.

To request permissions, contact the publisher at rights@stormpublishing.co

Ebook ISBN: 978-1-83700-293-1
Paperback ISBN: 978-1-83700-295-5

Cover design: Eileen Carey
Cover images: Arcangel

Published by Storm Publishing.
For further information, visit:
www.stormpublishing.co

ALSO BY RACHEL WESSON

The Resistance Sisters
Darkness Falls
Light Rises

Hearts at War (WWII)
When's Mummy Coming?
A Mother's Promise

WWII Irish Standalone
Stolen from Her Mother

Orphans of Hope House
Home for Unloved Orphans (Orphans of Hope House 1)
Baby on the Doorstep (Orphans of Hope House 2)

Women and War
Gracie Under Fire
Penny's Secret Mission
Molly's Flight

Hearts on the Rails
Orphan Train Escape
Orphan Train Trials
Orphan Train Christmas
Orphan Train Tragedy
Orphan Train Strike
Orphan Train Disaster

Trail of Hearts – Oregon Trail Series

Oregon Bound (Book 1)

Oregon Dreams (Book 2)

Oregon Destiny (Book 3)

Oregon Discovery (Book 4)

Oregon Disaster (Book 5)

12 Days of Christmas Coauthored Series

The Maid (Book 8)

Clover Springs Mail Order Brides

Katie (Book 1)

Mary (Book 2)

Sorcha (Book 3)

Emer (Book 4)

Laura (Book 5)

Ellen (Book 6)

Thanksgiving in Clover Springs (Book 7)

Christmas in Clover Springs (Book 8)

Erin (Book 9)

Eleanor (Book 10)

Cathy (Book 11)

Mrs. Grey (Book 12)

Clover Springs East

New York Bound (Book 1)

New York Storm (Book 2)

New York Hope (Book 3)

For the lost, the silenced, and the forgotten –
the women and children of the Magdalene laundries and all who suffered in their shadow.
You are remembered.

PROLOGUE

SUMMER 1912

Rosie's hooves clopped along the stony lane, ears flicking as though she knew the way to the sea. The trap rattled behind her, piled with baskets, buckets and spades, and a creel or two for any fish they might catch. Ellen sat between Mam and Da, breathing in the morning air, storing up the feeling of being pressed between her parents, listening to Patrick's tuneless whistling as he dangled his legs over the side, and Seamus joking as he sat holding a spade like a soldier's pike.

Days like this didn't come often anymore, not with everyone so busy.

Five miles was a long way with loads to carry, but Rosie made short work of it. At the last field before the strand, which was busy with other families unloading their traps, Da pulled Rosie to a halt. They unhitched the trap, left her tied where she could graze on sweet seagrass, and went on the rest of the way on foot.

Already other families were on the move, the whole parish drifting seaward like pilgrims. John Power tramped alongside his parents, catching Ellen's eye as he passed. The smile he gave her made her stomach feel funny. Frank Tierney pushed his handcart, and Jack – Frank's cousin from Ballycluan – strode cheerfully over to walk with them, boasting that his pub was ready to stand the men a bottle of porter after the work was done. "Guinness if you've a taste for it," he said, "but my own brew will warm you better." That earned him a cheer and a joke or two from Da, who never minded a free drink.

The smell of salt met Ellen before the sight of the water did, and then the bay opened wide, shining and streaked with weed. The children scattered the moment their feet hit sand. Seamus lunged after Sarah Tierney, who shrieked and darted away, her braids flying. "I'll catch you yet!" he roared, though Ellen knew he'd never try too hard – he liked the chase too much.

Ellen watched as Patrick, determined to show off, scrambled straight for the rocks. He'd barely prised a mussel loose when his foot slipped on the weed, and down he went, backside first into a tide pool. Water splashed high.

"Saints preserve us, Patrick!" Mam gasped, though her mouth twitched.

Seamus folded his dripping arms. "If you wanted a bath, you could've asked."

Even Da chuckled. "You'll frighten the fish back to America with that carry-on."

Patrick scrambled up, sputtering, while Sarah laughed so hard she nearly toppled over herself. Ellen pressed her lips tight to hide a grin, but her eyes watered from holding it back. Her fool of a brother – always trying to prove himself, always ending up wet. She loved him for it, even when he was being thick.

Work soon took over: mussels filling buckets, cockles dug from the sand, winkles plucked into tins. Mam crouched low to gather carrageen for her cures, Da and Jack hacking kelp for the cabbages. Sarah gnawed dillisk like toffee. Her brother, Brian, bragged about a crab, and Patrick claimed the biggest cockle – though Brian slipped it into his own pocket.

John worked near Ellen, their hands occasionally brushing as they reached for the same cluster of mussels. Each touch sent a flutter through her that had nothing to do with the cold.

"You're quick with those," he said, nodding at her nearly full bucket. "I'd wager you could gather the whole strand yourself if you'd a mind to."

Ellen's blue eyes sparked with mischief. "And leave nothing for the rest of you? Where's the sport in that?" She plucked another mussel free. "Besides, someone has to leave a few for the slow ones."

"Slow, is it?" John grinned, reaching for the same cluster she was eyeing. Their fingers collided, and this time he didn't pull back. "Maybe I'm just being careful. Quality over quantity."

"Quality?" Ellen arched an eyebrow at his half-empty bucket. "Is that what you're calling it?"

"I call it being distracted by better things." His brown eyes held hers a moment longer than was proper.

The warmth that bloomed in her chest had nothing to do with the morning sun. Ellen turned back to her work, but she could feel his gaze on her still. "Then you'd best focus, John Power, or you'll go home with an empty bucket and an empty belly."

"Worth it," he murmured.

By noon, a driftwood fire steamed a pot of mussels, shells popping open one by one. Fishermen's wives arrived with baskets of herring, and Mam traded eggs for two silver fish. Barter done, the laughter carried easily across the strand.

As the young men gathered on a flat rock overlooking the Atlantic, Ellen drifted close enough to listen to them.

Patrick stood with his arms spread wide, pointing at the endless water. "Look at it," he said, eyes bright. "America's out there waiting. Fortune to be made, adventures to be had. I'll go one day, see if I don't."

"Aye, and Mam will box your ears for the suggestion," Seamus said, but his tone was fond. "Not me. Ireland's my home. I'll not leave her, not for all the gold in California."

John stood slightly apart, hands in his pockets. When his gaze found Ellen's, something shifted in his expression.

"What about you, John Power?" Patrick asked. "Would you take the ship to America?"

John never looked away from Ellen. "Depends. I'd only go if I had reason to."

The look he gave her made her cheeks warm. Ellen watched John turn back to the sea, the wind ruffling his hair. What had he meant by that look? Was he saying...? But no, that was daft thinking. They weren't even walking out together. Da would give her legs a good slap if he caught her even thinking about a boy.

When the tide crept in again, they heaved their loads back toward Rosie and the trap. The baskets were heavier now, but the thought of Jack's pub put a spring in the men's steps.

Ballycluan's main street smelled of turf smoke and sea air. Jack leaned in his doorway, bar rag slung over one shoulder, malt-scent drifting out. "You'll be dry within," he called. "One round on the house, and no arguing."

The women settled on the low wall outside, shawls pulled close, children clambering up beside them to swing their legs. Ellen watched enviously as Seamus and Patrick followed the men inside. John paused at the door, glancing back at her with a quick smile before disappearing into the warmth and laughter.

Rosie stamped at the hitching post, tugging at the last of the seagrass.

From outside, Ellen heard the muffled rise of laughter and the thump of a hand on the counter. Someone shouted something about Patrick, his name carrying through the door, followed by more laughter. She could imagine them in there, pints in hand, teasing him about his tumble. Another burst of laughter, lower this time, and she guessed that was about Seamus and Sarah. She hugged her knees against the chill, Sarah humming beside her. John's smile kept floating back to her, making her stomach do funny things.

She'd have to tell Isabella Russell about it, though her friend would only tease her something awful. They shared all their secrets and Bella knew Ellen liked John. A lot. Sometimes Ellen forgot the line between them until Isabella's mother's voice cut through the laughter, calling her daughter away. But when it was just the two of them, barefoot and breathless from running across the fields, they were only girls, not lady and servant's child.

Ellen wondered what Isabella would make of all this. The young lady up at the big house had never been to the strand with everyone, never dug for cockles or eaten fish cooked over driftwood, sand getting in everything. Imagine having all that money and missing this. Isabella said the sea at Brighton was grand, but how could it be better than their own bay with everyone here together?

ONE

SOUTH CAROLINA, NOW

"Has Bridget summoned you again?" Caitlin heard the familiar mix of sympathy and amusement in Donna's voice as she approached the nurses' station at Southern Oaks Care Center.

Through the window behind Donna, Charleston's May afternoon stretched humid and still, the palmetto fronds hanging motionless in the thick air.

"You know Grammy too well." Caitlin shifted the bouquet to her other hand. The ribbon bit into her palm. She loosened her grip before she left sweat marks on the paper.

Donna smiled, her eyes twinkling. "She's probably matchmaking again. She was just telling me the date you had with the doctor didn't work out. I told her I'd mentioned my nephew, but you wouldn't even look at his photo. I may be biased, but he is cute and, for his age, not carrying too much baggage."

Caitlin sighed. *We're all carrying baggage.* "I'm happy being single." The lie sat sharp on her tongue. The name she would not say rose anyway, a cold flick behind her ribs.

"You keep telling yourself that, girl, and someday you might believe it." The nurse got up from her desk and gave Caitlin's arm a reassuring squeeze before walking away.

As her footsteps echoed down the hallway, Caitlin's gaze flicked to the EXIT sign – a habit her body kept even as her mind rolled its eyes at it.

Gathering her thoughts, Caitlin took a deep breath before opening the door to her grandmother's room. She eased it shut again without letting it latch hard. Noise still had a way of finding her nerves.

Her grandmother lay in the bed, eyes closed, looking too innocent by half. The rhythmic beeping of the heart monitor filled the quiet space. Caitlin sat down in the bedside chair.

"Finally. Good job I wasn't at death's door, otherwise you'd have been late." Grammy's voice broke the silence, raspy but filled with its usual sharpness.

"Grammy." Caitlin smiled as she leaned in closer. The teasing tone loosened the knot in her chest. As she kissed her grandmother's cheek, the familiar rose lotion wrapped around her like a blanket.

"You look beautiful, Caitlin. Those colours really suit you. But you should schedule a visit to the hairdresser, tidy up those roots, and brighten up those highlights. Did I tell you about the new..."

Exasperated, Caitlin stood up. "Grammy, stop it. I told you, I'm not interested in dating anyone, least of all the newest doctor. I swear, if one more nurse gives me that pitying look, I'll start carrying a sign: 'Single by choice, not defective.' It's getting ridiculous now. Every time I come through the hospital doors, the staff are eyeing me up and down, wondering what's wrong with me." As she spoke, Caitlin removed the old dead flowers from the vase, cleaned it and refilled it with fresh water before arranging the new bouquet. "If I wanted a man in my life, I could have one." She tried for a grin. It wobbled. "I could pick one off the cardiology rack if I felt like it."

"But..."

"Enough. Now, tell me, how are you? Why are you hooked up to that machine again? I thought the doctors were happy with your new meds."

"They are. That's just a twenty-four-hour monitor, to be sure." Her grandmother picked at a loose thread in the sheets, not meeting Caitlin's eyes.

Caitlin's hands stilled. They'd promised to be honest with one another, yet her grammy was hiding something. Then again, Caitlin hadn't been entirely truthful either. She'd told her about the shooting, but not about the nights when her shoulder locked, or how the pin in her leg still tugged like an old promise whenever the weather turned – her thigh throbbing now, a barometer for bad news. "What is it? There's something you're not telling me."

"Stop fussing."

"Grammy, tell me right now or I'll go ask your doctors. We had a deal. No more secrets."

Caitlin held her gaze until Grammy looked away, colour climbing her cheeks. She'd hidden her heart issues from Caitlin before. Caitlin had returned from a trip to find her grandmother unconscious on the floor. She'd counted compressions with shaking arms, pretending not to hear the clock marking out the seconds she might lose her. The metronome of it lived in her wrists. *One, two, three.* Now she flexed her fingers until the ghost of it stopped.

Grammy shifted in the bed to face her directly. "I need to tell you something. You won't like it, but please listen to me before you lose your cool."

Caitlin locked her ankles together under the chair. *Come on, Grammy.* The soft hum of the machines filled the silence. She matched her breathing to the monitor. In, out. Keep the line steady.

"Are you going to tell me, or do I have to beat it out of you?" Caitlin said, hoping her grandmother couldn't hear the anxiety in her voice. Her comment was meant to break the lingering silence but, to her horror, a tear fell down Bridget's cheek, followed by another. She never cried, not even when...

"Grammy, what's wrong? What did the doctors say? We can get a second opinion. I can..."

Her grandmother reached for her hand, warm and trembling.

"I'm not dying – well, not today, but we both know that we don't need a second opinion. I'm old and have had a good life. But..." She rubbed her fingers up and down Caitlin's wrist, eyes pleading. "I need to tell you something before I die. I thought about writing you a letter for you to find, you know, after. But that's the coward's way out. You are a brave, strong, beautiful young woman. Now I need to borrow some of your strength."

Caitlin's stomach tightened; she pressed her tongue to her molars. Why might Grammy need her strength?

"I sent away for one of those DNA packages I saw advertised."

A laugh rose, she bit it back. Her grandmother had never wanted to know her background before, saying she wasn't interested in the family tree. There'd been a project at school one year, and Bridget had become defensive when Caitlin had asked for details of her family. With her mom and dad dead, all she had was her grandparents. Grammy had given names, dates, and little else. But now, her grandmother had arranged a DNA test?

The antique clock on the mantel ticked louder than usual, each tick marking the passing seconds. *Tick.*

Bridget's grip tightened, surprisingly strong. The touch brought a flood of old memories and a fresh edge of unease.

"Why now, Grammy?"

"I've kept secrets, Caitlin. For too long. I thought it was to protect you, but maybe it was to protect myself." Her voice cracked, then steadied. "I lied to you about not knowing my parents. I did know, or at least I think I knew my mother... I was about two years old, the last time she sang to me. I don't know if I remember her face or if it's from looking at her photograph. My adoptive parents were given one photo of her. You remind me so much of what I believed her to be: strong, fearless, impatient, stubborn. You even look like her."

"Why tell me you were an orphan?"

"It was easier. I didn't want you to know of my shame."

Something pinched behind Caitlin's breastbone. She squeezed

the wrinkled hand gently. "Shame" was a heavy word in this room. She wanted to shoulder it and throw it out the window.

"Mam left me. She said she'd come back but she never did." A tear slid down Bridget's cheek. "My adoptive parents told me the nuns said my father didn't want anything to do with either of us. That I was wicked, and Mam didn't love me. That she was a sinner."

"How could you be anything but innocent, Grammy? You were a child."

"From what the nuns said, I suspect my mother was not married; at least, not when I was born. It was different back then. People were cruel, especially to women in her situation. The stigma was unbearable. She must have been desperate, to leave me there, and maybe she planned on coming back. But she never returned, and I was left to face the harshness of the orphanage alone." Bridget gave a weary sigh. "At least, that's what I believed all my life. Gavin says it wasn't really an orphanage – it was one of those homes for mothers and their babies."

Caitlin felt a chill run through her. She'd heard about those places, seen one of the films that had made people cry in theatres. But that was history, she'd thought. Other families, other sorrows. Not hers. Not Grammy's.

Bridget shuddered. "Maybe they were right. She forgot about me. I was a weight around her neck, a constant reminder of her so-called sins."

Heat climbed Caitlin's throat. Little Bridget with her chin up anyway, taking the blame that did not belong to her. "I can't imagine how hard that must have been for you. But you survived, and you built a life here. You raised me. You're the strongest person I know."

Her grandmother gave a small, sad smile. "Survival isn't the same as living, Caitlin. I've been haunted by those memories, by the feeling of being unwanted. I never wanted you to see me as weak or tainted by my past."

"But you're not weak, and your past doesn't taint you," Caitlin said, her grip tightening. "It's part of who you are, but it doesn't define you. You've always been my hero."

Her grandmother's eyes shimmered, the tears making them look green rather than hazel. "Thank you, dear. I was lucky in lots of ways. I came to America and although my parents weren't kind people, they gave me a home. If I hadn't come to live in Charleston, I wouldn't have met your grandfather." Her gaze flicked to the bedside photo. "He was a very special man who loved me anyway."

"Of course he loved you. I love you. Everyone here thinks you're incredible." Outside, a mockingbird ran through its repertoire from the live oak that shaded Grammy's window, its new leaves still half-unfurled, yellow pollen dusting the cars below. "Please don't let what happened in the past upset you. It's not good for you to be stressed." She lowered her voice, as if calm could be caught.

"Can you get me the folder in the top drawer of my desk, please?"

Caitlin crossed to the small desk by the window. She opened it, breathing in the scent of old paper and lavender. A small folder rested on top, edges softened with age. As she lifted it, a photograph slid out and landed on the desk face up. But for the clothes, she could have been looking at herself. Her scalp prickled. It felt like being seen from the other side of time.

"Is that her?" Caitlin said, holding up the photo so Grammy could see.

"Your great-grandmother, Ellen McGrath."

"She looks just like me," Caitlin whispered as she moved back to her grandmother's bedside and gave her the folder. "I'd love to hear about her, Grammy. I've always been curious. But why now? What's changed?"

Bridget drew out a printed family tree and handed it over. "I never knew I had a brother. Until now."

Caitlin studied the chart. "Seán Power, born 1924."

"Maybe he's still alive, but I don't believe so. I'd feel it here, wouldn't I?" Grammy touched her heart.

Caitlin did not argue. She set her jaw until the thought passed.

"Did the genealogy site send you these documents? I didn't think they got involved in specific cases."

"No, dear. A cousin, second or third, sent them. When our DNA matched, he emailed me through the site and we've been corresponding since. He lives in Australia but was recently in Ireland, visiting family."

Of course Grammy was emailing. The secret-keeping stung. Especially after the last six months when Caitlin would have sworn there were no more secrets between them. Grammy was all she had left. Her job was gone. The friends who could not look at her the same way, anymore. The future she had thought was mapped out. The word *retirement* still felt like a door slamming.

Grammy's fingers worried the edge of the blanket, her mouth pulling tight at the corners. "I know you're upset."

"I'm fine." Caitlin turned her eyes on the small window in the door, watching a nurse hurry past in the corridor.

"No, you're not. Look at me, pet." When Caitlin turned back, Grammy's eyes were bright with unshed tears. "I was going to tell you, but I wasn't sure where the exchange would lead. I knew my mother's name was McGrath, but I could never trace anything beyond her birth certificate in that name. I wrote to the nuns at the convent that arranged my adoption, but they said they couldn't help me. I drew a complete blank and gave up, imagining she didn't want to be found." She sighed. "Then Gavin's letter arrived yesterday. He's a kind man."

"You trusted a stranger online? That was dangerous." The words came out sharper than Caitlin had intended. This Gavin person had been exchanging emails with Grammy for who knew how long, learning family secrets while Caitlin had been kept in the dark

"Maybe a little, but it worked out. You'd have done the same thing if you were in my position." Grammy lifted her chin, into that stubborn set Caitlin knew so well. "Everything I thought about my mother was wrong. She was married – both my parents' names are on my baptismal certificate. I wasn't illegitimate. I wasn't a bas – I cannot say that word." She pressed her hand to her chest, breathing shallow. "My brother was a baby at the same home. Mam went to the nuns to have him. She died in childbirth the year I was admitted." Grammy held the handwritten letter out to Caitlin but continued talking. "She did love me. She died. Otherwise, she would never have left me. I remember her holding me and crying. I blocked out those memories for a long time but you do not forget. She used to sing to me and kept repeating, *A chuisle mo chroí, thug Dia chugainn thú*."

"What does that mean?"

"It doesn't translate straight into English. Something like, 'Child of my heart, God gave you to us.' Even then she spoke in terms of 'us'. She must have meant her and my father." Her eyes darkened. "Those nuns told me a pack of lies. They never told me about my brother or Mam dying. Why would they do that?"

"Maybe they thought you were too young to know. You were so little. I'm sure they did not mean to hurt you, Grammy." Even as Caitlin said it, anger needled her again. "But, Grammy, how did Gavin know about Seán if the convent kept everything so secret?"

Bridget's fingers traced the edge of her father's death certificate. "Patrick, my uncle and Mam's brother. The local doctor knew a nun at the convent. She wrote to Dr Casey and he must have given the letter to Patrick. Gavin found the letter with Patrick's papers. His family, even though only distant relatives, inherited them when Patrick died in 1951. Never married, the poor man."

This was like something out of the movies. "What did the letter say?"

"That Ellen had died giving birth to a son. The doctor thought Patrick should know, since he was head of the family after their parents died." Grammy's voice turned bitter. "Patrick wrote on the envelope that he tried to find us, but the convent wouldn't say where we'd been sent."

Caitlin squeezed her grandmother's hand. Another tragedy in a story full of them. An uncle who'd spent twenty-six years living with the knowledge that his sister's children were out there somewhere, unreachable, their story locked behind convent walls.

"He kept that letter until he died," Grammy whispered. "Maybe hoping someday he'd find us. And now, seventy years later, he has."

TWO

Grammy's hands shook as she passed Gavin's letter to Caitlin. "Read what he says about my mam—? Imagine being allowed to do that."

Caitlin read the paragraph Grammy pointed to and then read it again. "Not registering a death is a crime. Why would they have done that?"

"If you read on, Gavin says it was common practice in those days. Seems there have been some programmes on Irish television about these homes. The nuns often didn't register births or deaths under the correct names, to avoid questions from the state or clergy superiors about the woman's identity or cause of death. They also wanted to protect their reputation."

"Why? Surely giving a home to women and children in need was a Christian, kind thing to do?"

Tears slid down Grammy's cheeks. "There was nothing good or Christian about those homes. They didn't care what they did to families."

The room went still except for the clock ticking on the wall. Caitlin didn't know what to say. All her life, Grammy's past had been a locked room – now she'd cracked the door, and the air spilling out was full of sorrow.

"I can't change what happened," Grammy whispered, dabbing at her eyes. "But maybe we can finally understand it. Caitlin, I need you to do something for me."

The older woman squeezed her hand. "I want you to go to Ireland. Find out what happened to my family. Why did I, or rather we, end up in one of those mother and baby homes? I looked it up on Google and it says they were for unmarried women, but my parents were married. Did my brother live? Did he have a family? Was he happy? I cannot travel, but you can. It might even do you good. Get you away from here, from the memories, from Mark, from all of it."

Frustration tangled with fear in Caitlin's chest. She was alive, she was here, she was all the family Grammy had and Grammy wanted her to leave? Four thousand miles away when anything could happen? The last time she had gone anywhere, she had come home to find Bridget on the floor. "I can't leave you, Grammy. I told you I would look after you." Her leg ached at the thought of hours in the air. First class or not, metal hated altitude.

"I do not need looking after," Grammy said sharply. "I need answers." Then she looked contrite. "Sorry. That was rude... What I mean is... I am very well looked after here. I have plenty of money. I do not need anything but answers. And you, my darling girl, are the only person who can get them." She took Caitlin's hands and squeezed them. "You need perspective on your life and your plans. I will fund the trip. Enjoy my beautiful homeland. It is stunning, and the people are lovely. You may even meet a handsome Irishman who steals your heart. Not everyone is like Mark."

Caitlin glared. Matchmaking, again?

Bridget reached out, fingertips brushing Caitlin's cheek before dropping her hand. "Give me one good reason you cannot go. Your retirement is official. You will travel first class so you can rest your leg. You don't have a mortgage to pay – thank God your grandfather bought you the house outright on your twenty-first. No ties, not even a pet. I am happy here. So..."

The comment stung. Was that really all her life amounted to?

No ties, no roots? She had friends, didn't she? But when she tried to name them, her mind came up empty. Since the retirement, since the warehouse, since Mark, they'd all quietly disappeared.

"What if you take a turn and I am not here? I couldn't bear that."

"Oh, sweetheart, come here." Grammy held her arms open.

Caitlin moved into the embrace and let her grandmother hug her tight.

"Nobody knows when we are going to die," Bridget murmured. "I could go to sleep right now and not wake up. I worried about you for years. Would you come home alive, injured? Or would two officers show up at my door? I still had to let you go and live your life. I love you more than anything, Caitlin. I won't ever leave you. Even if I die while you are in Ireland, I will still be here." She pressed her hand to Caitlin's heart. "Every time your heart beats, that's me loving you. Distance can't change that. Please, *Alannah*," she said softly – the old Irish word for *my darling*. "Will you go?"

Caitlin nodded. She glanced at the photograph of Ellen McGrath in the folder, those familiar eyes looking back at her across a century of silence. She imagined calling her grandmother from a rain-bright Dublin street, saying the words that might mend an old bruise. *I've found her. I know the truth.*

Maybe it was time to bring the voices home.

Caitlin sat at her kitchen table in Charleston, the folder from Grammy spread before her like evidence at a crime scene. *Old habits die hard.* She'd already organized everything chronologically, cross-referenced the dates, made notes in the margins. The photograph of Ellen McGrath stared up at her, those eyes that could have been her own.

Before booking flights, before making any plans, she needed to know what she was walking into. The ex-cop in her demanded reconnaissance. No more walking blind into situations. Not after the warehouse.

She pulled out her laptop and searched for St Brigid's Convent, Galway. Grammy's cousin Gavin had mentioned it in his notes as the place where Ellen had died in childbirth.

The website was sparse, mostly historical information and Mass times. But there was a contact number for "Historical Inquiries."

Her hand hovered over her phone. *Just make the call, O'Shea. It's just information gathering. Nothing like—*

She cut off that thought and dialled.

"St Brigid's Convent, Mrs Walsh speaking." The voice was pleasant but formal, with that particular Irish lilt Grammy sometimes slipped into when she was tired.

"Hello, my name is Caitlin O'Shea. I'm calling from the United States. South Carolina."

"How can I help you, Ms O'Shea?"

"I'm researching my family history. My great-grandmother, Ellen McGrath Power, was at your convent in the 1920s. She died there in 1924, giving birth to my grandmother's brother." Caitlin kept her voice professional, the way she used to when calling for case information. "I was hoping to access any records you might have about her."

A pause. The kind of pause that told Caitlin everything she needed to know before Mrs Walsh even spoke.

"I see. That's quite some time ago."

"Yes, but I have documentation. Birth certificates, baptismal records. My grandmother – Ellen's daughter – is ninety-one and in poor health. She's just learned she had a brother she never knew about, and I'm trying to find information for her before..." Caitlin let the sentence hang.

"I understand, and I sympathize with your grandmother's situation." Mrs Walsh's tone had shifted to something carefully neutral. "However, I'm afraid I can't discuss any individual cases over the phone."

"Could I make an appointment when I arrive? I'm planning to fly to Dublin next week."

"Any request for historical records has to go through our archivist, Ms O'Shea. You'd need to submit a formal written application, along with proof of relationship – birth certificates showing the family connection, your identification, that sort of thing."

Caitlin picked up a pen, her fingers automatically positioning for note-taking. "And once I submit the application...?"

"It goes to our archive committee for review. They meet monthly to assess applications."

"Monthly?" Her pen stilled.

"Yes. And then, if approved, the actual retrieval and preparation of records can take additional time. Many of our older files are stored offsite and need special handling."

"How long are we talking about in total?"

"We typically advise people to expect six to eight weeks from the time we receive their written application. Sometimes longer if the records are particularly complex, or if there are... complications."

Six to eight weeks? Grammy might not have six to eight weeks.

"Is there any way to expedite the process? Given my grandmother's health—"

"I'm afraid not." Mrs Walsh's voice was sympathetic but firm. "The process is the same for everyone. These records contain sensitive information about women who were in very difficult circumstances. We have a duty of care to protect their privacy, even posthumously. And there are data protection regulations to consider."

Caitlin set down her pen. In her experience, bureaucracy like this usually meant they were hiding something. "What if I just wanted to visit? See where she lived?"

"The buildings from that period are no longer in use. The old laundry buildings were demolished in the 1980s."

Of course they were. Everything she'd read online said the religious orders had tried to bury the past, but the Irish government had finally started pushing back. "Can you at least confirm that Ellen McGrath was there? That she died there in 1924?"

"As I said, I can't discuss any individual cases over the phone. If you submit a formal request with proper documentation, our archivists will research what records we have."

"And that takes six to eight weeks."

"At minimum, yes. I can post you an information pack with the application forms if you'd like, or I can send you a download link."

"Please send the link," Caitlin said. The sooner Grammy signed them, the sooner the process would start.

After ending the call, she stared at Ellen's photograph again.

Six to eight weeks of official channels and red tape. But she'd be in Ireland for a month. There had to be other ways to find information: local parish records, newspaper archives, people who remembered the stories their grandparents told. The official records might be locked behind bureaucracy, but memories had a way of surviving in small communities.

She pulled up the airline website. If she couldn't get Ellen's records through proper channels, she'd have to do it the way she'd learned to work cases when official sources dried up: talk to locals, follow leads, piece together the truth from fragments.

Sometimes the best information came from the people who lived with these stories, not the institutions that tried to bury them.

She booked the flight to Dublin. One month to find answers. Grammy deserved that much. Whatever secrets the convent was protecting behind its six-to-eight-week wall of bureaucracy, Caitlin would find another way in.

She'd failed to see the truth about Mark until it was too late. She wouldn't fail Grammy.

Not this time.

THREE
1916

"Seamus, are you here? Is anyone home?"

Isabella's voice carried on the air across the stone-walled fields. Ellen looked up from her mending while Mam paused at the stove, flour still dusting her hands. They exchanged a worried glance. Their landlord's daughter hadn't come to their cottage in years. Clonbarra House was on the opposite side of the village to their cottage.

They rushed outside, their footsteps pounding against the stone path. Ellen stopped short at the sight of Isabella on horseback before them, her usually immaculate riding habit dishevelled and dirt-streaked, her complexion white as milk beneath streaks of mud. Was that blood too? Ellen's heart beat faster. Something was terribly wrong for Isabella to come here in such a state. Her auburn hair hung loose around her shoulders in damp tangles, so unlike the careful coiffure she usually wore, that Ellen could only stare.

Mam spoke first. "Miss Russell, what's happened? If you don't mind me saying so, you look a mess. Are you hurt?" She wiped her flour-dusted hands on her apron, worry lines creasing her face.

"Not me, Mrs McGrath, but there's been an accident. Edward was riding Duchess, and he fell."

Seamus came running from the backfield, shirt clinging to his back with sweat, and for a moment Ellen frowned at the sight of him. When had her brother grown so broad in the shoulders? "I heard shouting. What's wrong?"

"Duchess is hurt." Isabella's voice trembled.

"How bad is she? What has he done?" Seamus's hands fisted at his sides, muscles tensing beneath his rolled-up sleeves.

Ellen put a hand on her brother's arm, feeling the coiled tension. She knew that look, the same fierce protectiveness that made him sit up all night with sick lambs. But Edward was the master's son, and that fury had to stay buried.

"Seamus, you know what he's like. Always has to win. To be the best." Isabella struggled for control. "Duchess needs you."

"I'm not a vet." His green eyes flashed with barely contained anger.

"No, but Dr Shandon would contact Father, and that would put the cat among the pigeons." Her green eyes, wide with fear, locked on to his, conveying the urgency that went beyond the injured mare. "Can you please come and look? If you still think we need him, I'll ride for him myself."

Ellen knew her brother wouldn't be able to say no to Isabella's pleas for help.

"Let me grab some things." He strode back to the house with those long-legged strides that ate up ground, reappearing with what Mam called his doctoring satchel – Granny's battered leather bag that smelled of herbs, even from here.

Seamus helped Isabella dismount, then rubbed Prestige's velvety nose as the black stallion butted his head into Seamus's jacket. Laughing, Seamus withdrew a withered apple from his pocket. "Where is Duchess?"

"At the bottom of Long's field," Isabella whispered.

Ellen's heart sank. The wall. The one Seamus had warned Edward about.

"Did he try to jump the wall?"

Isabella glanced at Ellen, despair etched on her fine-boned face. The tension made Ellen's skin prickle. Mam grabbed Ellen's hand with rough fingers. They both knew how Seamus's level-headedness vanished when animals suffered.

"I'll kill him," Seamus swore, already moving toward the field.

Ellen's pulse quickened. She could see it already: Seamus confronting Edward, the consequences that would rain down on their family. The eviction notice. Her parents' faces as they lost everything.

"Mam, can you get Isabella a drink of water?" Ellen turned to Isabella. "We'll follow Seamus across the fields. It's the quickest way."

Mam ushered Isabella inside. Moments later, she returned, face washed and hair a little tidier, though curls still escaped around her temples. The transformation struck Ellen. Even dishevelled, Isabella looked nothing like them. "Thank you, Mrs McGrath. I'm sorry to put you out like this." She caught Ellen's eye, and for a moment Ellen saw not their landlord's daughter but a frightened girl who genuinely cared. "Can I leave Prestige here and collect him later?"

"Of course, Miss Russell. Go on now, be careful. Ellen, mind your brother." The warning in Mam's voice sent a chill through Ellen. They couldn't afford to upset Lord Russell.

The two girls hurried after Seamus, their footwear squelching in the muddy ground as they half ran across the fields. Isabella lifted her riding skirt to keep pace, and Ellen matched her stride.

"Will Duchess have to be destroyed?"

Isabella shook her head, slightly breathless from their quick pace. "I'm not sure. There was a lot of blood but it might not be as bad as it looks. Edward wasn't badly hurt." The frustration in her voice suggested she wished otherwise.

Ellen didn't particularly care whether Edward was hurt. The eldest Russell son was demanding and heartless with everyone. But those thoughts had to stay locked away.

They moved quickly through the wet grass, Ellen's prayers tumbling over each other. *Help for Duchess, restraint for Seamus.*

At the field boundary, they climbed the wooden stile.

Isabella glanced down at her ruined habit and laughed shakily. "This is just like when we climbed the orchard wall in our good dresses."

Ellen smiled weakly, aware of her own brown wool dress, faded and practical next to Isabella's burgundy riding jacket, fine even when mud-covered. "Except no one ended up bleeding that time."

"No, just covered in apple juice and twigs. Your mother was furious."

"So was yours." For a moment the years fell away, and they were just two girls who'd been friends long before the world taught them their places.

The smell hit Ellen first. The sharp tang of blood and something sour that might have been fear. Above it all, the air thickened with coming rain.

Duchess lay in the wet grass, sides heaving, crimson oozing steadily from a dark gash marring her chestnut flank where she'd hit the wall.

Seamus knelt beside her, his hands moving with the same careful touch Ellen had seen him use on sick lambs, his face tight with strain that made her own chest ache.

"How bad is it?" Isabella whispered, dropping to her knees near Duchess's head.

"Bad."

The single word made Ellen's stomach clench. She moved closer, stroking Duchess's muzzle. Cold seeped through her dress from the wet ground, but the mare's laboured breathing mattered more.

Edward paced nearby, crop slapping against his palm, the sound setting Ellen's teeth on edge. His face twisted in irritation, as if the horse's suffering were no more than an inconvenience. For a heartbeat his eyes flicked to Duchess. Was that guilt in them? Ellen couldn't tell before he looked away.

"Are you going to send for Shandon?" Ellen kept her voice low.

Seamus met her gaze, and the pain there made her chest

tighten once more. "You know what he will do. He'll put her down. I can't... let him do that."

"It's not up to you, Seamus," Ellen whispered fiercely. "Duchess is his lordship's favourite. If anything happens, he'll blame you. And Mam and Da by association."

"Don't you think I know that? That idiot has done this, but nobody will hold him responsible." He reached into his bag, pulling out clean bandages and Granny's salve. The familiar herb scent made Ellen's eyes water.

"What are you doing, McGrath? Can you fix her or not?" Edward's nasal whine grated.

Seamus ignored him, whispering to Duchess in Irish. Something passed between them that made Ellen shiver. An understanding that went beyond words.

Isabella inched closer. "Please try to help, Seamus. I'll deal with Father. Don't let her die." Her voice cracked with tears.

Ellen caught Isabella's cold hand. Strange how different she was from her father and brother. She'd always been so, even as a little girl, playing with the tenant children when no one watched.

Seamus looked up. "I think you should fetch Dr Shandon. Even if I can treat her, Duchess can't stay in this muddy field. She needs warm stables."

Isabella stood, determination replacing fear. "Edward, go and fetch Dr Shandon."

Edward spun around, his thin face flushing. "You go."

"This is your mess, Edward. Sort it out, or I will tell Father you were warned about this wall. Go on. The sooner you get the vet, the better Duchess's chances are."

"I can't walk through the village like this. What will people think?" His fingers fussed with his cravat, and Ellen wanted to shake him.

"Then run. That way." Isabella pointed across the fields. "That's the fastest way to the village, and on to the house. You'd better tell Father too."

Edward's mouth fell open, his pale eyes wide with shock.

"Go on. What are you waiting for? It's going to rain soon. Duchess will catch a chill."

He opened his mouth, closed it, then stormed off, his fancy boots squelching with each step.

"Now he's gone, do what you have to do." Isabella touched Seamus's forearm. "Please, Seamus. If we lose her because I was too much of a coward…"

He nodded, shoving damp hair from his forehead with a bloodied hand. "I need some long sticks for a splint. The leg might not be broken but she keeps moving it and that makes the gash bleed more."

The two girls hurried to an old ash at the field's edge, its grey bark deeply furrowed and branches reaching wide. Ellen had sheltered under those spreading limbs during sudden summer showers. Isabella snatched up branches, her fine kid gloves snagging and tearing. The sight jolted Ellen. The landlord's daughter, scrabbling in the muck like any of them.

"Do you think these will work?"

"Yes, they should." Ellen took them and they ran back, the darkening sky pressing down. Wind whipped loose strands of hair across her face.

"Will these do?" The cold had stolen her breath.

Seamus examined them with careful fingers. "These will do fine. Thank you."

He bent over Duchess, murmuring low and steady, the gentleness in his touch so at odds with his size that it caught at Ellen's throat. She clung to the herb smell of Granny's salve, praying it would be enough.

Ellen cradled Duchess's noble head, whispering nonsense words of comfort while the mare's breath warmed her hands. Isabella paced, then stopped. "I'll go and see if they're coming back. Edward must have found them by now."

She returned with slumped shoulders. "There's no sign of them." The first fat raindrops splattered down. "What will we do now?"

"We need to move her. Now." Seamus wiped his hands on his already-ruined shirt. "The rain will make things worse. But we can't risk it without help. You girls won't manage her weight safely."

Much as Ellen wanted to argue, to prove she was just as capable, she knew the truth of it. Before she could suggest alternatives, Isabella's voice rang out with relief. "I hear them. They're here."

FOUR

Ellen flinched at the thundering hooves. Through the grey curtain of rain, Lord Russell led the charge on his black hunter. Even in these circumstances, his riding coat remained neat, perfectly tailored, his grey hair tidy beneath his riding hat. The sight of the local landowner and landlord to most in the village made her stomach tighten with dread. Here was the man who held their lives in his hands, who could evict them with a word. Mr Lynch, the head groom, followed, with stable hands close behind. No sign of Edward or Shandon.

"You, boy, what are you doing to my horse? If you have caused her any harm, you will pay. Your family too." Each syllable fell like ice into Ellen's belly.

Ellen silently begged, *Please, Seamus, show him respect. Please don't let your pride destroy us.* But Seamus didn't stand. He continued checking Duchess's pulse and breathing. Ellen held her breath, fingernails digging into her palms as she willed him to stand and show the deference Lord Russell demanded. Her brother pretended the landlord wasn't there, attention focused on the injured mare. She saw the tension in his broad shoulders, his jaw tight. All signs of the temper he fought to control.

"Sir, that's Seamus McGrath. Healing hands he has. No better man around for taking care of Duchess." Mr Lynch jumped down, boots squelching as he handed his reins to a young lad.

Seamus finally stood, his full height impressive as he ignored Lord Russell and addressed the head groom directly. Ellen noticed his hands balled into fists at his sides, knuckles white against tanned skin. "Mr Lynch, it's bad. I did everything I could, but I'm not sure it will work. The leg isn't broken, but it's a deep gash. I cleaned it and packed it, but she needs taking out of this rain. She'll catch a chill – if she hasn't already – from lying in the mud."

The mare's rasping breaths filled the air, each exhale creating small clouds in the cold. The scent of blood and wet horse mingled with the smell of mud in Ellen's nostrils, and her stomach turned.

"She's lying on your coat, lad. That will have helped. Let me have a look at her." Mr Lynch's lined face was creased with concern. "Ellen, go out on the road and keep a lookout for Tom Clancy and the wagon. Miss Isabella, you're soaked through. One of the men can give you his horse."

"I want to stay with Duchess." Isabella's plea came out broken with emotion.

"Don't be silly, girl," Lord Russell shouted. "Go home before your mother sees the state of you."

"Don't anger your father." Ellen gripped Isabella's elbow, feeling her friend shake with cold or distress. Their eyes met, and Ellen tried to pour all her sympathy into that look. Despite the gulf between their stations, they understood each other. "Seamus will bear the brunt."

Isabella nodded, understanding. She squeezed Ellen's hand briefly. The small gesture warmed Ellen despite the cold. Isabella allowed a stable boy to help her mount and headed back to the big house.

Ellen gave her brother one last look. His jaw remained tight with suppressed anger. She headed out to the road as Mr Lynch had instructed, finding shelter under the ancient ash tree. Its thick trunk provided some protection, though water still dripped steadily from its bare branches. She pulled her thin shawl tight around her shoulders against the increasing cold. Every so often she glanced back at the group in the field, too far away to hear anything. She prayed Seamus was keeping out of trouble. Lord Russell wouldn't be happy if Seamus started telling him how Edward didn't deserve to clean out stables, let alone get on a horse. One word, one wrong look, and they could all be thrown out before nightfall.

A whistle startled her from worried thoughts.

"You asleep there, Ellen? You should be at home, girl, not out here in this weather. Your mam will be worried." Tom Clancy approached on the wagon seat, his eyes surprised to see her there. The old carter looked small and wiry in his patched brown coat and battered hat. The wagon wheels creaked through the mud.

"'Tis more than rain she has to be concerned about. Tom, Duchess is hurt bad and it was all Edward's fault. He tried to get her to jump Long's rear wall." The words tumbled out, her voice shaking.

Disgust filled Tom's face. "That *amadán* is a curse. Why couldn't he have stayed in England at that fancy school?"

"I'm worried sick." Ellen's voice caught. She swallowed hard against the lump in her throat. "Seamus did what he could but if Duchess dies, it will be blamed on him."

"Now, girl, don't be carrying on like that. Hop up beside me and let's go and see how the horse is doing."

Ellen climbed up, her wet skirts heavy and clinging. The wagon seat felt hard and uncomfortable, but at least she was off the muddy ground. They soon drew up next to where the horse lay.

Ellen tried to catch her brother's expression, but shadow hid it. The mare lay still. Too still. Was the horse dead? Ellen's heart pounded so hard she was sure everyone could hear it.

"About time, Clancy. I told you to put your back into it." Lord Russell's voice cut like a whip.

"Yes, your lordship." Clancy tugged his forelock, eyes staring straight ahead, not a hint of his earlier warmth visible. Ellen saw his hands tighten on the reins.

"Right, Lynch – you, Clancy and the lads get the horse onto

that wagon. Go easy, mind. It's bad enough that lad could have damaged her without you adding to it." Lord Russell gestured dismissively toward Seamus, who was carefully applying a fresh bandage to Duchess's wound, speaking in Irish as he worked.

Ellen caught some of his words, recognizing the ancient blessings for healing her mother had taught them both.

She watched Lord Russell linger at the edge of the group astride his horse while others knelt in the mud. Heat flared in her chest at the unfairness of it.

Tom and some grooms removed sturdy wooden planks from the wagon to create a makeshift ramp and covered it with straw. The sweet scent of it couldn't mask the metallic tang of blood that clung to everything.

Mr Lynch examined Duchess carefully, conferring with Seamus. Ellen noticed how he treated her brother with respect, unlike their employer. "Do you think she can walk, or should we use a blanket to slide her?"

Seamus shrugged. "Both ways involve a risk, but given her size and weight, I think we should try to avoid her walking. We'll have to roll her onto the blanket."

"For sure." Mr Lynch nodded.

"Lynch, what are you doing asking him? You're in charge of the stable, aren't you?" Lord Russell's voice dripped with disdain.

"Yes, sir, but Seamus has a way with animals. Always has done."

Lord Russell glared and turned away with a dismissive, "Hmmph."

Mr Lynch ignored his employer's displeasure and gestured to the grooms. They gathered around the injured mare. With Seamus at Duchess's head, they carefully rolled the horse onto the blanket. Ellen heard him murmuring: "Easy now, *a stór*. We'll have you right as rain soon enough. That's my brave girl."

They used thick ropes to secure her. Then each man heaved together, grunts tearing from their throats, necks corded and backs straining under the weight. Ellen pressed her palms to her temples, the raw sounds slicing through her. When Duchess gave a high-pitched squeal of agony, tears flowed down Ellen's cheeks. She noticed wet tracks on the men's weathered faces too, their rough features softened by compassion.

Seamus kept murmuring words of comfort to the horse in Irish, his voice low and steady as he bent close, his touch light as a feather on her neck.

Once the horse was secured, Seamus settled down beside her, his large frame folding into the cramped space, still soothing her with gentle strokes. Ellen saw how tender he was, how different from the angry young man who'd faced Lord Russell. This was the brother she knew. The one who'd rescued injured birds as a child and cried when their old dog died.

Mr Lynch and the others distributed extra straw and heavy woollen blankets around Duchess for padding and warmth, pulling a waterproof canvas over the horse. The men worked with practised efficiency, but Ellen could see worry in their movements.

Tom got into the driver's seat, his small frame dwarfed by the large wagon, and took up the leather reins with shaking fingers. Mr Lynch rode in the back with Seamus and the horse, his experienced eyes watching for any signs of distress. A sandy-haired, freckled young groom climbed up beside Tom, ready to help navigate the muddy roads, as the rest mounted their horses and headed back to prepare for the injured animal's arrival.

"I'll ride ahead and make sure that Shandon is on hand to meet us. Drive carefully, Clancy." Lord Russell wheeled his black hunter around, not sparing another glance for the injured horse that was supposed to be his prized possession.

Clancy touched his forelock again, but Lord Russell had already ridden off, his straight back rigid with displeasure.

Ellen was going to ask if she could follow but decided not to. Asking meant they could say no. Instead, she would just turn up at the stables.

As the wagon lurched forward, Ellen prayed all the way back to the big house, shoulders hunched against the rain, jaw clenched until her teeth hurt. She prayed the horse would survive and that Lord Russell would ignore her brother's impudence. Even God might struggle to get the landlord to thank Seamus for his care.

Ellen stood in the dimly lit stables, her heart racing as she watched Seamus. His jaw was set with determination as he focused on Dr Shandon examining Duchess.

The magnificent mare lay on thick, fresh straw, her chestnut coat dull with sweat and mud, sides still heaving with each breath she took.

The stable felt warmer than outside, filled with the comforting smells of hay and horses. But the warmth couldn't ease the tension that pressed against Ellen's chest, heavier than the damp air. Other horses shifted restlessly in their stalls, sensing distress. Lamplight flickered on whitewashed walls, casting dancing shadows that made everything seem more ominous.

Isabella came in behind her, having changed into a simple blue dress. Her friend's face was pale, eyes red-rimmed from crying. She clutched Ellen's hand as they watched the men, both girls afraid to breathe too loudly. Ellen squeezed back, grateful for the contact, for this small rebellion against the rules that said they couldn't truly be friends.

Edward stood near the stable door, having found time to change into a pressed white shirt and cream-coloured breeches while his horse lay suffering. Ellen felt disgust surge through her. He'd caused this tragedy and couldn't even stay in his wet clothes long enough to see the outcome. He stared at his father with nervous anticipation, but Lord Russell had eyes only for the vet and horse.

Dr Shandon stood slowly, rubbing his hands on a cloth stained scarlet before tossing it carelessly to the straw-covered ground. Ellen hated the way he dragged it out, every movement deliberate, as if he wanted them all to squirm.

Lord Russell broke the heavy silence. "Well? Will she recover?"

"She's alive, but she'll never race again." Shandon kept his tone professionally neutral. "Perhaps if I'd been called sooner..." The implication hung in the air like a blade.

Ellen stared at her brother. The muscle in his jaw jumped, a telltale twitch in his cheek betraying the storm inside. She willed him to remain quiet, knowing any word now could spell disaster for their family. *Please, Seamus. Think of Mam. Think of Da. Think of what will happen to us if you speak.*

Lord Russell took a step nearer the horse but barely glanced at Duchess, his expression focused more on financial loss than the living creature before him. "Destroy her. She's no use to me now."

"No!" The word tore from Ellen's throat before she could stop it, her voice echoing in the stable rafters. The horses in nearby stalls whinnied nervously at her outcry.

Lord Russell turned toward her with a withering glare that made her step back instinctively. She felt as if she'd been doused with ice water, her whole body shaking with the force of his displeasure.

Isabella quickly moved in front of her, her slender frame providing a shield. Despite her fear, Ellen felt a rush of affection for her friend. Isabella might be their landlord's daughter, but in moments like these, she proved where her heart truly lay.

"Please, Father. Let's wait a couple of days and see how Duchess is." Isabella's voice was steady despite the tears threatening to spill. "I couldn't bear..."

"You shouldn't be here. Women are too sentimental." Lord Russell looked around the stables with cold eyes, as if the very walls offended him. "I'll give her two days. If she hasn't shown significant progress, it's off to the knacker's yard."

Seamus drew a sharp breath, chest rising too fast, his shoulders drawn taut as bowstrings. Ellen saw Mr Lynch shift closer, his presence a steadying weight beside Seamus. A silent warning not to let fury loose. She held her breath, watching the struggle play out on her brother's body. Pride warring with prudence.

"We'll look after her, your lordship. Thank you for your mercy." Mr Lynch's voice was calm, respectful, though Ellen caught the slight emphasis on "mercy."

"Fancy a drink, Shandon?" Lord Russell was already turning away, dismissing the injured horse and everyone who cared for her.

The vet nodded, hefting his leather bag with one hand and adjusting his spectacles with the other. "I'd enjoy that greatly. My son is heading to France and I know you, being in the War Office, may have news of his regiment."

They didn't even look back. Ellen watched them go, already talking of war and politics while Duchess lay broken in the straw.

Edward slunk after them like the coward he was.

Isabella walked over to Seamus with determined steps, her chin lifted despite her tears. "Make her better, please."

"I'll do my best." Seamus's voice was gentle now, all trace of anger gone when speaking to Isabella.

Isabella gave the stable staff a small, sad smile. "Thank you all for your hard work and dedication. My father appreciates all your efforts, he just…" She gave up trying to cover for her father, her shoulders sagging.

Ellen watched as Isabella walked slowly toward the house, no doubt crying for the horse she loved. Her friend's dress dragged over the small patches of straw and mud of the stable yard, but she didn't seem to notice or care.

"Pity she isn't the person in charge, isn't it? At least she has a heart." Tom's sun-browned face showed his admiration.

"No more of that talk, Clancy. You don't want his lordship to hear of it. Now get back to work, all of you. Seamus, what do you think we should do next?" Mr Lynch spoke with authority, but his eyes were kind.

"Not much we can do, Mr Lynch, but wait and pray. The salve takes time to work, but Duchess is strong and healthy. I'll stay with her." Seamus coloured slightly as he remembered his manners. "If that's alright with you, Mr Lynch."

"It is, lad." Mr Lynch's voice dropped to a whisper. "Let's try to keep that butcher Shandon away from her for now." He turned to Ellen. "About time you got home, girl. Your mam and da will be worried sick. Tell them I'll take care of Seamus and make sure he gets some food and rest."

Ellen nodded, but she moved closer to her brother first. "Seamus," she whispered, "you did well to hold your tongue."

He looked down at her, and for a moment his face softened. "Go home, Ellen. Tell Mam not to worry."

She walked out by the side gate, glancing up at Clonbarra House. Was Isabella hidden behind one of those high windows? Or Edward, with his cold stare? The thought made her shiver. The house loomed above the village, its pale stone glowing even on the dullest day. The sweep of gravel drive and the lions flanking the steps spoke of wealth that would never be hers.

To Ellen, the windows always seemed like unblinking eyes, rows of them staring down at the cottages below, reminding everyone who truly ruled this land.

She picked up her skirts and ran.

FIVE

Ellen's boots squelched through mud as she made her way along the stone path to their cottage, her shawl pulled tight against the evening chill. The rain had finally stopped, but heavy clouds hung low in the darkening sky. The familiar sight of their whitewashed cottage should have comforted her, but tonight the thatched roof sagged more than usual, and the stone walls looked smaller against the vast landscape.

The comforting aroma of boiled potatoes and turf smoke drifted from the chimney. The scent wrapped around her like a warm embrace, but it couldn't ease the tension knotting her shoulders since leaving the stables. She paused at the door, suddenly aware of the mud caking her boots, her black hair escaping from its braid in wet tendrils. Her fingers fumbled at the latch, clumsy with cold and something else. Lord Russell's icy stare still burned in her memory.

Before she could announce herself, her mother's voice called out, worn but still holding that note of concern. "Ellen? Is that you, child? Come in out of that cold before you catch your death."

Ellen pushed through the wooden door. The warmth hit her immediately, along with the familiar scents of home. But then she saw her father.

Paddy McGrath sat hunched over the rough wooden table, his shoulders shaking with a violent coughing fit. His calloused hands gripped the table's edge until the knuckles went white. The sound was wet, rattling, like something clawing out of his chest.

"Da?" Her voice came out small and frightened. She'd never seen him look so fragile, this man who'd always seemed as solid as the stone walls of their cottage.

Mary hurried over with a cloth, her movements gentle as she rubbed her husband's back. "There now, Paddy. Easy does it." She looked up with tired eyes that held fear. The flickering oil lamp cast shadows across her mother's face, deepening the lines around her eyes. "Your father's been like this most of the day. That dampness gets into his chest something fierce."

Paddy finally stopped coughing, wiping his mouth with the back of his hand. As he pulled it away, Ellen caught a glimpse of blood. When he looked up, she could see how pale he'd grown beneath his weather-beaten tan. But his blue eyes still held their familiar warmth, though rimmed with exhaustion.

"Don't be fussing over me, Mary. I'm grand." His voice was hoarse, each word an effort. "Ellen, girl, what's this I hear about Duchess? Your mam said there was trouble."

Ellen moved to warm her hands by the small peat fire, steam rising from her wet clothes. The heat felt good against her chilled skin, but it couldn't warm the cold dread in her bones. "Edward tried to make her jump Long's wall, Da. Seamus said it was too high, but you know how Edward is." Anger hardened her voice. "The poor creature has a terrible gash on her flank."

"And how is our Seamus managing?" Mary's ladle shook slightly as she served the potatoes. She had to pause twice, steadying herself against the table. "That temper of his will get him into trouble one day, mark my words."

"He kept his head, Mam. Though I could see it was a struggle." Ellen took her place at the table, accepting the bowl gratefully. Plain potatoes, a scrape of butter. She remembered when Mam scraped bacon fat over them. Those days felt far away now. "Mr

Lynch made sure to praise his healing touch in front of Lord Russell." She paused, the next words sticking in her throat. "But Duchess... Dr Shandon says she'll never race again. His lordship wanted to destroy her right there."

Paddy's eyes flashed with anger, colour flooding his pale cheeks. "That heartless—" Another coughing fit seized him, worse than before, his whole body convulsing.

"Paddy McGrath, you mind your tongue." Mary's words came sharp, but Ellen caught the quick glance that gave her mother away. She moved behind her husband again, rubbing his back, but the fear in her mother's eyes grew. "We can't afford to have talk like that getting back to the big house."

"Aye, and when has holding our tongues ever helped us?" Paddy gasped between laboured breaths. His fist crashed on the table, making the dishes rattle. "The Russells treat us like we're nothing more than the dirt under their boots. That son of theirs ruins a fine horse through stupidity, and who'll be blamed if she dies? Our Seamus."

Ellen watched her parents with growing concern. Her mother's movements were jerky as she returned to her seat. Her father listed to one side as if staying upright required too much effort. The cottage felt smaller tonight, the low ceiling pressing on her shoulders, walls too close with all their worries.

"Isabella stood up to her father," Ellen said, remembering the squeeze of her friend's hand. "Made Edward fetch the vet himself. She has a kind heart, that one."

"Aye, well, it's not Miss Isabella who holds the purse strings." Mary settled into her chair with a weary sigh. "Her father has the final say, and you know how he feels about tenants getting above their station."

Paddy reached across the table to squeeze Ellen's hand. His palm felt too hot, feverish, but his grip was still firm. "You did right helping today, child. Animals shouldn't suffer for human foolishness." His voice grew stronger with conviction despite his obvious illness, and Ellen saw a flash of the man he used to be. "No living thing should suffer under the boots of our betters."

"Paddy..." Mary's voice held a warning tone, but Ellen could hear the exhaustion beneath it.

"What, Mary? Am I to pretend the world is different than it is? That our sons don't deserve better than to spend their lives bowing and scraping to the likes of Russell?" His eyes burned with pride – the same look Ellen had seen in Patrick's face before he left for Dublin. "Patrick sees it clear enough. There's change coming, mark my words. Ireland won't be under the English thumb forever."

Mary's face drained of colour as her fingers found the small cross at her throat. "Don't speak of Patrick, not with talk like that. These walls might be thick, but words have a way of travelling."

"Patrick's a grown man, Mary. He can make his own choices."

"And what good will those choices do him if he ends up in prison? Or worse?" The words came out ragged, tears threatening. "First Patrick with his politics, now Seamus getting too close to the gentry's business. And you with this cough that's getting worse by the day. How am I supposed to keep this family safe?"

Ellen's spine stiffened. She'd never heard Mam sound so defeated, so afraid. Rising from her chair, she wrapped her arms around her mother's thin shoulders.

Mary tucked a wet tendril behind Ellen's ear. "You're frozen, love."

"Mam." She tried to inject confidence into her voice. "Seamus will be careful. He knows what's at stake. And Da will get better once the weather clears."

But even as she spoke, the words echoed hollow in the small room. The cough plaguing her father for weeks showed no signs of improvement. She'd seen how he winced when he thought no one was looking, how he pressed his hand to his chest as if trying to hold something in. As for Seamus, she knew her brother's protective instincts. If Duchess took a turn for the worse, no amount of caution would keep him from trying to save her.

"That's my good girl," Paddy said, his voice softer now, affectionate despite the rasp. "Always looking for the bright side." Another coughing fit overtook him, and there was red on his handkerchief before he tucked it away.

He pushed aside his plate, having barely touched his meal. Ellen stared at the untouched potatoes, remembering how her father used to clear his plate and ask for seconds. Now he couldn't manage even one portion.

Mary poured water for him, each movement precise despite the slight tremor in her grip. "You need your rest, Paddy. This dampness has settled in your chest, and arguing politics won't cure it."

"Aye, perhaps you're right." Paddy stood slowly, his movements stiff and painful. Ellen noticed how he gripped the table edge for support, how his breath came in short gasps. "Ellen, you help your mam with the washing up. And say a prayer for that horse. If she dies, it'll go hard on our Seamus, no matter whose fault it really was."

As her father shuffled to their parents' bedroom, Ellen began clearing the table. The simple meal sat heavy in her stomach. She thought about Patrick up in Dublin. Had he met up with John? Not that the two boys were friendly. John was quieter, like Seamus. Kind too. And handsome. She plunged her hands into the hot water. There was little point in mooning over a boy.

Outside, the wind picked up again, rattling the cottage windows, and she shivered despite the warmth of the fire. Her mother tutted at the way she was washing the dishes and took over, handing Ellen a cloth to dry.

"Mam, how bad is Da's cough really?" The question escaped before she could stop it.

Mary's hands stilled in the water. Only her father's harsh breathing from the next room broke the silence, punctuated by coughing that shook the thin walls. When her mother finally spoke, her voice was barely above a whisper. "I don't know, child. I ought to fetch the doctor but your da won't hear of it. He's worried about the expense." Mary scrubbed at the pot with more force than necessary. "I put your grandmother's salve on his chest and boiled up turnips with sugar, but nothing seems to help. I'm going to write to Patrick. It's time he came home."

Ellen's heart sank. If Mam was calling Patrick home, things were worse than she'd thought. "But him and Da will start arguing again. They might both believe in a free Ireland, but Da can't abide violence, and you know Patrick believes the time may come when Irishmen take up weapons again. You know how they get."

Her father had always backed John Redmond, saying no Irishman should rebel while Britain fought the Germans – that helping now would earn Ireland her freedom later. But Patrick called that a fool's bargain. He said the only time to strike was when England was too busy bleeding on foreign fields to crush them at home.

Mary set the now clean pot aside and reached for a biscuit tin, where she kept paper and a pencil stump. "Patrick will be too busy helping with the farm to argue, and your father doesn't have the energy for their usual rows. At least if I get Patrick home, I can keep an eye on him. Better here than running around Dublin with those Volunteers he writes about."

As she dried the last bowl with a cloth mended too many times to count, Ellen didn't dare voice her suspicions. Patrick wouldn't listen to their mam any more than he'd listened to Da. Her eldest brother's letters had grown different lately, full of pride and talk of freedom, of a teacher named Pearse who was stirring the young men's hearts. Patrick had fire in his blood, the kind that made men do dangerous things. And with Edward Russell back from England, having Patrick home might bring more danger than help.

The wind howled outside. From the bedroom came another racking cough. Ellen closed her eyes and said a silent prayer for Duchess, for Seamus, for Da's health, and for Patrick to stay away just a little longer. But even as she prayed, the wind rattled the windows again, like a warning.

Storms were coming. Ellen just didn't know if they'd break first over the big house or her own roof.

SIX

A week later, Ellen looked up from the washing bucket at the sound of hooves. Her hands were raw from the lye soap, and she welcomed the excuse to pause. The morning was still sharp with coolness.

Isabella rode toward them on her chestnut mare, picking carefully through the muddy patches left by last week's storms.

As she drew near, she called, "Ellen, is Seamus here?"

"He's up in the top field helping Da. Can I do something for you?" Ellen wiped her hands on her apron as the older girl dismounted. She still wasn't riding side-saddle. Lady Russell would have a fit if she knew.

"I wanted to tell him Duchess is doing much better. Father is going to use her as a brood mare, on Mr Lynch's advice. I thought Seamus would like to know. After all, he saved her." Isabella's face lit with gratitude.

Relief washed through Ellen. Duchess alive meant one less worry for Seamus. She dipped her head. "I'll tell him. It was kind of you to come."

Isabella smiled. "You don't have to be so proper. You used to call me Bella. I'd like us to be friends again."

Ellen hesitated, then managed a small smile. They had been

friends, as children. She had missed Bella, perhaps not as much as she missed John, but enough. "It's good to see you, Bella."

"You can tell Seamus that Father has insisted Edward enlist. Mother kept him out of the war so far but Father says it will make a man out of him."

Isabella lowered her voice. "The servants were saying Patrick might be coming home from Dublin. Is it true?"

Ellen's hands stilled against her apron. Isabella knew already? A small chill ran through her. Mam had only written last Saturday. Gossip travelled faster than the post. "Mam persuaded him to come back. She's worried about Da's cough."

"I hope your father gets better soon." Isabella glanced at the gathering cloud. "I'd best get back before Miss Nugent wakes from her nap. Father always finds the dullest governesses in Europe. I wish I could go to the local school, like you."

Ellen shook her head, smiling despite herself. The idea of Miss Isabella Russell at the village school was beyond imagining. Lord Russell would as soon walk to London barefoot.

She held Isabella's horse for her as she mounted.

"I hope I'll see you soon, Ellen," Isabella called out as she rode off.

Ellen watched her race away, hair flying, and felt a pang. For all her fine clothes, Bella looked lonely. Cook said she sometimes slipped bread to hungry families, but never when Lady Russell was watching.

Her mother's call pierced her thoughts. "Ellen, what are you doing standing around staring into space? There's plenty of work to be done."

Mary stood in the doorway, shoulders stooped. She had no time for loneliness. Ellen shook herself back to work. She returned to the washing, plunging her hands back into the harsh water. Patrick would be home soon. What changes would that bring? She hoped his presence would ease Mam's fears and provide the support their da desperately needed.

It took hard work to make a small farm meet the rent and feed a family. Patrick had helped by sending some of his wages home from Dublin, but since losing his well-paid job in the lockouts in 1913, he'd only managed to find odd jobs on the docks. The lockout had broken more than wages – factory doors barred, men blacklisted for standing with the unions in Larkin's strike, families queuing for bread. Patrick had come home thinner, but proud he hadn't bent. Ellen had thought her brother would take the king's shilling and join the army, like so many others who were desperate to feed their families. But not Patrick. He'd said he'd starve before betraying Ireland by fighting for the king.

A sigh escaped her. It was alright for a single man like Patrick to hold such views. But men like poor Jack Hurley hadn't the same choices. She thought of Jack with ten children to feed, and only one arm left to hold them with when he came back from the Front. Half his mind gone, if shouting at shadows was anything to go by.

As the afternoon wore on, Ellen watched the lane frequently, hoping to catch sight of Seamus returning from the fields. The sun was beginning its descent when she finally spotted him walking alongside their father. Paddy seemed smaller beside Seamus's growing height.

When they reached the cottage, exhaustion was etched in her father's face. The day's work had taken its toll, and each breath came harder than usual.

"How are you feeling, Da?" Ellen helped him settle into his chair by the fire.

"Grand, child. Just grand." His eyes tightened, then the cough came again, rattling through him.

Seamus shot Ellen a meaningful look. "Da pushed himself too hard today. I told him to rest, but he wouldn't hear of it."

"A man doesn't rest when there's work to be done." The words dissolved into a coughing fit that left him gasping.

Mary emerged from the kitchen, wiping her hands on her apron. Her eyes immediately went to her husband, and Ellen saw her lips thin. "Paddy McGrath, you're pale as milk. Ellen, fetch your father some water."

As Ellen moved to comply, she heard her mother say. "Seamus, I got a letter back from Patrick today. He says he'll be home by week's end."

"And Da? How's he taking the news?"

"He's relieved about the help with the farm." Mary's voice was tight with worry. "But you know how those two are when they're in the same room for more than five minutes."

Ellen returned with the water, pretending she hadn't overheard the conversation. But as she handed the cup to her father, she caught Seamus's troubled expression. He knew. They all did. Patrick's return would bring its own complications. Patrick and Da had always butted heads – about the farm, about Patrick's ambitions, about everything.

Later that evening, as the family came to the table for their modest supper, the conversation naturally turned to their absent son and brother.

"When exactly did Patrick say he'd arrive?" Ellen asked, passing a cup of tea to her da.

"By week's end, but you know Patrick. He's never been one for keeping to schedules." Her mother set out bowls of boiled potatoes and turnips.

Her father attempted a reassuring smile despite his fatigue. "It'll be good to see the boy again. And we'll need his help with the spring planting. Where is Seamus? It's not like him to miss a meal."

"He's away with the hurling." Ellen watched her da's hand shake as he added some food to his bowl. "They have a match coming up, and he said he needed the practice. The others keep comparing him to Patrick, and he's determined to be recognized as a talented player in his own right."

Paddy nodded approvingly. "That boy is always measuring himself against Patrick. We all have our gifts. Patrick may be a gifted sportsman, but Seamus has a way with animals most can only dream of."

Ellen and her mam exchanged a smile. They knew Seamus might prefer to have a gift with a hurl and a *sliotar*, if his comments about getting the local girls to pay more attention to him were anything to go by. But her da didn't need to know his youngest son was growing up.

Mary set down her spoon, her expression growing serious. "Patrick needs to understand that things have changed since he left. Your father's health, the farm... we can't afford any of his political nonsense."

"Mary," Paddy warned, his voice rough.

"No, Paddy. I won't pretend otherwise. If Patrick comes home spouting rebellion and stirring trouble, it won't just be him who suffers. We'll all pay the price." Her voice trembled slightly as she spoke. "Dreams don't feed a family. They just bring soldiers to the door."

The scrape of spoons on bowls filled the silence, louder than words. Somewhere up the hill, Isabella would be eating with silver cutlery off porcelain plates. Ellen tore her bread in half and passed it to her mam.

Ellen slept badly that night and was up before the cockerel, the dawn light filtering through the thin curtains. She dressed quickly and headed outside, the cool morning air offering a welcome respite from the stuffiness indoors.

She found Seamus in the top field, already busy with the scythe, the blade moving in steady rhythm through the grass.

"Seamus," she called out, waving. He had only got back last night after she had gone to bed, and she had things to tell him.

He straightened, wiping his brow with the back of his hand, alarm flashing in his eyes. "What's wrong? Is it Da?"

"No, he's fine." Ellen steadied herself before continuing. "Duchess is doing much better. Isabella came by yesterday with the news. Her father is going to use Duchess as a brood mare on

Mr Lynch's advice. She thought you'd like to know – after all, you did save her."

Seamus's face broke into a smile. "That's good to hear. I'm glad she's on the mend. Duchess is a fine horse."

"Oh, and Isabella also mentioned that her father has arranged for Edward to enlist. To make him a man."

He chuckled. "Not sure anyone could make that eejit grow up. But it's good news. Let's hope he is sent to France at the head of his men. He's got such a big head the Germans will have no problem finding their target."

"Seamus! You can't say things like that. It's wrong to wish a man dead."

Seamus only grinned. "Just saying what half the village thinks. Are you going to help, or heading back to the house?"

Ellen spent the rest of the morning helping Seamus in the field, their conversation drifting between work, the war, and the uncertain future. The rhythm of the work was soothing, with him cutting and her raking the grass into neat piles.

Despite the hard work, she enjoyed spending time alone with her favourite brother – even as her thoughts kept drifting to the changes Patrick's return would bring to their small, close-knit world.

SEVEN
DUBLIN, NOW

"Ladies and gentlemen, we're beginning our descent into Dublin."

Caitlin unclenched her fingers from the armrest one by one. Eight hours of flying and her leg was already lodging a formal complaint. Grammy would want to know everything. Did she sleep, did they feed her properly, did she talk to anyone nice? The answer to all three was no, but she would find a way to make it sound better. She rolled her ankle, testing what the pins would tolerate.

Ireland spread below her like one of those postcards in Grammy's desk. All that green. Stone walls dividing the fields into neat little packages. Nothing like the marshland around Charleston.

The wheels hit the tarmac with a jolt that shot straight up her bad leg. Welcome to the homeland, courtesy of Aer Lingus and a metal pin that did not appreciate altitude changes.

Dublin Airport was exactly what Grammy had described: organized chaos in two languages. Signs in Irish and English, announcements she half understood, the smell of coffee mixing with something that might have been breakfast rolls. The terminal buzzed at a level just shy of a siren. She breathed through it.

Customs moved efficiently. When her turn came, the officer

looked up with eyes the colour of summer rain. Dark hair, easy smile. Trustworthy at first glance. She knew better.

"Céad míle fáilte go hÉireann."

"Go raibh... míle maith agat?" she managed.

He smiled kindly. "Fair play to you for trying. You'll get the hang of it."

"My grandmother would be mortified. She tried teaching me for weeks."

"Family back home then?" He flipped through her passport.

"My grandmother. She sent me to play detective."

"Ah, roots hunting. Half of America's at it." A stamp, a flourish. "Have a brilliant time. Mind yourself on the roads. We drive on the proper side."

A smile tugged at her lips. "I'll try to remember that." She stepped aside, keeping the flow moving.

At baggage claim, she grabbed for her black suitcase, put too much weight on her bad leg, and pain fired up her thigh. The handle slipped.

"I've got it." A man in his sixties hauled it down. "Heavy enough to hold half of America."

"Just essentials." Her hand went to her hip out of habit. Empty. No badge. Just the ghost of it.

"First time over?"

"Is it that obvious?"

"You'll fall in love with the place soon enough. They all do." He grabbed a trolley before setting the suitcase on it.

"Thank you," she managed, as her shoulder instinctively tensed, muscles locking against the subtle pain of the old bullet wound as she reached for the trolley. Kindness still caught her off guard, like a gentle touch received after months of bracing for a blow.

The rental counter ran like a drill. Forms, a smile and a reminder about roundabouts, keys. The compact hire car smelled like pine and other people's vacations. She tested the pedals before pulling out. *Trust the leg, then the lane.*

Wrong side of the road. Wrong side of the car. Everything backward. But the traffic was patient. She kept to the left like it might disappear if she glanced away.

She found her hotel tucked between a coffee shop and a bookstore, blue against a grey sky. Inside, she absorbed the warmth and smell of something baking.

"Miss O'Shea?" the clerk said, her auburn hair escaping its bun. "Siobhan", according to the badge. "You're early, but your room's ready." A quick flick of her eyes took in Caitlin's stance, then her professional gleam returned. "Lift to your left, breakfast seven to ten. Wi-Fi on the card. If you need ice packs, dial zero. We keep some for the jet-lagged and the sporty."

"That would be great. Thank you," Caitlin said, with a grateful smile.

"First time in Dublin?"

"First time anywhere in a while."

"You must be wrecked. We can send your bag up."

"Please."

Room 323 was small and clean, its window over a narrow street. Caitlin kicked off her shoes and lay back. Her leg throbbed its familiar rhythm. She propped it on a pillow and waited for the heat to dull.

She looked at her phone. Two missed calls from Grammy. Three texts, too. Caitlin hit dial.

Grammy answered on the first ring. "Finally. I was starting to think you'd been kidnapped by leprechauns."

She laughed. "It's past midnight there. You should be asleep."

"Sleep is overrated. Tell me everything. Was the flight awful? Did they feed you? You did eat something, didn't you?"

"The flight was fine. Yes, they fed me. No, I didn't eat it."

"Caitlin Rose O'Shea—"

"I know. I'll order room service. The hotel is nice. Very Irish."

"Are the people friendly? Donna says Irish men are terrible flirts."

"Actually, the Customs officer *was* pretty charming. Complimented my terrible Irish."

A delighted gasp. "Was he handsome?"

"Grammy."

"I'm old, not dead."

"Dark hair, nice smile. Patient with jet-lagged Americans."

"Did you get his name?"

"They don't wear name tags at Customs. And it wasn't a date."

"Missed opportunity. Any nice young men at the hotel?"

"You're incorrigible."

"I am invested in your happiness. How is the leg? Truth."

"Sore. Ice will do."

"You're taking your medication?"

"Yes."

"And you will be careful? No overdoing it."

"I promise."

"One more thing," Grammy said. "I have been thinking about Mam all day. Your great-grandmother. Do not hide the truth from me. Even if it is bad."

"I'll find out what happened to her, Grammy."

"I know you will. You are my brave girl."

Brave. The word landed strangely. She had hidden in her apartment for months. She couldn't wear her badge anymore. "Grammy—"

"Order room service. Put your leg up. And if you see that Customs officer again, get his name."

"Good night, Grammy."

"Good night, love. Call me tomorrow. Any time." The line clicked off.

Caitlin looked at her paperwork but she was too tired to achieve anything. She'd deal with it tomorrow. Tonight, she would ice her leg and eat, relieved she had managed to sound so normal to Grammy when she felt anything but. It was amazing how easy it was to be Grammy's granddaughter, and not the woman who flinched at doors that slammed.

Caitlin's stomach growled as she looked at the room service menu. Eleven months since the ambush, since Mark, since everything fell apart. And here she was, three thousand miles from home, chasing ghosts for a ninety-one-year-old who still called her "brave".

EIGHT

Dublin woke up outside Caitlin's window with all the subtlety of a brass band. Car engines, footsteps on wet pavements, someone's alarm going off three times before they finally shut it off.

She showered fast. Good water pressure for an old building. She pulled on jeans and a plain grey hoodie. Her leg complained when she stood. Time to walk it off before it seized up completely.

The lobby buzzed with German tourists trying to understand the bus system while Siobhan drew them a map that looked more like abstract art. Caitlin slipped out before anyone could ask if she'd slept well. She didn't want to disappoint them with her answer.

The morning air bit sharp and clean, nothing like Charleston's humidity that clung to you like wet clothes. A violin played somewhere, the kind of sad Irish song that made you homesick for places you'd never been. She headed for St Stephen's Green because the hotel map said it was close and because she had nowhere else to go.

The park gates opened onto paths that probably meant something to people who belonged there. She didn't. Just another American tourist looking for roots that might not exist.

The lake stretched as grey as the sky. A bunch of school kids pressed against the fence, pointing at swans.

"Stay back from the edge, Cian Murphy, or I'll be tellin' your mam why you came home like a drowned rat!"

The teacher's accent made Caitlin smile despite herself. Grammy would love it here. She'd probably already be chatting with the teacher about the children, sharing stories about her days volunteering at a local school.

She found a bench facing the water and sat before her leg could make the decision for her. The wood was damp, but everything so far in Ireland seemed to be.

"Anyone sittin' there, love?"

An elderly woman stopped beside the bench, carrying a handbag big enough to smuggle a body and wearing a headscarf that had seen better decades.

"All yours." Caitlin scooted over.

"Ah, you're a dote." The woman plunked down with the confidence of someone who owned the bench through sheer habit. "Maureen Corr, though everyone calls me Mo. Come here every mornin' for me lunch. Can't be payin' those prices in the cafés, not with what they charge now."

She unwrapped a sandwich that smelled like real butter and ham – nothing like the processed garbage Caitlin had been living on since her discharge from hospital.

"Visitin' Dublin?"

"First time. I'm Caitlin."

"American! I can tell by the vowels. They come out all flat." Mo's eyes crinkled. "You've picked the right country, I'll give you that. See that?" She pointed at a patch of blue fighting through clouds. "That's what we call summer."

Caitlin surprised herself by laughing.

"Are ya hungry? Ham sandwich?" Mo held out half without waiting for an answer. "I always pack extra. Me mother survived the rationing, taught me never to eat alone if someone else might be hungry."

Every safety rule Caitlin had learned said *no. Don't take food from strangers. Don't engage. Don't trust.* But Mo's face was so open, so genuinely kind, that refusing felt like kicking a puppy.

"I couldn't..."

"Course you could. If not the sandwich, try a fairy cake. Made them fresh this mornin'."

The cake was still warm, dense with currants and butter and something that smelled like Sunday afternoons at Grammy's kitchen table. Caitlin bit into it and made an embarrassing sound.

"That good, is it?" Mo beamed. "My old dog Joe loved them too. Now me husband – waste of space that one was. Threw him out years back and good riddance." She cackled at Caitlin's expression. "Sorry, love. Probably shouldn't speak ill of the eejit. You'll think I'm mental."

Caitlin nearly choked on the cake. When was the last time she'd laughed like this? Really laughed, not using the polite version she'd perfected for hospital staff?

"What brings you to Dublin then? Besides our glorious weather?"

"Family research. Looking for my great-grandmother."

"Ah, another one searchin' for roots. Can't blame ye. Where was she from?"

"Clonbarra. Near Galway."

The woman looked pensive. "Don't know it meself, but the west is gorgeous altogether. Wild and lonely, all cliffs and stories." Mo scattered seeds from a paper bag, and ducks appeared like she'd summoned them. "Never give them bread. Kills the poor things."

An hour passed without Caitlin noticing. Mo talked about everything: her hip replacement, the price of milk, her neighbour's terrible singing. All delivered with the easy intimacy of someone who collected people like others collected stamps.

"Right, I'm off to the hospital. Mrs Brady's had her hip done and her son's about as useful as a chocolate teapot." Mo gathered her things. "Lovely meetin' you, pet. Your parents raised you right."

If only she knew. If only Caitlin could remember her parents well enough to know if that was true, or if everything good in her came from Grammy.

Alone again, guilt crept back. Grammy in the nursing home bed while Caitlin sat in a Dublin park eating cake with strangers. What if something happened? *What if...*

Stop. Grammy had practically ordered her to come. The same woman who'd survived her daughter's death, husband's death, who'd raised a granddaughter from a baby and never complained. If Grammy said go, you went.

Her leg had stiffened. Caitlin stood carefully and headed for Grafton Street, where a guy with a guitar was murdering "Whiskey in the Jar" for tips. The rich smell of cooked food pulled her toward a pub that looked old enough to have served James Joyce.

Inside was warm and loud and exactly what she needed. She found a corner table and ordered fish and chips and, because she could, a half-pint of Guinness. No Mark to correct her order, to explain why she really wanted water and a salad, to manage her choices in a way that was disguised as caring.

"First time?" As the server put her Guinness on the table in front of her, Caitlin noticed she had purple streaks in her hair and a grin that said she'd seen it all. "That determined look gives it away."

"That obvious?"

She grinned. "Don't worry if you hate it. Takes practice." She lowered her voice. "I can't stand the stuff meself, but don't tell me boss."

The beer was bitter and strange. The fish was perfect. Caitlin ate slowly, watching Dublin through the window. Normal people living normal lives. She wanted that so badly it hurt.

Back at the hotel, she spread Grammy's documents across the bed. Birth certificates, death records, Gavin's emails. Ellen McGrath, born 1901. Married John Power. Two children.

A whole life reduced to a sheet of paper.

It was pointless going to St Brigid's as Mrs Walsh had told her, she'd have to wait. Maybe she should go straight to Clonbarra, where Ellen had lived. She bit her lip as she wondered where to start. She looked at the map on Google, and found the seaside called to her. Neutral territory. Easier to face the ocean than empty rooms or curious villagers.

She searched online for accommodation and found a cottage rental in a village called Ballycluan, about five miles from Clonbarra. White walls, windows facing the Atlantic, far enough from neighbours that no one would ask questions. A month to find Grammy's truth. She booked it before she could overthink it.

Her phone buzzed. Grammy.

"Did you eat today?"

Caitlin shook her head as she laughed. "Yes, Grammy. Made a friend. Her name's Mo."

"Already making friends! I knew this trip would be good for you. Any progress with your search?"

"I decided to stay in Dublin for a few days. I want to search the births, marriages and deaths registers. The paperwork Gavin found will give me a good starting point. I spoke to a helpful researcher at the General Register Office. He advised me to come in on Tuesday when it is open to the public. I can spend all day there and see what I find."

"I wish I could be there with you."

"Grammy, he said the records aren't always accurate so don't get your hopes up."

"I'll do my best."

Patience had never been Grammy's strength. But who could blame her for wanting answers now. "Good night, Grammy."

"Good night, love. Drive careful when you go west. Text me when you get there."

Outside, Dublin settled into its evening rhythm. Pub doors opening, laughter spilling onto streets that had seen worse and survived. In two days, she'd leave this city for the edge of Ireland, where the Atlantic met the sky and secrets waited in the salt air.

For tonight, she'd try to sleep without dreams of gunfire or betrayal. Try to believe Grammy was right; that some journeys were about finding your way home, even when you'd never been there before.

Caitlin found the brass plate on the red-brick terrace: **General Register Office, Research Room, Werburgh Street.**

Inside, the air smelled of old paper and floor polish. A radiator ticked. Two other researchers were already hunched over terminals, coats on the backs of chairs, notebooks open.

"Photo ID?" the receptionist asked.

Caitlin slid her passport across. "I'm looking for birth, marriage, and death records for my great-grandmother's family."

"You can search on the PCs. When you're ready, fill the pink order slips for research copies. We take debit or credit cards." A pause, gentler. "Write down exact names, dates if you have them, and any known addresses."

Caitlin chose a terminal near the window. St Werburgh's bell gave a single note outside, thin through the glass. She opened her folder, set Ellen's photograph beside the keyboard, and started with the civil indexes.

She searched the deaths using both of Ellen's surnames, McGrath and Power, but nothing appeared. To check the accuracy of the records, she searched for Patrick and Seamus and found their details. So why was Ellen not listed?

She must have sighed louder than she realized, as one of the other people searching looked over. "Having problems?"

"Yes, I can't find my great-grandmother's death certificate. I know the year she died, her parents' and brothers' names, but I'm drawing a blank."

"Did she die in Ireland?"

"Yes, in a home run by nuns." This was ridiculous – why was she ashamed to tell someone her great-grandmother had been in what they called Magdalene laundries? "She died in a mother and baby home. I don't know why she was there, as she was a widow. She was married in a church."

The man scratched his neck with his pencil. "Have you found her marriage certificate? Maybe her surname was misspelled and that's why you can't find a death record?"

"No, there's no marriage certificate. A friend who did some family research – he's a cousin of sorts – thought they might not have married. But how can that be when they are both named on my grandmother's baptismal certificate? See?" Caitlin held out a copy of the church registry.

"You're right to question it. In those days, no priest would give a child a baptismal record listing both parents if he didn't believe them to be married in the church. But, in order to be legal, marriages in Ireland had to be registered. If there is no record of your great-grandmother on the church register, in the eyes of the law, she was never married. I'm sorry. Sometimes our rules are hard for visitors to understand."

"Please don't apologize. You've been very helpful."

The man shook his head sadly. "After all the media coverage lately about those homes, I'm not sure what went on in the hearts and minds of those who ran those institutions."

His phone beeped and, with a look of apology, he stood up and left the room to take the call.

A clerk passed with a stack of bound indexes, their cloth spines frayed smooth. "If you need to confirm a variant spelling, the books are there," she said, nodding to a long table. "And keep an eye on informants, witnesses – any names you find when you get the certs. They tell you more than people think."

Caitlin looked back at her notebook. Four lines. Four slips. She added a fifth note in the margin: *Compare informants and addresses across all events.* If the address repeated, it could tie them to a district hospital, a county home, a workhouse infirmary. Names could lie. Addresses left footprints.

At the counter she handed over the pink slips. "Research copies, please. Full certificates."

"Of course." The clerk checked her passport again, typed, then slid a card machine forward. "If any are out for scanning, it may take a little longer. We will email where possible."

"Email is fine." Caitlin tucked her passport away. "Can I verify the informant names here when they arrive?"

"You can. Often it is the same priest, the same neighbour, the same matron. Look for patterns. They tell you who stood in the room."

Caitlin returned to the terminal and pulled up the entries again, copying every small thing she had skipped at first: superintendent registrar district, quarter, reference numbers, any middle initials. She kept trawling until the clerk advised they were closing.

Outside, Werburgh Street was bright and cold. She paused on the steps, the city moving around her in small purposeful currents. Somewhere behind her, in a room of humming screens and cloth-spined books, her family had begun to line up on paper.

NINE

1916

Seamus pulled Ellen's braid. "Did you hear John Power's back? He's staying with his uncle Frank at the pub, helping him in the stables."

Tierney's public house sat at the crossroads, its whitewashed walls and green-painted window frames cheerful despite the grey sky. The building housed both the pub and the stables, connected by a cobblestone courtyard that always smelled of hay and horses.

Ellen looked away before Seamus saw his teasing had hit a raw nerve.

John had been Ellen's childhood friend until his father was killed in France two years ago. His mother, unable to bear the reminders, had taken him to Dublin.

John had been the thoughtful boy who shared Ellen's books and taught her to whistle like a lark. She remembered too the day he'd left, how she'd cried into her pillow that night, mourning the loss of the one person who understood her love of stories and dreams of a world beyond their small village. They were both older now, would they feel the same?

The boy who returned was lean and watchful, sandy hair catching the light, eyes that saw everything but gave nothing back. The new sharpness in him made Ellen's pulse jump when their paths crossed. She found herself taking extra care with her appearance each morning, braiding her hair more carefully, pinching her cheeks for colour before she might encounter him.

Since he'd started helping at the stables, she timed her walks past Tierney's when the horses were out, her heart leaping whenever she caught a glimpse of John's familiar figure.

"Ellen," her mother called from the kitchen, breaking into her daydreams, "take this broth over to Mrs O'Brien. The poor woman's been poorly all week."

Ellen wrapped her shawl around her shoulders and took up the covered pot, grateful for the excuse to walk through the crossroads where the four lanes met, then up the gentle rise into Clonbarra proper, where the church spire served as a beacon above the thatched roofs. The main street was wide enough for two carts to pass, and she knew John often exercised the horses along the lane at this hour. Her heart quickened at the thought.

Sure enough, as she returned from Mrs O'Brien's cottage, she spotted him leading a bay mare along the path. Her breath caught at the easy grace of him, the strength in his shoulders under his work shirt.

He looked up, and the careful smile she remembered so well spread across his face. It transformed his watchful features, making him look younger, more like the boy she'd known.

"Ellen. How are you keeping?" His voice had deepened since Dublin, taking on a richness that sent warmth spreading through her chest.

"Grand, thank you." She felt heat rise in her cheeks but pressed on, not wanting this moment to end. "And yourself? Are you settling back into Clonbarra life?"

John's expression grew thoughtful, and she watched the play of emotions across his face, something she'd always been able to read, even as a child. "It's... different than I remembered. Smaller, perhaps. But peaceful." He paused, his brown eyes studying her face with an intensity that made her skin tingle. "Would you care to walk with me a while? If you're not needed at home."

Ellen's heart leaped. She thought of the chores waiting, of her mother's expectations, and dismissed them all. "I'd like that."

They walked in comfortable silence toward Ellen's home, stopping at an old oak tree near it, where they'd often played as children. Ellen felt acutely aware of everything: the way he slowed his steps to match hers, the warm scent of horse and hay, the brush of his sleeve that sparked through her arm. When their hands accidentally touched as they navigated a narrow part of the path, neither pulled away.

"Do you still whistle like a lark?" he asked.

Ellen tried, but the sound that emerged was more crow than lark. John laughed. "It's worse than I remember."

"Then you'd better remind me how to do it," she said, and he showed her, the clear notes threading between them like a private tune.

"You've changed since Dublin," she said, eyeing the shadows under his eyes.

John glanced at her. "Have I? In what way?"

"You're more... serious, I suppose. Like you've seen things that most people our age haven't." She paused. "But you're still you. I can still see the boy who taught me to skip stones and shared his books with me."

John didn't answer straightaway. When he spoke, his voice was rougher. "Perhaps I have seen things. But, Ellen..." He stopped walking, turning to face her. "You've changed too. Grown more beautiful. Your hair so dark, your eyes..." He blushed.

The words sent heat flooding through her. She'd dreamed of him saying something like this, but the reality was overwhelming. "John..."

They'd reached the oak tree, and he helped her settle on the grass beneath its spreading branches. The gesture was courteous but intimate, his hands lingering on her arms a moment longer than necessary. She could feel the calluses on his palms, the strength in his touch.

He seated himself beside her. "Ellen," he began, then stopped, seeming to wrestle with his words. She watched his throat work as he swallowed, noticed the way his hands clenched and unclenched in the grass. "There are things about Dublin, about what I've been doing... things I can't speak of."

Ellen's pulse quickened. She reached out instinctively, placing her hand over his. "Are you in some kind of trouble?"

He turned his hand palm up, interlacing their fingers. The simple touch sent warmth racing up her arm. "Not trouble, exactly. But... dangerous times call for young men to make difficult choices. Some choices that others might not understand."

The weight of his words settled between them. Ellen thought of her brother Patrick's angry politics, of the whispered conversations that stopped when she entered rooms at home, of the tension that seemed to thicken the air whenever certain names were mentioned.

"You're talking about the Easter Rising in Dublin."

John's jaw tightened, but he didn't deny it. His thumb traced circles on her palm as he spoke. "I'm talking about Ireland. About what kind of country we want it to be. About whether we're content to remain on our knees forever."

Fear and excitement knotted in her. His eyes blazed even as his voice stayed controlled. She found herself leaning closer, drawn by more than just his words.

"What are you saying?"

"I'm saying that there are those of us who believe Ireland should be free. Truly free, not just allowed to exist at England's say-so." He rubbed his other hand over his face, his eyes staring into the distance. "I was there, Ellen. In Dublin. At Stephen's Green with Commandant Mallin and Countess Markievicz." His voice caught. "They executed Michael Mallin. A good man who died for believing Ireland deserved better."

Ellen's breath caught. She'd heard whispers about the executions, but to hear it from someone who'd been there. Without thinking, she squeezed his hand tighter, offering what comfort she could.

"That's why you came back. You're hiding."

John nodded grimly. "I managed to get away when they were rounding up the others. Made it back here, but I know they're still looking." He lifted their joined hands, studying them as if they held answers. "But I'm also saying that I care about you, Ellen McGrath. More than I probably should, given..."

"Given what?" Her voice came out breathless.

"Given that caring about someone makes you vulnerable. Makes you careful when perhaps you should be bold." His thumb traced across her knuckles, and she shivered despite the warm evening. "Makes you hope for a future that might not be possible."

Ellen's breath caught. She turned her hand in his, gripping tighter. "John..."

"I know I have no right to ask anything of you. I know I'm just a stable hand with dangerous ideas and no prospects to speak of. But, Ellen, I've thought of you every day since I left. When things were darkest in Dublin, when I thought I might not survive, it was memories of you that kept me going."

"Don't," she whispered, her free hand coming up to touch his face. His skin was warm beneath her fingers, rough with a day's stubble. "Don't talk about having no right. You have every right to... to hope."

He leaned into her touch, his eyes closing briefly. When he opened them again, the raw emotion there made her heart race. "If I asked you to wait for me, if circumstances required me to go away for a while, would you?"

The question sent a chill through Ellen. She could feel the desperation beneath his careful words, the fear he was trying to hide. "How long?"

"I don't know. Perhaps months. Perhaps... longer."

Ellen studied his face, memorizing every detail: the small scar above his left eyebrow from a childhood fall, the way his hair fell across his forehead, the gold flecks in his brown eyes. "John, what aren't you telling me?"

Before he could answer, the sound of raised voices from the

cottage behind them made them both turn. Ellen recognized her father and Patrick's voices, carrying clearly through the evening air.

"They failed, the whole country is against them!" The frustration in Paddy's voice was evident. "See what the *Tribune* says!"

"They are patriots."

John's entire body went rigid, his hand tightening almost painfully on hers. "Your brother's talking too loud."

Ellen's stomach dropped. "John, please..."

"Da, I don't care what those newspapers say. The men are heroes and in time everyone in Ireland will see it, just mark my words."

John stood abruptly, pulling Ellen to her feet. His face had paled, and there was something almost frantic in his eyes. "Ellen, listen to me. Your brother needs to be more careful about what he says and where he says it. Calling the rebels 'heroes', defending them so loudly... there are ears everywhere, and not all of them friendly."

"Where are you going?" came Mary's worried voice from the cottage.

"Out!" Patrick's reply was sharp with anger.

The cottage door slammed, and Patrick strode past them without acknowledgment, his face dark with fury, down the lane toward the village crossroads.

John watched him disappear down the lane, his expression troubled. "Anger without caution gets men killed. Or worse, their families destroyed." He turned to Ellen, cupping her face in his hands. The gesture was so tender, so desperate, that it made her eyes sting with unshed tears. "Promise me you'll warn him. Tell him to watch his tongue, especially around strangers."

Ellen covered his hands with hers, feeling the tremor in them. "How do you know..."

"Promise me," he insisted, his forehead coming to rest against hers. "Please."

"I promise."

For a moment they stood there, breathing the same air, so close she could see the pulse beating rapidly at his throat. Then John stepped back, though his hands lingered on her face.

"I should get you home before your mother worries."

They walked up the path of the McGrath cottage in a silence heavy with things unsaid. Ellen's hand found his again, and this time there was nothing accidental about it. She memorized the feeling: the roughness of his palm, the strength in his fingers, the way their hands fit together perfectly.

At her door, John paused. In the fading light, his face was all planes and shadows. "Ellen, whatever happens in the coming days... remember that some things are worth the risk. And remember that you're the best part of being home."

Before she could respond, he lifted her hand to his lips, pressing a kiss to her knuckles. Heat rushed through her.

Then he was gone, disappearing into the gathering dusk, leaving Ellen standing at her door with her heart pounding and the ghost of his kiss burning on her skin.

That night, after the dishes were done and her parents had retired, Ellen caught Patrick by the door as he prepared to go out again.

"Watch your tongue outside, will you?" she said quietly.

Patrick looked at her, and for a moment his anger softened. "You too now?" he said, weary rather than angry. "I'll be careful, Ellen. Enough for you?"

It wasn't enough, but it was all she could win from him.

The next evening, when Da had gone to the pub and Mam was out visiting a sick friend, Ellen heard a low whistle, clear and lilting like a lark's call. She slipped out of the house, leaving her brothers arguing by the fire.

John stepped from behind the tree, a grin tugging at his mouth. "Thought that might bring you out."

"You'll have the neighbours talking, meeting me out here after dark."

"They already talk," he said, moving closer until she could see the faint stubble along his jaw. "May as well give them something worth gossiping about."

"Ah, don't be cheeky. Is that what I am? Someone to cause talk?"

He shook his head, the teasing fading. "No. You're someone I can't stop thinking about."

The words hung between them, startling and wonderful. John turned toward the tree then, drawing his pocket knife and carving carefully into the bark, just under where they had once carved their initials.

"What are you doing?"

"You'll see."

She stepped closer and saw the small bird taking shape beneath his blade, wings lifted mid-flight.

"A lark," she murmured.

He smiled. "I haven't given up teaching you to whistle. Seemed fitting."

When he finished, he ran his thumb over the carving, then looked at her again, his expression softer. "You'll think of us when you see it."

He reached for her hand, and for a moment she saw in his eyes the same boy who had shared apples with her beneath the summer trees, who had taught her to whistle like a lark when they were barely tall enough to see over the stone walls. But this, the way his thumb traced her knuckles and the careful way he drew her closer, was something altogether different from their childhood games.

The kiss that followed was gentle and uncertain, a promise rather than a claim. When they parted, he smiled, still close enough for her to feel his breath.

Ellen's fingers curled against the rough bark behind her, seeking something solid in a world that had suddenly tilted. Her eyes stayed closed a heartbeat longer than his, and when she finally opened them, she found herself blinking as if emerging from deep water.

"Now the neighbours will have something to talk about."

She laughed, but it came out breathy and strange, nothing like her usual confident humour. "Let them."

At her gate, he lifted her hand to his lips. "I'll marry you one day, Ellen McGrath," he whispered.

Before she could speak, he disappeared down the lane, whistling the same tune.

Ellen touched her fingers to her lips, holding the warmth there, then noticed her hand trembling slightly. She pressed it flat against her skirt and drew in a deep breath of the cool night air, trying to steady herself. The world felt different somehow. The familiar gate, the lamp in the window, even the sound of her brothers' voices drifting from inside all seemed touched by something new and wondrous.

She slipped back into the house, grateful for the dim light that might hide the flush she could feel warming her cheeks and neck.

TEN

Days later, Ellen was hanging laundry out to dry when she heard a motorcar approaching at speed. The sheets billowed around her like white flags of surrender as she looked up to see a dark touring car racing toward Tierney's pub, dust rising in its wake. Her blood turned to ice.

She dropped the wet shirt she'd been holding, barely noticing as it fell into the dirt. John. They'd come for John.

By the time she reached the village centre, a small crowd had gathered. Two Royal Irish Constabulary constables in dark green uniforms had emerged from the motorcar and were speaking urgently with Frank Tierney at the pub door.

"Where is he?" one constable demanded, his voice carrying across the square.

"I don't know what you're talking about," Frank's voice lacked conviction.

"John Power. We have information that he's been hiding here since returning from Dublin. Proof he was involved in the recent troubles there." They pushed their way roughly into the pub.

Ellen's legs nearly gave out beneath her. She clutched at Tom Clancy's arm for support, and the old man's face creased with sympathy.

"They've been asking questions about the lad for days," he whispered. "Someone in Dublin gave them his name."

The constables emerged from the pub, their expressions frustrated but determined. "If you're harbouring a rebel, Tierney, you'll answer for it same as him," one warned before they climbed back into their motorcar and drove off, deeper into the countryside, no doubt to search the fields and hidden places where John might be concealing himself.

Ellen watched them go with her heart hammering against her ribs. Somewhere out there, John was running or hiding, and she might never see him again.

The arrest came two days later, just before dawn. Ellen woke to the sound of shouting and a motorcar engine echoing from the direction of the village. From her window at the McGrath cottage, she could see lights moving on the main street, a quarter mile away but clear in the pre-dawn darkness. She flew from her bed, not even stopping to put on shoes, and ran outside in her nightgown with only a shawl thrown over her shoulders.

Desperation spurred her on. She didn't even notice the stones of the lane cutting into her soles as she raced down the familiar path, past the field where her father's sheep used to graze, through the crossroads where four lanes met, and up the slight rise into the village proper. The cottage sat in a hollow, so she couldn't see what was happening until she crested that final hill.

On the main street, parked outside Tierney's pub, the same motorcar idled, dark and purposeful, its engine's hot-oil reek turning her stomach. John was already in shackles, face bloodied but defiant as the constables loaded him in. A crusted thread of blood at his collar, a torn cuff. Even battered, he held himself straight, chin raised. Their eyes met across the gathering crowd, and time seemed to stop.

In that moment, Ellen saw love and desperation in his face.

Ellen pressed her hand to her heart and nodded, as if answering a question he'd asked.

Then he was gone, the motorcar disappearing down the lane toward the county jail, and Ellen stood barefoot in the early light, knowing he might never return.

Frank Tierney approached her as the crowd dispersed, sorrow etched deep into his face. Without a word, he draped his coat around her shoulders. Only then did she feel the shaking in her body. "He asked me to give you this," the publican said, pressing a folded piece of paper into her hand. "If they took him."

Ellen unfolded the note with trembling fingers:

Ellen,

If you're reading this, then they've found me. I'm sorry I couldn't tell you everything, sorry I couldn't stay. But I need you to know that these past weeks, getting to know you again, falling in love with you, they've been the best of my life.
I loved you as a boy, but I love you as a man now, with everything I have. You're brave and beautiful and true, and you deserve better than a rebel with a price on his head.
I don't know where they'll send me or for how long. But if you're willing, if you can find it in your heart to wait, I'll come back to you. I swear it on my life.
Will you write to me? Will you let me hope?

Forever yours, John

Ellen pressed the letter to her chest and closed her eyes, feeling her world tilt on its axis. When she opened them again, Frank Tierney was watching her with kind, understanding eyes.

"He's a good lad, Ellen. Foolish, perhaps, but good. And he loves you true. I could see it in his eyes every time he spoke of you. The boy was half-mad with it."

"Do you know where they'll take him?" Her voice was barely a whisper.

"Likely back to Dublin first for questioning, then to England for trial. These political prisoners... they don't keep them close to home." Frank's voice gentled. "But I'll find out, child. I'll make sure you have an address where you can write to him."

Ellen nodded, not trusting her voice to remain steady. As she walked back to her cottage, John's letter clutched in her hand, she made a silent promise. However long it took, however dangerous it became to love a rebel, she would wait.

A month later, Frank Tierney appeared at the McGrath cottage door with news that made Ellen's hands shake. She'd been kneading bread, and flour still dusted her arms as she wiped them on her apron.

"John's been tried in Dublin, convicted of participating in armed rebellion against the Crown, and sentenced to imprisonment. He's being transferred to Frongoch Internment Camp in Wales, along with hundreds of other Republican prisoners."

Ellen felt her mam's stare like a hand at her throat, but she kept her attention on Frank, knowing that one glance at her mother's face would shatter what little composure she had left.

Her mother had made her feelings clear when she'd caught Ellen returning from the oak tree one evening, John's kiss still warming her lips. "That Power boy will bring nothing but trouble to this house," she'd said.

"I'll pray for him and your family, Frank. Can I get you a cup of tea? Something stronger?" Mary's question went unanswered as Frank continued speaking.

"At least he wasn't executed. The boy's young age likely saved him from the firing squad. I've got the address where you can write to him, though the letters will be read by the prison authorities."

Ellen stared at the address written on the small slip of paper Frank handed her:

Prisoner 847, Frongoch Internment Camp, Bala, Wales.

Her John was now just another number in a British cell.

That evening, Ellen sat at the kitchen table with paper and pencil. Her mother's lips pressed into a thin line. "Writing to imprisoned rebels now, are we?" But she turned back to her mending without forbidding it, which was as close to permission as Ellen would get.

What could she possibly say that would pass the censors? That she missed him so much it felt like a physical ache? That she woke each morning with his name on her lips? That the village felt empty without him?

She started three different letters and crumpled them all up. Finally, she just wrote what was in her heart:

Dear John,

Frank told me where you are. I'm keeping my promise. I think of you every day and pray for your safe return.
The oak tree misses you too.

Yours always, Ellen

"What are you doing, love?"

Ellen jumped at her da's voice. Flushing, she looked up. "Writing to John."

Her da coughed before taking a drink of water. "He's a decent lad. Kind, and comes from a good family – but his heart rules his head." Da's coughing started again. "He's for Ireland, and I can't be against him for that."

On impulse, Ellen leaned over and kissed her da on the cheek. "I'm glad you like him."

"Now don't be getting ideas, miss. You're too young for courting."

Ellen sighed before her da added, "Still, nothing wrong with sending a few words of comfort to a lad in a strange land, is there?"

ELEVEN
NOW

The cottage sat at the edge of Ireland like it was waiting for her.

Caitlin turned off the engine and sat for a minute. Three hours of wrong-side driving through countryside that looked like Grammy's postcards. Stone walls, sheep that didn't care about right of way, villages with names she couldn't pronounce. Now this. A red door that belonged on a tourism website. White walls, green shutters, the Atlantic stretching beyond toward America.

She grabbed her phone. Two texts from Grammy:

> Did you make it safely?

> Remember to eat lunch. Real food, not just coffee.

The car door protested when she opened it. Salt air hit her immediately, its freshness still surprising her after Charleston's swampy heat. Wildflowers grew everywhere around the cottage perched above the beach, like nobody had told them about property lines. Purple ones, yellow ones, some white things that might have been weeds but were still beautiful. She wished she could identify them. Grammy would know their names.

Barking echoed from nearby, and she groaned to herself. *Great.*

Neighbours. She wasn't ready for the whole "friendly Irish village" thing yet.

A man appeared on the path from the beach, carrying a surfboard and followed by what looked like a small bear. *German shepherd*, her brain corrected, even as her body tensed. The dog spotted her and launched itself over the low stone wall that separated the property from the beach path as if it had springs for legs.

For one awful second, she was back there. Wet pavement, Nemo's weight in her arms, blood everywhere.

"Finn, no! Down!"

The dog was already on her, paws on her chest, tail wagging so hard his whole back end moved. Not aggressive. Just... enthusiastic. His nose was cold and wet against her hand as she stumbled backwards, just managing to keep her balance.

"Jesus, I'm sorry." The surfer reached them, breathing hard. "He thinks everyone wants to be his friend. You okay?"

She made herself breathe. Made herself see this dog, not the one in her head. "Fine."

"You sure? You've gone a bit pale." His accent was local: softer than Dublin's. She turned to him and took in the dark hair still dripping from the ocean, water running down his neck in a way that made her notice the strong line of his shoulders. The wet suit clung to him, leaving little to the imagination. Mid-thirties, maybe. The kind of tan that said this was a daily routine, not a vacation.

Her face heated. When was the last time she'd noticed a man like that?

"Your dog needs better training." The words came out sharper than she'd intended, defensive.

"You're right. Sorry about that." He clipped a lead to Finn's collar, and she caught herself watching his hands. Strong, capable. No wedding ring.

Stop it, Caitlin.

"I'm Conor. You must be renting Annie Murphy's place."

"Caitlin." His handshake was warm. She let go quickly.

"American." Not a question. A smile played at the corner of his mouth, and she found herself staring at it. "Let me help with your bags. Least I can do after Finn's assault."

He was already lifting her suitcase from the trunk before she could stop him. His eyes flicked to the way she shifted her weight as they began to move towards the house. A tiny pause, then he slowed his stride to match hers without a word. No fuss, no comment, just quiet adjustment. Heat prickled the back of her neck, not from pain this time, but from the fact he'd noticed. Most people pretended not to.

She followed, trying not to notice the easy way he moved, the strength in his shoulders as he carried her overpacked bag like it weighed nothing. *Get it together*, she told herself. *You're here for Grammy, not to ogle the locals.*

The cottage key was exactly where the rental company said it would be: under a rock shaped like a turtle.

"The Aga's temperamental," Conor said, setting her case inside the door. His arm brushed hers as he pointed to the instructions on the wall, and she caught the scent of salt water and something else – clean and male. Her pulse jumped. How did he know about the stove? Was Annie Murphy his mother?

"Do you own the cottage?"

At her question, he turned to face her. "I wish. I grew up near here. My mam and Annie are friendly. She lives in a nursing home now but when we were younger, my brothers and I were sent over to help Annie with chores like fetching turf for the stove. There's instructions on the wall, but basically you just talk nicely to it and pray. Ballycluan's fifteen minutes that way" – he tipped his head, indicating the way along the coast road – "if you need anything."

"Thanks." Her voice came out breathier than intended.

"No bother." He whistled for Finn, who was investigating the garden with the dedication of a detective. "Maybe see you on the beach. Good walking when the tide's out."

He paused at the gate, and their eyes met. Held. Something

shifted in the air between them, electric and unexpected. "Hope you find whatever brought you here."

She stood in the doorway longer than necessary, watching him walk away. The wet suit really left *nothing* to the imagination.

Grammy would have a field day with this.

Inside, the cottage was charming. Low ceilings with exposed beams that would brain anyone over six feet. White walls that looked freshly painted, blue cushions on a worn sofa, and a scrubbed pine table by the window where Caitlin could spread Grammy's documents out properly. A kitchen from the 1950s, complete with a stove that looked like it required an engineering degree. No dishwasher, no microwave – none of the conveniences that Mark would have insisted on.

Good.

The living room had a stone fireplace and bookshelves stuffed with paperbacks left by previous visitors. Romance novels in six languages, thrillers with broken spines, and... she pulled one out. *A History of Coastal Galway*. Maybe Grammy's answers were sitting right here, waiting between water-damaged pages.

Later. First, she needed to text Grammy back.

> Made it safe. Cottage is perfect. Already met a neighbour and his attack dog.

The response was immediate:

> Was he handsome?

> Grammy. I'm here to research your family.

> You can do both. Send pictures!

Caitlin shook her head but found herself smiling. Ninety-one years old and still convinced romance could fix everything. Maybe that was true for some people. But not for someone who'd been played so thoroughly she'd almost died from trusting the wrong person.

Unbidden, however, her traitorous mind kept circling back to water dripping down a strong neck, warm hands, that moment at the gate...

Caitlin got up, needing to distract herself by moving, and went to explore the upstairs rooms. The bedroom window framed the ocean. She could see the beach path where Conor had appeared. No sign of him now, just gulls fighting over something in the waves. Ellen McGrath could have known this view. Could have walked that beach with Grammy as a baby, before everything went wrong.

Her leg was screaming from the drive. She dry-swallowed two ibuprofen and changed into jeans and sneakers. The beach could wait for tomorrow. Or next week. Or...

No. Grammy had sent her there to find answers, not hide in a cottage feeling sorry for herself. Or think about surfers in wet suits.

The path to the beach was steeper than it looked. Her leg protested every step, but the view was worth it. The bay opened wide, miles of sand mixed with smooth pebbles that shifted under her feet. Empty now, but she could imagine how it must have looked a century ago, families spreading across the strand, gathering mussels and cockles, children chasing each other through the rock pools.

The water was grey-blue, streaked with weed at the tide line. When the sun broke through, the waves turned the colour of old glass bottles. She could see the distant shore across Galway Bay, just a smudge on the horizon. Waves crashed against the rocks, same as they would have in Ellen's time.

This was what the edge of the world looked like.

She walked slowly, favouring her good leg. The sand was firm near the water, easier than the loose stones higher up. Shells and wet seaweed tangled where the tide had left them. No broken glass, no tourists, no one asking if she was okay.

Ellen McGrath might have walked here. What had broken her so badly that she'd ended up in the care of the nuns?

"Find out what happened to my family," Grammy had said. Like it was simple. Like the past wasn't buried deeper than old bones.

The wind picked up, bringing the smell of rain. Time to head back before her leg gave out entirely. Tomorrow she'd drive to Clonbarra, see what was left of Ellen McGrath's world.

At the cottage gate, she turned for one last look at the ocean. Somewhere out there was home. Somewhere behind her were answers.

TWELVE

1916

Why? Why did God have to let Da die? What had he ever done to anyone? Everyone loved him.

Ellen kicked the base of the old oak tree, the one that stood alone in the field beyond their cottage, its gnarled trunk scarred by decades of Atlantic storms. She'd run there since childhood, whenever the world pressed too heavy. The rough bark bit into her boot.

Her chest ached with more than grief. If John were here, he'd know what to say. He'd rest his hand on her shoulder in that quiet way of his, not needing words. But he was locked away across the water, and she couldn't even tell him. The thought of him reading about Da's death in one of her carefully worded letters made her come out in goosebumps. How did you write such news when you know the prison censor would be reading it?

"Ellen? What is it? What's the matter?"

Ellen scrubbed the tears from her face before turning to face Isabella. "My da, he's dead. I... I..." She crumpled, allowing Isabella to draw her into a hug.

Isabella rubbed her back while murmuring words of condolence. "I liked your father, he was a kind man. He always had a smile for me. Remember when he taught us both to whistle using grass blades, right here under this tree?"

Ellen nodded, hiccupping as she tried to get her emotions under control. The memory – Da's patient demonstrations, Isabella's frustrated attempts, their laughter carrying across the fields – made the loss sharper. "I should get back home. Mam will need help with... well, you know. I shouldn't have left her but I just couldn't bear it. They stopped the clocks and opened the windows."

"I never understood why Catholics do that."

"It's to let his spirit go to heaven." Ellen rubbed her eyes and started walking toward her home.

"Ellen, wait. What can I do? Please let me help in some way. I know my presence wouldn't be welcome: at least, the villagers wouldn't feel comfortable with me being there... But I'd like to do something for your father. For you."

Ellen couldn't think of what to say. There was no point in challenging Isabella's opinion – it was the truth. Having a Protestant – never mind the fact she was Lord Russell's daughter – at the wake would be inappropriate.

"Maybe you could get some bread? It must be white."

"I'll go to O'Sullivan's now. Please pass on my condolences to your mother and brothers on their loss. I'll... I'll see you soon." With a quick hug that lingered just a moment longer than usual, Isabella walked over to her horse, mounted and rode off in the direction of the village.

Ellen made her way home, her fingers unconsciously seeking the small piece of paper in her pocket – John's last letter, worn soft from reading. "*Keep your courage up, mo stór,*" he'd written. "*Your da would want you strong.*" But how could he have known? The letter was weeks old. She'd write tonight, after the prayers. Tell him about Da's last days, how he'd asked after John, called him "a fine lad with a true heart." Maybe the censors would let that through. She'd heard they only passed letters to prisoners when they felt like it. Would the death of an Irishman stir pity – or satisfaction? Ellen walked into her parents' bedroom where her Da was laid out on the bed. The room smelled of turf smoke and beeswax, the two candles at Paddy's head sending shadows up the whitewashed wall. His hands lay folded round the rosary Mary had pressed into them, the knuckles swollen from years of work on land that never gave enough back. A sprig of cherry laurel, wet from the holy water dish, glistened on the blanket.

Despite everything, Ellen found herself almost smiling. Da would have hated the fuss, would have grumbled about good candles being wasted. "Sure, I can't see them anyway," he'd have said, and Mam would have swatted him with her dishcloth.

Sometime later, they heard the sounds of a bicycle. Seamus put his head around the door. "Mam, come and see this."

Mrs O'Brien looked at Mary. "You go on, love. I'll stay with Paddy."

Ellen went to the kitchen followed by her mam. Seamus and Patrick unloaded the contents of two boxes. "O'Sullivan sent his delivery boy over with it. Says Miss Russell paid for a wake order. There's a few pounds of tea, sugar, white bread loaves, currant brack and biscuits. She's even included a bottle of whiskey – the good stuff – and a gallon of porter."

Patrick lifted the whiskey bottle, examining the label with raised eyebrows. "This costs more than we see in a month."

Her mam picked up some of the packages. "She even thought of the snuff, the tobacco and the clay pipes. Paddy will have a fine send-off thanks to her generosity."

"Least she can do after all her family put him through all these years." Patrick sniffed, opening the whiskey and pouring a glass for himself and Seamus.

"You mind your manners, son. Your da valued kindness and we will too. There was no call for Miss Russell to do this. We won't make light of her actions."

Patrick opened his mouth but at a look from Seamus shut it again. Now wasn't the time to be arguing with Mam. Not when the love of her life was laid out in the other room.

"Remember the time Da caught you with grandfather's pipe?"

Seamus said suddenly, looking at Patrick. "You were green as grass for hours."

Patrick's stern expression cracked slightly. "He made me smoke the whole bowl. Said if I was man enough to steal tobacco, I was man enough to finish it."

"Then he sat with you all night while you were sick," Ellen added softly, with a sad smile. "Told Mam it was something you ate."

The kitchen fell quiet, each lost in their own memories.

Ellen knelt beside her mother, lips moving with the rosary decades, though her gaze clung to her father's face. The chin band cut a strange line along his jaw: too tight, too final. From the kitchen drifted the scrape of chairs, men coughing low into their pipes. Patrick and Seamus had gone out among them, filling clay bowls, passing the snuff box keeping to the old ways.

Someone had covered the mirror with a length of dark cloth. Ellen's gaze kept straying to it, the heavy folds shivering when the door opened or the fire spat. She had an urge to lift the cloth, just to see herself, to make sure she was still there and not gone after him. But she remembered what the old ones said – that a soul might get caught in the glass, or that she'd see his face there, waiting. She crossed herself quickly and bent lower over her beads.

From the kitchen came the murmur of voices and the steady rhythm of prayer. The neighbours were taking turns by the bed, men and women alike, keeping the candles burning so her father would not lie alone.

On the table in the kitchen, Mary had set out the feast Isabella had supplied: sliced white bread spread with jam, the currant loaf, a pot of strong tea black as porter. The women of the village poured and poured again, the clink of cups rising above the murmured prayers.

Every neighbour who crossed the threshold dipped the sprig,

shook droplets over Paddy's folded hands, and bent close for a moment of silence.

Old Mr Donnelly pressed Ellen's hand. "Your father helped me bring in my harvest last year when my back gave out. Wouldn't take a penny for it." His eyes were wet. "We won't forget."

When the older women began the keening, the sound caught in Ellen's chest – a rise and fall like the tide in the bay, naming his name, crying out the hard years and the small mercies.

Mary's shoulders trembled, but her hands never left the beads.

Grey light seeped into the room when the men lifted Paddy from the bed into the rough coffin Seamus and Patrick had hammered together by candlelight. Mary's hands clutched the rosary as Ellen stood close, numb with the smell of resin and new planed wood, her brothers steadying the box as if afraid to let go.

Patrick, Seamus and four other men, carried him out feet first, shoulders bent beneath the weight. No one spoke. The lane outside was lined with neighbours, caps pulled low, women with shawls drawn tight against the morning chill. The air was hung with pipe smoke and the tang of damp earth.

At the threshold, old Mrs Reilly dipped the laurel once more and scattered drops over the lid of the coffin. Someone began the rosary, voices rising in a rough unison that followed the bearers down the boreen. Ellen kept step beside her mother, skirts brushing the wet grass, her eyes on the coffin swaying against her brothers' shoulders.

At the crossroads they paused, as was the way, heads bowed while the prayers wound to a close. Then the men shifted their grip and moved on, the sound of boots and murmured Hail Marys carrying Paddy toward the churchyard and the last bed he would take in Clonbarra soil.

THIRTEEN

In the days after the funeral, grief lay over the cottage like the spring mist that drifted in from the bay. Turf smoke curled through the rafters as it always had, yet to Ellen it seemed heavier now, as though sorrow had seeped into the very air. Beeswax lingered on her sleeve from the candles that had burned at Da's head, a scent she couldn't wash away.

Each morning, after Patrick and Seamus left to work the farm, Isabella arrived carrying her basket from the big house kitchens, full of bread, broth and cooked chicken or ham.

At first Ellen bristled: more charity, more reminder of their place. But Isabella stayed, perching on a stool or kneeling beside the wash as if she belonged.

On the third day Ellen nearly laughed outright when Isabella plunged her pale hands into the suds. "You'll ruin your dress," Ellen warned.

"Then I'll ruin it," Isabella replied, wringing out a sheet so clumsily she splashed herself head to toe.

Ellen barked a laugh before she could stop herself. Isabella laughed too, and for the first time since Da's death the weight on Ellen's chest lifted, just a little.

That afternoon they sat by the window, with the basket of

mending between them. Isabella pricked her finger almost at once and stuffed it in her mouth with a grimace.

"Miss Nugent would have apoplexy if she saw you now," Ellen said, in a prim imitation of Isabella's governess.

The two of them collapsed into giggles until Ellen glimpsed her mother in the doorway, her face drawn and disapproving, and the laughter froze like ice.

"Perhaps you shouldn't come here every day," Ellen said softly. "Your parents might not approve."

"Let me worry about my parents," Isabella answered, though uncertainty flickered in her eyes. Both of them knew the truth: if her parents knew where Isabella was, everyone would be in trouble.

A week later Mam called Ellen into the kitchen. The cottage felt smaller, the air close. Mary sat at the table, hands trembling even in stillness. The rosary beads were never far from her fingers now.

"Sit down, child. We need to talk."

Ellen obeyed, her stomach tightening.

"I've secured you a position at the big house. Chambermaid under Mrs Murphy. You start the fifth of June."

Ellen nodded, having half expected it. Her schoolbooks still lay neatly stacked by her bed, but she knew they would gather dust now.

"It wasn't what your da and I wanted for you." Mary's voice cracked. "We hoped you'd stay in school longer. Maybe be a teacher. But now, we can't afford to refuse it."

The word *charity* flared in Ellen's head. Was this what Bella's kindness had bought them?

"Mrs Murphy would have preferred a younger girl, but she's taken you as a favour. You'll start as a chambermaid. It's beneath what you should be doing at fifteen, but Da's death has changed everything."

Ellen swallowed, thinking of Miss Fallon's praise, of her dreams to be a teacher.

"There's one blessing. Her ladyship will be away in England for a month. She'd usually go for the London season, but with the war... well. At least you'll have time to learn before she returns." Mary's voice sharpened. "But, Ellen, there'll be no more visits with Miss Isabella. No more chatting. Do you hear me?"

"Mam..."

"No." Mary's hand struck the table, rattling the cups. "Listen to me. We are tenants on Russell land. Our cottage, our farm, our very livelihood, depends on their goodwill. If Lord Russell thinks his daughter too familiar with the likes of us, we could lose everything. Do you understand?"

Heat rose in Ellen's cheeks. She nodded, swallowing the words that would only make things worse.

"She's a lady. You'll be a servant. That's the way of the world."

The words stung because they were true. Ellen thought of Isabella's laughter with the washing, her warm shoulder on the cottage step, and knew all of it had to end.

"You need to stop her coming here, Ellen. Today."

When Isabella arrived with another basket that afternoon, Ellen met her at the door. "I can't invite you in today. Mam's resting."

Isabella's face fell. "Perhaps we could walk?"

Against her better judgement, Ellen found herself heading with her toward the oak tree. The hedgerows were heavy with May blossom, their sweetness mingling with the earthy smell of ploughed fields. Ellen plucked a daisy and pulled at the petals, whispering John's name under her breath.

"It's wrong, you know." Isabella's voice was suddenly passionate.

Ellen looked up from her flower. "What?"

"Are you even listening to me?" Isabella put her hands on her hips, her cheeks flushed with sudden emotion.

"Of course, milady." Ellen gave a mocking half-curtsy, the gesture more bitter than playful.

"Stop teasing me. It's wrong: me living in that big house, having so much, when some of the village children don't have enough to eat. They don't have shoes, Ellen. Children walking around barefoot because their families can't afford proper clothing."

Ellen looked down at her own feet, encased in the stiff leather shoes her mother had insisted on buying for her new position. They pinched her toes and rubbed blisters on her heels. Scrunching her toes against the confining leather, she said, "I miss walking barefoot. Feeling the grass between my toes, the cool mud after rain. But Mam says I have to behave like a proper servant now."

The irony wasn't lost on either of them.

"Be serious," Isabella pressed on, her hands trembling slightly as she clasped them together. "I want things to change. If women had the vote, the world would be a better place, wouldn't it? We could make laws to help people like your family."

Ellen shrugged, her fingers still working at the daisy petals. The flower was nearly bare now, white petals scattered at her feet. "I don't think it would make much difference to my life."

"Why not? You could be anything you wanted to be. You're clever, Ellen. Cleverer than half the boys in the village. You could be a teacher, or a nurse, or..." Isabella stared at her, eyes wide.

"Hardly, Bella." Ellen's laugh was sharp and humourless. She threw the stripped daisy stem to the ground with more force than necessary. "I had to leave school and get a job. At your house. I wanted to stay at school. Now I need wages. I'll work until I marry, then I'll leave to have children, and someday my daughter will become a housemaid too. And likely her daughter after that. That's how it works for people like us."

Isabella's cheeks flushed. "Don't you have any ambition? Any dreams of something more?"

Ellen stared at her friend, frowning at Isabella's complete lack of understanding. Dreams? Of course she'd had dreams: of staying in school, of becoming a teacher like Miss Fallon, of having books and learning and a life beyond scrubbing floors and emptying chamber pots. And she'd had dreams of John coming home, of them building a life together that wasn't defined by servitude. She'd dreamed of teaching their children to read, of breaking the cycle that trapped generation after generation.

"Ambition is for those with money." Ellen turned to face Isabella fully, heat flooding her cheeks. "You know I wanted to be a teacher. But that was just a foolish dream when Da was alive. Now it's impossible. Some of us have to live in the real world."

Isabella stepped back as if she'd been slapped, her face draining of colour. The spring breeze lifted loose tendrils of her copper hair, and Ellen could see tears gathering in her green eyes. She blinked rapidly, the way she did when trying not to cry. "I... I was only trying to..." Isabella's voice broke slightly. "I thought we were friends. I thought you understood that I want to help."

Ellen felt a stab of regret, but she forced herself to continue. This had to end, and it was better to end it cleanly than to let it drag on, to let Isabella believe things could be different. "Help?" She laughed bitterly. "You want to help? I start Monday week in your house. I'll scrub floors you'll walk on. I'll be emptying your chamber pot, and you'll be the lady giving me orders. That's reality."

Isabella's tears were flowing freely now, but her chin lifted with stubborn pride. "I never... I would never treat you like that."

"You won't have a choice. Your parents will expect it. The other servants will expect it. Even I will expect it, because that's how the world works. Not because you want it, but because it's how things are."

Isabella turned, skirts brushing the grass, and walked away with her head held high.

Ellen watched until she disappeared, then bent to pluck

another daisy. The wind caught the torn petals, lifting them like pale butterflies. "He loves me, he loves me." She repeated the words over and over, fighting the tears until they won.

FOURTEEN

Ellen walked the long path toward the big house, a basket of eggs balanced on her hip. The weight pulled at her side, and she shifted it higher, feeling the smooth shells shift against the woven sides. The morning sun cast long shadows across the manicured lawns, and the scent of early roses mixed with freshly cut grass. Her worn boots crunched on the gravel drive, so different from the confident whisper of ladies' heeled shoes. Days had passed since their quarrel under the oak tree. If Isabella was home, maybe Ellen could apologize for hurting her; try to explain why their worlds were so impossibly far apart.

The garden gates stood open, their wrought-iron curves cool under her hand. Through them, she spotted a familiar figure beneath an old apple tree, copper hair gleaming in dappled sunlight.

Isabella sat with a book open in her lap, but Ellen could tell from the stillness of her that she wasn't reading.

Isabella looked up, and Ellen's breath caught. Relief flooded her friend's face, followed by something that looked like joy. "You came."

The simple words held so much weight. Ellen's throat tightened. "I had eggs to deliver," she said, lifting the basket slightly, aware of how foolish the excuse sounded.

A smile touched Isabella's mouth. "Of course you did."

Without discussion, they walked together toward the back of the house, away from the windows where curious eyes might be watching. Ellen was conscious of every step, every glance, knowing that servants would gossip and word might reach Lady Russell. But Isabella's presence beside her, the familiar rhythm of their matched steps, made the risk feel worth it.

They settled beside the old summer house just as they had in childhood, when they'd shared secrets and dreams before the world taught them their places. Their skirts brushed in the grass: Isabella's fine silk whispering against Ellen's rough wool. The contrast wasn't lost on either of them, but for a moment, it didn't matter.

"Have you heard from your brother?" Ellen asked gently, trying to find safe ground between them.

Isabella's expression darkened, her fingers tightening on her book. "Mother took to her bed with vapours until Father agreed to pull some strings to get him reassigned. Edward's back from France, back to the safety of the War Office." Her voice carried a bitter edge that Ellen had never heard before. "It's all very well for other men to die fighting for king and country, but she draws the line at her own son."

Ellen tried to find something kind to say, though the mention of Edward made her skin crawl. "I think all mothers would want to protect their children."

"Mother isn't thinking of Edward as a person. If he had married and sired an heir, she couldn't care less if he rotted in France. It's all about keeping the estate intact, preserving the bloodline." She plucked at the grass with agitated fingers, shredding the blades. "He was back here for a week, strutting about the place like a peacock. He barked orders at everyone, terrifying the maids in particular. Thankfully, he's gone back now."

Ellen said nothing, though she knew too well of what Edward

was capable. The memory of Duchess lying broken in the field rose unbidden.

Isabella glanced at her before dropping her voice. "I wanted to come to you after... after our quarrel. But Father's been watching everything I do. He says this is no time for 'mingling with peasants,' especially with what's happening in Dublin."

Ellen's mouth twitched despite the gravity of the moment. "So we're back to that word again."

Isabella flushed, the colour rising from her neck to her cheeks. "You know I don't think of you that way." She leaned closer, and Ellen caught the scent of her perfume. Something French and expensive that probably cost more than Ellen's family spent on food in a year. "Ellen, can you imagine it? Connolly, so broken they had to tie him to a chair to shoot him. And Plunkett, dying of consumption, and still they killed him. The cruelty of it... No wonder the Irish hate the English. They're barbarians."

The passion in Isabella's voice, the genuine horror, caught Ellen off guard. "Be careful who hears you speak of the Rising with sympathy. These are dangerous times." Ellen said no more. The words rose to her lips, but she swallowed them. Most folk wouldn't see a difference between Bella and the English she condemned. An Anglo-Irish name was enough to damn you, no matter what your heart believed. How could she ever make Bella understand what the Rising had *set loose*? The neighbours whispering after the executions, soldiers stopping men on the roads, asking questions that had no right answers. What were you supposed to say when they asked if you believed Ireland should be free? Or if you supported the men and women who'd taken a stand? If the British hadn't answered rebellion with firing squads, it might all have faded away. Instead, every bullet they fired had turned more hearts toward the cause for Independence.

Isabella leaned forward, her green eyes bright with sudden fervour. "Have you read the Proclamation? They were promising equal rights to both men and women. All people were to be free, regardless of class or creed. Can you imagine it, Ellen? A world where you and I could truly be equals?" Her voice dropped to an excited whisper. "Surely you support that? Your family too?"

Ellen shifted uncomfortably, acutely aware they were treading on dangerous ground. This was exactly the kind of conversation that could destroy her family if overheard. Her brothers would be furious if they knew she was discussing politics with Lord Russell's daughter. Patrick especially, with his secret meetings and fierce pride. She closed her eyes for a second, remembering John at the tree warning her to tell Patrick to keep quiet. "Bella..."

"I've been writing to Countess Markievicz," Isabella interrupted, her words tumbling out in excited whispers. She gripped Ellen's hand, her fingers soft against Ellen's work-roughened ones. "I wrote once. I posted it from the village to avoid Father seeing it. I don't know if it got past the censors at her prison."

Ellen knew the countess had been sentenced to death for her part in the Rising. She also knew that when her sentence had been commuted to life imprisonment because she was a woman, she had told her captors she wished they'd had the decency to shoot her with her comrades.

Ellen pulled her hand away, looking around frantically to ensure they were truly alone. "You can't be serious. If your parents discover this..."

"But that's just it! Mother introduced me to the countess years ago!" Isabella's eyes sparkled with the thrill of her secret rebellion. "You know how Mother is, always trying to curry favour with titled families. She was practically fawning over Sir Josslyn and Countess Markievicz at charity events. Father even complimented the countess's horsemanship during fox hunts." She lowered her voice conspiratorially, leaning so close Ellen could smell her minty breath. "A fact he, no doubt, is careful to keep from his London cronies, now that she's a convicted rebel."

"Bella, listen to me." Ellen gripped her friend's wrist urgently, feeling the delicate bones beneath silk and skin. "If your parents discover you've been corresponding with her, they won't just blame you. They'll blame *me* for filling your head with Irish nonsense.

My family could lose everything. Our cottage, the land. We're hanging by a thread as it is."

Isabella's face fell slightly, but her jaw remained set with stubborn determination. "I don't care what they say. I've missed you terribly, Ellen. These past days have been the loneliest of my life. I won't let their prejudices keep us apart."

The raw sincerity in her voice made Ellen's chest ache with answering emotion. She studied Isabella's face: the fine white skin that marked her as gentry, the faint freckle on her jaw that powder couldn't quite hide, the earnest hope in her green eyes.

This girl, who had everything, still somehow needed their friendship as desperately as Ellen did.

"I've missed you too."

They sat in comfortable silence for a moment, bees humming lazily in the blossoms about them. The sun warmed Ellen's face, and for these few precious minutes, she could pretend they were just two girls again, before the world had shown them how wide the gulf between them truly was.

Isabella nudged Ellen's arm playfully. "So, tell me what's been happening in the village. Any interesting gossip? Has Molly O'Brien finally noticed your brother making eyes at her during Mass?"

Ellen felt a pang thinking of all the things she couldn't share: Patrick's mysterious absences that had their mother pacing the floor until her breathing turned ragged, the way Mam clutched her chest whenever someone mentioned the rebels being rounded up, the letters Ellen posted to a Welsh prison. How could she explain one without revealing them all? Each secret was another wall between them.

"Nothing much worth telling," she said, forcing lightness into her voice. "Though Patrick did turn red as a beetroot when Molly smiled at him last Sunday."

Isabella laughed, the sound bright as silver bells. "Poor Patrick. He should—"

"Isabella Florence Russell, what is the meaning of this?"

The voice cut through their conversation like a blade. Ellen scrambled to her feet so quickly she nearly dropped the egg basket. She curtseyed automatically, even as her mind reeled with panic.

Lady Russell stood on the garden path like an avenging angel, her face white with fury. Her elaborate morning dress of burgundy silk seemed absurd in the garden's soft green hush, the dark colour unsuited to the warm morning. Her eyes, cold as winter frost, were fixed on Ellen with undisguised disgust.

"Mama…" Isabella began, rising more slowly, her chin lifting with defiance.

"Don't 'Mama' me," Lady Russell snapped, her cultured voice sharp enough to cut glass. "When Nellie said you were seen from the morning room, consorting with a tenant girl in our garden, I could scarcely credit it. I had to see this disgrace with my own eyes." Her gaze raked over Ellen. "I am thoroughly ashamed of you, Isabella."

"Mother, please don't speak of Ellen that way. She's my friend." Isabella stepped forward, placing herself slightly between Ellen and her mother's wrath.

"She is no friend of yours and has no business on these grounds." Lady Russell's voice rose dangerously, carrying across the manicured gardens. "Mr Pierce!"

The butler appeared from behind a hedge as if he'd been waiting for the summons. Ellen's heart sank further. Pierce had never been unkind, but, like all the servants, he couldn't afford to lose his position.

"Yes, my lady?" His voice was carefully neutral.

"Escort this person off the premises immediately. I never want to see her here again. Is that understood?"

Ellen found her voice, though it came out smaller than she'd intended. Her hands trembled as she lifted the basket. "But the eggs, my lady. Your cook was expecting…"

"Cook can find another source." Lady Russell snatched the basket from Ellen's hands with such force that Ellen stumbled. Without hesitation, she hurled it to the ground.

Eggs smashed against the stone path, shells shattering and bright yolks spreading into wasteful gold across the grey stones. Three days of laying, gone in a heartbeat.

Ellen stared at the ruin, something inside her cracking along with the shells. Each broken egg was a meal they wouldn't eat, a penny they wouldn't earn. She thought of her mother's tired face.

"Get out of my sight." Lady Russell's voice dripped with venom.

"Mother, you can't..." Isabella stepped forward, her face flushed with anger and embarrassment. Ellen had never seen her friend so furious, her usually gentle features transformed by rage.

"I can and I will. You are confined to the house until further notice." Lady Russell's voice was ice, each word precise and cutting. "And if I hear of you attempting to contact this... person... again, there will be consequences far beyond your imagination. Do I make myself clear?"

Ellen curtseyed one more time, her legs shaking so badly she nearly fell. Pride kept her upright, kept her voice steady. "I'm sorry to have disturbed you, my lady."

She looked at Isabella one last time, trying to memorize everything: her friend's stricken face, the tears gathering in her green eyes, the way her hands clenched her silk skirts. This might be the last time they saw each other, and they both knew it.

Then Ellen turned and walked away with as much dignity as she could muster. Behind her, she could hear Isabella's voice rising in protest, words like "cruel" and "heartless" carrying on the morning air, but the exact words were lost in the rushing sound of her own heartbeat.

She didn't look back, didn't run despite the burning desire to flee. She walked steadily down the long drive, past the ornate gates with their Russell coat of arms, and onto the muddy lane that led back to her world. Her eyes burned with unshed tears, but she wouldn't give Lady Russell the satisfaction of seeing her cry.

"Ellen, girl! Wait a moment there."

She turned to see Tom Clancy hurrying after her, his quick

steps eating up the distance between them. The small, wiry groundskeeper moved with surprising speed for his age, his patched brown coat flapping in the breeze. His kind face was creased with concern.

"Mr Clancy, I'm sorry you had to..."

"Hush now." He glanced back toward the house, then fell into step beside her. His breathing was slightly laboured from hurrying. "That was a terrible thing to witness. I've worked these grounds for forty years, and I've never seen such cruelty. Her ladyship had no call to treat you so, no matter what the circumstances."

Ellen felt fresh tears threaten. The kindness in his voice after Lady Russell's viciousness was almost too much to bear. "It was my fault. I shouldn't have come. I knew better."

"Nonsense. You're a good girl, Ellen McGrath, and anyone with eyes can see that young Miss Isabella thinks the world of you." Tom's kind eyes were troubled, deepening the wrinkles around them. "Though I fear this means you won't be starting in the kitchens come Monday."

Ellen's stomach lurched as the full reality of what had happened hit her. In her shock over Lady Russell's cruelty, she'd forgotten about the position. "Oh, God. What am I going to tell Mam? We need that position. The wages..." Her voice broke. Without those wages, they couldn't pay the rent. Without the rent paid, Lord Russell would evict them.

Tom touched her arm gently, his hand paternal in its comfort. "There might be another way, child. O'Sullivan's shop in Clonbarra. Young Michael's just enlisted, the fool boy. Off to France with the Connaught Rangers, leaving his father short-handed. Old O'Sullivan's asked me, just this morning, if I knew of someone to help mind the store. Shop work pays better than chambermaid wages."

Ellen wiped her eyes with the back of her hand, hope flickering despite everything. "Do you think he'd consider me? I can read and write well, and I'm good with figures. Miss Fallon always said I had a head for numbers."

"I'd say you're exactly what he needs. A bright girl who can handle the books and deal with customers proper-like." Tom's voice grew warmer. "I could put in a word for you, if you'd like. Tell him you're from good people who've fallen on hard times through no fault of their own."

"Would you really?" Hope flickered in Ellen's chest despite Lady Russell's cruel words. A shop position would mean staying in the village and seeing her family every evening, instead of being trapped in service at the big house.

"Ah, sure, child. I'll stop by O'Sullivan's tomorrow on my way to market." Tom glanced back toward the house once more, his expression darkening. "What happened here today... it's not right. That woman's got a heart like a stone. But perhaps it's for the best. Working under that woman's roof would have been no kindness to you. I've seen what happens to young girls in service there. Better you're away from all that poison."

As they reached the lane that led to Ellen's cottage, Tom tipped his battered hat. "Keep your chin up, Ellen. Things have a way of working out, even when they seem darkest. And that young lady won't forget you, mark my words. Real friendship doesn't die just because the high and mighty wish it so."

Ellen watched him walk back toward the big house, his small figure growing distant against the grand backdrop of the Russell estate. She thought of Isabella, probably locked in her room by now, raging against the bars of her golden cage.

They were both prisoners in their own ways.

With a heavy heart, she turned toward home, dreading having to tell her mother about the lost position but clinging to the hope of O'Sullivan's shop. At least she wouldn't have to empty Lady Russell's chamber pot. Or pretend Isabella was a stranger.

FIFTEEN
NOW

After the best night's sleep she'd had in months, Caitlin woke up paying for yesterday's stupidity. Her leg screamed, and her shoulder felt like someone had taken a hammer to it. A long flight, three hours of driving, then that beach walk.

Brilliant, Caitlin. Real smart for someone with metal holding her bones together.

Coffee first. Think later.

The cottage owner had left a stack of local brochures on the counter. Restaurants, tourist traps, and... Restorative Motion Physio. She flicked through the brochure and then grabbed her phone, opened the map and punched in the address. No point calling. She needed groceries anyway.

Ballycluan looked like Ireland's tourist board had designed it personally: fishing boats bobbing in the harbour, pink flowers tumbling from window boxes, thatched cottages that probably charged a fortune in rent. People smiled and nodded as she passed but didn't stop to chat. Perfect. Friendly, but without the interrogation.

The physio clinic sat in a white house with a thatched roof and red gates. As she stepped in she registered the air conditioning, clean lines, and that particular smell of antiseptic trying to hide under lavender. *Fairy tale outside, medical efficiency inside.*

The reception desk was empty. She took a seat and scrolled through her phone. Grammy had sent six texts already.

A door opened and she looked up to see Conor walk out wearing scrubs.

Her stomach did something complicated.

"Caitlin! I wasn't expecting to see you." He looked genuinely surprised. Good surprised or bad surprised? "Is everything alright?"

She caught sight of the certificates on the wall. His name on every one. Heat crawled up her neck. "You're the physiotherapist?"

"Guilty as charged." That smile again, the one that made her notice his eyes were the same blue-green as the ocean. "I saw you favouring your leg yesterday but thought it might be the flight. My next patient has just cancelled. Want me to take a look?"

"I could come back when there's someone else available." She glanced at the certificates again. "A woman, maybe?"

"Sorry, it's just me. My partner left six months ago. Haven't found a replacement yet." He gestured to his qualifications. "I promise I'm fully trained. But I understand if you'd prefer to wait."

The pain won. "No, it's fine. I need help."

His bright and airy office had windows overlooking the village – nothing like the clinical torture chambers she'd gotten used to in Charleston.

Conor pulled up a file on his computer, all business now. "I'll need some basic information. How did you injure yourself?"

"It's nothing. Just travel catching up with me."

Conor tilted his head, steady, not buying it. "You carry yourself like someone used to pain. And used to hiding it."

She felt her cheeks flush and she crossed her arms. "I don't owe you my life story."

His voice softened. "You don't. But if I'm going to treat you, I need the truth."

She looked at him for a moment and then handed over the medical summary she kept in her wallet. Easier than explaining. "I was shot. The shoulder's mostly healed. The leg... work in progress."

His professional mask slipped. "Shot?"

"One bullet caught my shoulder, just below the collarbone. Tore up the muscle pretty good. The other one went through my thigh and shattered the femur." She kept her voice flat, clinical. Just facts. "I've had extensive PT back home, but between the flight and that walk yesterday..."

"Jesus." He scanned the papers, and she watched his face change as he absorbed the medical terminology. Multiple surgeries. Metal pins. Permanent damage likely. "I feel like an idiot now – yesterday, assuming you were just another tourist. You're a cop?"

"Was. Ex-cop." The word still tasted bitter. "And I'd appreciate it if you didn't mention that to anyone. I'm trying to leave it behind."

"Of course." He stood, and she was suddenly aware of how tall he was. "If you're comfortable with it, take off your jacket and lie on the table. I'll examine the injuries. I haven't treated many gunshot wounds – not much call for it here, thank God. But trauma's trauma, and I've worked with plenty of that."

She shrugged off her jacket and settled on the table. The paper crinkled under her. *Here we go again.* Another stranger's hands on her body, prodding at the damage. At least this stranger had eyes like sea glass and hands that looked...

Stop it.

"What medication today?" He was washing his hands, sleeves rolled up. She absolutely did not notice his forearms.

"Just Tylenol."

"We call it paracetamol here." He dried his hands, then paused. "I'll put up the 'Closed' sign so we're not interrupted. This might take a while."

When he returned, she was ready for the usual routine. Cold hands, clinical distance, that careful professional wall. Instead, his touch was warm, gentle but confident as he worked through the scar tissue on her shoulder.

"Tell me about the pain level."

"Fine." She bit back a gasp as he found a knot.

"Liar." But he said it softly, adjusting the pressure. "You don't have to be tough here. I need to know what hurts."

His hands moved across her shoulder, finding every place the bullet had torn through. She focused on breathing, on not noticing how careful he was, how his fingers seemed to know exactly where the damage was worst. When was the last time someone had touched her with such—?

No. Medical procedure. Nothing more.

"Better," he said finally. "Let's look at the leg now."

This was always worse. The leg that betrayed her, that wouldn't hold her weight when it mattered. She tensed as he began working on the tight muscles, but his hands were patient, coaxing rather than forcing.

"You're holding your breath," he murmured. "Try to relax."

Right. Relax while an attractive man had his hands on her thigh. While she was acutely aware of how close he was, how she could smell that clean ocean scent again. *Get it together, O'Shea.*

"The doctors back home were optimistic at first," she heard herself saying. "Full recovery, they said. Then it became 'improved mobility.' Then 'manage expectations.'"

His hands stilled for a moment. "What do you think?"

"I think they gave up."

"Well, I don't give up easily." He went back to work, finding trigger points she didn't know existed. "With consistent treatment, proper therapy... I've seen worse injuries than this make remarkable progress. Some people think my methods are a bit alternative, but the results speak for themselves."

"I'll try anything to walk normally again."

"When did this happen?" His voice was carefully neutral.

"Eleven months ago." *Please don't ask more.*

He didn't. Just nodded and continued working. The silence

was comfortable somehow, broken only by her occasional sharp breath when he hit a tender spot.

"There," he said finally, stepping back. "That should help. You shouldn't drive any further than from here to the cottage for at least a week. Give your leg time to recover from the flight and the long drive from Dublin."

"But I've got research to do."

"Can it wait a few days? We've only started. We'd need regular sessions to make real progress."

She sat up slowly, testing the leg. It did feel better. Looser. It couldn't hurt to postpone her research trips a week. "Thank you."

He handed her some tissues to wipe the excess lotion from her leg. "Take a moment to get yourself sorted, then meet me at reception. We'll sort out payment and scheduling." He paused at the door. "And, Caitlin? Ballycluan's small. People talk. But I keep patient information confidential. Your story's safe with me."

At the reception desk, he pulled up a calendar. "Three times a week would be ideal. More if you can manage it."

"I'm here for a month. Looking into family history." She watched him input her information, noticed he was left-handed. Why was she noticing that? "Speaking of which, is there someone local who might help with genealogy research?"

He looked up, that smile playing at his lips again. "Delia Tierney. Runs the pub by the marina with her husband. Both families have been here forever. Actually..." He glanced at his watch. "I haven't had lunch yet. I could introduce you if you like."

"Are you asking me on a date?" The words were out before she could stop them.

He leaned against the desk, eyes dancing. "That would be highly unprofessional, wouldn't it? Your physiotherapist asking you out?" He let that hang for a beat. "But lunch between new neighbours who happen to be going to the same place? That's different entirely."

She found herself smiling. Actually smiling. "Very smooth."

"I have my moments. So?"

"Why not? I need to eat anyway."

The pub was exactly what she'd imagined an Irish pub should be: dark wood, low ceilings, photos covering every inch of wall space. The smell of fish and chips made her stomach growl. They claimed a table near the window just as another couple was leaving.

"That's Delia behind the bar," Conor said, nodding toward a woman with silver hair, and arms that said she'd been pulling pints for decades. "She's the one you want, but wait until the lunch rush dies down."

Caitlin studied the menu, aware of him watching her. "What's good?"

"Everything. But the fish is caught this morning. Can't go wrong."

While they waited for food, she examined the photos on the walls. Black and white snapshots of the village, boats, families posed stiffly for long-exposure cameras.

"Are these all local?"

"Mostly. Some from Galway and around." He shifted his chair closer to point at a particular photo, and his knee brushed hers. Neither of them moved away. "You should look properly when it quiets down. Might recognize someone."

"I only have one photo of my great-grandmother, but you never know."

Their food arrived, and to her surprise conversation flowed more easily than it should have. He asked about Charleston, she asked about growing up here. Safe topics that skirted around gunshots and ex-partners. But she kept catching him looking at her when he thought she wasn't watching, and she was pretty sure she was doing the same.

"Conor Kelly, you devil!" Delia appeared beside their table, kissing Conor's cheek with the familiarity of long friendship. "And with a beautiful woman too. About time, boy."

Conor's ears turned pink. "Delia, this is Caitlin O'Shea. Just arrived from America. She's researching her family history. Her great-grandmother was Ellen McGrath."

Caitlin watched Delia's face change, the warmth flickering into something else. Recognition? Fear?

"Ellen McGrath." Delia repeated the name like she was tasting something bitter. "Well, now. That's a name I haven't heard in a while." She was already backing away. "I'd love to chat, pet, but as you can see, we're run off our feet. Come by tomorrow morning, would you? Early, before the lunch crowd. We'll have tea and a proper talk."

She was gone before Caitlin could respond, disappearing into the kitchen like she was being chased.

"That was odd," Conor said, frowning.

"You think?" Caitlin watched the kitchen door swing shut. "She looked like I'd said my great-grandmother was Jack the Ripper."

"Small towns have long memories. Could be nothing." But he didn't sound convinced. "Could be something."

"Grammy sent me here for answers." She pushed food around her plate. "I'm starting to think I might not like what I find."

His hand moved across the table like he might touch hers, then stopped. "Whatever it is, you don't have to face it alone. Ballycluan looks after its own, and you're one of us now. Temporarily, anyway."

She looked at him then, really looked. Saw the genuine concern in those sea-glass eyes, the careful way he was offering help without pushing. "I'm not great at accepting help."

"I noticed. But the offer stands."

Grammy would like him, she thought suddenly. Would be inviting him to come to Charleston. The thought should have sent her running. Instead, she found herself saying, "Same time Thursday?"

His smile was answer enough.

SIXTEEN

NOW

"Are ye pulling yer hair out yet? The internet can get a bit spotty at times."

Caitlin looked up from Grammy's documents spread across the pub table. Delia stood there with a tray, the smell of warm scones making Caitlin's stomach growl despite her late breakfast.

"I thought you might be hungry. The sea air gives most visitors an appetite." Delia set the tray down, two delicate teacups clinking against their saucers. "You mentioned Ellen McGrath last night —?" Delia settled into the chair beside her. "I can't abide weak tea, so if that's the way you like it, speak up now."

Caitlin wasn't about to admit she preferred coffee. "Strong is fine."

"Good woman." Delia poured, the steam curling up between them.

Caitlin stirred her tea, suddenly nervous about what Delia might tell her. "I suppose you get lots of Americans looking for their Irish roots?"

"If I had a euro for every American claiming to be Irish, I'd be rich enough to retire." Delia sipped her tea, studying Caitlin over the rim. "Don't take that wrong. I love Americans. Most are so friendly, so eager to connect. Though Hollywood has them believing we all live in villages from *The Quiet Man*."

Heat crept up Caitlin's neck and she bit her lip. She'd watched that movie the night Grammy had asked her to go to Ireland.

Delia's laugh was warm. "It's a common misconception. The real Ireland's better anyway. Now, what do you know about your grandmother's family?"

Caitlin's cop instincts flared. Delia was hiding something, or at the very least reluctant to tell her what she knew. But why?

"Just her name. My great-grandmother, Ellen McGrath. My grandmother just discovered she has Irish roots, and she sent me to find out more. Ellen's family came from a place called Clonbarra."

"Clonbarra's about five miles up the road. Not much left of it now." Something sad crossed Delia's face before she forced it away. "I've lived here all my life. Know most of the local families and their histories."

"Any help would be appreciated."

"Anytime, love. Now, these scones won't eat themselves." Delia broke one open, butter melting into the warm centre. "And if you're not a tea person, we've got coffee too. Hospitality's our specialty."

Caitlin bit down on her impatience. She knew Delia had recognized her great-grandmother's name. She needed her to open up, and if that took making small talk for a while, then so be it. "Your family's been here a long time?"

"Born in the village. My father and his father before him. My husband's family, the Tierneys, have been here even longer. Survived Cromwell and all the troubles since."

"Cromwell? Was he a recent visitor?"

Scone crumbs flew as Delia laughed. "Oliver Cromwell, love. Arrived in Dublin in 1649. By September, he'd killed four thousand people in Drogheda alone. Hated the Irish, Catholics especially. Those he didn't kill lost their lands. Some got shipped to Virginia and the Caribbean as indentured servants."

Caitlin stayed quiet, fascinated.

"The Irish who stayed were forced west. That's how Cromwell freed up land for English loyalists. Banned us from owning property, practising our religion, holding office. Tried to make us second-class citizens in our own country." Delia's eyes sparkled. "But he learned what others have since. The Irish don't bow to anyone. Took the English eight hundred years to figure that out."

An old man shuffled past their table. Worn tweed jacket, patched elbows, cap in hand. Despite the threadbare clothes, he carried himself with dignity.

"Ah, Delia, don't start. You know the English are grand people."

Delia winked at Caitlin. "That they are, Harry Bennett, except for the likes of you giving them a bad name."

Instead of taking offence, Harry laughed. "Go away with you. You know you love me. Now stop nattering and pour me a pint."

"Sorry, love, duty calls." Delia headed for the bar, still laughing.

The lunch rush hit hard. The pub filled with locals and tourists, voices rising over the clink of glasses. Delia worked alone, her face flushed from the heat of the kitchen. Without thinking, Caitlin started clearing empty tables.

"You can't be doing that. You're a guest." But Delia's protest was weak, gratitude clear in her eyes.

"I waited tables in college. Let me help. Call it payment for information about my family."

Something troubled flickered across Delia's face. "Be careful what you wish for, love. But the help would be mighty appreciated." She smiled gratefully. "I can put your laptop in the office for safekeeping."

Caitlin fell into the rhythm easily. Clear tables, take orders, deliver food. Muscle memory from her college days kicked in. She left the tricky Guinness pours to Delia but managed everything else. The kitchen staff, aprons splattered with the day's work, promised her the best club sandwich in Ireland as thanks.

"Have you the thirst bad today, Harry?" Delia called out as the old man raised his empty glass. "That pint didn't touch the sides."

"Are you my mother or the landlady? Maybe you should hear confessions instead of pulling pints. Might suit you better!"

The banter flew back and forth, insults wrapped in affection. Grammy was right about the Irish and their *slagging*, that easy teasing that always came with a grin. Everyone gave as good as they got.

By three o'clock, the pub had emptied. Caitlin's ears rang in the sudden quiet.

"I don't know what I'd have done without you today." Delia wiped down the bar with practised strokes. "You're a McGrath all right. Just jumped in where needed. Usually young Declan and Deirdre help, but they're both down with flu. Told them the water's too cold for surfing without wetsuits, but would they listen?" She pointed to a corner table. "Sit yourself down. Now, what'll you have? On the house."

"The club sandwich would be great."

"Coming up." Delia headed for the kitchen as Harry raised his glass in salute.

"You're a grand *cailín* for an American."

Caitlin laughed.

Paddy, Delia's husband, emerged from the kitchen and was greeted with a barrage of insults.

"About time you showed up. Tell that wife of yours to mind her tongue. Nearly had me saying novenas for a pint."

"Go away with that. My Delia knows prayers are wasted on you, you old scoundrel."

Caitlin grinned as they traded insults. She could have listened all day.

Delia returned with a loaded plate and, surprisingly, a mocha alongside the tea. "My daughter-in-law says these are all the rage."

"Perfect, thank you." The sandwich was heaven. Real bacon, crisp lettuce, ripe tomatoes, proper mayonnaise.

Delia waited until she'd finished eating, then pulled out a worn photo album. "So, you said you didn't know much about your great-grandmother?"

"My grandmother never spoke about her until last week." Caitlin explained Grammy's discovery, watching Delia's face grow more troubled with each word.

"Last night, I found this." Delia opened the album to a yellowed photograph. Young people standing outside what was clearly an earlier version of the pub, faces serious in that old-photo way.

"This was 1920. That's my husband's distant cousin, Sarah Tierney." She pointed to a dark-haired girl. "And that's Seamus McGrath beside her. Recognize the woman next to him?"

Caitlin's breath caught. "That's her. That's Ellen." She pulled out Grammy's photo to compare. Identical faces stared back at her across a century.

"You're the image of her." Delia's voice was soft.

"So Seamus is my great-uncle?" The man in the photo had something familiar about his jaw, the set of his shoulders.

"He was."

"Who are the others?" A striking young woman dominated the centre of the group, even in sepia tones.

"Isabella Russell."

But Caitlin's attention caught on another figure, half turned from the camera. "And him? Is he something to Ellen?"

"Patrick McGrath. Their brother."

Her heart sped up. "You knew my family."

"I knew of them." Delia closed the album carefully. "If things had been different, we'd have been related by marriage."

The pub felt suddenly cold despite the afternoon sun streaming through the windows.

"What I have to tell you isn't a happy story." Delia's vibrant energy had drained away, leaving someone who looked older, sadder. "Are you sure you want to hear it?"

Caitlin thought of Grammy in her bed, clutching those documents. "She needs to know what happened. Why her mother took her to St Brigid's."

Delia nodded slowly. "Then I'll tell you what I know. But you might wish I hadn't."

SEVENTEEN
1917

"You've an eye for colour, Ellen. My wife was the same. She used to arrange the drapery counter to show the fabrics off in the best possible light. She'd be pleased to see you looking after it so well."

Mr O'Sullivan's gruff voice carried unexpected warmth, and Ellen felt heat rise in her cheeks. She smoothed the emerald silk she'd been arranging, the fabric cool beneath her fingertips. After nearly a year working in the shop, praise still caught her off guard, especially coming from such a large man. When she'd first started, his broad shoulders and booming voice had frightened her half to death. Now she knew better.

"Thank you, Mr O'Sullivan." She loved her job more than she'd ever expected. The scent of tea and tobacco, the feel of different fabrics, the satisfaction of balancing the books at day's end; it was worlds away from the chambermaid position she'd nearly taken. Mr O'Sullivan was a taskmaster but patient, especially at the start when it seemed she made more mistakes than anything else. He hid his kind heart behind a gruff exterior, but she'd noticed how the poorer women often ended up with a couple of slices more bacon or an extra few cups of flour when he was measuring out their orders.

He treated everyone the same, whether they were the cook

from the big house or the doctor's wife: professional service, but no fawning over the rich like some of the townspeople. And unlike working at the Russells', here she was a person with a name, not just another servant to be ordered about.

He shared news from the letters he got from his son, Michael, reading snippets aloud during quiet afternoons. "Still in France," he'd say, his voice carefully neutral. "Says the food is terrible but the lads keep each other's spirits up." Recently the silences between letters grew longer, and Ellen had learned not to ask when one was overdue.

The bell rang over the door just as she was about to go on her lunch break. She looked up from the counter, ready with her shopkeeper's smile, and her heart stopped.

"Hello, Ellen."

It was John's voice, but that was about the only thing she recognized. The man in the doorway was a ghost of the boy who'd been arrested outside Frank Tierney's pub. He'd lost so much weight his cheekbones looked sharp enough to cut paper. His sandy hair, shorn to prisoner length, was starting to grow out in uneven tufts. But it was his eyes that made her chest tighten: those warm brown eyes she'd dreamed about were shadowed and dull.

Her gaze swept over him, taking in every terrible detail. The marks of hard labour on his hands, the way his clothes hung loose on his frame, the slight tremor in his stance – as if he wasn't sure he was really there.

His confident smile faded as she stood frozen, unable to speak past the lump in her throat.

"Do you not recognize me?" His voice carried a note of uncertainty that broke her heart.

"John Power, as I live and breathe... of course I recognize you." The words came out as barely more than a whisper. "What did they do to you?"

She pushed up the wooden counter divider without thinking, stepping out onto the shop floor. Every instinct screamed at her to run to him, to throw her arms around him and never let go. She would have done it too, but for Mr O'Sullivan arriving from the back stores.

"Ellen, I thought I heard the door—" He spotted the newcomer and his eyes widened. "My God, John! You look like you'd fall over in a strong wind." Mr O'Sullivan's careworn features drew together in genuine concern. "Ellen, shut the door and turn the sign to 'Closed'. We'll take our lunch now. You'll join us, won't you, John?"

John's eyes flickered with gratitude and something else: relief, perhaps, at being welcomed rather than turned away. "I don't want to impose, Mr O'Sullivan."

"Nonsense. Any friend of Ellen's is welcome at my table. Besides, you look like you could use a proper meal." Mr O'Sullivan's voice was gruff but kind. "Come on through to the back. Ellen's become quite the cook since she started here."

They settled around the small wooden table in the room behind the shop, the familiar scents of fried fish and boiled cabbage filling the space. Ellen's hands shook slightly as she served generous portions, noting how John's fingers trembled as he picked up his fork. He ate slowly at first, as if his stomach had forgotten how to handle real food. She wanted to reach across the table, to touch his hand and assure herself he was really there, but Mr O'Sullivan's presence kept her still.

"Frank Tierney said you came home yesterday," Mr O'Sullivan said, cutting his fish with deliberate care. "Must be good to see your uncle again."

John nodded, swallowing carefully before he spoke. "Uncle Frank's been kind. More than kind, really, taking me in when..." He paused, his jaw tightening. "When my mother passed last winter, back in Dublin."

Ellen's fork clattered against her plate. The sound rang out in the small room like a bell. "John, I'm so sorry. I didn't know." How had she not known? All those months of writing to him, and she'd been addressing letters to a man whose mother was dead.

"Pneumonia. They wouldn't let me out for the funeral." His

voice was flat, carefully controlled, but Ellen could see the pain flickering in his eyes like candle flame. "Said it would be a security risk."

The cruelty of it made her stomach turn. To lose your mother and not even be allowed to say goodbye, to stand at her grave...

Mr O'Sullivan cleared his throat gently. "Your mother was a good woman, John. I remember her from church, before she went to Dublin. Always had a kind word. She was proud of you, lad. Anyone could see it."

"Thank you." John's voice was rough. "That means a great deal."

John's gaze wandered to the small, framed photograph on the mantelpiece: Michael O'Sullivan in his British army uniform, his smile confident beneath his military cap. *The elephant in the room*, Ellen thought. *The Irishman who'd chosen to fight for Britain while John had chosen to fight against her.*

Mr O'Sullivan followed his gaze and cleared his throat. "Michael's still in France. His last letter said they were near someplace called Passchendaele."

John studied the photograph, his expression carefully neutral. "I remember him. Good with a hurl, always fair in his dealings. I hope he comes home safe to you."

"You lads took different paths," Mr O'Sullivan said quietly. "Each following what you thought was right."

"Yes." John met the older man's eyes directly. "And I pray his path leads him home. Too many good men won't be coming back from France."

The sincerity in John's voice seemed to satisfy Mr O'Sullivan. The tension in the room eased slightly.

"Tell me about the camp, then," Mr O'Sullivan said, his tone lighter. "Frank mentioned some of the lads had been organizing things, keeping spirits up and such."

John's face brightened slightly, the first real animation Ellen had seen since he'd walked in. "Michael Collins had us organized within weeks. The man's a force of nature, Mr O'Sullivan. The

British thought they were punishing us by locking us all up together, but Collins turned Frongoch into a university of sorts." He took another bite, more confident now.

Ellen glanced up sharply at the name. Patrick had spoken of Collins in the same awed tone – half soldier, half legend. She'd pictured someone old and battle-worn, not a young man with enough energy to turn a prison camp into a training ground for freedom.

"Military drills at dawn, Irish language classes, lectures on everything from engineering to politics. Collins said if we were going to fight for Ireland, we needed to be worthy of her. 'Every man a soldier, but also a scholar,' he'd say."

"And the hurling?" Mr O'Sullivan leaned forward with genuine interest. "I help run the local team here, you know. Always looking for good players."

John's smile was genuine for the first time since he'd walked in, transforming his gaunt face. "Collins made sure we kept playing. Said the Irish needed to be fit in body as well as spirit. I was never much good before, but after more than a year of training..." He flexed his lean arms with rueful humour. "I might not look like much now, but I can run farther and hit harder than I ever could before."

"Well, then, you'll have to come to practice next week. We would benefit from some fresh talent." Mr O'Sullivan glanced between John and Ellen, and she knew he'd noticed the way they kept stealing glances at each other. "Ellen, why don't you take the afternoon off? It's been quiet today, and I'm sure you and John have a lot to catch up on."

Ellen felt heat rise in her cheeks. "Are you certain, Mr O'Sullivan? I don't mind staying..."

"Go on with you both. Youth doesn't last forever." The older man's eyes were kind but knowing. "Just make sure you're back by six to help me close up."

. . .

They walked in silence toward the old oak tree, their feet finding the familiar path without conscious thought. The June air was soft and warm, filled with the scent of wild roses and cut hay. But Ellen noticed how John kept glancing around, his body tense as a drawn bow, as if expecting police to materialize from the hedgerows.

"You can relax," she said as they settled on the grass beneath the spreading branches. The same spot where they'd sat that evening before his arrest. "No one's coming for you."

John's laugh was bitter. "It's hard to believe sometimes. Over a year of looking over your shoulder, of counting every word, of wondering if today would be the day they decided to make an example of you... it doesn't just stop when you walk out the gates."

Ellen studied his profile, cataloguing all the ways prison had changed him. The new lines around his eyes, the way his shoulders never quite relaxed, how his hands kept moving: drumming against his knee, pulling at grass stems, never still. "Was it very bad?"

For a long moment, John said nothing. A blackbird sang in the branches above them, and somewhere in the distance, she could hear children playing. Just the sounds of a normal day, but John seemed to exist outside of it all.

Then, quietly: "The worst part wasn't the cold or the hunger or the hard labour. It was the silence. They used it as punishment, you see. No mail, no visitors, no word from home." His voice grew rough. "They'd tell us our families had forgotten us, that Ireland had turned its back on the Rising. Some of the men from Dublin, they got word their shops had been looted, their families evicted. There were days I almost believed them when they said no one cared anymore."

"But you got some of my letters?" Ellen held her breath, remembering all those carefully worded pages, trying to say everything while saying nothing the censors could object to.

John turned to look at her directly, and she saw tears gathering in his brown eyes. "Four. In over a year, I got four of your letters. They were..." He paused, struggling for words. "Ellen, they kept me alive. When I wanted to give up, when the guards would wake us in the middle of the night for no reason but to remind us we were prisoners, I'd remember your words. That you were waiting. That someone still believed I was worth waiting for."

Ellen reached out and took his hand, feeling the rough calluses from prison labour, the thin scars that hadn't been there before. His fingers were cold despite the warm day. "I wrote every month. Every single month, John. I'm so sorry they didn't let you have them all."

"Some of the Welsh guards were decent men." John's thumb traced across her knuckles, the familiar gesture making her heart ache. "There was one, Davies his name was, who used to slip us extra food sometimes. Had a son about my age fighting in France. I think... I think he saw his boy in us. He's the one who made sure those four letters reached me."

They sat in silence for a moment, hands intertwined. Ellen could feel the tremor that ran through him, constant as a heartbeat.

"And now?" she asked finally. "What happens now?"

John stared out across the fields toward the village, and she saw him catalogue every building, every path, as if memorizing home. "I don't know," he admitted. "Collins says there's more work to be done, that the fight isn't over. He's already planning..." He stopped himself, old habits of secrecy hard to break. "But, Ellen, I'm tired. So desperately tired of fighting and hiding and watching good men die for dreams that seem as distant as the moon."

"Then don't fight, at least not for a while. Build your strength back up. Redmond says Ireland will have Home Rule when the war ends. The British promised. Wait and see what happens. Ellen said, surprising herself with the fierceness in her voice. "Stay here. Help your uncle with the stables, play hurling for Mr O'Sullivan's team, live a quiet life. There's no shame in that."

John smiled sadly. "Is that what you want? A quiet life with a broken-down rebel who jumps at shadows?"

Ellen moved closer to him, close enough to see the amber flecks in his brown eyes, close enough to catch the faint scent of soap and something indefinably John beneath it. "I want you alive, John

Power. I want you here, with me, building something real instead of chasing ghosts. I want Sunday walks and ordinary worries and the chance to grow old together."

"And if they come for me again?"

"Then we'll face that when it happens. But for now, for today, you're free. You're home. You're here with me." She cupped his face in her hands, feeling the sharp angles of his cheekbones, the roughness of stubble. "That has to be enough."

John closed his eyes and leaned into her touch, and for a moment Ellen saw something of the boy she'd fallen in love with flickering beneath the surface of the man he'd become.

"I used to imagine this," he whispered. "In the camp, when things were darkest. I'd close my eyes and imagine sitting here with you, just like this. Sometimes it was the only thing that kept me sane."

"I'm real. This is real. You're home. Stay," she whispered. "Please stay."

"I'll try." His voice was fierce with a desperate kind of hope. "God help me, Ellen, I'll try."

They sat there as the afternoon shadows lengthened, not speaking, just holding on to each other as if they could make the world stop turning through sheer force of will. Ellen knew there would be challenges ahead. John may not be able to stay out of the fight as the political situation was far from settled. But for now, for this perfect moment, they were together.

When the church bell chimed five, Ellen reluctantly pulled away. "I should get back. Mr O'Sullivan…"

"I know." John stood and helped her to her feet, his movements careful as an old man's. "Ellen… thank you. For waiting. For writing. For…" He gestured helplessly. "For still seeing me as someone worth loving."

Ellen felt the reluctance in every muscle as she pulled away, her fingers trailing along his sleeve. The thought of walking back to the shop, of returning to ordinary life when nothing about this felt ordinary, made her chest ache. She studied his face in the evening light. Part of her wanted to keep him here forever, safe beneath their tree, away from whatever darkness still chased him. But the church bell was insisting, and Mr O'Sullivan would be waiting.

"Always. Walk me back?" The words came out smaller than she intended, a question when she meant it as an invitation.

He offered her his arm, and together they made their way back toward the village. Ellen noticed he walked easier now, his shoulders not quite so tense.

It was a start.

As they reached O'Sullivan's shop, John paused. "I'll come by tomorrow, if that's alright. Maybe... maybe we could take another walk?"

"I'd like that." Ellen squeezed his hand. "And, John? Welcome home."

The smile he gave her then was worth every lonely month of waiting.

EIGHTEEN

NOW

Caitlin wiped her eyes with the back of her hand. *Great. Crying in public. Real professional.*

"I'm sorry, love." Delia squeezed her hand across the table. "I warned you it's not a happy story."

"I'm just being silly. But to send a boy – that's all he was really – to jail, in Wales, and not even let him go to his own mother's funeral... That's barbaric. Especially when he was just fighting for his country."

Delia's face grew thoughtful. "John was lucky, really. Others were executed for their part in the Easter Rising in 1916. Someone must have spoken for him."

"Did Ellen and her brothers get involved in the Rising?"

"No, and that led to more trouble. But for now, let's stay with Ellen. She was devastated when they arrested John." Delia shook her head. "That poor girl. Lost her father not long after John was sent away. And her brothers, well, they got more involved in the cause."

"The cause?"

"The fight for independence. Everyone was, really. Even the women." Delia stood, returning moments later with another photo album. "Here. Look at this."

The photograph she showed Caitlin was of a crowd of people marching, banners held high. One banner was dated 1918. Delia tapped the photo. "The conscription crisis. The British wanted to draft Irishmen to fight in their 'Great War'. The whole country said no but it was the women who marched. They weren't letting their men be cannon fodder for the oppressors."

Caitlin leaned closer. There, in the middle of the crowd, stood Ellen. Young, fierce, determined. "She marched with them?"

"She did. The priests encouraged them from the altar. It was one thing everyone agreed on: Irish boys weren't dying for the British Empire."

A life of purpose and passion, so different from the broken woman who'd taken Grammy to a home.

"What happened to her? To make her abandon Grammy?"

Delia closed the album carefully. "That's a story for another day, love. Some wounds are too deep to probe all at once."

Her phone buzzed. Grammy:

> How are you getting along?

What could she say? *I've found out your father was jailed after 1916. Your mother was a rebel who marched against conscription.* She couldn't – not via a text message, anyway.

She typed back:

> Learning lots. Can't talk now. Speak later?

"You are welcome to get copies of the pictures. If you want to send them to your grandmother?" Delia stood. "I'd better get back to the kitchen. Paddy will think I've abandoned him. What are your plans for the afternoon?"

Nice deflection. "Back to the cottage. Maybe a walk on the beach."

"Good idea. Nothing like the sea to clear your head. Thanks again for helping at lunch. If you want to make it regular, let me know." She headed for the bar, then turned. "Oh, your laptop. I'll fetch it."

Delia returned with the laptop, her smile not quite reaching her eyes. "Safe and sound. You take care now. And, Caitlin? Sometimes the past is better left buried. But I understand why you need to dig."

Outside, the afternoon sun felt too bright after the pub's dim interior. Caitlin walked slowly back to the cottage, favouring her leg. The physio session had helped, but she'd been on her feet too long.

Back at the cottage, Caitlin spread the photographs Delia had lent her to get copies, across the table. Ellen McGrath, standing with her community against an empire. Where did that courage go? What broke it?

The cottage was quiet, just the sound of waves through the open window. She spread Grammy's documents on the table again. Birth certificates, death records, that single photo of Ellen. Not much to build a life from.

Her phone rang. Conor.

"How did the lunch investigation go?" His voice was warm, teasing.

"Interesting. I ended up waiting tables."

"Of course you did." She could hear his smile. "Delia put you to work?"

"They were slammed. I couldn't just sit there."

"Most people could."

Heat crept up her neck. "It was nothing."

"If you say so. Listen, I was wondering if you'd eaten dinner yet?"

She checked her watch. "It's four in the afternoon."

"I know, but I'm heading to Galway for supplies. There's this place that does incredible seafood. Thought you might want to come, unless you're sick of my company already?"

She should say no. Keep it professional. Patient and therapist, nothing more.

"What time?"

"I'll pick you up at six—? Gives you time to rest after your waitressing shift."

After they hung up, Caitlin stared at the phone. What was she doing? She was here for Grammy, not for dinner with men who had kind eyes and gentle hands.

But Grammy would approve. *Hell, Grammy would already be picking out wedding china.*

The thought made her smile, despite everything. Maybe that was answer enough.

She looked at the scattered documents one more time, then turned them face down. Even cops knew when to clock out.

She had just over an hour. Time enough to shower, change, and try to shift her mind from the past to the present.

In the shower, the hot water helped wash away some of the day's weight. She chose jeans and a soft sweater, nothing that screamed "date." Because it wasn't. Just dinner. Between neighbours. Who happened to have chemistry that made her nervous.

Conor arrived right on time, dressed in jeans and a button-down that made his eyes look even more blue-green. His smile was easy, warm. "You look nice."

"It's just jeans."

"I meant you look relaxed. Better than this morning, when your leg was obviously flaring."

The drive to Galway took forty minutes along the coast road. They talked about safe things. His practice, her research, the weather that couldn't decide between rain and sun. But underneath ran that current of awareness. The way he handled the car with easy confidence. How her pulse jumped when he laughed.

The restaurant sat right on Galway Bay, windows overlooking the water. Nothing fancy, like he'd said, but the smell alone made her stomach growl.

"Trust me?" he asked, when the server appeared.

"With dinner choices?"

"Start small." That grin again. "Work up to the big stuff."

He ordered for both of them in Irish, the language rolling off his tongue like music. The server, a woman old enough to be his mother, beamed at him, replying in Irish.

"She says you're too pretty to be trusted," Conor translated. "But she'll feed us anyway."

"Did she really say that?"

"No. She said I better be treating you right or she'd have words with my mother." His ears went pink. "Small towns. Everyone knows everyone."

"Your mother lives here?"

"Just outside Ballycluan." He studied her. "What about you? Family besides your grandmother?"

The automatic walls wanted to go up. But the way he asked, like he actually wanted to know, made her answer openly. "Just Grammy. Parents died when I was a baby. Car accident."

"I'm sorry."

"It was a long time ago. Grammy and Grandpa raised me. Did a pretty good job, all things considered."

"I'd say they did an excellent job."

The food arrived before she had to respond. Fresh oysters, brown bread still warm from the oven, seafood chowder that tasted like the ocean had been distilled into a bowl.

"Oh my God." She didn't mean to moan, but the flavours were incredible.

Conor grinned. "Wait until you try the main course."

He was right. The salmon was perfect, the vegetables fresh; everything simple but exactly right. They talked between bites. His hand brushed hers reaching for the bread, and neither pulled away.

"Can I ask you something?" He set down his fork, giving her his full attention. "This morning, at the pub. What did Delia tell you?"

"Family history. Not the happy kind."

"Ah." He didn't push, just waited.

"My great-grandmother had a hard life. Lost people. Had to make impossible choices." She thought of Ellen marching against conscription, young and fierce. "I'm starting to think Grammy won't like what I find out. It'll break her heart, even if it makes her proud."

"Sometimes knowing is better than what we imagine."

"She needs to know. Before—" She stopped. She couldn't think about Grammy being gone, never mind talk about it.

"—before it's too late." Conor said it gently. "My gran was the same. Waited until she was in her eighties to tell us about her first marriage. The one that ended when he died in the War of Independence. She'd carried that story for sixty years."

"Did it help? Telling it?"

"I think so. Secrets are heavy things."

The server cleared their plates, asked about dessert. Caitlin was too full, but Conor ordered something anyway.

"To share," he said. "You can't come to Galway without trying their apple tart."

It arrived with two forks and cream so thick you could stand a spoon in it. The first bite made her close her eyes.

"You're going to make those noises again, aren't you?" His voice was teasing, but lower than usual.

She opened her eyes to find him watching her with an expression that made heat pool in her stomach. "Problem?"

"No." His gaze dropped to her mouth. "No problem at all."

The drive back was quieter, charged with something that hadn't been there before. He walked her to the cottage door, hands in his pockets like he didn't trust them.

"Thank you. For dinner. For not pushing about the family stuff."

"Anytime." He stepped closer, and she caught that ocean scent again. "Caitlin?"

"Yeah?"

"I know you're here for your grandmother. And I know you've got..." He gestured vaguely. "History. We all do. But I'd like to see you again. Not as your physiotherapist. Just as... this."

She should say no. She was leaving in less than a month. She had trust issues that could fill a library. But standing there in the Irish twilight, with this kind man who made her laugh and didn't push for more than she could give, she found herself nodding.

"I'd like that too."

His smile lit up his whole face. "Brilliant. Friday? There's a music session at the pub. Nothing fancy, just locals with instruments. You might enjoy it."

"Okay."

He leaned in, and for a moment she thought he might kiss her. But he just squeezed her hand, gentle and warm, then headed back to his car.

Inside, she leaned against the closed door, heart racing like she'd run a mile. She was here for Grammy, not for... whatever this was.

Her phone buzzed. Grammy:

> Hope you ate proper food today. Any nice people?

Caitlin laughed out loud. Even from three thousand miles away, Grammy knew.

She typed back:

> Had dinner with the physiotherapist. He's nice.

The response was immediate:

> 'Nice?' That's all? Send pictures!

NINETEEN

APRIL 1918

"Come on, sleepy head. I'll walk you in. I've a few hours' work at Tierney's."

At Seamus's call, Ellen yawned, pushing back the bedcovers, shivering as her feet touched the cold stone floor. While she enjoyed her job at O'Sullivan's, it was tough on dark wet mornings to get up at the crack of dawn. It would be easier if her mam would let her live above the shop. But as O'Sullivan was a widower who lived alone, that was not going to happen. The priest would never approve.

"Drink that down you, love. It will heat you up." Her mam handed her a cup of hot tea, placing a bowl of porridge in front of her. "Hurry up now."

Seamus grabbed their mam, twirling her around. "Where would we be without you looking after us, Mam?"

Her mam smiled but Ellen could see it was forced. The light had gone out of her mother's eyes the day they buried Paddy McGrath. The woman was skin and bone, getting thinner every day. Ellen knew her brothers worried just as she did, but there was nothing that could be done.

The sister and brother left the cottage, and walked in companiable silence for a bit. Then: "Why are you working at Tierney's, Seamus? I thought Patrick needed you on the farm."

"We need the cash."

Ellen eyed her brother. The wages for casual workers in a stables attached to a public house weren't known to be generous.

"Are you working in the pub too?"

"Only if Tierney needs us. He and Sarah have things under control most of the time."

"It wouldn't be Sarah that's causing you to be spending time there, would it?"

Ellen was only teasing but Seamus grabbed her arm, pulling her around to face him. "Don't be talking like that. You keep those comments to yourself. Do you hear me?"

"Seamus! Stop it, you're scaring me." She rubbed her arm – he hadn't hurt her, not really, but his reaction had frightened her.

He let go and took a step back, running a hand through his hair. "I'm sorry. I didn't mean to frighten you. It's just…"

Ellen blinked, the truth sinking in. "You love her."

He gave a small, helpless laugh. "I do. And God help her, she loves me." He glanced around before adding in a lower voice.

"Ellen, it's dangerous. If people were to find out… Sarah could be in danger."

"What people? Frank Tierney doesn't think you could put a step wrong."

"Frank isn't the problem. You've heard what the British do to those who help the Volunteers. Imagine what they would do to the woman they love?"

Ellen nodded, trying to ignore the shiver of fear running through her. John had been imprisoned for taking part in the Rising. Now her favourite brother confirmed he had joined the movement too.

They walked the rest of the way in silence. When they got to the store, Mr O'Sullivan had the shutters open.

"Morning, Seamus, Ellen. Busy day today."

Market day always was. Ellen said goodbye to her brother,

hung her coat on the rack and, taking down a clean apron, tied it around her plain black dress, her mind already running through the chores she needed to get done before they opened. She began dusting down the counter and the shelves.

As the clock turned eight, there was already a small queue outside the door. For the next couple of hours, she was run off her feet: slicing bacon, weighing out sugar or flour, packing parcels in brown paper, recording purchases in the ledger – while keeping her eye on the customers. Locals could be trusted, but market day always brought strangers and they could be light-fingered.

Jimmy, their errand boy, was kept busy cycling out with the deliveries.

Just before lunchtime, a telegram arrived for Mr O'Sullivan. Ellen watched his face pale as he opened the envelope, swaying as he read the contents. She moved quickly, pushing a chair behind him as she pulled him into it.

"Aw, Michael, *a stór*. Not you. Not *you*."

The telegram fluttered to the floor. Ellen picked it up, seeing it was from the War Office, although she didn't need to read it to know its contents.

Rapidly, Ellen served the last of the customers before closing the door and turning the sign to "Closed". She ignored the people who banged on the door. Helping Mr O'Sullivan, she took him back into the kitchen where she made him a cup of tea with plenty of sugar. She poured him a measure of whiskey too.

"My poor boy. He thought it would be exciting, you know. But look at him. Dead and buried over there in Flanders. Thank God his mother is dead, as this news would have her in the ground."

"You stay here. I'll go for the priest. He'll know what to do."

"But the shop?"

"The shop can stay shut for a couple of hours. It won't hurt anyone to wait a while. I'll fetch Seamus to help me. Mr Tierney will understand. Now you sit there until I come back. Promise?"

The large man, who had once intimidated her with his size and strength, seemed to fold in on himself. She didn't even know if he heard her. Taking off her apron, she grabbed her shawl and ran to the church.

Ellen found Father Murphy in the sacristy, polishing the silver chalice with careful, reverent movements. His ink-stained fingers, the same ones that had blessed her father's coffin, worked with practised precision. The priest had looked up as she burst through the door, his kind eyes immediately registering her distress.

"Ellen McGrath, child, what's wrong?"

"Father, it's Mr O'Sullivan. He's had terrible news – his son, Michael, is dead. Killed in France." The words tumbled out breathlessly. "He's in a bad way, and I don't know what to say to comfort him."

Father Murphy set down the chalice immediately, his face grave. "Ah, poor man. Michael was a good lad." He reached for his coat, hanging on a peg by the door. "You did right to come for me, child. These are burdens too heavy for young shoulders to bear alone."

"There's something else, Father. I need to fetch Seamus from Tierney's stables to help mind the shop, but Mr O'Sullivan can't be left alone."

The priest nodded approvingly. "You have a good head on your shoulders, Ellen. Your father would be proud. I'll go to O'Sullivan now – you fetch your brother and meet us at the shop."

Ellen hurried through the village, her shawl pulled tight against the spring wind.

She made her way around to Tierney's stable yard, breathing in the familiar scents of leather, oats, and warm animal bodies. The sound of horses whickering and stamping their feet in their stalls was comforting somehow, a reminder that life continued even in the face of tragedy.

"Seamus?" she called, peering into the dim interior.

"Back here, Ellen." His voice came from one of the far stalls where he was rubbing down a bay mare, his shirtsleeves rolled up, revealing the strong muscles of his forearms. Sweat beaded on his forehead despite the cool air.

"I need you to come with me." She told him the news. "Father Murphy's with Mr O'Sullivan now, but I need help minding the shop."

Seamus straightened immediately, his face sobering. "Jesus, Michael's dead? We used to play hurling together when we were lads." His voice caught slightly. "Poor Mr O'Sullivan – Michael was all he had left in the world." He patted the mare's neck gently. "Let me just finish here and I'll grab my coat."

"Seamus? Is everything alright?" A soft voice came from the stable entrance, and Ellen turned to see Sarah Tierney approaching with a cloth-covered basket. At seventeen, Sarah had the confident bearing that came from helping run her father's pub since she was little more than a child. Her warm brown hair was pinned neatly beneath a simple white cap, and her intelligent hazel eyes quickly assessed the situation.

"Hello, Ellen," Sarah said, warmly, though her eyes remained concerned. "What's happened?" She held up the basket. "I was just bringing Seamus his lunch, but something's clearly wrong."

Ellen noticed how Sarah's eyes lingered on Seamus, and how her brother's entire demeanour seemed to gentle in the young woman's presence. There was something tender and protective in the way he looked at her, as if she were something precious that needed safeguarding.

"What's happened?" Sarah asked again, noting their serious expressions.

"Michael O'Sullivan's been killed in France," Seamus explained, shrugging into his coat. "Ellen needs help with the shop while Father Murphy tends to the old man."

Sarah's face filled with sympathy. "Oh, the poor soul. Michael was such a lovely lad – always polite when he'd come in for a pint before he enlisted." She turned to Ellen. "Is there anything I can do to help? Perhaps I could prepare some food for Mr O'Sullivan? People need to eat, even in their grief."

Ellen felt a surge of gratitude for this girl's kindness. "That would be wonderful, thank you."

As they prepared to leave, Sarah caught Seamus's arm gently. "Be careful," she said, and Ellen caught something in her tone – a weight of worry that seemed to encompass more than just the afternoon's sad duty.

"I'm only helping in a shop, Sarah," Seamus replied, but his voice was equally quiet, equally weighted with unspoken meaning.

Sarah nodded, but Ellen noticed she didn't look entirely reassured. Sarah nodded, but Ellen noticed a change in her expression, a flicker of resolve as though she had just made up her mind. "There was... something happened last night in the pub that you both should know about."

Ellen and Seamus exchanged glances. "What is it?"

Sarah glanced around to ensure they weren't overheard, then lowered her voice. "There's been more talk of conscription coming to Ireland. Last night, Constable Clarke was nursing his pint in the corner when one of the garrison soldiers started ranting about how they need more men for the front, and that Ireland's been getting off too easy."

Ellen felt a chill that had nothing to do with the weather. "Surely they wouldn't dare?"

"The locals went dead quiet when the soldier raised his voice," Sarah continued. "But then old Tom Clancy muttered under his breath, 'They'll never take our lads.' The tension in that room could have been cut with a knife."

Seamus's jaw tightened. "What did the constable do?"

"Clarke just stared into his pint like he hadn't heard anything. But his knuckles were white where he gripped the glass." Sarah's eyes were troubled. "The soldiers don't understand what they're walking into if they try to force Irish boys to fight for the Crown. But I fear some of our own lads might do something foolish in response."

Ellen looked between Sarah and her brother. There were

tensions here she didn't fully understand, but she could feel the undercurrent of danger.

"We should go," Seamus said. "O'Sullivan needs us."

When they reached O'Sullivan's shop, they found a small crowd had already gathered outside. There was Mrs O'Brien with a fresh brown bread cake under her arm, while Dr Casey waited with his medical bag. Tom Clancy held his hat in his work-worn hands, his face creased with sympathy.

"How is he?" Ellen asked, as Father Murphy emerged from the shop.

"Bearing up as well as can be expected," the priest replied. "The shock has passed, but the grief will take time. It's good the community is rallying around him – no man should face such loss alone."

Ellen watched the neighbours file into the shop, each bringing what comfort they could offer. In the face of tragedy, the village came together as it always did, setting aside differences and disagreements to care for one of their own.

But she couldn't forget Sarah's words about conscription, or the weight of worry in the girl's eyes when she'd looked at Seamus.

Change was coming to Ireland, whether they wanted it or not. And Ellen had the sinking feeling that the death of young Michael O'Sullivan in the mud of Flanders was only the beginning.

Three days later, the church bells tolled solemnly across Clonbarra as the community gathered for Michael O'Sullivan's mass. Without a body to bury, the ritual felt incomplete somehow, but Father Murphy had insisted that the young man's soul needed the prayers of his neighbours, even if his earthly remains lay somewhere in the mud of France.

Ellen sat with her mother and Seamus in their usual pew, noting how the church was packed beyond capacity. Even those who rarely attended Mass had come to pay their respects. Mr O'Sullivan sat in the front row, his large frame somehow diminished, flanked by Mrs O'Brien and Dr Casey, who had appointed themselves his guardians for the day.

The service proceeded with familiar solemnity – prayers for the dead, hymns sung in voices thick with emotion, and Father Murphy's gentle words about Michael's young life cut short.

But as the priest moved toward his final blessing, he paused, gripping the edges of the pulpit. "Before we conclude," Father Murphy said, his voice carrying clearly to every corner of the packed church, "I have been instructed by his grace the Archbishop to read a statement regarding a matter of grave concern to all Irish families."

A rustle of tension moved through the congregation. Ellen noticed how several of the younger men sat straighter, their faces alert. In the back pew, she spotted Constable Clarke, his uniform conspicuous among the dark mourning clothes.

Father Murphy unfolded a sheet of paper, his voice taking on the formal cadence reserved for official pronouncements. "The bishops of Ireland, in union with the clergy and laity, wish to make known our unanimous opposition to any attempt to impose conscription upon the Irish people. We consider such a measure to be an oppressive and inhuman law, which the Irish people have a right to resist by every means that are consonant with the law of God."

The silence in the church was profound. Ellen could hear her own heartbeat, could feel the collective held breath of the community. Even baby Margaret O'Toole, who usually fussed during services, seemed quieted by the gravity of the moment.

"However," the priest continued, his voice carrying a note of warning, "we call upon our people to resist this unjust measure through constitutional and peaceful means only. Let every parish organize prayer vigils and lawful demonstrations, but let no man take up arms in anger, for violence begets only more violence. Our resistance must be that of a Christian people, firm in our convictions but guided by the principles of our faith."

Ellen glanced toward Constable Clarke again, noting how his

face had gone pale. The man was caught between his duty to the Crown and his position in a community that was clearly united against conscription. His hand trembled slightly as he reached up to loosen his collar.

As Father Murphy returned to the altar, Ellen felt the weight of history settling over them all. Michael O'Sullivan's death had been tragic enough, but now the war that had claimed him was reaching across the Irish Sea with grasping fingers, seeking more young Irish lives.

After the final blessing, the congregation filed out in unusual quiet, small groups forming on the church steps to discuss what they had heard in hushed, urgent tones. Ellen noticed how the younger men seemed to gravitate toward each other, their conversations intense and purposeful.

"That was a brave thing for Father Murphy to do," her mother said, as they walked back to the cottage.

Seamus said nothing, but Ellen caught the look that passed between him, Patrick, and several other young men. She thought of Sarah's warning about the pub conversation, the tension that had been building for weeks, and her brothers' strange behaviour lately, and she shivered as they hurried home.

TWENTY
APRIL 1918

The newspaper headline had been as stark as a death warrant: **CONSCRIPTION BILL EXTENDED TO IRELAND** and **MILITARY SERVICE ACT TO APPLY TO ALL MEN AGED 18–50.** Ellen still remembered the silence that had fallen over O'Sullivan's store when she'd read the announcement aloud; how the handful of customers had stood frozen, as if the very words could reach out and snatch their sons.

Now, as Ellen hugged her arms to her chest, the last of Father Murphy's Latin faded into the hush outside the church. Once again, the priest's sermon had been carefully worded, supporting the bishops' statement while avoiding direct defiance, but everyone understood the message: *The British want our boys for cannon fodder. We will not let them take them.*

Women filtered into the churchyard in twos and threes, lips pursed, eyes down, yet with a current running through them, something strong and shared. The very air seemed charged with defiance.

Sarah stood with arms crossed near the church door. "Will you sign it?"

Ellen eyed the folded table where Miss Fallon, the schoolmistress, arranged the petition papers like they were the

Gospels themselves. The carefully penned words at the top read: *"We, the undersigned women of Clonbarra Parish, do solemnly pledge our opposition to the forced conscription of Irish men into the British Army..."*

"Do you have to ask?" Ellen smiled, but her mam suddenly gripped her arm.

"Ellen, let's go home."

"Mam?" Ellen stared at her mother in disbelief. "You heard the priest. We must stop them. They can't take Seamus and Patrick. If they're sent to France, they could end up like Michael, or worse. Come home in a state, like poor Jack Hurley."

Her mam closed her eyes and made the sign of the cross, her face etched with the kind of exhaustion that came from losing too much already. Ellen could see her thinking of Patrick's politics, of Seamus's stubborn streak, of all the ways this new threat could destroy what remained of their family.

"Mam, if Da was here, he'd be stopping every person leaving until they signed. You know that."

Mary McGrath's shoulders sagged, but she nodded wearily. "Aye, he would." And she stepped forward and signed her name with a trembling hand, her signature small and careful. Then she turned toward the graveyard. "I'm going to have a few words with your father. Tell him what's happening to his boys."

Ellen watched her mother walk away, then turned back to add her own signature to the growing list. Around her, other women were doing the same. Mothers, sisters, sweethearts, all united by the fear of losing their men to a war that wasn't theirs.

Sarah nodded approvingly. "Then we'll march too."

Near the gate, the Anti-Conscription banner fluttered in the spring breeze: **NO KINGS, NO CONSCRIPTION, NO SURRENDER**. It had been stitched in the nights by women from Clonbarra, women who'd never once raised their voices in public until the British dared threaten to draft their menfolk.

Ellen stepped forward to join the forming procession and froze.

A bicycle skidded to a halt on the lane, and off swung a figure not in a shawl, but in uniform. Isabella Russell dismounted with practised grace, but she was transformed from the girl Ellen had once known.

Gone was the fine silk and careful coiffure of the landlord's daughter. Isabella's brown boots gleamed beneath a green *Cumann na mBan* tunic, her Sam Browne belt worn like she'd earned it through drill and discipline rather than birthright. A tricolour ribbon was pinned beneath her collar, and a small pistol holster hung at her hip, though it was conspicuously empty. Her copper hair was braided back severely, and her green eyes held a determination Ellen had never seen before. She found herself wishing she'd worn her *Cumann na mBan* uniform too.

The women went quiet, rosary beads stilling in their hands.

Sarah's jaw dropped. "Is she lost?"

"No," Ellen whispered, unexpected pride for her old friend filling her chest. "She knows exactly where she is."

Isabella strode forward through the parting crowd and met Miss Fallon's eye directly. "Have you room for another name?"

Miss Fallon, to her credit, didn't blink. Her voice was steady as granite. "We do."

Without ceremony, Isabella took up the pen and signed her name in bold strokes: *Isabella Russell, Clonbarra House.* The scratch of her pen seemed unnaturally loud in the churchyard silence.

Then she turned to the watching crowd and gave a short nod. "I've trained in first aid, map reading, and arms drill with the Volunteers. I stand with Countess Markievicz, I stand with you." Her refined English accent cracked slightly on the next words. "With Ireland."

The silence stretched. Women turned to one another at the name of the countess who had been condemned to die following her part in the Easter Rising, who had until recently been imprisoned by the British. Ellen's heartbeat thundered. Around her, she felt the collective assessment of these women who had every reason to distrust a Russell. The old Lord Russell's politics were well known, and Edward's reputation was damning. But if Countess Markievicz trusted Miss Russell, shouldn't they?

Finally, old Mrs Cassidy stepped forward, her black shawl stark against her grey hair. "And will your brother, Edward, stand with us too?"

"God forgive us all," someone muttered from the back of the crowd.

Ellen didn't turn to acknowledge that comment, her eyes on Isabella's face. A few sharp, bitter laughs rose from the crowd, but Isabella didn't flinch. Her jaw tightened, but her voice remained steady. "He doesn't speak for me," she said simply. "He never did."

Ellen found herself stepping forward before she'd consciously decided to move. The crowd parted for her, and she could feel every eye on her as she approached Isabella. She embraced her, brief, fierce, and wholly improper.

"Walk with us," Ellen said, holding out the small white badge she'd been handed moments before.

Isabella took the badge and pinned it over her heart, right next to the tricolour ribbon. Her hands were steady, but Ellen noticed her fingers trembled slightly as she secured the pin.

They set off then, a procession of women unlike any Clonbarra had ever seen. Shawled mothers walked beside farmers' daughters, shopkeepers' wives beside servant girls, and in their midst, a landlord's daughter in Republican uniform. Ellen noticed how the other women glanced at Isabella – some curious, some approving – all aware that something unprecedented was happening.

A steady whisper of rosary beads began, the measured tread of feet on stone, voices murmuring the familiar words.

Isabella walked in silence, her lips pressed together, clearly not knowing the prayers. But her presence spoke louder than any words. Their shoulders brushed as they walked, and Ellen could feel the tremor running through her friend despite her ramrod posture. When Bella glanced sideways at her, Ellen saw her own determination reflected back. Two girls who'd once played together in the Russell gardens, now women choosing to stand against an empire.

Ellen reached out, briefly squeezing Bella's hand. The gesture was fleeting, but Isabella's grateful smile made Ellen's chest swell with something fierce and protective. They were all soldiers now, in their own way.

The village seemed to hold its breath as they passed. Curtains twitched in windows, faces appeared and disappeared behind glass. Mrs O'Brien stood in her doorway to watch, still in her Sunday best. Ellen caught her eye and saw the small, approving nod. Not every woman dared to march, but plenty still stood with them.

TWENTY-ONE
NOW

The waves thundered against the shore as if matching Caitlin's sense of frustration. She knew the reasons for her not driving were sound but it felt confining to be in Ireland and only able to do research via a laptop. Caitlin sat with her boots off, the hem of her jeans damp from where she'd walked too close to the edge. Wind lifted her hair, carrying the salt and something faintly floral from the dunes behind her.

"Not the worst view in Ireland," a voice said behind her, amused but kindly.

She turned. A tall man in his late fifties stood on the path above the beach, collar glinting white beneath a navy windcheater. His face was lined, brown from the weather, eyes a sharp blue that spoke of long hours spent watching skies for storms.

"Sorry," he said, stepping down onto the sand. "Didn't mean to startle you. Father Tom Brady."

Caitlin smiled faintly. "You must be the local priest."

"Guilty. And the local historian, depending who you ask. Delia mentioned you were researching some family history and may need some help. Thought I'd better come make sure you're not writing lies about us."

"I'm just trying to understand. My great-grandmother was born near here in the early 1900s. I'm filling in the blanks."

"Ah." He folded himself down beside her, joints creaking. "Then you've chosen a rough period to untangle. Nothing simple about those years."

"Delia has explained a little about the Easter Rising and I found out my great-grandfather was imprisoned for his part in it. When he came home, I think he got involved in other things."

He scooped up a handful of sand, letting it fall slowly through his fingers. "After the Rising in 1916, most Dubliners cursed the men who led it. The city was in ruins, families lost their homes, food was scarce. People thought the rebels had brought disaster on their own. But then the British started executing them – one by one, day after day. Pearse, Connolly, Clarke... you can only shoot so many young men before the country's heart turns."

Caitlin listened, watching the grains slide from his hand. "So the Rising failed but changed everything?"

"That's about the size of it." He smiled. "When the First World War ended, thousands of Irishmen came home – if they came home at all. Some were missing limbs, some just... missing inside. They'd fought for the Crown because John Redmond promised Home Rule after the war. The British Parliament had already passed it in 1914, but suspended it 'for the duration.'" His fingers curled into the sand. "When the war was over and they still delayed, the promise turned to dust."

"So the anger grew."

"It did. You had men who'd fought for Britain side by side with men who'd been jailed for fighting against her. They came home to the same parishes, the same lanes. And then you had Michael Collins and others like him – young, fierce, organized. They took what was left of the old Irish Volunteers and forged it into the IRA, the Irish Republican Army. No more parades or speeches. This time it was intelligence work, ambushes, and counter-spies."

Caitlin hugged her knees, thinking of Ellen's photograph in her bag. "Would there be records of that? Of what Collins did?"

Father Tom nodded. "Bits and pieces. Reports in the Bureau of Military History, witness statements, old intelligence files. Some are digitized now. Collins was clever – he wrote little down himself, but others wrote plenty about him. You'll find his name in police lists, RIC memos, even court-martial transcripts. But remember, every record's written from someone's side of the story."

Caitlin swallowed hard. "My great-grandmother marched in the anti-conscription protests," she said quietly. "In 1918. Delia shared some photographs."

Father Tom's eyes warmed. "Ah, one of the brave ones. We hear too little about what the women of Ireland did. The IRA would've failed without them. It was the women who sheltered the Volunteers, smuggled messages under loaves of bread, fed men on the run. The servants who listened at doors, the office girls and cleaners up in Dublin Castle – they risked their lives in silence."

Caitlin looked toward the water, imagining Ellen among the crowds, a banner in her hands. "I don't think she saw herself as brave."

"Most heroes don't," Father Tom said gently. "They just do what needs doing."

"Father, how would someone like her end up in a mother and baby home?" Caitlin hesitated, then continued. "I found a church record, a baptismal record for my grandmother with both parents' names but no wedding entry for my great-grandmother. Years later, when she was pregnant again, they sent her to a mother and baby home. My grandmother, aged about two, was taken there too. I can't make sense of it. I assume you had to be married in a church to have your child baptized. How could she be married in a church and still end up there?"

Father Tom's gaze softened. "Ah, that would've happened more than you'd think. Back then, the priest registered the Church ceremony. Sometimes, they forgot or the records went missing, particularly in the turmoil of war. Without proof of her marriage, a woman could be branded unwed." He looked out toward the horizon, voice low. "And once the State decided a woman was unmarried, well... everything that followed was branded sin, no matter what vows she'd taken before God."

She hesitated, twisting her fingers together. "Father, would you have any influence with a convent called St Brigid's? I need answers, and my grandmother's in her nineties. They said it may take two months or more, but I don't have that kind of time."

He studied her for a moment, the sea wind ruffling the grey in his hair. "Some doors take more than a knock to open," he said at last. "But I can try a few I know. The Church has a long memory – not all of it proud."

Her throat tightened. "Thank you."

He gave a small nod. "If you're chasing truth, you'll find it, though it might not come gentle." He glanced back toward the village path. "Call up to the presbytery tomorrow. I'll see what I can do."

Caitlin watched him walk away across the sand.

The next morning, Caitlin sat at the small kitchen table in the presbytery, the smell of tea and boiled cabbage mingling in the air. Father Tom poured two cups, added milk to both, then set his aside.

"Right," he said, wiping his hands on a tea towel. "Now, let's make a phone call or two." He glanced over his glasses at her. "Whom did you speak to?"

"A Mrs Walsh," Caitlin said. "I got the sense she was reading from a script as soon as I mentioned my family history."

"No doubt," he murmured, lifting the receiver. "They're all told what to say these days. Too much press coverage. Some of it deserved, some not. Doesn't make it easier to open old wounds."

He dialled, waited, then smiled when the line clicked.

"Could I speak to Mrs Walsh, please?... Ah, lovely. It's Father Brady calling."

Pause.

"Mrs Walsh! And how are you keeping? I've heard great things about you from the Archbishop himself." He winked at Caitlin, mouthing *trust me*.

Another pause.

"He did indeed. Said you were the most organized woman in the country. Now, I won't keep you long, but I need a little help with a delicate matter."

He leaned back in his chair, tone easy, almost conversational.

"Yes, it concerns an old parishioner – or rather, her daughter. The woman was born not far from here, many years ago now. For reasons I'm hoping you can clarify, she and her pregnant mother ended up in St Brigid's. Her name was Ellen Power, née McGrath. I'm wondering if her file might be located and reviewed as a matter of urgency."

A short silence, then his expression sharpened slightly.

"Yes, I understand you've had a request for this before. I just wanted to ensure you're aware of the time sensitivity. The daughter, the one making the inquiry, is in her nineties. We can't afford a delay."

He gave a faint chuckle. "Yes, almost ninety years since the events themselves. Hard to believe, isn't it?"

Another pause, then his eyes softened.

"Ah, that's wonderful, Mrs Walsh. I'm very grateful. I'll be sure to tell the Archbishop how helpful you've been. God bless you for your time."

He replaced the receiver gently and reached for his tea.

"There now," he said with a grin. "You'd be amazed what a little flattery can do when wielded in the service of justice."

"You make it look easy."

Father Tom shrugged. "It isn't. But some walls fall faster to kindness than to kicking. I hope you find the answers you need but be prepared, those places weren't happy ones. They brought out the worst in people, particularly those who should have been more Christian. If you don't get a response soon, please come and find me. I have a few more tricks up my sleeve."

TWENTY-TWO

JANUARY 1919

The Armistice had brought peace to Europe, but not to Ireland. The war was over, yet the promises made to this country were already being broken, and unrest was brewing again. With no sign of Home Rule being introduced, rumours abounded that Sinn Fein would not recognize the British Government but would instead set up a new government in Dublin. John could no more give up the fight for Ireland than he could breathing. He was involved with Michael Collins, training men in readiness to take up arms.

Ellen stacked a crate of tea tins behind the counter. A low, throaty rumble of a motorcar rolled down the street, unlike the clip of hooves or the groan of cartwheels she was used to. Curious, she wiped her hands on her apron and stepped outside.

The motorcar had drawn up at the kerb, its dark body shining despite the dust of the road. The chauffeur climbed down, tall and thin, with the measured movements of someone used to being watched. He opened the back passenger door, and Isabella Russell stepped gracefully onto the street.

"Ellen!" Isabella's face lit, her voice warm with delight. "I hoped you'd be here."

Ellen smiled back and watched the chauffeur help Isabella onto the pavement. As she did so, she noticed something pass between them – a moment that stretched like a fiddle string pulled taut, as Isabella's fingers lingered in his grasp a heartbeat too long, her cheeks blooming pink. And, for a moment, the man's professional mask slipped, revealing such naked longing that Ellen felt like an intruder.

It was over in a blink. Isabella released his hand, smoothing her gloves with brisk composure. Yet the softness in her eyes lingered, and Ellen's smile faltered just a little. She had never seen Isabella look quite like that before. But it couldn't mean anything. Gossip spread by the maids from the big house had Isabella dancing till dawn in the arms of dashing majors and captains in Dublin Castle – the centre of British administration and intelligence in Ireland.

She turned to Ellen, arm extended as she made the introductions. "Ellen, this is Fintan Murphy. He hails from Cork. Cook needed some provisions urgently. She couldn't wait on the usual delivery. We came to collect them."

Ellen bit her lip trying not to laugh. The excuse was as flimsy as bringing eggs up to the big house the day Lady Russell banned her from Isabella's company. Lady Russell was now a permanent fixture in England, thank goodness.

Isabella held Ellen's gaze, a beseeching look in her eyes. "I thought you might have the kettle on. Fin—" She caught herself, colour deepening. "I mean, Murphy didn't have a chance to have breakfast. Father sent him on an errand at dawn."

Ellen noticed the awkward silence that followed, the way Fintan studied the shop window with sudden fascination while Isabella twisted her gloves. Taking pity on them both, Ellen stepped back toward the door.

"Come inside. Mr O'Sullivan likes a cup of tea about this time."

Fintan straightened. "If you're sure, miss. I could wait with the motor."

"Nonsense." Isabella shook her head, perhaps too quickly. "And nobody will touch it. It's quite safe. Come inside."

Ellen held the door open as the couple walked in.

Fintan's eyes immediately landed on the picture of Michael O'Sullivan in his Connaught Rangers' uniform. "Is he here? I served in the same outfit."

Before Ellen could respond, Mr O'Sullivan emerged from the back of the store. "My son, Michael. He fell at Passchendaele. Were you there?"

"Yes, sir. I'm sorry for your loss."

"That's a Cork accent. What has you so far from home?"

"Mr O'Sullivan, this is Fintan Murphy," Isabella interjected smoothly. "Father recently employed him as my chauffeur, bodyguard and general spy." Her tone was light, teasing, but Ellen caught the quick glance she shot at Fintan.

Instead of being shocked, Fintan merely smiled, a professional, appropriate smile this time. "Lord Russell was kind enough to offer employment when I returned from France, sir."

"Ellen, will you turn the sign and put the kettle on?" Mr O'Sullivan gestured toward the back room. "We'll have an early lunch, if you don't mind joining us, Mr Murphy? If it doesn't cause you too much pain, I'd like to hear what it was like over there, from someone who served with my son. You didn't come across him, did you—?"

Mr O'Sullivan caught himself. "My apologies, Miss Russell. I should have checked with yourself before making assumptions."

"Please don't worry, Mr O'Sullivan. If you and Mr Murphy wish to catch up, it will give Ellen and myself time to chat." Isabella's relief was palpable. "Just don't let us leave without Cook's provisions, or my life won't be worth living."

Ellen busied herself with the tea things while the men settled at the small table in the corner. She could hear Fintan's measured voice recounting a story about trenches and mud, keeping his tone neutral, revealing nothing of his own opinions about the war or its aftermath.

Isabella helped arrange the cups, moving with the easy familiarity of their friendship despite the fact they hadn't seen each other in almost a year. But Ellen noticed how her friend's attention kept drifting to the corner table, how her hands trembled slightly when Fintan's voice rose in laughter at something Mr O'Sullivan said. Isabella had always been the most composed girl Ellen knew, unflappable even when her mother raged or her father thundered. But this morning her movements were too quick, her voice too bright. And her eyes – they held a restless hunger that no amount of tea or conversation would satisfy.

"This is dangerous," Ellen murmured, low enough that only Isabella could hear.

"I know." Isabella's response was barely a whisper. "But some things can't be helped, can they?"

"From what I heard, you've been having a wonderful time up in Dublin dancing the nights away with eligible bachelors." Ellen didn't add those bachelors all shared one common feature – they were all members of the British Army.

Isabella flushed but Ellen wasn't sure if it was embarrassment. Was it anger? But why? They'd once teased each other all the time.

Isabella rose. "We really must collect those provisions and return. Father will wonder what's become of us."

Ellen wrapped the requested items while Fintan shook Mr O'Sullivan's hand, thanking him for the tea. As they left, Ellen caught the briefest touch of Fintan's fingers against Isabella's back, guiding her through the door – an intimacy that made Ellen's chest tight.

The motorcar rumbled away, leaving a cloud of dust and the faint scent of fumes. Ellen stood in the doorway, watching until they turned the corner.

Just as she was about to step back inside, she spotted John striding up the street. He paused mid-step as the motorcar passed, and through the settling dust, Ellen caught something – a flicker of recognition in his face, there and gone. But it vanished so quickly she wondered if she'd imagined it. But Ellen had the strangest feeling, as if something delicate had shifted inside her, knocked slightly out of place.

John simply touched his cap and continued toward the shop, his expression perfectly neutral.

"Ellen, love." He kissed her cheek as he reached the doorway, but his eyes were still on the road where the motorcar had disappeared. "Was that the Russell motorcar?"

"It was. Isabella came for provisions with her new chauffeur." Ellen studied his face, searching for that flicker she'd seen, but John's features gave nothing away.

"Ah." Just that single sound, but something in it made Ellen's unease deepen. "Are you free this evening? I thought I'd walk you home. The long way." John's wink pushed all suspicions out of her mind as she giggled. "I'll take that as a yes. Go on, then – get back to work, Miss McGrath, and stop proving such a distraction to us working men."

John walked on whistling their tune – the one from the night he'd first kissed her under the oak tree.

Ellen walked back into the store to be met by a concerned look on Mr O'Sullivan's face.

"That's trouble brewing. Mark my words, no good comes from the gentry mixing with their servants, no matter how many stripes he earned in France."

Ellen didn't reply. What could she say? She should warn Isabella. Mr O'Sullivan wouldn't gossip, but certain ladies in town would have a field day.

Ellen helped her employer clear the tea things. As she worked, Mr O'Sullivan's mood seemed to darken.

"Speaking of trouble," he muttered, gesturing at the morning papers still spread on the counter. "Have you seen this?"

Ellen moved closer, reading over his shoulder. The headlines spoke of the Paris Peace Conference, of new nations being carved from old empires.

"Lies and more lies." Mr O'Sullivan shook his head, arranging the newspapers with sharp, angry movements. "Wilson speaks of freedom for small nations while the British keep us in chains. Home Rule was promised, but where is it now that the war's done?"

Ellen nodded grimly. "Mrs Branigan was saying the same at Mass yesterday. Even she's talking about supporting the boys now, and she used to call them troublemakers."

"The whole village is turning. The British are showing their true colours, and they're uglier than many imagined." Mr O'Sullivan's lined face hardened. "My Michael died for their empire, and this is our thanks: more broken promises, and contempt."

Ellen thought of John, her brothers, of all the young men gathering in secret. The tide *was* turning, she could feel it. Even those who'd been reluctant to support armed resistance were beginning to change their minds.

"There'll be fighting again soon."

Mr O'Sullivan met her eyes. "Yes, girl. And this time, I think the whole country will be behind it."

TWENTY-THREE

Ellen lay on a blanket beside the river with John, enjoying one of their rare afternoons together. The late September air was soft and warm, and golden light filtered through the willow branches that brushed the slow-moving water. John's head rested in her lap, his eyes closed, his breathing steady at last.

Moments like this felt impossibly precious, made even more so by the flawless weather. Between her shifts at O'Sullivan's and John's frequent, unexplained trips with Collins's men, they rarely found time to be alone. Ellen cherished the weight of him against her, the quiet hush of the river, the distant hum of village life.

"I wish your mam would give us permission to get wed." John ran his fingers through her hair, sending delicious sensations through her body that made it difficult to think.

"I do too, but she's worried. She thinks the country will be at war soon, and you'll be gone, and she doesn't want me to be a widow – with a child or two." She blushed, thinking of them having children.

"I understand. But God knows, you could die in childbirth; I could get run over by a horse and cart. There are no guarantees in life." He kissed her, then broke off the kiss with a growl of frustration. "I hate not being able to be with you. Properly."

He rested his forehead against hers. "When it's over – when Ireland's ours – we'll grab your mam and your brothers and stand in front of the priest and take our vows. Assuming you still want to marry me."

She kissed him deeply. "I will always want to marry you." Emotion clogged her voice.

"You always say *when*, never *if*," she said, trying to smile.

"Because I have to believe it." His voice was rough. "If I didn't, none of this would be worth fighting for."

She nodded, though a chill ran through her despite the sun. Love and danger had become the same thing.

John spoke without opening his eyes. "How much do you know about Isabella?"

Ellen's fingers paused mid-stroke in his hair. "What do you mean?"

"Her friendship with Countess Markievicz. Her politics. All of it."

Ellen watched a fish leap and fall, ripples widening across the surface of the water. "Not much, if I'm honest. She came with us for the anti-conscription march, wore her *Cumann na mBan* uniform. Caused quite a stir – but she hasn't worn it since. Said someone warned her off. Probably her father." She hesitated. "It's hard to know what to make of her these days. She's in Dublin more than here, always off to some dinner or dance. I've heard she's popular with the officers. British ones."

The comment sounded more critical than she meant it to be. It made no sense. One day she was walking out with a chauffeur, the next she was laughing with British officers.

She shifted slightly beneath John's weight. "I suppose she's doing her best to manage things. Her parents have gone back to England, and Edward's still in London. She's on her own."

John sat up suddenly, his eyes sharp and serious. The shift in him was so quick, Ellen's heart stuttered. "You can't repeat this to anyone. Not even to Seamus or Patrick."

"But they're on your side. They support the cause."

"They do. But the fewer who know, the safer we all are. This isn't about trust, Ellen."

He took her hands in his, rough and warm, his thumbs tracing circles on her palms in a gesture meant to soothe, but which only made her more aware of him. "Isabella is working for Collins. She's spying for us. And Fintan, he's her connection. He drives her to those Dublin parties, yes, but she's not there to dance. She's gathering information – military plans, troop movements, things mentioned over port by men who think she's just decoration."

Ellen's breath caught. She pressed a hand to her chest, feeling her heart race beneath her palm. "Isabella? A spy?"

"She moves in circles we could never reach. Collins thinks she's one of our best assets. People speak freely around her. They see the dress, the title, and assume there's nothing behind it." His voice dropped. "The same way they ignore the shop girl at the counter. Or the maid sweeping the floors. Women are invisible, Ellen. That's their advantage."

Ellen's thoughts raced. She remembered Isabella's guarded glances, her bright smile that didn't quite reach her eyes. The nerves, the slips in speech. It all suddenly made sense.

"The chauffeur thing, that's just cover? I knew you recognized him, that day they came to the store."

John didn't argue. "Fintan really was in the British Army – Connaught Rangers, like Michael O'Sullivan. But Collins recruited him not long after he came home. The attraction between him and Isabella? That's real. Not planned, but it helps the cover story."

Ellen thought of Isabella staring at Fintan, how her hand had lingered in his just a little too long. "So when she's in Dublin..."

"She's listening. Watching. Reporting. And if she's caught..." He didn't finish.

A chill ran through Ellen despite the warm September air. She swallowed hard. "You think I could help too. That's why you're telling me—?"

"No!" In one swift movement, John rolled to his knees, looking at her fiercely as he retook her hands. "It's too dangerous. You're already exposed. Your brothers, me, the company you keep. If you started passing information, you'd be marked. I wouldn't risk that."

She frowned. "But then why tell me?"

"Because you need to know the truth. You were judging her. She hasn't turned her back on Ireland. She's risking her life for it." He let go of her hands and looked out toward the water. "And because I need someone I trust to listen. If anyone starts to question her, why she's in Dublin so much, why she's never without that chauffeur, we need to know."

Ellen nodded slowly, her mind still spinning. "What should I be listening for?"

"Rumours. Suspicion. Especially from the *polis* or anyone with connections to the garrison. Anything that might suggest they're looking too closely at her or Fintan."

"And the way she feels about him?" Ellen asked. "Doesn't that make things harder?"

John gave a rueful smile. "Love always makes things harder. But Collins thinks it helps. People will be too busy gossiping about the lady and the chauffeur to suspect her of anything else."

"People may think she's just a plaything, John. But you and I both know better. She's a kind, wonderful young woman and she's in love. What will happen to her if her father hears the gossip?"

John's face softened with regret as he picked up her hand. "Would you prefer he heard the truth?"

She gasped at his blunt words.

He took her hand again. "I'm sorry, that was uncalled for. I know she is your friend, but nobody forced her to do what she's doing. She knows the risks and has accepted them." He lifted her hand to his lips, kissing her knuckles gently. "You're the best of us, Ellen McGrath."

Then he lay back down, resting his head in her lap again. "All I ask is that you keep your ears open."

Ellen resumed stroking John's hair, but her thoughts were miles away. Isabella, her childhood friend, the landlord's daughter who'd once wept over broken eggs, was now risking her life as a spy for Irish independence. It seemed impossible. And yet, the signs had been there all along. Ellen remembered that day, years ago, when her mother had said Isabella would never be "one of them", that she'd always be the landlord's daughter first. Lady Russell had held similar views, banning her daughter from speaking to her. Now Ellen understood: Isabella had found her own way to be "one of them" after all, in a manner more dangerous and committed than anyone could have imagined. The uniform she wore once and never again. The nervous glances. The slip of "Fin" on her lips. It wasn't cowardice, Ellen realized, it was courage, carefully hidden behind gloves and good manners.

"I'm proud of her. Scared for her, but proud."

Isabella was deceiving British officers who could have her shot. When had her friend become so brave?

"As you should be." His voice was drowsy now, his body warm and heavy against her legs. "She could've stayed safe. But she didn't."

Ellen looked out at the water, sunlight catching on its surface. It was more than that. By standing for the Irish, Isabella was risking rejection from everything and everyone she'd ever known. And even with her bravery, there were some Irish who'd never accept her. She'd always be British and therefore an object of hate to them.

Somewhere, Isabella was smiling across a ballroom, laughing at some officer's joke while memorizing names and dates that could save lives. The least she could do was try to help protect her friend and support her when possible.

"I'll listen. I'll tell you if I hear anything."

John murmured, "That's all any of us can do – protect each other. And hope it's enough."

TWENTY-FOUR

DECEMBER

Ellen had just closed the cottage door when the low growl of an engine carried up the lane. She stilled, heart lifting. A motorcar, at this hour? She pushed the door wide again, and headlamps spilled light over the yard.

The Russell car idled by the gate, its headlights cutting pale beams across the stone wall. In the three months since John told her Isabella's secret by the river, Ellen had kept her word. She'd watched her friend come and go with Fintan, biting her tongue when Patrick made cutting remarks about their landlord's daughter playing at politics.

Isabella climbed down, her cloak pulled close against the December chill. In her hands she carried a neat wicker basket. Behind her, Fintan steadied the load until she had it balanced, his touch careful, lingering just a shade longer than it needed to.

"Ellen!" Isabella called, voice bright as though nothing in the world was amiss. "I've been in Dublin and thought of you."

She pressed the basket into Ellen's arms – spices, dried fruit, sweet biscuits tucked beneath tissue paper. "For your mother," Isabella explained. "I heard she's been ill. I thought... a few little things might tempt her appetite. It's almost Christmas after all."

Ellen blinked hard against the sudden warmth in her chest. "That's very kind. She'll be touched."

Fintan tipped his cap, face composed, though his eyes followed Isabella with an intensity Ellen could not mistake. Then his gaze swept the lane, the hedgerows, always watchful for danger even here.

Ellen hugged the basket close as she studied her friend. Isabella was thinner and paler than she'd been in September, shadows beneath her eyes that powder couldn't quite hide.

"Will you come inside?" Ellen asked, although she knew her friend would refuse. Isabella hadn't been in the McGrath home since those few days after Ellen's da had died.

"Ellen, I... would you step into the car? I need a quiet word."

Heart thudding, Ellen placed the basket carefully by the front door before following Isabella and climbing inside the car. The leather seats were cold, the air sharp with the scent of petrol and Isabella's French perfume. Only once Fintan had taken his seat did Isabella speak.

"Patrick's in trouble. I can't tell you how I know but you need to warn him to lay low for a bit. He can't be involved in any more actions against the RIC."

Ellen's stomach dropped. "What about John? Is he—?"

"I don't know." Isabella's voice was gentle but urgent. "My information was specifically about Patrick. But, Ellen, you *must* make him listen."

Ellen hesitated. The words John had made her swear burned in her throat. Should she tell Isabella she knew what she was doing up in Dublin, or would that mark her as someone incapable of keeping a secret?

Isabella solved it for her. "Fintan" – Isabella smiled at the man sitting in the front of the car, though tension lined her face – "told me you know my story. What I'm really doing when I go to Dublin. He said you are part of my protection."

"Thank God. I wanted to tell you I was proud of you and scared at the same time. But John told me not to tell Patrick and

Seamus about you. So how do I warn Patrick so that he listens to me?"

Isabella's fingers twisted in her lap. "Tell him the truth. He's become suspicious, and he's less dangerous if he knows."

Ellen understood immediately. Patrick asking questions, poking around, could expose the entire network.

"The risk is real," Isabella continued. "Tell him the action planned for December 29th must be cancelled. Make him see. Won't you?"

"I'll try, but you know my brother."

Isabella gave a rueful smile. "He's almost as stubborn as mine." She sighed. "I don't know if I will be here in the next few weeks. Father... Father is ill and they don't expect him to last much longer. I've been summoned to London."

Ellen pulled Bella into her arms seeing the tears shining in her eyes. Whatever anyone else thought of Lord Russell, he was still Isabella's father.

"I envied you your father, Ellen. He was such a kind man. Whereas mine... well, he's anything but. But he's still my father. I have to go."

Ellen could see Fintan's hands tighten on the steering wheel. His pain for Isabella was written in every line of his body, unable to offer comfort while maintaining his role as merely the chauffeur.

"When do you leave?"

"Tomorrow morning. The boat from Queenstown." Isabella pulled back, composing herself. "Ellen, if something happens while I'm gone—"

"Nothing will happen," Ellen said firmly, though dread pooled in her stomach.

"If it does," Isabella insisted, "Fintan will know how to reach me. And, Ellen? Thank you. For understanding. For keeping my secret. For being my friend despite everything."

The motorcar pulled away into the darkness, leaving Ellen standing by her gate with a heart heavy with foreboding.

Inside the cottage, she could hear Patrick's voice raised in laughter over something Seamus had said.

How was she going to make him listen? How could she protect him when he thought himself invincible? If only John were here – he always knew how to steady Patrick when no one else could. But he was away with the Volunteers, working under Michael Collins, travelling from parish to parish, recruiting and training new men for what they were beginning to call the Irish Republican Army.

She picked up the basket and went inside to face her brother. She would have to find the words, and pray they were enough.

TWENTY-FIVE

NOW

Hearing a car pull up outside, Caitlin opened the door to find Conor standing there with a canvas bag and an expression somewhere between "determined" and "nervous". He was wearing a grey Henley that stretched across his shoulders, and morning stubble shadowed his jaw in a way that made him look less "polished physiotherapist" and more like the surfer she'd first met coming from the beach.

"Morning." He held up a piece of paper. "I've been thinking."

"Dangerous habit." She stepped back to let him in, suddenly conscious of her bare feet on the cold floor, not to mention her fluffy PJs.

"About your treatment. I can't be your physiotherapist if I want to..." He paused, colour rising above the stubble on his cheeks. "If we're going to be seeing each other socially."

"Oh." Her stomach dropped. Was he backing out already?

"So I called a colleague in Oranmore. Tessa Quinn. She's excellent, specializes in trauma recovery." He handed her the paper with contact details. "I explained your case in broad terms. No names, no specifics. She can see you tomorrow if you're interested."

"You're firing me as a patient?"

"I'm referring you to someone who can be objective." He set the bag on her table, the movement making the Henley pull taut across his back. "Which I'm finding to be increasingly difficult."

Something fluttered in her chest. "Is that so?"

"Very much so." He unpacked the bag, producing several small jars. The morning light threw shadows under his cheekbones, making him look older, more serious than usual. "These are for you. Old family remedies. My gran swore by them for her arthritis."

Caitlin picked up one jar, the dark contents visible through the glass. "What is it?"

"Bladderwrack salve." He opened the lid, and immediately a sharp, briny smell filled the kitchen. "You warm it up, rub it into the sore muscles. This one's carrageen moss poultice for tightness. And fish oil." He wrinkled his nose. "That one's pretty pungent. But it works."

"You made these?"

"My gran's recipes. She learned from her mother, who probably learned from hers." He pushed up his sleeves as he demonstrated, revealing forearms corded with muscle – the kind that came from paddling through waves, not lifting weights. "You take a small amount, warm it between your palms first..."

His hands moved to show her, and she caught herself staring at them again. Those careful, capable hands – long fingers moving with the particular grace of someone who understood bodies and how to heal them.

"The smell takes getting used to," he warned. "Very... maritime."

"I live by the ocean. I think I can handle maritime."

He smiled at that, and it changed his whole face, softening the serious lines. "Fair point." He closed the jar, wiped his hands on a cloth he'd brought. "Tessa's excellent. She'll take good care of you. And this way..."

"This way?"

He stepped closer, and she was suddenly aware of the height

difference between them, how she had to tilt her face up to meet his gaze. "This way I can do what I've wanted to do since Finn knocked you over."

Her breath caught. "Which is?"

"This." His hand came up to cup her jaw, warm and steady, but gentle too. "If that's okay?"

Instead of answering, she leaned in, rising slightly on her toes. The kiss was soft at first, tentative, like he was giving her every chance to pull away. When she didn't, his other hand found her waist, drawing her closer.

When they finally broke apart, they were both breathing harder. She could see the pulse jumping in his throat, the way his chest rose and fell under the soft cotton of his top.

Her voice trembled despite her best efforts to keep it steady. "I've been thinking about that since dinner."

"I've been thinking about it since you stood up to Finn with that fierce look on your face." His thumb traced her cheekbone with professional precision but decidedly unprofessional intent. "Even pale and favouring your leg, you looked ready to take on the world."

"I was terrified."

"I know. That's what made it impressive." He kissed her again, more briefly this time, but she felt it all the way to her bare toes on the cold floor. "I should go. I have patients. Real ones, who I'm not desperate to kiss."

She grinned, pushing her sleep-mussed hair behind her ear. "Smooth talker."

"Only with you, apparently." He gathered his things, pausing at the door. The light caught the strong line of his profile, the way his dark hair fell across his forehead. "The salves really do help. And Tessa's wonderful."

"Thank you. For the referral. For these." She gestured at the jars. "For..."

"For finally getting to kiss you properly?" That grin again, transforming him from serious medical professional to the man who'd caught her attention that first day when she'd arrived. "Entirely my pleasure."

After he left, Caitlin touched her lips, still feeling the warmth of him. She checked the time. Nine thirty here meant it was only four thirty in the morning in Charleston. Grammy would kill her if she called now.

She busied herself organizing the salves, reading Conor's handwritten labels. Instructions for warming the bladderwrack, how much carrageen to use. His writing was careful, precise, just like his physio work.

Caitlin's phone rang at noon. Grammy, right on schedule.

"Well? How was dinner with the nice physiotherapist?"

"He's referring me to someone else for treatment."

"What? Why? Is he not good at his job?" Grammy's voice rose with indignation.

Caitlin smiled. "He's very good. That's the problem. Can't date patients. Ethical rules."

The delighted gasp on the other end made her hold the phone away from her ear. "So he wants to date you properly! Oh, Caitlin, I knew it! Tell me everything. Start from the beginning. What did he say exactly?"

Caitlin looked at the jars of traditional remedies lined up on her counter. "He brought me seaweed salve and kissed me."

"Seaweed salve? Is that romantic in Ireland?"

"Apparently. Smells like low tide."

"But the kiss was good?" Grammy's voice held that particular tone that meant she was already planning the wedding.

Caitlin thought about the way he'd cupped her face, gentle but certain. The way he'd admitted to wanting to kiss her from the beginning but waited until it was appropriate.

"Yeah, Grammy. The kiss was good."

"Oh, I'm so happy I could dance – if my heart, or Donna, would let me. When do you see him again?"

"Friday. Local music at the pub."

"Wear something pretty. And put your hair down. You hide behind that ponytail."

"Grammy..."

"Don't 'Grammy' me. I know what I'm talking about. Is he tall? He sounds tall."

"How does someone *sound* tall?"

"You're deflecting. That means he's handsome. Oh, this is wonderful. My granddaughter finally meeting a nice man who brings her seaweed medicine. Very practical." Grammy paused, her tone shifting. "But tell me, what have you found out about Mam? About Ellen?"

Caitlin's stomach tightened. "I've learned some things. Your father, John Power, was sent to prison in Wales after the 1916 Easter Rising."

"Sent to prison?" Grammy's voice went quiet.

"Yes, but he was lucky. Some were killed for the roles they played. Your mother... Grammy, she was brave. She marched against conscription in 1918. Fought for Irish independence."

"She did?" Wonder crept into Grammy's voice. "My mother?"

"I saw photographs. She was right there with everyone else, protesting the British trying to draft Irishmen for their war."

"What else?"

Caitlin hesitated. How much to share over the phone? "Her father died not long after John was sent away. Things were hard. But I'm still piecing it together. Delia at the pub has been helpful. She knew the families."

"Keep looking, love. I need to know... I need to know why she left me." Grammy's voice cracked slightly. "But for now tell me more about this young man with the seaweed medicine."

They talked for another ten minutes, Grammy steering the conversation back to safer ground, but Caitlin could hear the emotion underneath. By the time they hung up, her face hurt from smiling, but her heart ached for the questions Grammy still needed answered.

Some things never changed. Grammy, playing matchmaker from her hospital bed, still knowing exactly what to say. Maybe it was hereditary, this faith in love despite the evidence against it. Ellen had loved and lost. Grammy had loved and been left alone with a granddaughter. Caitlin had loved and nearly died for trusting the wrong person.

She pushed Mark from her mind. She was in Ireland, holding jars of seaweed salve, lips still tingling from a kiss she hadn't seen coming.

Maybe the McGrath women were just slow learners when it came to matters of the heart. She remembered Grammy at Grandpa's funeral, back straight, refusing to let anyone see her break. Later that night, Caitlin had found her on the porch, clutching his coffee mug, whispering, "I'd do it all again, every minute." Even knowing how it would end.

Either way, she had a physio appointment to make in Oranmore. And a date to prepare for on Friday.

TWENTY-SIX
MAY 1919

The May sun warmed Ellen's face as she climbed down from the cart, her boots sinking into the sandy ground where the road met the shore. The Atlantic spread before them, a sheet of hammered silver under the clear sky. She breathed deep, tasting salt.

John had found a sheltered spot behind the old boathouse to leave Rosie and the cart, well away from the main road. Fintan pulled the Russell motorcar in beside them, hidden from any passing patrols.

"Would you look at that," Sarah breathed beside her, shading her eyes against the glare. "Why do we not come here more often?"

Isabella alighted from the motorcar, and Ellen caught how her friend's eyes immediately sought Fintan as he helped secure the vehicle. Four months since her father's death, and the strain of maintaining their secret showed in the careful distance they kept.

"Ladies." Patrick tipped his cap, already restless. "We'll be at Tierney's if you need us. Business to discuss."

"Business," Ellen repeated, flatly. "On a Sunday?"

John caught her eye, a silent plea for peace. He'd organized this outing as a respite, a chance for their circle to simply exist without the weight of their cause for one afternoon. But Patrick could no more stop plotting than the tide could stop turning.

"Just a pint and a chat," Seamus assured her, though his grin suggested otherwise. "We won't be long."

The four men set off toward the village, their forms soon swallowed by the dunes. With a flash of irritation, Ellen watched them go. Even here, even on a day meant for pleasure, the work consumed them.

"Shall we walk?" Isabella suggested, already moving toward the strand. "The air will do us good."

They made their way down to the water's edge. Ellen sat on a smooth rock to unlace her boots, tucking her stockings inside before placing them well above the tide line. The cool sand between her toes was heaven after months of winter boots. Sarah and Isabella did the same, Isabella laughing as she wiggled her pale feet in the sand.

"Mother would be scandalized," Isabella said, lifting her skirts just enough to keep them dry. "A Russell going barefoot like a fisherman's daughter."

"Then it's lucky she's in Bath," Ellen replied, linking arms with her friend.

They strolled along the tide line, Sarah beside Ellen, their feet leaving prints in the wet sand. Seamus's girl had grown quieter since Christmas, when her brother, Brian, had been arrested in a raid. He'd been released after questioning, but the experience had aged her.

"Tell us about London," Sarah prompted Isabella. "Was it very grand?"

"Cold," Isabella said, simply. "And full of people who looked at me like I'd grown a second head when I opened my mouth. 'Anglo-Irish', they'd say, as if it explained everything *wrong* with me."

Ellen heard the bitterness beneath the light tone. Isabella's inheritance from her father had come with conditions: time in England, meetings with solicitors, her mother's attempts to find her a suitable match among the Protestant gentry. All while her real work, her real life, waited here.

"But you're back now," Ellen said. "That's what matters."

"For now." Isabella bent to collect a shell, turning it over in her gloved fingers. "Mother has plans. A season in Bath, she says. As if I'm still some debutante to be paraded about."

They walked in companionable silence, Ballycluan visible in the distance but their focus on the sea and sand.

"Remember when Patrick fell into that tide pool when we were children?" Sarah said suddenly, giggling. "He was trying to show off, climbing on the rocks, and went straight into the water."

Ellen smiled at the memory. "Mam and Da were happy that day. We all were."

"They'll be in there for hours," Sarah predicted, glancing toward the village. Her gaze grew distant, perhaps thinking of Seamus and the danger the men were in. "Plotting and planning, as if no one notices."

"Let them have their councils," Isabella said. "We have our own ways of working."

Ellen knew she meant the intelligence networks, the careful cultivation of sources among the Castle staff and the military wives. Work that required Isabella to play her part perfectly: the loyal daughter, the society beauty, even as she memorized troop movements and supply schedules.

They found a sheltered spot among the rocks, spreading Ellen's old quilt on the sand. The sun climbed higher, warming the air until Isabella unpinned her hat.

"Sometimes I wonder what we'll do," Sarah mused, "when it's over. When we've won."

"If we win," Ellen corrected gently.

"When," Bella insisted. She turned to face them fully, sand still clinging to her hem, her copper hair coming loose from its pins in the sea breeze. There was something almost fevered in her expression, as if the belief itself could make it true. "We have to believe it, or what's the point of any of this?"

Ellen thought of Patrick's bruises from his last encounter with the Black and Tans, those rough English recruits the British used for its dirtiest work, of John's careful maps hidden beneath his floorboards, of Fintan's steady hands on a rifle. The cost already paid, and the cost yet to come.

"Patrick says he'll farm," she offered. "Take over the land properly once—"

"Your brother wouldn't know what to do with peace if it knocked him on the head," Isabella interrupted, not unkindly. "None of them would. They're warriors, the lot of them. What happens to warriors when the war ends?"

It was a question Ellen had pondered often, watching John clean his revolver with the same care another man might tune a fiddle. The work had shaped them all, carved them into instruments of purpose. What would they become without it?

The afternoon wore on, the women content in their sheltered spot, talking of everything and nothing. When shadows began to lengthen, they gathered their things and made their way back through the village. The ghost of sand still clung between Ellen's toes even after she'd brushed them clean and pulled her stockings and boots back on.

"There they are," Sarah pointed.

The men emerged from Tierney's, Patrick's voice carrying as he gestured at something Seamus had said. They met the women in the street, John's eyes finding Ellen's immediately.

"Good walk?" he asked.

"Lovely," Ellen replied. "Business all settled?"

"For now," Patrick said, curtly. "We should head back."

As they started back to where the vehicles were hidden, Jack Tierney appeared in his doorway with a box-camera. "Hold there a moment," he called. "Let me get the lot of you. Stand just here, by the door."

"Jack," Patrick warned, glancing up and down the street.

"It's Sunday afternoon." Jack waved off his concern. "You're just friends out for a day at the seaside. Nothing suspicious in that."

They assembled awkwardly against the whitewashed wall of the pub, Ellen careful to place the quilt out of sight of the shot. The painted sign reading "Tierney's" creaked softly above their heads. The late afternoon sun cast long shadows across the ground. Isabella naturally commanded the centre, her presence drawing the eye even as she tried to blend with the others. Sarah stood beside Seamus, her dark hair pinned severely back. Ellen found herself between John and Patrick, achingly aware of John's nearness, trying not to lean toward him though she wanted to. Fintan held himself straight, near Isabella but with that careful distance that only made his devotion clearer.

"Closer together," Jack instructed, fiddling with his apparatus. "You'd think you were strangers instead of friends."

Patrick shifted impatiently, angling his body as if ready to bolt. "We haven't all day, Jack."

"Hold still, would you? This is for posterity."

John's hand brushed Ellen's sleeve as they steadied for the photograph. The fleeting touch set her pulse racing. She didn't dare look at him, but the heat of it lingered.

"That's it now," Jack called. "Don't move."

The shutter clicked. They broke formation almost at once, Patrick striding off ahead as if romance and photographs were both indulgences he had no time for. Seamus bent to lift the quilt, Sarah's laughter spilling bright as she teased him for being slow. Isabella lingered, brushing a strand of damp hair back into place, her eyes drawn to Fintan despite her careful composure.

"We shouldn't linger," Patrick called back, sharply.

They walked quickly through the village to where Rosie and the motorcar waited. John helped Ellen into the cart, taking a seat beside her. The boathouse disappeared behind them as they took the back road home, away from the sea, and back to the war that waited for them in the shadows.

TWENTY-SEVEN
AUGUST 1920

"Ellen, leave the front door."

Ellen looked up from sweeping, catching something in Mr O'Sullivan's tone. He stood in the doorway to the back room, one hand gripping the frame like he needed the support. "Don't lock it yet. We'll have..." he paused, glanced toward the windows where Mrs Cassidy's hunched figure was disappearing down the street, "visitors."

The word scraped down her spine. She didn't need Mr O'Sullivan to explain. Since Michael's death she'd caught the silences, the men who slipped in after dark, the parcels that vanished without record. She gripped the broom tighter, wishing she could sweep away the truth pressing in on her.

"Should I—"

"Stay. Your being here makes it look ordinary." O'Sullivan moved to the front windows, not quite closing the curtains but angling them to block clear sight lines. "Owner and his shop girl, working late. Nothing strange in that."

Ellen nodded, though her hands had started trembling as she propped the broom against the counter. Michael's photograph watched from the mantelpiece – her employer's dead son in his

British uniform the perfect disguise for what O'Sullivan had become.

Over the next hour, they arrived one by one through the back entrance. Ellen heard each arrival. The soft signal at the rear door, muffled voices, footsteps moving through the storeroom. First John, then her brothers, finally two strangers whose accents marked them as Cork men when O'Sullivan made quiet introductions.

Ellen continued her evening routine, sweeping, wiping down surfaces, arranging stock. Playing her part.

In the stockroom, replacing some jars, Ellen breathed deeply to calm her nerves. The smell of dried herbs and tobacco filled her nostrils. Normal shop smells that couldn't quite mask the tension radiating from the main room.

The taps on the door this time jolted through her like a spark: three, then two. Her breath snagged. Her nerves quivered so tightly she thought even the barrels of flour might hear them.

"That'll be Miss Russell," O'Sullivan murmured, going to open the door.

Isabella slipped inside the moment he opened the door, stumbling slightly. Her dove-grey coat was mud-streaked, her hat askew. Dark hair escaped its pins in damp tendrils.

"Thank God." Isabella's composure cracked for a second. "I thought I'd never make it."

Ellen grabbed her friend's arm, felt the tremor running through her. "What happened?"

"Train delay. Military transport. Had to walk the last three miles cross-country." Isabella was breathing hard, her expensive boots caked with mud and worse. "Fintan's waiting with the motorcar near Oranmore. We couldn't risk him being seen here. Saw lights moving in patterns on my way. They could be preparing an ambush."

They moved through the storeroom toward the main shop. Ellen's heart hammered against her ribs. In the golden lamplight, the five men who'd been waiting rose as they approached. John's brown eyes found hers immediately, relief and fear warring in his expression. Seamus stepped forward respectfully as Isabella entered, his broad frame casting shadows across the wooden floor. Patrick remained seated until the last moment, cigarette burning between his fingers. The two Cork strangers stood apart from the others. Lean men with closed faces and careful eyes.

"Miss Russell." Seamus nodded as they entered. "Safe journey, I trust?"

"Safe enough." Isabella was already reaching inside her coat. "But we haven't much time. I saw lights moving in formation on my way here. It could be a patrol, maybe more. As far as I could tell, they were moving away from the village."

The men exchanged sharp looks.

Patrick's cigarette stilled halfway to his lips. "How many?" he asked, tersely.

"Hard to say in the dark." Isabella's hands were steady now as she produced a folded letter. "Just in case, we need to be quick."

"Liam O'Brien," Patrick said, gesturing to one of the strangers. "Tomás Flanagan. IRA, Third Battalion."

O'Brien's gaze fixed on Isabella, his expression wary. "You're sure about her?" he asked Patrick.

"She's proven herself," Patrick replied. "More than once."

"Aye, but she's still—"

"Gentry. Anglo-Irish?" Isabella's voice was steady despite the challenge in O'Brien's tone. "I can't change my parents, but I was born in Ireland. It's my country too."

Flanagan studied her mud-caked boots, her dishevelled appearance. "Fair enough, miss. Takes courage to come out on a night like this."

O'Brien nodded grimly. "Miss."

The letter Isabella had produced was an innocent-looking thing covered in flowery script. "It's coded. 'Dear Kitty, it was simply splendid to see you at the races...'" She translated: "Royal Fusiliers... Colonel Redmayne."

Flanagan swore. Actually swore, forgetting where he was for a moment. "That butcher."

"How did you get this information?" John asked quietly.

Bella's voice sounded steady but Ellen caught a slight tremor. "Lord Pembroke's dinner party. Colonel Winters arrived late – he'd just come from the castle, where they'd been planning this. They were speaking freely, as ever assuming I was just another empty-headed socialite more interested in the women's gossip than their conversation."

"Thirty Auxiliaries. Moving west through Ballinrobe." Isabella's finger traced the innocent words that meant death for so many. "Three-pronged attack. North, east, south."

The hiss of the stove filled Ellen's ears. She fought to steady her breathing. Across the counter, O'Sullivan bent to his ledger – calm as ever, except for the whiteness of his knuckles around the pen.

John stubbed out his cigarette. Ground it into the ashtray – sharp, vicious twists that made Ellen think of wringing necks.

"When?"

"Tuesday morning."

"Jesus." Seamus ran both hands through his hair. "There's a column of Volunteers in the Partry Mountains. If they're surrounded—"

A motorcar engine growled outside, growing louder. Everyone froze. In the silence, they could hear the vehicle slowing.

"Back room," O'Sullivan whispered urgently. "Ellen, stay here with me."

The men moved quickly but quietly toward the storeroom. Ellen heard the soft shuffle of feet, the careful closing of the connecting door. She was alone in the shop now, praying for safety as the motorcar's engine idled just outside.

Footsteps on the pavement. Getting closer.

Ellen forced herself to move, tidying the counter with shaking hands. Just a shop girl, working late. Nothing to see here.

The footsteps passed. The engine revved and faded into the distance.

She waited another minute before opening the storeroom door. "They're gone."

"Patrol," O'Sullivan said. "They'll be back."

Isabella was staring at the letter in her hands. "There's more. Colonel Winters mentioned safe houses. Said they had new intelligence."

Ice in Ellen's stomach. John's eyes found hers across the room.

"Specific names?" O'Sullivan asked. His voice stayed level, but Ellen caught the tightness.

"No. But he was confident about rolling up the network. He mentioned 'the loyal families – those still in mourning.'" Isabella's voice dropped. "Men like you, Mr O'Sullivan."

O'Sullivan's pen paused over his figures. For just a moment, Ellen saw his mask slip. Saw the rage underneath.

"Let them come," he said. "They killed my boy for their king. Let them learn what that cost them."

O'Brien stood abruptly. "We need to move. Get word to Tom Barry."

Flanagan was already reaching for his coat. "The old drove road through the bog?"

"Aye. I'll sketch you the path." O'Sullivan pulled out a scrap of paper.

Ellen wrapped bread and meat in brown paper. Her hands moved automatically, muscle memory from feeding travelling men these past months.

John caught her wrist as she passed. "Be careful," he whispered. "If they're watching places like this—"

"I know." She wanted to say more but couldn't find the words.

One by one, the men slipped out the back. Isabella fed her letter to the stove's flame, watching weeks of dangerous work turn to ash.

"It's done," Ellen said. The words felt hollow.

Isabella slumped in her chair, the careful spy facade cracking to show the frightened young woman underneath. "I hope it's enough."

O'Sullivan was still writing in his ledger. Playing his part to the end. Outside, footsteps passed on the street. A drunk singing off-key. Normal village sounds masking revolution.

"What if they suspect you?" Ellen asked.

O'Sullivan looked up. Michael's photograph seemed to watch him from across the room. "Then they'll see what loyalty to the king really cost me."

Ellen stared at the dark panes. It felt like the night itself was leaning close, listening, waiting for them to slip.

TWENTY-EIGHT

"You'll both stay the night," O'Sullivan said to Isabella. It wasn't a question. "It's too dangerous to travel now, with patrols increased."

Isabella nodded, exhaustion finally showing in the set of her shoulders. "Thank you."

"Ellen, take the spare room. My wife... there are some of her things in the chest of drawers. I'll bank the fire and check the locks." O'Sullivan was already moving through his routine, every action designed to make the shop look exactly like what it was supposed to be: a grieving man's business, closing for the night.

Ellen led Bella up the narrow stairs to the small room above the shop. It held a single bed, a washstand, and a chair that had seen better days. The window overlooked the back lane, useful for watching who came and went.

"Here." Ellen pulled a clean nightgown from the chest. "It's not silk, but it's warm."

Bella accepted it gratefully. "After tonight, I'd sleep in a potato sack and be grateful." She began unpinning her hair, copper strands falling around her shoulders. "Ellen, help me with these buttons, please? My hands won't stop shaking."

Ellen moved behind her friend, working the small pearl buttons down Bella's spine. The expensive fabric was mud-stained and torn, her fine dress ruined by her cross-country journey.

"When did you last eat?"

"This morning. Early." Isabella's voice was thin with exhaustion. "There was breakfast at the hotel in Dublin, then the train, then..." She gestured vaguely at her dishevelled state.

"I'll bring you something. Bread and butter at least."

"Stay. Please." Bella caught Ellen's hand. "I don't want to be alone just yet."

Ellen settled onto the narrow bed beside her friend. The mattress creaked under their combined weight. Through the thin walls, she could hear O'Sullivan moving about downstairs.

"Are you frightened?" Ellen asked, quietly.

"Terrified." Bella's honesty was stark in the shadowed room. "Every time I attend one of those dinner parties, every time I smile and laugh while they discuss troop movements over wine... I feel like they can see right through me."

Ellen thought of her own fear, that sharp, constant edge under everything. "But you keep going."

"What choice do I have? This is my country too, like I said to O'Brien. I can't stand by and watch them crush it." Isabella was quiet for a moment. "Besides, there's Fintan now."

The name settled between them like a weight. Ellen remembered the first time she'd seen them together, how Fintan had helped Isabella from the motorcar and their eyes had held a beat too long, how Isabella's careful society mask had slipped for just a moment. Even then, Ellen had known this would be trouble. Beautiful, dangerous trouble.

Something new threaded through Isabella's voice when she spoke his name: softer, vulnerable in a way the confident spy never allowed herself to be.

"You love him." Ellen didn't need to ask.

Bella's blush could be seen even by the dim light from the window. "Is it that obvious?"

"To me, maybe. I know what it looks like." John's hands flashed through her mind, the way her heart stuttered every time she heard his voice. "The others probably just see a good cover story."

"It started as that. A perfect arrangement, lady and her chauffeur, him driving me to social events, both of us gathering intelligence." Isabella's fingers twisted in the bedsheets. "But somewhere between Dublin and Cork, between pretending to be his employer and actually trusting him with my life..."

"He feels the same?"

"I think so. Hope so." Isabella's voice dropped to barely above a whisper. "Ellen, when he looks at me, I forget I'm supposed to be acting. When he helps me from the motorcar, when his hand touches mine... God, I sound like a schoolgirl."

Ellen smiled in the darkness. "You sound like a woman in love. And here I thought nothing could ruffle the composed Miss Russell." Isabella's surprised laugh was worth the gentle teasing. "There's nothing wrong with that."

"There is when it could get us both killed." The weight in Isabella's voice pressed down on them both. "If my feelings make me careless, if I start trusting him too much, if we're discovered because we're too busy staring at each other to notice a patrol..."

"But you can't help it."

"No. I can't." Isabella turned to face Ellen fully. "What about you and John? How do you bear it? The constant worry, never knowing if he'll come back from wherever Collins sends him?"

The wind rattled the window frame. Ellen searched for words to capture the gnawing fear. "Some days I can't. Some nights I lie awake convinced I'll never see him again. Then he appears at the shop or sends word through Seamus, and it's like I can breathe again."

"Do you think about after? When this is all over?"

"Sometimes. A little cottage somewhere, maybe children..." The future tasted strange on her tongue, like something that happened to other people. "Do you?"

"I try not to. It seems like tempting fate." Isabella pulled the thin blanket up to her chin. "Besides, what kind of life could we have? I'm Lord Russell's daughter, he's a Republican fighter. Even if Ireland wins her freedom, where would we fit?"

The gulf yawned between their worlds, too wide for even love and shared danger to bridge. They lay in silence for a while, each lost in her own thoughts.

Finally, Isabella spoke again. "Ellen, there's something else. Something I couldn't say in front of the others."

The shift in her tone made Ellen's skin prickle. "What?"

"More intelligence. From the same dinner party where I heard about the troop movements." Isabella's voice dropped even lower. "They have someone here. In Clonbarra. A mole."

Ice crystallized in Ellen's chest. "What?"

"Colonel Winters was discussing how they'd managed to track some of the safe houses. He mentioned having 'a reliable source in the villages,' someone providing information about Republican activities." Isabella's words tumbled out now, urgent whispers in the darkness. "He didn't give a name, but he was very pleased with the intelligence they'd been receiving."

Ellen's thoughts scattered like startled birds. A mole in Clonbarra. Someone who knew about the meetings, the safe houses, the men involved. Someone who'd been watching, listening, reporting back to the British.

"Anyone could be..." Her throat closed around the words. "God, Isabella. That means tonight—"

"—could have been a trap. I know." Isabella's voice cut sharp. "That's why Fintan and I have been trying to identify them. We think it's someone with access to information but not quite at the centre of things. Someone who can observe, without being suspected."

"A shopkeeper. A publican. A priest, even."

Isabella sat up, her silhouette rigid against the window. "We're close, I think. Fintan's been tracking patterns in the intelligence they've been acting on, trying to figure out what our source would have had to know to provide it."

Nausea rolled through Ellen's stomach. Every meeting they'd

held, every man who'd passed through O'Sullivan's shop, every conversation she'd overheard – any of it could have been reported. Lives hung in the balance, and they didn't even know who to trust.

"What do we do?"

"Be careful. Watch for things that don't fit, meetings that are discovered too easily, patrols that show up at just the wrong time." Isabella lay back down, but tension was once again radiating from her like heat from a forge. "And, Ellen? Don't tell anyone else yet. Not even John or your brothers. If there really is a mole, the fewer people who know we're looking for them, the better."

"But if it's someone we trust..."

"Then we'll deal with that when we find them." A hardness Ellen had never heard before edged Isabella's voice. "Whoever they are, they've been sending Irish boys to their deaths. When we catch them, there'll be a reckoning."

Silence pressed down on them. Outside, a dog barked in the distance. British patrols moved through the darkness. And somewhere in Clonbarra, someone they knew, someone they might even like, was betraying everything they fought for.

Ellen stared at the ceiling, her mind churning. Every face in the village seemed masked, hiding something from her. Every friendly conversation could be interrogation in disguise.

"Bella," she whispered finally.

"Hmm?"

"What if the mole knows about the meeting, knows you brought intelligence?"

The quiet stretched so long Ellen thought Isabella had fallen asleep. When she finally spoke, her voice barely disturbed the air. "Then by morning, they'll be coming for all of us."

The wind picked up outside, rattling the window frame with increasing urgency. Ellen pulled the blanket closer and tried not to think about the dozen ways their world could end before dawn.

TWENTY-NINE
SEPTEMBER 1920

"Morning, Ellen. Are your boys ready for the game tomorrow? We need them on top form, especially when John gets back from America. Don't you go distracting him now, when he returns."

Ellen looked up to see Tom Clancy coming up the lane from the village.

She blushed at his teasing, though her heart ached at the mention of John. He'd been gone five weeks now. On paper, John worked for McKenna & Sons, a livestock export company that shipped beef to Boston and New York. He carried invoices, manifests, and quarantine certificates – all perfectly respectable. Only she knew the real reason for his absence: fundraising for the cause among Irish-Americans who still remembered the old country's struggle.

"Isn't he always ready to prove his team are the best!" she replied, forcing a smile.

Ellen walked on, down the lane toward the village.

Ellen was painfully aware of how much she missed John's steady presence. As she passed the field beside the church, she watched grown men batting a ball around. The way they carried on, you'd think they were kings.

Just as she came to O'Sullivan's store on the main street, she froze, sensing someone staring at her.

Glancing up, she met the cold stare of one of the Black and Tans, his hard gaze enough to chill her blood. Everyone knew what they were for. She forced herself to look away rather than give him the dirty look he deserved. Those men were dangerous, and it wasn't good to engage with them in any way.

"Well, if it isn't the lovely Ellen McGrath."

She stilled, hearing her name. Chills ran down her spine. She'd heard Edward Russell was back and had gone out of her way to avoid him. Now he stood in front of her, blocking her way, dressed as a British officer.

"Cat got your tongue? The Ellen I remember wasn't always so quiet."

Ellen looked around under her eyelashes, but the streets were still quiet. No doubt the townspeople were avoiding trouble.

"Excuse me, I have to get to the market."

"Tell me, Ellen, is what I've been hearing about your brothers true?"

Ellen forced herself to look at him innocently. "Patrick is a real talent at hurling – best player for miles around. Seamus is almost as good. I didn't think you took an interest in sport."

"I love real sport. Soccer, rugby, horse racing. They take talent." His pale eyes glittered with malice. "But it isn't Patrick's sporting prowess I'm interested in. Give my regards to Patrick when you see him. Tell him I've been catching up with old friends in Tuam and Tullaghmore. Mícheál Breathnach sends his regards as does Moran and O'Hanlon. Fascinating conversations we've been having."

Ice chilled her spine as the Englishman named the leaders of the local Volunteers. How could Edward know those names?

"I've no idea what you're talking about. I'm not my brother's keeper."

"Pity. I thought you had more brains than the rest of your family." His smile was cold as January frost. "Such interesting times we live in, don't you think? So many people to keep track of, so many... movements to monitor."

"Can I go now?" Ellen held his stare. She wasn't going to let this brute know he had rattled her.

He stood back, bowing in a mocking way. "Of course, milady, the road is yours."

Ellen walked on, ignoring the whistles and coarse comments from his men. Shaken by her encounter, she thought about heading straight home, but that could make things worse. If they were watching her, they would know his words had met their mark. She continued with her walk toward the market, nodding and smiling at the people she recognized.

"What's the matter with you? You almost walked into me." Sarah pulled on her elbow. "Lord above, Ellen, you're shaking and white as a sheet. What happened to you?"

"Edward Russell. He stopped me back along the road." She dropped her voice. "He was toying with me, Sarah, but he knows."

"Knows what?" Sarah whispered, as she took Ellen's arm and walked along by her side.

"He mentioned Michael Moran and the others. He said he's been having conversations with them."

Sarah greeted someone loudly, the cheer in her voice too bright, then lowered it again. "He's just playing with you. If he or his men had been talking to the IRA leaders, we'd have been warned. He can't know anything for sure. Nobody around here would talk to the likes of him. Remember what he was like when we were younger? Always picking on people or animals."

Ellen tried to take reassurance from her friend, but in her heart, she knew Edward. She could still see Duchess's broken body in the field.

Ellen filled her basket with the usual assortment of vegetables and goods from the market. She had been looking forward to catching up with Sarah and the other women, but after the encounter with Edward, she wanted to get home. Maybe Patrick would take her concerns more seriously than Sarah had.

With a wave, she bid her friends goodbye and started back down the dusty road toward the farm. The sun was beginning to set, casting long shadows that danced on the path ahead.

As she walked, a lorry filled with Black and Tans sped past her, the engine roaring, making her skin prickle.

Suddenly, the sharp crack of gunshots pierced the air and the tang of powder burned her nose. Bullets ricocheted off the stones nearby, sending chips of rock stinging against her legs.

Ellen froze, her mind screaming at her to find cover, but her body wouldn't obey. Her ears rang with a high-pitched whine that drowned out everything except the thundering of her own heart.

Screams echoed around her, a horrific symphony interspersed with cruel laughter from the lorry, which quickly disappeared down the road. She stood rooted to the spot, unable to move or speak, panic clawing at her throat.

A man, rugged and breathless, grabbed her shoulders. "Are you hurt, love? Were you hit, Ellen?" It was Tom Clancy.

Ellen shook her head, her voice trapped in her chest.

"Come on then, child," Tom said, his eyes full of worry. "Let's get you home to your mam. If she hears about this, she'll be worried sick."

Ellen allowed Tom to guide her down the road, her legs feeling like jelly beneath her.

Everyone whispered about what the Black and Tans were capable of, but opening fire on market folk? That was a new low.

As they approached the farm, Ellen saw her mother feeding the chickens. The colour drained from Mary's face as she spotted them.

"Ellen, what is it? Tom, what are you doing here? What happened? Are you hurt, child?"

"She's a bit shook up," Tom replied, guiding Ellen into the house. "Have you a drink? The soldiers opened fire in the town."

Mary swayed, her hands flying to her mouth. "Dear God in heaven," she whispered. She quickly fetched a cup of water and handed it to Ellen, her hands trembling.

"Mary, she wasn't hit, just shocked," Tom reassured her. "Plus, I noticed Russell talking to her earlier on. Seemed to have a lot to say for himself."

"He was asking after the boys, Patrick in particular," Ellen managed to say, her teeth chattering as she spoke. Her chest tightened at the mention of her brothers.

Mary's face hardened. "What did he want to know?"

"He was just showing off. P-playing with me like a cat with your w-wool," Ellen stammered. Her mam had enough to worry about without telling her what Edward had really said. "You know how much he hates us, especially Seamus. After the incident with Duchess. He blames us for his father sending him to war."

Mary hugged her daughter tightly. "Thank God you're all right." Over Ellen's head, she asked, "Thank you for bringing her home, Tom. Was anyone hurt?"

Tom's face darkened as he shrugged. "I don't know. I heard screams, but whether it was from someone hit or fear, I'm not sure. I'll head back and find out. I wanted to get this one home first. Stay safe, Mary. Ellen, you take care now."

As he walked away, Ellen felt the first tears slip down her cheeks. She clung to her mother, the reality of what had just happened sinking in. Mary stroked her hair, whispering soothing words.

The air was thick with the mingling scents of turf smoke from the hearth and the savoury aroma of the potatoes simmering over the fire. The oil lamp threw restless shadows across the walls, making the kitchen feel uneasy, as if even the house couldn't settle.

"They'll be back any minute." Ellen glanced up at her mam's words but said nothing.

Her brothers were late.

Ellen took the potatoes off the fire and put them to one side before placing another piece of turf on the fire. She kept busy by setting the table for the four of them. The bowls were cracked but clean. She filled a jug with water.

The door swung open with a gust of cold wind, and Patrick

and Seamus entered, their faces etched with grim expressions. Their boots were muddy, and their clothes damp from the misty rain that had started to fall.

"Siobhan Carey, and her eight months pregnant, was shot dead." Seamus's voice trembled with anger. "Those murdering ba—"

"Watch your mouth, Seamus McGrath," Mary interrupted sharply, her tone firm despite the weariness in her eyes.

Ellen's stomach lurched. She remembered Siobhan from church, always slipping extra pennies into the poor box when she thought no one was looking, her gentle hands smoothing her daughters' hair during Mass.

"Sorry, Mam." Seamus's face flushed under the reprimand, and he looked down, the firelight reflecting off his freckled cheeks.

Mary turned to her eldest son, Patrick, her expression a mixture of sorrow and determination. "Why did they shoot her?"

"Who knows? Maybe she looked at them the wrong way," Patrick replied, his jaw clenched. "Carey is left with three motherless girls. Father Murphy was with him when I left."

Ellen, standing by the hearth, grabbed the pot and began ladling the potatoes into the four bowls, the wooden spoon scraping against the pot.

Seamus took a seat at the table, one hand on his spoon, although he knew better than to start without saying Grace.

Mary sighed, wiping her hands on her apron. "I'll head over there now. He'll be needing help with the children and laying her out."

"I'll go with you, Mam," Patrick offered, but Mary shook her head.

"No, Patrick, you stay here with Ellen. Seamus will accompany me, won't you, son?" Her tone brooked no argument.

Seamus looked longingly at the food, then nodded, pushing it away. "Yes, Mam," he said with a sigh, knowing that refusal was not an option.

After their mother and Seamus had left, the farmhouse fell into a heavy silence, broken only by the occasional pop and crackle of the fire and the sounds Patrick made as he ate his meal. Ellen couldn't stomach eating. She waited for him to finish. He pushed the bowl aside and grabbed the bottle of whiskey, pouring himself a glass.

"Edward Russell was in town today," she said, her voice low and urgent. "He was asking about you."

Patrick put a cigarette in his mouth, and Ellen noticed how his hands trembled slightly as he struck the match. The flare briefly illuminated his face before he took a deep drag, blowing the smoke into the air, where it mingled with the other household scents.

"Patrick, did you hear me? He told me he'd been having conversations with Moran and O'Hanlon. He even dropped Mícheál's name..."

"Mícheál Breathnach," Patrick interrupted. His voice caught slightly as he dragged on his cigarette again.

"I'm scared. He knows, Patrick," Ellen said, her voice shaking.

"He knows nothing," Patrick replied, though something in his voice made her doubt him.

"You're planning something. Someone talked. Isabella said she thought there might be a mole. He knows. I know by the look in his eyes," Ellen insisted, her hands clenching.

Patrick didn't even glance her way. He picked up his glass of whiskey and took a long drink. He grimaced as he swallowed.

"Please listen to me. Things are getting worse. It's like a tinderbox. Take Seamus and get away from here. Go to Dublin or even across to Britain. Just for a while. Until things settle down," Ellen pleaded, tears burning behind her eyes.

"Seamus has nothing to do with it. And how would running away make that happen?" Patrick snapped, grinding out his cigarette. "I didn't fight in the Easter Rising with Pearse and the other patriots, and that's something I'll regret to my dying day. I'm not going to make that mistake again."

"But..." Ellen's voice broke.

"But nothing, Ellen," Patrick cut her off, his eyes blazing with a fierce determination. "You think we are going to stand for those animals murdering a pregnant woman? They will pay. They have to. Until they and their like leave Ireland, we won't stop."

His words pressed against her chest, stealing her breath as the fire snapped in the grate. Patrick stood, his chair screeching against the stone floor.

"I have a meeting."

"Not tonight. Dear Lord, can't you..." Ellen's voice cracked with desperation.

Patrick put his hand on her arm, a gentle touch rather than a slap. "I know it's because you care, but you must stop telling me what to do. I'm the man of the house now. Do you think our da would stand back and let women be killed and not do anything? Let those animals burn our houses, our streets, our cities? You know what they did to Cork and Balbriggan up in Dublin. We're at war, Ellen."

She turned on him, eyes blazing. "Don't you think I know that? Do you think it's just the men who feel like you do? Me and every woman like me feels the same. None of us want those men here, but bloodshed only leads to more bloodshed. You may kill some of them, but they'll come for you and Seamus. You know they will." Tears ran down her face as her fists pummelled his chest.

Patrick pulled her toward him and hugged her tightly, his arms strong yet gentle. As he held her, he whispered "*mo stór*" the way their father used to when they were small and frightened, his hand stroking her hair with the same tender motion Da had used to comfort them after nightmares.

"I'll try to keep Seamus out of it, I promise. But I have to do this. You know I do. Ireland is ours, we must be free."

Ellen sobbed against his shoulder, her tears soaking into his shirt. She clung to him, her fear and frustration pouring out in waves. The warmth of the fire did little to chase away the cold dread that settled in her heart.

When Patrick spoke again, his voice was softer than she'd heard in months. "Ellen, I need you to be strong. For Mam, for

Seamus, for all of us. If we give in to fear, they win. I can't let that happen. Da wouldn't want that."

Ellen pulled back slightly, looking up into her brother's eyes. She saw their father's stubbornness staring back at her, his set jaw, eyes burning with the same fierce resolve Da once carried. It scared her as much as it stirred her.

"Just promise me you'll be careful," she whispered, her voice trembling.

"I promise," Patrick said, brushing a stray lock of hair from her face. "I'll be back in the morning."

He kissed her forehead, a fleeting moment of comfort before he turned and walked toward the door. The chill night air rushed in as he opened it, the darkness beyond a stark contrast to the warmth of the farmhouse. He paused at the threshold, casting one last look back at Ellen. "I do appreciate you trying to warn me, Ellen."

Ellen nodded, swallowing hard as she watched him disappear into the night. The door closed behind him with a heavy thud, and she stood there, feeling a profound sense of loss and helplessness. The silence of the farmhouse pressed in around her, broken only by the distant howl of the wind and the crackling of the fire.

She moved to the window, staring out into the darkness, biting her nails. *If only John were here.* She could almost hear his low chuckle, feel how he'd steady her with just a hand on her shoulder, that quiet strength that always made the world feel less tilted.

Taking a deep breath, Ellen wiped her tears away, steeling herself for what lay ahead. She turned from the window, the flickering firelight casting her shadow long against the walls. Patrick was right – she had to be strong, for John, for her family, for Ireland. The fight was far from over, and she knew that in the end, they would all have to pay a price for their freedom. She could only hope it wasn't too high.

THIRTY

The October wind cut through Ellen's coat as the train rattled toward Limerick, but it was nothing compared to the cold dread pooling in her stomach. The suitcases were too heavy. She'd known it the moment the young railway attendant had insisted on helping her onto the train at Galway station, his face reddening with the effort.

"Lord above, miss, what have you packed in here? Rocks?" he'd joked, struggling to push the second case into place.

Ellen had forced a laugh. "Mammy's preserves and some of her good linens. You know how mothers are."

Patrick's voice echoed in her memory from the night before: "*Act natural. You're visiting family in Limerick.*" Easy enough to say when you weren't the one sitting in a rattling train compartment with enough ammunition to arm a dozen Volunteers hidden above your head.

"*If there was any other way...*" That's what Patrick had said, gripping her shoulders with those calloused hands that never seemed to stop shaking anymore. "*They arrested Finnegan yesterday, and I can't risk it myself – too many of them know my face now.*"

So here she sat. Ellen McGrath, shopkeeper's assistant. Dutiful sister. Gun-runner.

The elderly priest across from her stirred in his sleep, his breviary sliding off his lap. Ellen's heart jumped. What if he woke during the inspection? What if those kind eyes saw too much? She pressed her gloved hands together to stop their trembling.

A widow in mourning black clutched her carpet bag, staring out at brown fields stubbled with autumn's remains. Safe in her grief. No secrets weighing down her luggage.

The train lurched. Ellen's stomach lurched with it.

Through the grimy window, khaki uniforms moved along the platform at Craughwell station like predators circling prey. British soldiers positioning themselves. Ellen had travelled this route twice before on legitimate business – visiting Mr O'Sullivan's sister in Oranmore, delivering letters for the store. She knew this inspection was routine.

Knowing didn't help the cold sweat gathering at the base of her neck.

The compartment door banged open. A young RIC constable stepped inside, Cork accent thick despite his official bearing. Behind him loomed a British sergeant, scanning passengers with pale, calculating eyes.

"Names and tickets, please. Routine inspection."

Ellen handed over her ticket, giving her name as Ellen McGrath of Clonbarra. The reason for her journey was as fabricated as the calm expression she fought to maintain.

"Business in Limerick, miss?"

"Family visit. My aunt's expecting her fourth child."

True enough. Aunt Margaret was indeed pregnant, though she had no idea her niece was coming. The perfect cover story. One that could be verified if anyone bothered to check.

The sergeant stepped forward. Something unsettling in his stare, like he could peel back her carefully constructed facade and see the truth beneath.

"Mind if we have a look? Standard procedure."

Ellen's heart stopped. Actually stopped. Then resumed at double pace. "Of course. Though it's mostly women's things."

The constable crouched beside the first suitcase.

Don't react. Don't breathe. Don't—

He lifted it. Grunted slightly. Ellen bit her tongue to keep from crying out. The case was impossibly heavy – far heavier than preserves and linens should be. She watched his face, waiting for realization to dawn.

"Your mother certainly believes in being thorough," he said, with a strained smile.

"She does indeed."

His hands moved to the brass latches. The first one clicked open like a gunshot in the enclosed space. The priest was watching now, mildly curious. The widow frowned at the disruption.

Ellen felt the world narrow to this single moment. The second latch began to give way.

Shouting erupted from the platform – someone trying to bolt, by the sound of it. Whistles. Running feet. The sergeant's head snapped toward the window.

"Constable! Leave that. We're needed on the platform. Now."

Training won over curiosity. The young man straightened, touching his cap. "Sorry for the inconvenience, miss. Duty calls."

Gone. Just like that.

Ellen's hands shook as she pushed the cases back into the luggage rack. The weight nearly broke her. Through the window, she glimpsed soldiers clustered around a ragged man they'd pulled from a freight car. His furtive manner had caught their attention. Saved her life.

The train lurched forward again. Ellen sank into her seat, legs suddenly useless.

"Terrible thing, these inspections," the widow murmured conspiratorially. "Though I suppose they're necessary, what with all the troubles."

Ellen nodded. The woman had no idea how close they'd come

to witnessing an arrest that would have made headlines across Ireland.

Countryside rolled past stone walls dividing into ancient patterns, scattered farmhouses with smoke curling from chimneys. Normal life. People going about their business while she carried revolution in her luggage.

Patrick's words came back: *"Every bullet could save a life. Every grenade could protect a family. You're not just carrying weapons, Ellen. You're carrying hope."*

Then, quieter: *"Just don't tell John about this. Not yet. He'd try to stop you."*

John. Ellen closed her eyes, imagining his reaction when he found out. The fury in those brown eyes that had seen too much already. The way his jaw would clench, hands fisting at his sides. Patrick was right. John would have locked her in the cottage before letting her take this risk.

But John wasn't here.

The train began slowing as Limerick's outskirts appeared. Ellen gathered her handbag, smoothing her skirt with movements that felt disconnected from her body. At the station, a young man would be waiting. Someone who knew her by the white ribbon pinned inside her coat collar. A stranger claiming to be her cousin.

The transfer would be swift. The suitcases would disappear into a grocer's wagon, hidden beneath vegetables. Ellen would spend one night maintaining her cover story before returning to Galway.

Simple. If you ignored the part where discovery meant hanging.

The priest touched her arm as they prepared to disembark. "Safe travels, my dear. I'll say a prayer for your aunt's safe delivery."

"Thank you, Father."

Ellen stepped onto Limerick platform, her legs still unsteady. The suitcases dragged at her arms like dead weight.

"Miss? You alright there?"

A young man approached, concern creasing his freckled face. Something about his eyes – too alert, too knowing.

"I'm looking for my cousin," Ellen said carefully. "Dermot Flynn?"

The man's expression shifted almost imperceptibly. His gaze flicked to her coat collar, where the white ribbon lay hidden. "Ah, you'd be Ellen, then. Come on, I've got the cart waiting."

Ellen was mucking out the hen shed, a horrible, dirty job, when angry voices carried from the front of the cottage: John's rising dangerously, Seamus's deeper rumble, and Patrick's defensive tone cutting through both. The argument was already well underway by the time she rounded the corner, finding them on the front step.

"—absolutely mad if you think—"

"You had no right!" John's face was flushed with fury, his hands clenched at his sides. "No right at all to ask that of her!"

Patrick stood his ground, jaw set stubbornly. "She's my sister, and she was the right person for the job. End of discussion."

"Volunteered?" Seamus's voice cracked like a whip. "Good God, Patrick. What did you expect her to say when you told her it was for Ireland?"

Patrick shrugged, unmoved. "She said yes, didn't she? That's what matters."

Ellen took a deep breath and stepped into view, and all three men turned to her. John's brown eyes were blazing with an anger she'd never seen before – not the cold fury he'd carried back from prison, but something hot and protective and desperate.

"Tell me it's not true," he said, his voice barely controlled. "Tell me you didn't carry guns on that train."

Ellen lifted her chin. "I can't tell you that."

John made a sound like he'd been punched. Seamus ran both hands through his dark hair, turning away from her.

"Ellen, do you have any idea what could have happened?" John stepped toward her, his voice breaking. "If they'd caught you

—" He stopped, unable to voice what they all knew. What happened to women in Black and Tans custody wasn't something spoken of in polite company, but the whispered stories were enough to turn any man's blood cold. "There are things worse than execution, Ellen."

"They didn't."

"That's not the point!" The words exploded out of him. "Do you know what the Black and Tans do to girls they catch? What they did to Mary Fitzgerald in Cork? To the O'Sullivan girl in Kerry?" His voice cracked. "Ellen, death would be a mercy compared to—" He couldn't finish the sentence.

Patrick moved between them, his expression cold. "She was perfect for the job. Young woman travelling to visit family – completely above suspicion. It was tactically sound."

"*Tactically sound?*" John's voice rose dangerously. "She's not a *weapon*, Patrick. She's not expendable."

"Everyone's expendable if it means Ireland gets her freedom." Patrick's green eyes were hard as flint. "You of all people should understand that."

John lunged forward, catching Patrick around the middle and driving him backward into the cottage wall. Patrick grunted as his back hit the stone, but he recovered quickly, shoving John away with both hands.

"You selfish fool!" John swung wildly, his fist connecting with Patrick's jaw more by luck than judgement. "She could have died!"

Patrick stumbled but came back swinging, catching John in the ribs. "She did what needed doing! That's more than I can say for some people."

They grappled against the wall, both breathing hard, throwing punches that landed more often than not.

Seamus stepped forward to intervene, but Ellen was faster.

"Stop it!" She pushed between them, her hands flat against John's chest. "Stop it right now!"

John froze, his chest heaving. A trickle of blood ran from his split lip, and his knuckles were already swelling. Patrick leaned against the wall, one hand pressed to his jaw, his green eyes still defiant.

"This is exactly what I was trying to avoid," Ellen said, her voice shaking with anger. "You fighting over me like I'm a child who can't make her own decisions."

"Ellen—" John began.

"No." She whirled on him. "Nobody made me get on that train, John. Nobody forced me to carry those suitcases. Patrick asked, and I said yes."

"Because you're too noble for your own good," John shot back. "Because you can't say no when someone wraps it up in talk about Ireland and duty and—"

"Because I wanted to!" The words came out louder than she'd intended. "Because I'm tired of sitting safely at home while men die for something I believe in too."

John stared at her, something breaking in his expression. "Ellen, you don't understand what you're risking—"

"Don't I?" She stepped closer to him, her blue eyes blazing. "You think I don't know what happens to gun-runners? You think I don't know about the executions?" Her voice dropped to a whisper. "I know exactly what I risked. And I'd do it again."

The fight went out of John all at once. His shoulders sagged, and he reached for her with trembling hands. "Ellen, please. I can't... I can't lose you too."

The raw pain in his voice undid her. She let him pull her against his chest, feeling the way his hands shook as they buried themselves in her hair.

"You're not going to lose me," she whispered against his neck.

"You don't know that. None of us know that." His arms tightened around her. "Good heavens, Ellen, when Tom told me what you'd done... I've never been so terrified in my life."

Over his shoulder, she could see Patrick wiping blood from his mouth, his expression showing no trace of guilt – only cold calculation. Seamus stood apart, his face grim with dawning understanding.

"I'm not sorry," Patrick said, his voice flat. "The mission succeeded. The Volunteers got their weapons. That's what matters."

John pulled back enough to look at him, his brown eyes filled with disgust. "Listen to yourself. You sound exactly like—"

"Like what?"

"Like Edward Russell." The words fell like stones into water. "Calculating. Ruthless. Deciding other people's lives are worth less than what you want."

Patrick's face flushed with anger. "Don't you *dare* compare me to that English—"

"Why not? You both think you're entitled to use people in whatever way suits your purposes." John's voice was quiet now, which somehow made it worse. "The only difference is what cause you're serving."

Ellen stepped between them again, her hands on John's arm. "John, please."

"Sorry, Ellen, but he needs to be told. He goes too far." John turned his attention back to Patrick, his voice deadly quiet. "If you ever put her at risk like that again, we're finished. All of us."

Patrick's jaw tightened. "The cause comes first, John. It has to. If you can't understand that—"

"Then I guess we have nothing more to say to each other."

Patrick touched his tender jaw, his expression unrepentant. "The mission was a success," he said, as if that justified everything.

John threw Patrick a dirty look before taking Ellen's hand. "Walk with me."

Without a word, she took his hand. They walked to their oak tree, a witness to many of their conversations.

"I know you're brave," he said, turning to her. "I know you're not a child. But, Ellen, I've seen what this war costs. I've seen good people broken by it, and I can't... I won't watch it break you too."

"Then don't let it," she said simply. "Help me stay strong enough to do what needs doing."

THIRTY-ONE
NOW

Caitlin picked up fresh cream cakes from the local store before heading to the pub. "Thank you for introducing me to Father Tom. He was onto St Brigid's, and I think it helped. Mrs Walsh rang me to make an appointment. I have to wait three weeks but that's better than the original timescale."

"Arra, you didn't have to bring anything but yourself." Delia patted her stomach. "I love cream cakes, though not as much as my waistline does."

She passed a mug of coffee to Caitlin. Steam rose between them in the cool pub air.

"I've about an hour this morning." Delia settled back into her chair, the old wood creaking. "Have you found out anything else about Ellen?"

"No. I went to the place you mentioned with the historical records. I found an old map of Clonbarra with pictures. The woman let me copy them to my phone. I want to visit it in person but have yet to find the courage. Silly really, don't you think?"

"Not at all, my dear. You know there are bound to be unhappy memories there. Are you ready to hear more about Ellen's Ireland?"

Caitlin nodded. Her throat felt tight already.

"The IRA in those days freed our country, but they paid a high price. Not just the men, but their families too." Delia stirred sugar into her coffee, the spoon clinking against ceramic. "We were lucky Jack Tierney survived, and this pub along with him."

The words hung heavy between them. Through the window, morning traffic passed by – people heading to work, living ordinary lives in the freedom Ellen's generation had bled for.

Delia's hand covered Caitlin's. Warm, steady. "I hate to tell you, but things got worse."

"Worse?"

Delia stirred her tea, eyes on the grey sky beyond the café window. "You have to understand what 1919 was like," she said quietly. "Ireland was already at war, even if no one called it that yet. The men who'd survived the Rising – the ones locked up after 1916 – had spent their time in those English prisons learning, planning. Collins used the place like a classroom, teaching them how to build a real army once they got home."

She shook her head slowly. "By 1919, those same men were back in Ireland, scattered through the counties, and they weren't making speeches anymore. They were burning RIC barracks, ambushing patrols, cutting telegraph lines. The British hit back with raids and arrests, beatings, house burnings. Anything to stamp it out. There were no battle lines, just ordinary people caught between the two sides. Everyone knew someone who'd disappeared or been dragged from their bed in the night."

She looked back at Caitlin, her voice quiet but certain. "That's the world your great-grandmother was living in. The war hadn't been declared, but it had already begun."

Caitlin couldn't believe what she was hearing. "It must have been horrendous."

"Violence doesn't change anything, really, love, does it? Just leaves us with legacies of long-term hurt and sadness." Delia leaned back, the chair protesting. "You have shadows in your eyes, Caitlin. Like someone who was badly hurt."

Caitlin's thumb found the scar tissue at her shoulder, an

unconscious habit she thought she'd broken. Some wounds showed. Others you carried where no one could see.

Delia smiled gently at her. "You don't have to tell me: you barely know me. But they say a trouble shared is a trouble halved."

"That's what you say when you want to know everyone's business."

They both jumped. Harry Bennett stood beside their table, one hand gripping a chair back for support.

"Be careful what you tell her, young lady. It'll be all around Ballycluan and halfway around the county before night falls."

"Harry! Don't be saying things like that."

"Why not? 'Tis true."

"No, it isn't, and you know better than to say otherwise."

Caitlin looked up at him. "Delia has been nothing but helpful. I'm trying to find out what happened to my great-grandmother and her family. My grammy only found out in the last few weeks she had a baby brother. His name was *Seán* Power but that may have changed if he was adopted. Ellen—"

She stopped.

Harry's face had gone grey, his grip on the chair tightening until his knuckles showed white through papery skin.

"Are you alright, Mr Bennett? You've turned a funny colour. Would you like to sit down? I can fetch some water, or maybe a doctor?"

"I don't need a doctor or women fussing over me." His voice came out strangled. "I'm fine. Or at least I will be when I get out of this place." He glared at them both. "No good comes from turning over old rocks. And you should know that better than anyone, Delia Tierney. Good day to you both."

They watched him shuffle toward the door, each step careful and deliberate.

"Will he be okay?"

"Don't worry, I'll send Paddy to check on him. Harry has lived on his own for a long time on that old farm of his, and he refuses to admit it may all be getting a bit much. He's in his eighties, you know."

"You might think I'm mad, but he seemed to recognize *Seán's* name, didn't he?"

Delia busied herself stacking their plates and cups. "I'd best get these back to the kitchen and spend a bit of time with Paddy or he'll be accusing me of abandoning him. What are you up to for the rest of the afternoon?"

Caitlin's first physiotherapy appointment in Oranmore was at two, but she didn't want to explain why she wasn't seeing Conor anymore. Not yet.

"I think I'll head out and explore a bit of the countryside."

"Good idea. Enjoy the fresh air." Delia squeezed her good shoulder. "I'm glad you came to Ballycluan."

Outside the pub, the May wind cut sharp off the Atlantic. Caitlin pulled her jacket closer and headed for her car, but Harry's stricken face stayed with her.

Seán Power. A name that made an old man's hands shake.

Some stones were better left unturned. But it was too late for that now.

THIRTY-TWO

Later that afternoon, Caitlin's bare feet pressed into the cool sand as she kicked at a piece of driftwood. What connection could Harry Bennett, an Englishman, have with her missing Irish great-uncle? *Stop reading into things that have no meaning.* Yet all her cop instincts told her he was hiding something. He'd recognized the name Seán Power.

"Hey. Was the physio that bad?"

She startled, nearly stumbling. Conor stood a few yards away, his brow furrowed, hand half raised as if to steady her.

"Sorry, I was miles away." Heat crept up her neck. "Tessa sends her regards, by the way. Said you trained her well." She tried for lightness but her voice came out breathier than intended.

"How did it go?" He studied her face, jaw tensing slightly as if bracing for bad news. She remembered those same eyes watching her over dinner, the way his thumb had traced her cheekbone after their kiss.

"Good. Not as good as you, but almost." The words slipped out before she could stop them.

The corner of his mouth quirked, fighting a losing battle against amusement.

"Where's the dog?" she asked, quickly.

"Over there." He pointed toward the waves where Finn bounded through the surf. "He's crazy for that ball. The most gorgeous lady dog could strut right past and he'd still be chasing after it."

Despite her mood, Caitlin laughed. Finn came racing back, practically grinning around the tennis ball clamped in his jaws. The moment he reached them, he shook himself vigorously. Water sprayed everywhere.

"Finn, you devil!" Conor lunged for the dog's collar, but Finn had already trotted to Caitlin. He dropped the ball at her feet and gazed up with liquid brown eyes that clearly said *please*.

She couldn't resist. Scooping up the ball, she hurled it toward the waves – then immediately winced as pain shot through her shoulder.

Conor was watching her carefully, concern on his face. "You alright? I saw that."

"Fine. I just forget sometimes." The lie came easily. *Too easily*.

His mouth tightened at the corners – he wasn't buying it – but he fell into step beside her, close enough that their arms occasionally brushed. Each accidental touch sent warmth through her – ridiculous for a woman her age. But then, everything about Conor made her feel like she was discovering something new.

Their eyes met and lingered longer than necessary before she turned her attention again to Finn attacking the waves with boundless joy.

"What do you think of Harry Bennett?"

Conor retrieved the ball and sent it flying further into the sea. "Harry's alright, most of the time. Gave me a hard time when I was a boy, though."

"What did you do?"

"What didn't I do, more like." His mouth did that thing – not quite a smile, not quite a smirk – that made her pulse skip. "Harry was the local cop. Didn't tolerate us young ones acting the mick. Drinking and diving off the pier was strictly forbidden."

"As it should be. That's dangerous."

"Haven't you ever done something you shouldn't? We were young and thought we were invincible." A distant look crossed his face, the muscles in his jaw working. "Nobody got up to any real mischief. Well, apart from the time we painted the Union flag on Harry's shed – you know, him being English. Or when we'd play 'Ding-dong Ditch'."

"What's Ding-dong Ditch?" she asked, a smile on her lips.

"Ring someone's doorbell and run away, to watch them answer. Great fun until my da got fed up of Harry turning up at our door." His shoulders tensed suddenly. "Couldn't sit down for a week after that hiding. My brothers got off with a talking to. Not me."

The shift in his tone was unmistakable.

Caitlin stayed quiet, sensing deeper currents.

They walked in silence, broken only by the crunch of sand and distant crash of waves. The sun hung halfway to the horizon now, painting everything gold.

Conor sighed, picked up a smooth stone, and sent it skipping across the water. "Growing up, I was always the odd one out. My parents had expectations, and my siblings fit the mould perfectly. Golden children, every one of them. Always excelling, always doing everything right."

The stone disappeared beneath the surface.

"Sorry." He rubbed the back of his neck, a flush creeping up from his collar. "Had a bit of an argument with the folks today, so I came out here to calm down. The beach is therapeutic for me. But I shouldn't be all doom and gloom – we've only just started..."

He trailed off, and she caught the unfinished thought. Only just started what? Dating?

"Don't mind me." Caitlin waved off his concern. "Sometimes it helps to talk things out. Family expectations and not living up to them – I understand that completely. My grandfather loved me, but he wanted me to follow him into his business. Couldn't understand why I wanted to be a cop."

His hand found hers, fingers interlacing naturally. This felt right. Dangerous, how right it felt.

The familiar ache settled in her chest. "His attitude was if you play in the dirt with criminals, it'll come back to bite you. He died a few years back, but I guess he got the last laugh. If I hadn't been on that job—"

"Shoulda, woulda, coulda." His thumb pressed firmly against her palm, grounding her. "That'll drive you nuts."

Fair point. Caitlin shrugged. "So what's your story?"

"Not as dramatic as yours." He smiled. "I just was different. Didn't want to follow the same path as my siblings – excel at school, university, qualifications. I loved the sea, the freedom it represented." His gaze went distant, focused on something beyond the horizon. "That wasn't what my family wanted. They saw it as wasted potential."

"Must have been tough."

Finn bounded back, fur glistening with seawater. Conor took the ball with his free hand, the tension in his shoulders easing as he threw it again, still holding onto her with the other.

"Eventually I had to leave. Needed to find my own way, away from their expectations. Ended up travelling the world, working on boats, taking odd jobs. Not the life they wanted for me, but it was mine. My choice."

Empathy tugged at Caitlin's heart. She'd loved her career. Letting it go still felt like an amputation. "Sounds like you found something you love, though."

"For a while. But the travelling got lonely. Then a few years ago, I had an accident. Hurt my back badly." He paused, watching Finn's joyful chase. "The physiotherapist who helped me get back on my feet – she changed my life. Made me realize I wanted to help others the way she helped me. So I went back to school, trained as a physio, and here I am. Back in Ballycluan."

"Sounds like you found your calling. You certainly helped me." The memory of his hands on her, professional yet tender, made heat rise in her cheeks.

The lines around his eyes deepened, crinkling with genuine pleasure. "Thank you. I think I have found it. Not easy, but fulfilling. Being back here, seeing the old faces – even Harry Bennett – it's grounding. Reminds me who I am and where I come from."

The sun had become a deep orange ball on the horizon, casting long shadows and a blazing path across the water. Finn returned, calmer now, dropping the ball at Caitlin's feet with that same imploring look.

She threw it with her good arm, watching him bound away again, then sat down in the cooling sand. Conor dropped down beside her.

"Why were you asking about Harry?"

"Met him today. In the pub."

"That wouldn't be unusual. He's a divil for the drink these days. Wasn't always that way – think his wife dying was the straw that broke him. Did he upset you? He can be outspoken, but usually doesn't rub people the wrong way."

"Not upset, exactly. He reacted strangely when I mentioned my grandmother had a brother. Like he recognized the name." She leaned into Conor's shoulder without thinking, then caught herself. When had she started seeking his comfort so naturally? "I probably overreacted. I do that."

His arm came around her, fingers spreading across her shoulder blade. "What did he say?"

"More how he looked. Went pale, then told Delia to leave the rocks lying as they were. Something about damage being done when people disturbed sleeping dogs."

Finn trotted back, content now to collapse alongside them.

"Harry was a brave cop. Back in the day, when the troubles were rife in the North, there were some around here who held pro-IRA feelings."

"I found out my family were involved with the IRA back in the 1920s."

Conor shook his head, the movement sharp. "Not that IRA. Most of us will admit to having family in the old IRA – those who fought for our freedom. They didn't kill women and children like the modern lot did. Don't get me wrong, I believe in a united

Ireland – we are thirty-two counties. But nobody should die in the fight to get our country back."

His voice roughened, and she felt the tension return to his frame. "Being a cop and an Englishman at that, Harry was a target of IRA supporters, especially after he found a safe house near the Sligo border. Many shunned him for arresting those men. Rumour had it his name was on some hit list, but they never got him. Still, he and his wife had to be careful. Used to see him checking under her car before she went out. Then the peace agreement was signed, and his work involved more regular criminals."

"Sounds like he had a rough time."

"He has. The drink's his way of coping, I suppose. Doesn't make it right, but it explains a lot."

Companionable silence settled between them as they stood again, and continued walking. Finn trotted happily beside them, occasionally darting off to chase a gull or investigate interesting seaweed.

"I wonder if Harry knew my great-uncle through his work. What if he was a criminal? That could explain why he didn't want to talk about it."

Conor stopped walking and faced her, both hands now holding hers. "Typical cop, jumping to that conclusion."

She bristled until she caught the way he bit the inside of his cheek, clearly trying not to laugh.

"You might have stopped being a cop, but you still think like one. He could have recognized the name because your man was a wonderful hurling player or a GAA football star. Maybe he was another cop?"

"I tried searching online already. Nothing came up for Seán Power in this area." She frowned. "It's like he never existed."

"Maybe you have the wrong name? Or the wrong spelling? Irish names get mangled all the time in records." He squeezed her hands gently. "Old parish records, census data – they're full of creative interpretations."

"Are you telling me how to investigate?" she joked, with a raised eyebrow.

"I wouldn't dare." He held his hands up in surrender.

She punched him lightly on the arm.

He caught her fist, rubbing his arm with exaggerated care, and she laughed. But the idea took root. "You're right though. I've been so caught up in the mystery I didn't think to do something that simple."

"See? I can be useful sometimes."

As they continued walking, the conversation shifted to lighter topics. Conor's favourite places in Ballycluan, the best spots for sunsets. He asked about her childhood memories, and she found herself sharing more than she'd intended, lulled by the rhythm of their steps and the warmth of his hand in hers.

The sky darkened, stars beginning to twinkle, and the air grew cooler.

"Do you ever think about leaving again?" Caitlin asked.

"Sometimes. But then I remember why I came back. This place, these people – they're part of me. I want to make a difference here."

"I understand that." The words came out softer than she'd intended. "I came here looking for answers for Grammy, but this place... it sounds silly, but I think I found something more. A sense of belonging."

"Ballycluan has a way of doing that. It's a special place." He stopped walking, turning to face her fully. "You're special too, you know. The way you jumped in to help Delia, how you care about your grandmother, even how you threw that ball for Finn despite the pain."

They reached a small rocky outcrop where waves crashed rhythmically. Finn settled at their feet, content to rest.

"You know, if you ever need help with your research, I'm just a call away." His fingers found that strand of hair the wind kept blowing across her face, tucking it behind her ear with deliberate slowness.

"Careful, or I'll be calling every day." She meant it as a joke, but his thumb stilled against her palm, and she felt his breathing shift.

"I wouldn't mind that at all."

The moment stretched between them, charged with promise. She could feel the pull between them, stronger than the tide.

Finn chose that moment to shake himself again, breaking the spell.

"Walk you home?" Conor asked, his fingers tightening around hers.

"I'd like that."

They turned back the way they'd come, the cottage lights visible in the distance. Friday couldn't come soon enough.

THIRTY-THREE
NOVEMBER 1920

"Thirty-two souls," Ellen whispered, as she and John emerged from Sunday Mass, the bronze voices of Clonbarra's bells echoing across the grey November morning. A week's worth of killing wrapped into a single Sunday. Each toll had counted another life lost – fifteen British intelligence agents assassinated in their beds across Dublin at dawn, fourteen innocent civilians gunned down at Croke Park in retaliation, and Father Griffin himself, murdered just a week ago.

Bloody Sunday, they were calling it.

John's jaw was set as they walked away from the church, his brown eyes scanning faces with that watchfulness she'd grown to recognize. "After what happened to Father Griffin..." His voice trailed off, but Ellen understood. The beloved Galway priest's murder had shaken the entire county. When Crown forces abducted him from his home, put a bullet in his head, and dumped his body in a bog, it crossed a line many thought even the Black and Tans wouldn't dare cross.

Ellen drew her black shawl close against the bitter wind. Around the churchyard, parishioners clustered in hushed, urgent whispers, their faces pale with shock. Mrs Cassidy gripped her rosary beads like a lifeline. Old Tom Clancy shook his head repeatedly, muttering prayers under his breath.

Ellen and John walked toward their oak tree without speaking. The November air cut sharp with dying leaves and cottage smoke, but she found no comfort in these familiar scents. Everything felt poisoned by what men could do to each other.

"Twelve thousand people at Father Griffin's funeral," she said, as they settled beneath bare branches. "In a town of fourteen thousand. Even the Protestant constables wept." John took her gloved hand. "And then children watching a football match." Her throat pinched tight, words breaking loose. "British forces shot *children*, John."

His fingers tightened around hers. "I know what they did."

Something in his tone turned the air heavy, pressing against her ribs. "Did you know this was coming?"

Long silence. When he finally spoke, his voice barely reached her. "Collins was planning something. The British intelligence agents – Collins nicknamed them the Cairo Gang – were getting too close. Too many of our good men disappearing." He met her eyes. "But the football match was pure revenge by the British."

Ellen's breath caught. The thought had been nagging at her all through Mass. "Isabella's intelligence – did her information help Collins find those agents?"

She watched John's face darken. She pictured Isabella's copper hair gleaming in some Dublin drawing room, while she quietly catalogued the men who'd be dead within hours.

"More than possible," he admitted. "She moves in exactly those circles. British officers, intelligence operatives. If she overheard their addresses, their routines..."

"Dear God." Ellen pressed her hand to her mouth. "She signed their death warrants."

"Those men hunted Irish patriots." John's grip tightened on her hand. "Sent them to their deaths. If she helped identify them, she protected lives. Our lives."

The newspaper images flashed through Ellen's mind. Bodies in

Dublin hotel rooms. Blood on Croke Park cobblestones. "Look what's happened now. They murdered civilians for revenge. How does this make anything better?"

John's laugh cut as bitter as the wind. "They've been murdering priests and pregnant women, Ellen. Burning towns. Torturing boys to death. How much worse could it get?"

She thought of the Loughnane brothers. Beaten, dragged behind a lorry, shot, burned. Dumped in a muddy pond like slaughtered animals. The whole of Galway was still reeling. "Patrick says this is what Collins wanted. To show the world what the British really are like."

John asked, "What do you think?"

Ellen watched a blackbird scrabble through fallen leaves. When she spoke, sadness seemed to rise from somewhere deep inside. "We're all becoming something we weren't meant to be. Isabella cataloguing men for death. You carrying messages that lead to ambushes. Patrick planning blood." She met his eyes. "Me carrying guns. We're all killers now."

John pulled free and stood abruptly. She watched him pace to the clearing's edge, boots crunching frost-brittle grass.

"What would you have us do?" His voice rose. "Submit forever? They've made it clear, no peaceful solution. Every political attempt met with violence."

"I know we have to fight." Ellen kept her voice steady despite the tears gathering. "But when does it end, John? When do we stop being soldiers?"

He turned back, and she saw something break in his expression. "When Ireland is free."

The words sounded hollow even to her. "When? Next month? Ten years?" Ellen stood, moved to him. "I'm not frightened of dying. I made peace with that on the train. I want to move on with my life. I want to marry you, have your children. Other couples marry in wartime. But you won't even discuss it."

Pain flickered across his face. "How can I make you a widow?"

"How can you make me wait for a tomorrow that might never

come?" The words burst out sharper than intended. "We could die tomorrow, John. Any of us. I want to live first."

He pulled her close. She felt the tremor in his body, breathed wool and November air. His heartbeat thundered against her ear, and she found herself pressing closer, wanting more than this careful embrace. Years of courtship, of stolen kisses and careful distances. How much longer would they have to wait? The thought of losing him before they'd ever truly been together made her grip tighten on his coat.

Over his shoulder, she could see smoke rising from the village chimneys, hear the distant sound of children playing. Normal life continuing despite the war that was consuming them all.

"The Country wants a truce," she murmured against his chest. "Some clergy too. Say the killing has to stop."

His arms tightened. "Collins will never agree. Not after this morning."

"Why not?"

"They're close to breaking British will. Today proved it. Collins struck their intelligence heart and they responded like cornered animals. That's desperation, not strength."

Ellen pulled back, searched his face for hope. "What about us? Isabella and Fintan, Sarah and Seamus. How many more must die?"

She saw pain flicker in his brown eyes. The church bells began tolling again, slow, measured, for the dead. Ellen counted silently. Thirty-two bronze notes echoing across the November landscape.

"I pray for them all," she said when silence returned. "British agents, Croke Park victims, Father Griffin, the Loughnanes."

"You'll pray for the *agents*?"

"Even them. They are someone's sons. Someone's husbands." Her voice stayed firm. "Whatever they'd done, they didn't deserve to die in their beds."

John studied her face with an expression she couldn't read. "You're too good for this war."

"None of us are good enough. That's the problem." Ellen took his hand again. "But we're here. We have to see it through. I just pray there's something left of us after."

Wind shook the bare branches above them. Last autumn leaves spiralled down like ash. "Come." Ellen pulled his hand gently. "Mam will worry if we're late."

Ellen thought of Isabella in Dublin drawing rooms, memorizing doomed faces. Of Patrick planning operations that would make more widows. Of all the ways war was changing them – harder, colder, willing to pay prices they'd never imagined.

But she thought too of Father Griffin's funeral. Twelve thousand people united in grief and defiance. Ordinary people showing extraordinary courage. Love that still existed between herself and John, between all of them, despite everything.

Maybe that was enough. That small flame of humanity, flickering but refusing to die. Maybe that's what they were really fighting for – not just political freedom, but the right to remain human in an inhuman world.

The bells had fallen silent, but their echo lingered in the cold air. A reminder of all they'd lost, and all they still hoped to save.

THIRTY-FOUR

MARCH 1921

Ellen threw some turf on the embers of the fire, the sod crackling and releasing its distinctive earthy aroma. The rich, smoky scent filled the small space, mingling with the lingering smell of last night's fish stew and the mustiness of old thatch overhead. She placed a blackened kettle full of water onto the iron hook, watching as the flames licked hungrily at it.

It was her day off from O'Sullivan's store, and she was catching up on household chores while Seamus fought off a chill in bed. His deep, rumbling snores echoed from the small adjoining room. Even illness couldn't quiet the sounds that would wake the dead. She glanced toward the wooden coat hanger by the front door, noting Patrick's absence. His worn brown coat wasn't there, which meant he hadn't returned from whatever Republican business had called him away the night before. Thank goodness Mam had gone to see her sister for a few days. She was too frail to fight a chill.

Pinning her long black hair up in a loose bun secured with the bone pins her mother had given her, Ellen pulled on her coarse linen apron. The washing needed doing, and there were potatoes to scrub for the midday meal. Every chore took longer with just her to manage everything, but at least Seamus was getting the rest he needed.

She was hanging wet clothes on the line behind the cottage when her name came, breathless and cracked through the morning air.

"Ellen! Is Seamus here? Please, he has to go!"

Sarah Tierney stumbled into the yard, clutching her side, her boots and the hem of her blue dress caked in mud. Normally so neat, she looked half undone, strands of dark hair stuck to her damp face.

Ellen's stomach turned. "Sarah, what on earth?"

"They've found Isabella and Fintan," Sarah gasped. "Down near Silverstrand. Dead."

For a moment, Ellen couldn't breathe. The wind tugged at the washing line, snapping the sheet like a whip, but the world had gone eerily still around her.

"Bella?" she whispered. "No, not Bella."

Images flooded her mind: Isabella's laughter echoing through the orchard, the two of them whispering under the oak tree, sharing dreams and secrets they'd never dared tell their mothers. Bella, with her copper hair and fierce green eyes, who'd risked everything to help Ireland in her own quiet way.

"Bella was my oldest friend," Ellen said hoarsely. "She believed in the cause as much as any of us."

"I'm sorry." Sarah's voice broke. "The soldiers are saying the IRA killed them, that Seamus led it. They're already on their way here."

Ellen stared at her. "The IRA? Killing Isabella Russell?" Her voice rose, incredulous. "She might've been the landlord's daughter, but she wasn't." She stopped herself. Even now, it was dangerous to speak too plainly.

Sarah shook her head helplessly. "They're saying she was loyal to the Crown. That Fintan turned her against her own kind. You know what they'll think of that."

Ellen's heart thudded painfully. It made dreadful sense: an Anglo-Irish woman dead beside her Irish driver. The British would never believe she'd taken Ireland's side. Easier to call it an IRA outrage, arrest a few local lads, and call it justice.

Tears blurred her vision, but there was no time to weep. "Sweet saints." She caught Sarah's arm. "Inside. Now. We've no time to talk."

Inside, Ellen rushed to Seamus's bedside, shaking him roughly.

"Seamus! Wake up! The soldiers are coming for you!"

He groaned, rubbing his eyes. His dark hair was damp with sweat, his face pale from fever. "What's going on, Ellen? You look like you've seen a ghost."

"Sarah says the soldiers are coming for you. You've been accused of abducting and killing Isabella Russell and Fintan Murphy."

Seamus's eyes widened, the sleep clearing in an instant. "That's madness! Why would I kill them? They were on our side."

"I know," Ellen said fiercely. "You couldn't have. You'd never hurt Bella." Her voice cracked on the name. "She was one of us, Seamus. She." But the words broke, splintered by the ache in her chest.

He swung his legs from the bed and pulled on his clothes with shaking hands.

"Seamus, go up into the loft and stay there. No matter what you hear. Go on. Now." Ellen's voice carried desperate authority as she pointed toward the ladder leading to the small storage space under the thatch.

"I'll not hide like a coward." Seamus's jaw set in the stubborn line she knew all too well, his green eyes flashing with defiance.

"Do it for me."

"No. I won't drag either of you down with me. You're already at risk with your *Cumann na mBan* membership."

Then it came, the sound she'd dreaded. The rhythmic thud of boots on the lane, the sharp bark of orders in clipped English accents. Each step drove another nail into her hope.

"Sweet Lord," Sarah whispered. She turned to Seamus, caught

his face between her hands, and pressed a quick, desperate kiss to his lips.

A pounding on the door followed. "Open up! In the name of the Crown!"

Before Ellen could stop him, Seamus strode to the door and flung it open.

The soldiers flooded in. They wore the mismatched green and khaki uniforms of the Black and Tans, their presence and their brutal reputation crowding into the small cottage. Their peaked caps cast shadows over grim faces marked by the casual cruelty that had made them infamous across Ireland. The smell of leather, sweat, and gun oil filled the room as their heavy boots scraped across the flagstone floor.

"What is the meaning of this?" Ellen demanded, her voice raw. "You can't just storm into people's homes!"

The men ignored her, rough and efficient. The officer's voice was clipped, polished. "Seamus McGrath, you are under arrest for treason and the murder of two loyal citizens of the Crown."

Loyal citizens. That was what they'd call Bella and Fintan now, wipe away everything they'd risked, everything they'd done for Ireland, and call them traitors to justify their deaths.

Two seized Seamus by the arms, wrenching them behind his back. The soldiers bound his wrists with rough hemp rope, the fibres already cutting into his skin and leaving red marks. Ellen moved to stop them, her protective instincts overriding caution, but Seamus's voice cut through her anger.

"Ellen, don't. It will only make things worse." He spoke in Irish, the musical cadences of their native tongue offering a small comfort in the face of English authority.

"Listen to your brother," said another voice, colder, smoother, and infinitely more dangerous.

Edward Russell stepped into the doorway, immaculate in his intelligence officer's uniform. The sight of him stopped her cold. The riding crop at his hip gleamed silver, the same one he'd carried as a boy while strutting through the stables, all arrogance and entitlement.

Ellen trembled, knowing how much he despised Seamus, and by extension, her entire family. The old wound of Duchess's accident, Seamus's insolence, their father's proud refusal to grovel, it all lived in Edward's cold blue eyes like banked coals waiting to flare.

She stared at him, seeing the cold hatred on his sharp-featured face, the gleam of satisfaction in his pale eyes. This was his revenge, years in the making.

"My brother had nothing to do with the abduction and murder of your sister. I'm sorry for your loss; she was a kind woman, and Fintan Murphy was a friend." The words tasted like ashes in her mouth, but in this situation, she had to speak carefully. Isabella had been more than kind, she was her oldest friend. She was brave, passionate, and committed to Irish freedom.

Ellen felt Edward's pale eyes boring into her like gimlets. She lifted her head and held his gaze, refusing to show the fear that made her hands shake. "*They* had nothing to fear from people like us."

His eyes flared at the emphasis on *they*, the implication that Isabella and Fintan had been the same at heart, despite their birth and position. His thin lips compressed into a bloodless line, but he ignored the barb.

"Your brother is a member of the IRA, as you well know." He turned his attention to Sarah, who took a step back under the sharpness of his gaze. "What are you doing here, Tierney? It's rather early for visiting."

"She came to get a good laying hen for her mother." Ellen's lie came smoothly, born of necessity and desperation. She couldn't let the English know Sarah and Seamus were involved, their secret relationship had been maintained precisely to protect each other from moments like this.

Ellen turned to the other officer, whose grey eyes held the flat disinterest of a man who had overseen many such arrests. "Where are you taking my brother?"

The officer didn't answer, merely gestured to his men, who dragged Seamus toward the door. Ellen and Sarah tried to follow, but a soldier blocked them with the butt of his rifle.

Ellen broke free from the soldier's restraining hands and ran after him, her worn shoes slipping on the frost-slick lane. Her voice cracked as she screamed after her brother, the sound echoing off the stone cottage like a banshee's wail: "Seamus, don't give up. We'll prove your innocence. You will be home before too long."

Their eyes met across the sea of uniforms. Even with his hands bound, his broad shoulders forced into a humiliating hunch, he held his head high. The morning light caught the darkness of his hair, making him look defiant despite his circumstances.

Ellen called to him again: "Stay strong. Our land will be free. It won't be long now."

Seamus glanced at Sarah, and Ellen could see the desperation in his green eyes – not for himself, but for the woman he loved and might never see again. The raw pain in that look nearly brought Ellen to her knees.

Ellen let out an anguished cry as her brother was thrown into the back of the lorry like a sack of grain. The metal doors slammed shut with a finality that seemed to echo across the countryside, the sound mixing with the rumble of the engine and the grinding of gears as the vehicle lurched forward.

She dropped to her knees on the cold lane, her wool dress soaking up the moisture from the morning dew. The lorry carried her brother away toward the British garrison. If he lived that long.

Sarah moved to help Ellen up from the ground, her small hands surprisingly strong as she gripped Ellen's elbow. The wool of her blue dress was warm against Ellen's arm as she guided her friend back to the cottage.

"Our men will do something. They will save him." Sarah's voice carried hope she clearly didn't feel, but Ellen was grateful for the attempt at comfort.

Back inside the cottage, the space felt empty without Seamus. Sarah made tea with shaking hands and pushed a cup toward Ellen, who wrapped her fingers around it without drinking.

"What about Patrick?" Ellen's voice was hoarse. "He's still not back from last night. If they're looking for Seamus, they'll want Patrick too. How do I warn him? How do I stop him from walking straight into their hands?"

"We need to contact John. This is an emergency if ever there was one. One of the lads can get a message to him. They'll know what to do."

Ellen nodded, her resolve hardening. John was supposedly away visiting a sick relative if others were asking, but was with Collins. He would know who to contact, what strings to pull.

Sarah squeezed her hand and despite her tears, said. "We'll bring him home, Ellen. One way or another." Sarah hugged her before heading back to the village.

Ellen fed another sod of turf to the fire, the smoke curling upward as if carrying her prayers with it. She stared into the flames, tears slipping down her cheeks for Isabella and Fintan, for Seamus, for Patrick – for Ireland itself.

Then she sank to her knees on the cold flagstone floor and bowed her head. "Keep them safe, Lord," she whispered. "Keep John safe too."

THIRTY-FIVE

NOW

Gunfire.

Caitlin jolted awake, sheets twisted around her legs like restraints. In the cottage darkness, echoes bounced off stone walls – sharp cracks that made her flinch even as consciousness dragged her back to safety.

Warm weight pressed against her chest. Fur. The scent of wet dog.

"Nemo?"

Nothing. Just wind through the eaves and waves whispering against the shore.

The memory slipped away before she could catch it. Left behind: the familiar hollow in her chest. Ghost-touch of something warm coating her palms.

She fumbled for the lamp. Yellow light flooded the room, harsh and sudden. Her hands trembled as she examined her palms, turning them over in the light.

Clean. No trace of red.

The large figures of 3:13 a.m. mocked her from her phone screen.

Caitlin sat on the bed's edge, waiting for her pulse to slow. The cottage felt tomb-quiet after the phantom gunshots. Empty after Nemo's imagined weight.

She pulled on her robe and padded to the kitchen. Moonlight silvered the research papers scattered across the table. Ellen McGrath stared up from a newspaper clipping, those familiar eyes holding secrets.

Tea. Normal things. She filled the kettle, struck a match, watched the blue flame catch. Settled in the chair by the window as darkness bled toward grey.

Sleep was done with her for the night.

By afternoon, it was finally late enough in South Carolina for Grammy to be awake. Caitlin had spent the morning walking the beach and researching, but now she could finally make the call she'd been wanting to make since the nightmare. Caitlin adjusted her laptop screen carefully, angling it away from the chaos of research papers scattered across the table. No need to worry Grammy with evidence of her obsessive digging.

"There you are, darling." Grammy's face filled the screen, looking more fragile than when Caitlin had left Charleston. The hospital bed's white linens made her skin seem translucent, but her eyes remained sharp as ever. "How's my Irish explorer this morning?"

"Grand, as they say here." Caitlin forced brightness into her voice. The nightmare's residue still clung to her like smoke, but Grammy didn't need that burden. "The cottage is perfect. You'd love it. Right on the water, and the sunrises are spectacular."

"And the locals? Are they treating you well?"

"Incredibly well. I told you about the local publican, Delia Tierney. She's taken me under her wing completely. Knows everyone, remembers everything." Caitlin paused, seeing Grammy lean forward expectantly. "She's related to a Sarah Tierney on her husband's side, some sort of cousin. Sarah was engaged to your uncle, a man called Seamus."

Grammy's eyes lit up, her fingers gripping the blanket with sudden eagerness. "Do they know anything about Seán?"

Caitlin hesitated, not wanting to get Grammy's hopes up.

"Caitlin, you look like you did when I caught you with your hand in the candy jar."

Caitlin blew her Grammy a kiss.

"There's an older man named Harry Bennett. He was a police officer here for years." Caitlin watched Grammy's hungry expression. "When I mentioned Seán Power, he went completely pale. Almost like he'd seen a ghost."

"What did he say about Seán? Did he remember him?" The questions tumbled out of Grammy faster than usual, her composure cracking with anticipation.

"Not much. He seemed... uncomfortable talking about it. But, Grammy, the way he reacted – I think there's more to the story than we know."

Grammy's face fell slightly. "Of course there's more to the story, darling. I was only three or four when I was left at the orphanage. There's eighty plus years of family history I know nothing about." Her voice grew wistful. "Did this Harry mention anyone else? Ellen McGrath perhaps? Or Patrick?"

"Not yet. But I'm going to keep digging." Caitlin smiled at Grammy's obvious disappointment. "There's a woman at the local historical society. Delia mentioned her. And I found some newspaper clippings online about the War of Independence period. Your family was definitely involved in some significant events."

"What kind of events?" Grammy's voice carried a mix of pride and worry.

"I'm still piecing it together. But, Grammy, Ellen McGrath was quite remarkable from what I can tell. Strong, independent, involved in the fight for Irish freedom."

Tears gathered in Grammy's eyes. "She loved me. I remember that much. She used to sing to me in Irish." Her voice grew soft with memory as she wiped her eyes. "Oh, Caitlin, thank you for doing this. For giving me back pieces of her."

Caitlin ached for her grammy, so far away.

"How are your pain levels, darling?" Grammy asked, after composing herself. "Have you been doing your exercises regularly? You know what happens when you skip days. How's the new physiotherapist? As charming as the old one?"

Heat crept up Caitlin's neck. "Tessa is a woman, Grammy. She's good."

Grammy's eyebrows climbed toward her hairline. "And the seaweed guy?"

The heat intensified. "He's wonderful." *And a fantastic kisser.* "Everything is moving quite fast, though."

"Hmm." Grammy's smile held volumes of maternal knowing. "Just remember, darling – not everyone is Mark."

The name hit hard. Caitlin's breath caught, her chest tightening with familiar panic. She forced herself to keep looking at the screen, to not let Grammy see how much the simple mention could still affect her.

"I know, Grammy." Her voice came out smaller than she'd intended. "I'm being careful."

Grammy's expression softened with understanding. "I didn't mean to upset you, darling. I just... I worry. You've been through so much."

"I'm okay. Really." Caitlin managed a smile that felt more genuine. "Conor's different. Not controlling. He's wonderful."

"Good. He sounds like a good man, Caitlin." Grammy's eyes grew heavy, and she stifled a small yawn. "I should probably rest now. These pain medications make me so drowsy."

"Of course. Sleep well, Grammy. I'll call you tomorrow."

After the call ended, Caitlin sat staring at the dark screen. Mark's name still echoed in the cottage silence, bringing with it the familiar weight of memories she'd thought she'd left behind in Charleston.

Not everyone is Mark.

She pressed her palms against her eyes, but the memories pushed forward anyway. Mark's smile in those early days. His hand on the small of her back at police functions. The way he'd made her feel chosen, special, worth loving.

Before he'd made her feel worthless.

Outside, seabirds called to each other over the waves. Normal sounds. Peaceful sounds. Nothing like gunfire or the phantom weight of a dying dog or the echo of Mark's voice telling her she was overreacting, being dramatic, imagining things.

Caitlin reached for Ellen McGrath's photograph. Those familiar eyes stared back, determined, maybe a little defiant. The kind of eyes that kept secrets.

"What did you do, Ellen?" she whispered. "What did you all do?"

Her phone buzzed. A text from an unknown Irish number:

> Hope the physio helped. Weather's perfect for another beach walk if you're interested. Conor

Despite everything, the nightmare, Mark's ghost, Harry's strange reaction, she found herself smiling. Grammy's voice echoed: *Not everyone is Mark.*

Maybe it was time to start believing that.

THIRTY-SIX

1921

The body was found at dawn by young Michael O'Brien, driving his father's cart to market. Later, he would tell anyone who'd listen how the sight had made him sick up his breakfast right there on the road. Seamus McGrath's once-powerful frame, twisted and broken, dumped like refuse beside the stone wall that marked the boundary between Russell land and the village proper.

Ellen was stacking folded fabric when Tom Clancy burst through the shop door, tears streaming down his cheeks. The bell above the door rang with unusual violence, and she looked up from the blue flannel she'd been folding to see his stricken face.

"Ellen, child..." His voice broke on her name.

She knew.

The fabric slipped from her hands to the shop floor, but she couldn't feel her fingers to pick it up. Couldn't feel anything except the terrible certainty settling over her like ice.

"Where?" The word came out as barely a whisper.

"The old road, near the crossroads. Father Murphy's with him now. And..." Tom's lined face crumpled. "They left a note pinned to his shirt. Says he was executed for treason against the Crown."

Ellen's legs gave out. She sank to her knees behind the shop counter, knocking into the shelf beside her. A bolt of cloth she'd been cutting for a customer earlier fell across her lap like a shroud, but she couldn't push it away. Seamus – gentle Seamus with his healing hands and stubborn streak, who had saved Duchess and argued with Patrick about tactics, who was secretly engaged to Sarah and planned to marry her after the war ended.

Gone.

The sound that tore from her throat wasn't quite human – a keening wail that seemed to rise from somewhere deeper than grief, older than words. It was the cry of every Irish mother and sister who had lost sons and brothers to this endless war, the sound of a heart breaking so completely that the pieces could never be put back together properly.

Bella's laugh broke across her mind, sharp as glass in the orchard sunlight, copper hair blazing. The memory gutted her anew.

Two graves now. Two voices she'd never hear again.

Tom knelt beside her among the scattered fabric, his calloused hands gentle on her shoulders. "There's more, child. Your mam... Mrs Cassidy went to tell her before I could stop her. When I left to find you, your mam had taken to her bed and wouldn't speak. Wouldn't eat. Dr Casey's been sent for, but..."

Ellen forced herself to stand, though the world still tilted dangerously around her. She had been here, cutting cloth and serving customers, while her mother learned their Seamus was dead. While Mam collapsed under the weight of another unbearable loss.

"I have to go to her. Mr O'Sullivan—"

"—is at the church with Father Murphy, arranging things. He told me to tell you to go home, that the shop can wait." Tom gripped her arm. "But, Ellen... where's Patrick? He needs to know, but he needs to be careful too. If they killed Seamus in custody, they'll be hunting for Patrick with a vengeance."

The thought cut through Ellen's grief like a blade of ice. Patrick – reckless, passionate Patrick, who would see Seamus's murder as a call to arms rather than a warning. He would want revenge, would throw himself into some suicidal attack that would only add his name to the growing list of martyrs.

"He's... he was supposed to return this morning from Cork. Sarah went to watch for him, to warn him." Ellen wiped her eyes with the back of her hand, forcing herself to think through the haze of grief. "Tom, will you help us bring Seamus home? He shouldn't lie on that road like... like a criminal."

"Of course, child. Father Murphy's arranging for the body to be moved to the church. I wish we could wake him proper like we did your da, but we can't take the risk of a Black and Tans raid. They will be keeping a close eye on things for a while, the vicious sons of—" He stopped himself just in time.

Death seemed to hang in the air when Ellen got home, still wearing her shop apron, her hands smelling of the lavender water she used to freshen the fabric displays. The fire had died to cold ashes, and her mother lay in the bed she had shared with Paddy McGrath, her face turned to the wall. Mary looked smaller than Ellen had ever seen her, as if grief had physically diminished her already frail frame.

"Mam?" Ellen sat carefully on the bed, her hand hovering over her mother's shoulder. The guilt was overwhelming. She had been arranging pretty fabrics for ladies' dresses while her mother learned her son was dead.

"Mam, I'm here. I'm so sorry I wasn't here when... I should have been here."

No response. Mary's breathing was shallow and laboured, her hands clutching the quilt that had been her wedding present thirty years ago. Ellen could see the rapid flutter of her pulse in the hollow of her throat, like a bird's wing beating against a cage.

"Dr Casey's coming, Mam. You need to drink some water, take some broth..."

"My boy." The words were barely audible, whispered into the pillow. "They killed my boy."

Tears spilled down her cheeks. "I know, Mam. I know."

"First Paddy, now Seamus. And Patrick..." Mary's voice broke. "They'll take Patrick too. I can't... I can't bear it, Ellen. I can't lose another son."

"You won't. We'll keep Patrick safe. We'll—"

Mary turned then, and Ellen gasped at what she saw. Her mother's face was grey as ash, her eyes sunken and glassy with fever. But it was the look in those eyes that terrified Ellen most – empty, hopeless, as if something essential had simply given up.

"There's no keeping anyone safe in this war," Mary whispered. "It takes and takes until there's nothing left."

Before Ellen could respond, she heard voices outside – familiar voices raised in argument. She recognized Patrick's angry tone and John's quieter but equally fierce replies. They were back, and they were fighting already. "Mam, I have to..." Ellen squeezed her mother's hand. "I'll be right back."

Walking out to the yard, she found them facing each other like fighters in a ring. John's face was pale with grief and fury, his brown eyes blazing. Patrick stood with his jaw set stubbornly, his green eyes cold as winter frost. Between them, the space crackled with barely contained violence.

"—told you this would happen!" John was saying. "Your recklessness, your bloody determination to escalate everything—"

"*My* recklessness?" Patrick's voice was dangerously quiet. "Seamus volunteered for the IRA. He knew the risks."

"Volunteered? Or did you volunteer him?" John stepped closer, his hands clenched into fists. "Just like you 'volunteered' Ellen to carry guns on that train. Seamus is dead because someone informed on him, Patrick. Someone who knew exactly where to find him and what to accuse him of."

"Are you suggesting I—"

"I'm not suggesting anything. I'm stating facts." John's voice trembled with rage. "You've been so busy playing war, so determined to prove yourself after missing the Rising, that you've stopped caring who gets hurt."

Ellen felt the world shift beneath her feet. "John, stop—"

"No, Ellen. Someone needs to say it." John turned his burning gaze back to Patrick. "Seamus is dead. Isabella Russell and Fintan Murphy are dead. All because Patrick McGrath had to have his grand gestures, his dramatic operations. How many more people have to die for your ego?"

Patrick's face whitened with rage, his hands clenching into fists. He took a step toward John, murder in his eyes.

"Stop!" Ellen stepped between them, her voice cracking with desperation. "Both of you, stop! You're grieving. We all are. Don't let them destroy us from the inside – that's what they want."

For a moment, the three of them stood frozen. Ellen between them like a barrier against the violence that would solve nothing.

Patrick stepped back slowly, his chest heaving. "Everything I've done has been for Ireland. For Seamus, for all of us."

Dr Casey arrived in the late afternoon, his medical bag heavy in his knotted hands. Ellen met him at the door, seeing her own fears reflected in his kind but worried eyes.

"How is she, Ellen? I'd have been sooner, but a bad birth..."

Ellen gave a small smile to silence him. "Fading," she whispered. "She won't eat, barely speaks. It's like... it's like she's willing herself to die."

The doctor nodded grimly. "I've seen it before. Sometimes the heart just... gives up. The body follows where the spirit leads."

He spent a long time with Mary, listening to her chest, checking her pulse, speaking in low, gentle tones. When he emerged from the bedroom, his expression told Ellen everything she needed to know.

"She's weak, has been since your father passed. This shock..." He shook his head sadly. "I can give her something for the pain but, Ellen, you need to prepare yourself. And your brother."

"How long?"

"Days, maybe hours. I'm sorry, child. After everything else..."

Ellen nodded, not trusting her voice. She walked the doctor to the door, then stood in the gathering darkness, listening to the sounds of the village preparing for night. Somewhere in the distance, she could hear women keening – news of Seamus's death had spread, and the traditional mourning had begun.

Ellen lifted her face to the stars beginning to appear in the darkening sky. Somewhere up there, she hoped, Da was waiting for Seamus. Waiting for Mam too, probably. The thought should have brought comfort, but all she felt was a vast, empty ache where her family used to be.

Behind her, she heard Patrick's and John's voices – the argument continuing, though quieter now. Two funerals to plan, if Dr Casey was right about Mam.

"We'll give him a hero's funeral," Patrick was saying, his voice rough with unshed tears. "The whole county will know Seamus McGrath died for Ireland."

And John's quieter reply: "Being a hero won't bring him back to Sarah. Won't comfort your mother. Or Ellen."

The war would end someday – had to end. But the price they were paying... would any of them be left to enjoy the freedom they were dying for?

Ellen wrapped her shawl tighter around her shoulders and went back inside. Tomorrow there would be wakes and funerals and the terrible business of continuing to live. Tonight, there was only grief and the fragile hope that somewhere in the darkness, love might still prove stronger than hate.

But as she sat beside her dying mother's bed, listening to the laboured breathing that might stop at any moment, Ellen couldn't help but wonder if they were all just fooling themselves. If this war would take everything they cared about and leave them with nothing but bitter memories and the hollow victory of a flag flying over empty graves.

The price of freedom, she thought, was higher than any of them had imagined when this all began. And the war hadn't finished collecting.

THIRTY-SEVEN
NOW

Caitlin changed her dress for the third time, finally settling on the blue one Grammy said brought out her eyes. Through the cottage window, she could see the sun beginning its descent toward the horizon, painting the sky in shades of amber and rose.

The knock came at exactly seven. She opened the door to find Conor standing there in dark jeans and a shirt that made his eyes look impossibly blue-green. He held a single wild rose, clearly picked from somewhere along the path.

"I thought we could walk along the beach," he said, offering her the flower. "It's beautiful this time of evening, and Tierney's isn't going anywhere."

Her heart did something complicated. "I'd like that."

She tucked the rose into a glass of water and grabbed her cardigan. As they set off down the familiar path to the beach, she wondered if Ellen had walked this same route with John Power, before everything fell apart. The thought should have been melancholy, but with Conor's hand finding hers as they navigated the steep section, it felt more like continuation than repetition.

The tide was out, leaving firm sand that made walking easy even with her leg. They talked about small things – his day at the clinic, her frustrating visit to the registry office – but underneath ran that current of awareness that had been building since their first meeting.

"Nervous?" he asked, as they approached the lights of Tierney's, music already spilling from its open doors.

"A little," she admitted. "This is my first proper date in... a while."

He squeezed her hand. "Mine too, actually. We can be nervous together."

The pub was busier than usual for a Friday night, but not packed. The regular crowd had gathered for the weekly music session – locals Caitlin was beginning to recognize, mixed with a handful of tourists. In the corner, three musicians had set up: a fiddle player she'd seen at the beach, an older man with a bodhrán, and a woman coaxing haunting melodies from a tin whistle.

"There you are!" Delia appeared at Caitlin's elbow, her knowing eyes taking in their linked hands. "And together too. Well, isn't that lovely?" Her voice carried just enough to turn a few heads.

Heat crept up Caitlin's neck.

"Delia," Conor said with fond exasperation, "could you be a bit more subtle?"

"At my age? Not likely." She winked at Caitlin. "Sit wherever you like, loves. I'll bring drinks over."

They found a small table near enough to hear the music but far enough for conversation. The pub's warm lighting cast everything in gold, and Caitlin found herself relaxing despite the curious glances from locals who clearly knew Conor well.

"Sorry about that," he said, but his eyes held amusement. "Small towns."

"I'm getting used to it." She was surprised to find it was true.

The music wove through their conversation – traditional tunes that seemed to pulse with the very heartbeat of the place. They talked about everything and nothing: his years travelling, her grandmother's latest matchmaking attempts via text, the way the village was slowly becoming familiar to her.

"Dance with me," Conor said suddenly, as the musicians struck up a lively reel.

Caitlin glanced at the small space where a few couples had begun to move. "I don't know the steps."

"Neither do half the people here." He stood, extending his hand. "Come on, I'll teach you."

She let him lead her onto the floor, acutely aware of eyes following them.

At first, she was stiff with self-consciousness. But as the music built and Conor's confidence seemed to transfer itself through his touch, something in her began to relax. She found herself laughing as he spun her, the movement sending only the slightest twinge through her healing shoulder.

"You're a natural," he called over the music.

"I'm terrible," she called back, but she was smiling, her cheeks flushed with exertion and something that felt dangerously like joy.

"Terribly wonderful," he corrected, spinning her again.

When the dance ended, they were both breathless. Without discussing it, they slipped outside for air. The night had fully arrived, stars blazing overhead with an intensity impossible in cities. They could still hear the music, muffled now but present.

"Thank you," Caitlin said, softly. "For tonight. For being patient with my two left feet."

"You were perfect." He stepped closer. "Caitlin, I—"

"Yes?"

"I'd really like to kiss you again."

Part of her – the wounded part – wanted to step back. But the woman who'd danced and laughed won out. "I'd really like that too."

He smiled and stroked her cheek gently before moving to kiss her. His kiss was gentle, questioning. She leaned into it, into him, allowing herself this moment of connection. When they parted, he kept her close.

They stayed outside for a few more minutes, neither eager to break the spell.

When they finally returned to the pub, Delia caught Caitlin's eye and winked. And Caitlin found she didn't mind.

"Walk me home?" she asked, as the evening wound down.

"I was hoping you'd ask."

They took the long way back, along the beach under the stars. The wild rose in her cottage window glowed like a promise in the lamplight, and when he kissed her goodnight at her door, Caitlin thought maybe – just maybe – Grammy was right about second chances.

THIRTY-EIGHT

1921

The church bells of Clonbarra rang out at precisely noon on 11 July 1921, their bronze voices carrying a different tone than usual. Not the mournful tolling for the dead that had become so familiar, but something lighter.

Ellen stood in O'Sullivan's doorway, watching people emerge from their cottages like creatures surfacing after a long winter.

"Would you look at that," Mr O'Sullivan murmured beside her. "Mrs Cassidy's actually smiling."

For the first time in months, no patrols marched down the main street. No rifles caught the sunlight. The lorries with their cargo of death had vanished. Even the children played without being hurried indoors by nervous mothers.

"Ellen!" Sarah Tierney came running, her dark hair escaping its pins. "Have you heard? They say it's really over!"

"The Truce," Ellen said, though a lightness rose in her, unbidden. "It's only paused. The politicians will meet now."

But even as she spoke the careful words, the weight pressing on her chest for so long began to ease. No more nights lying awake in the empty cottage, listening for gunshots. At twenty, she was truly on her own now, with only Patrick for family. Seamus and their mother had been dead for months, both casualties of this endless war.

"Where is he?" Sarah asked. "John, I mean."

Ellen hadn't seen John since he'd left days before on a "cattle-buying trip" with Michael Collins.

"There!" Mr O'Sullivan pointed down the lane.

John walked up the main street. Tall, lean, moving with that careful alertness that had become second nature. But something was different today. His shoulders weren't quite so rigid. When he spotted Ellen, his face broke into a smile she hadn't seen in months.

"Ellen." He swept her into his arms right there on the street while Sarah laughed and Mr O'Sullivan pretended not to watch. "It's over. The killing is over."

"The Truce—"

"More than that." John's brown eyes were bright with unshed tears. "Collins thinks we've won, Ellen. Not everything we wanted, but enough. There'll be negotiations now instead of bullets."

"And you? What will you do now?"

John's hands moved to frame her face. "I want to live, Ellen. I want to plan for something beyond the next mission."

He stopped, glancing around at the small crowd that had gathered in the street. Among them, Sarah was beaming, Mr O'Sullivan nodded approvingly; even Father Murphy had wandered over from the church.

"Walk with me." John took her arm.

They made their way to their oak tree in comfortable silence. The summer air was soft with growing things, and for once the countryside felt peaceful rather than threatening.

"Ellen, I need to ask you something." John turned to face her, his expression suddenly serious. "Something I should have asked long ago."

Ellen's heart began to race. "John—"

"No, let me say this." He took both her hands, his calloused fingers trembling slightly. "I've loved you since we were children, Ellen McGrath. Through the war, through everything that's tried to tear us apart. And now... now I think we might actually have a chance."

Ellen felt the world narrow to just them, standing beneath their tree with summer sun filtering through the leaves.

"I'm saying I want to marry you." The words came out in a rush. "Not someday when the war is over. Now. As soon as it can be arranged."

Ellen's breath caught. "John, I... I want that too. More than anything. Patrick—"

"—will refuse." John's jaw tightened. "I know. But, Ellen, you don't need his permission."

"He's the only family I have left."

John pulled her closer. "We tell Father Murphy that – that Collins could call me back any day. The Truce is fragile. No one knows how long it will hold. If negotiations fail, I could be gone tomorrow."

Ellen stared at him, swallowing the fear that rose in her throat. She wouldn't give this war any more of her tears. "You think he'd marry us without the banns?"

"Yes. I think he supports Collins too. We're promised to each other, aren't we? In our hearts, we're already married." John's voice carried desperation. "We're just asking him to make it official before Patrick can stop us, or the fighting does."

Ellen thought of the empty cottage, too quiet without Mam's gentle presence. Thought of Patrick's obvious dislike of John. Thought of all the couples who had waited for permission that never came.

"When?" she whispered, though guilt already gnawed at her.

"Tomorrow morning? Before dawn, in the church." John's smile was strained. "Father Murphy... he'll understand the urgency if we tell him we need to marry quickly."

"And after?"

"We could live together – Uncle Frank would give us the cottage behind the pub – but we'd have to let people think what they will."

Ellen looked into his brown eyes.

"The village will talk."

"Let them talk," John said. "Uncle Frank says love shouldn't have to hide in shadows. We'll be married in God's eyes, Ellen. That's what matters."

Ellen studied his face, seeing her own hopes and fears reflected there.

"Yes," she said, and felt something ease in her chest that had been tight for years. "Yes, John Power. Yes."

He kissed her, and she kissed him back with all the longing of their years of waiting.

"Absolutely not."

Patrick's voice was flat with finality as he stood in their kitchen that evening. Ellen had planned her speech, thought of all the arguments that might sway him, but the cold fury in his eyes told her none of it would matter.

The cottage felt too empty with just the two of them there. Ellen found herself glancing toward the bedroom door, still expecting to hear Mam's voice calling out to ask what all the raised voices were about. But there was only silence from that room now.

"Patrick, please—"

"I said no, Ellen. Not to him. Never to him."

Ellen felt her own temper rising. "What do you mean, 'not to him'? John is a good man. He's fought for Ireland just as much as you have."

"Has he?" Patrick's voice was sharp with contempt. "John Power talks a good game, but where was he when the real fighting was happening? Off in the USA while better men died."

"That's not fair and you know it. He was in Frongoch, he was with Collins—"

"He was following orders, Ellen. There's a difference between being a good soldier and being a leader." Patrick turned away from her, staring out of the small window toward the village. "I don't trust him. I don't trust his judgement, and I don't trust his commitment to the cause."

"This isn't about the cause, Patrick. This is about you not wanting to lose your housekeeper."

Patrick whirled to face her, his eyes flashing dangerously. "What did you say?"

"You heard me." Ellen stepped closer, her chin raised defiantly. "You like having me here to cook your meals and mend your clothes and keep house for you. It's convenient, isn't it? Having a woman to do all the work while you play at being a revolutionary."

"How dare you—"

"It's true, isn't it? When Mam was sick, who took care of her? When she died, who arranged the funeral and cleaned the house and made sure you were fed? Not you, Patrick. You were too busy with your meetings and your grand plans."

Patrick's face had gone white with anger. "Everything I do is for this family, for Ireland—"

"Everything you do is for Patrick McGrath's idea of what a hero looks like." Ellen's voice was rising now, months of resentment spilling out. "You didn't like John before the war, you didn't like him during the war, and you don't like him now. This has nothing to do with his politics and everything to do with your pride."

"My *pride*?"

"Yes, your pride. You can't stand that John might have done things you didn't do, seen places you haven't seen, earned respect you haven't earned. You can't stand that I might choose him over you."

They stared at each other across the small kitchen, brother and sister who had once shared everything, now divided by years of unspoken resentments. The empty cottage seemed to echo around them.

"The answer is no," Patrick said, his voice cold as winter. "You're my sister, my responsibility since Da and Mam died. I won't give my permission for you to marry that man. And frankly,

Ellen, I need you here. This house, this farm – it needs a woman's hand. You have duties here."

Ellen nodded slowly, though tears stung her eyes. "I thought you might say that."

"Good. Then we understand each other."

"We do." Ellen wiped her eyes with the back of her hand. "We understand each other perfectly. You need me here to cook and clean and keep house. John needs someone who can fight beside him, not behind him. And I need... I need to choose my own life."

Patrick's eyes narrowed. "What does that mean?"

"It means I'm going to marry John Power whether you approve or not. In secret, if I have to. In the eyes of God, even if not in yours."

The silence that followed was deafening. Patrick's face went through a series of expressions – surprise, anger, betrayal, and finally a fury so cold that it made Ellen step back despite herself.

"If you do this," he said, "if you sneak around behind my back like some common tart, you're no sister of mine."

The crude word hit Ellen like a slap, but she forced herself to stand tall. "If wanting to be loved makes me a tart in your eyes, then we have nothing more to say to each other."

He stepped closer, looming over her. "You want to marry him? Fine. But you'll do it without me. I'll never agree. You'll stay here and do your duty to this family."

"And if I refuse?"

"Then you can leave. Tonight. With nothing but the clothes on your back." Patrick's smile was cold. "See how long your precious John's love lasts when you come to him with empty hands and no dowry."

Ellen stared at her brother, seeing a stranger in the familiar features. This wasn't the boy who had taught her to fish, who had held her when she cried over Da's death. This was someone harder, colder.

"You would really throw me out? Your own sister?"

"I would protect what's mine," Patrick said simply. "This

house, this land, this family. John Power is not family. And if you choose him over your blood, then neither are you."

Ellen felt the walls of the cottage closing in around her and she sank into her father's old chair by the fire, tears flowing freely now. The cottage full of memories and silence. But beneath the grief was something else – a cold anger at being trapped, at being treated like property instead of a person.

And then another thought struck her – one that made her sit up straighter in the chair. She didn't have to stay. She didn't have to submit to Patrick's threats and manipulation. She had a job, a place where she was valued for more than her ability to cook and clean.

Ellen wiped her eyes and stood, moving with sudden purpose to the small chest where she kept her few possessions. If Patrick wanted to threaten her with being thrown out with nothing, then she'd leave on her own terms.

As Ellen packed her few clothes into a carpet bag, listening to the sounds of celebration of the Truce that drifted from the village, she made her decision.

Tomorrow, before dawn, she would meet John at the church. Father Murphy would say the words that would make them husband and wife. Tonight, she would ask Mr O'Sullivan if she could take the small room above the shop that he'd offered before.

Patrick could find himself another housekeeper. She was finished with being treated like an unpaid servant by her own brother.

So what if it wasn't the life she'd dreamed of as a girl? Dreams were for peacetime, and they'd had so little of that. This was real. John was real. And love, Ellen knew now, was sometimes the most revolutionary act of all – especially when it meant choosing freedom over family obligation.

Mr O'Sullivan looked up from his ledger as Ellen knocked softly on the shop door, her carpet bag in hand and tears still drying on her cheeks. Even in the lamplight, she could see the concern that immediately crossed his face.

"Ellen, child, what's happened? It's past nine o'clock."

"Mr O'Sullivan, I'm sorry to disturb you so late, but I need... I was wondering if your offer still stands. About the room above the shop." The words tumbled out in a rush.

"Slow down, slow down." The older man stepped aside to let her in, noting the bag and her obvious distress. "What's brought this on? Has something happened with Patrick?"

Ellen set down her bag and tried to compose herself. "We had a disagreement. About John. Patrick won't give his permission for us to marry, and he... he made it clear that I'm more valuable to him as a housekeeper than as a sister."

Mr O'Sullivan's face darkened. "Did he now? And what did you tell him?"

"That I wouldn't be his unpaid servant anymore." Ellen lifted her chin, though it trembled slightly. "I know it's not proper, a young woman staying the night alone above a shop, but I have nowhere else to go, and I thought perhaps—"

"Nonsense about proper," O'Sullivan interrupted gruffly. "You're a good worker and an honest girl. If Patrick McGrath can't see that his sister deserves better than to be treated like hired help, then he's a bigger fool than I took him for."

Ellen felt fresh tears threaten. "Then you'll let me stay tonight?"

"Course I will. The room's been empty since my Mary died, and it'll be good to have someone in the house again." He studied her face carefully. "This John business. You're set on marrying him?"

Ellen nodded. "Tomorrow morning, if Father Murphy will perform the ceremony. It won't be legal without Patrick's permission, but it'll be real in God's eyes."

O'Sullivan surprised her by nodding approvingly. "It'll be legal too, child. Patrick has no say in Church law. You're over twelve and Father Murphy's a priest – that's all you need. John Power's a good man. Steadier than your brother, if you ask me. Less inclined to grand gestures and more focused on the people he cares about." His voice grew softer. "If my Michael had come home, I wouldn't have stood in his way. No matter who he wanted to marry."

The unexpected blessing broke something loose in Ellen's chest. "Thank you," she whispered.

"Don't thank me yet. Patrick won't like this, and he's not the type to let go of what he considers his easily." O'Sullivan picked up her bag. "But you're welcome here as long as you need, Ellen. A girl should be able to choose her own path, especially one with as good a head on her shoulders as you."

As they climbed the narrow stairs to the small room above the shop, Ellen felt something she hadn't experienced in months – hope. Tomorrow she would marry John in secret. Tonight, she would sleep under a roof where she was valued as more than a servant.

Father Murphy was waiting for them in the church when Ellen and John arrived before dawn the next morning, along with Sarah and Frank Tierney. The sacred space was lit only by a few flickering candles, casting long shadows across the wooden pews. The priest had unlocked the church quietly, and they entered through the side door to avoid being seen.

Sarah squeezed Ellen's hand as they approached the altar. "Are you certain about this?" she whispered.

Ellen nodded, grateful beyond words that her friends had agreed to witness this secret ceremony. Frank stood beside John.

"The boy's earned the right to happiness," Frank had told Ellen a few minutes before. "And if Patrick McGrath can't see what a treasure he has in you, then he's a fool."

"You came to me with urgent need," Father Murphy said, his expression sombre in the candlelight. His eyes searched their faces. "This is a serious matter. Marriage is a sacred sacrament, not to be entered into lightly, even under... difficult circumstances. But I've buried too many young men these past years. I know why you cannot wait for banns."

"If fighting starts again, Father, I could be gone tomorrow." John's hand tightened on hers. "We love each other, Father. We want to do right by God and by each other."

The priest studied them both. Finally, he nodded slowly. "Then let us proceed. But understand – this marriage, hastily performed though it may be, is binding in God's eyes. There will be no going back from the vows you speak today."

"We're certain, Father," Ellen said, her voice steady despite the tremor in her hands. "More certain than I've ever been about anything."

John squeezed her fingers again, his hands warm and strong in the morning chill. "More certain than we've ever been about anything."

The priest nodded slowly, opening his book to pages he seemed to know by heart. "Then in the sight of God, though in haste and secrecy, let us join these two souls in holy matrimony..."

The ceremony was whispered rather than spoken. When John slipped a simple ring onto Ellen's finger – his grandfather's signet ring, worn smooth with age – and when she promised to love and honour him through whatever storms might come, Ellen felt something click into place in her chest.

They were married. Secret, complicated, impossible – but married.

Sarah wiped tears from her eyes. Frank shook John's hand.

Frank Tierney stepped forward, his craggy face breaking into a smile. "Come home with us, Ellen. The cottage behind the pub – it's yours now. Both of you." He glanced meaningfully at John. "It's time this family had some happiness."

Ellen felt fresh tears threaten. "Mr Tierney, are you certain? People will talk—"

"Let them talk." Frank's voice was firm. "You're married in God's eyes, and that's good enough for me. John's family, which makes you family too." His expression grew serious. "Patrick won't like it, and there'll be those in the village who'll whisper. But there'll be others who understand that love shouldn't have to hide in shadows."

As they prepared to leave the church together, Ellen looked down at the ring on her finger, catching the candlelight.

She stepped out into the dawn light, a married woman. The Truce held, the sun was beginning to rise over Clonbarra, and somewhere in the distance she could hear church bells beginning their morning call. It wasn't peace, not yet. But it was hope. *And sometimes*, Ellen thought, as John's arm came around her waist in the growing daylight, *hope is enough to build a life on*. Especially when it came with the support of those who truly understood that love was worth fighting for, whatever the cost.

Father Murphy would keep his own counsel about what had happened in his church before dawn, but his gentle smile when he encountered the young couple in the days to come would speak volumes to those wise enough to read between the lines.

THIRTY-NINE
DECEMBER 1921

The baby kicked hard enough to make Ellen wince. Six months along, and their child seemed determined to remind her of its presence at every moment. She pressed her hand to her side, trying to ease the sharp jab under her ribs as she arranged the morning's deliveries behind O'Sullivan's counter. "Easy there, little one," she murmured, though part of her was grateful for the distraction. The news from Dublin had everyone on edge, and even the baby seemed to sense the tension crackling through Clonbarra like lightning before a storm.

The shop bell chimed. Sarah Tierney stepped inside, her usual bright smile strained around the edges. These days, Ellen saw the same look on every face – brittle cheerfulness, as if everyone feared the world might crack again.

"Morning, Ellen. How are you keeping? You look tired."

Ellen shifted her weight, trying to ease the constant ache in her lower back. "Well enough, considering." She gestured ruefully toward her rounded belly. "This little one seems determined to keep me awake at night."

Sarah's face softened. "Not much longer now. Are you nervous?"

"Terrified," Ellen admitted.

"That's only natural. First babies are frightening enough without all this political upheaval." Sarah squeezed Ellen's hand gently. "But you're strong, and you have John. You'll manage fine."

Ellen gave her a grateful smile. Sarah had never once flinched at the mention of the wedding or the cottage.

"I came for some tea and sugar, but mostly to see how you're managing with all this Treaty business. Da's been in a right state since the news came from Dublin."

Ellen nodded, measuring out the tea with hands that trembled slightly. The Anglo-Irish Treaty, signed just days ago on 6 December. Already the cracks were showing. Not just in Dublin, but right there in their small village.

"John thinks it's the best deal Ireland could get," Ellen said carefully. "A stepping stone, he calls it."

"And what do you think?" Sarah asked.

Wrapping the tea in brown paper, Ellen said, "I think I'm tired of young men dying for dreams that always seem just out of reach. If this Treaty stops the killing, even if it's not everything we wanted..."

"But we're not a republic," Sarah said. "We'll still swear allegiance to the English king. And the partition – six counties in the North left behind!"

"I know." Ellen's voice dropped. "But John says Michael Collins was set up. That de Valera knew the terms Britain would accept and sent Collins to take the blame for signing them. Collins thinks he was signing his own death warrant, but he did it anyway because he thought it was Ireland's only chance."

The shop bell chimed again. Mr O'Sullivan emerged from the back room, his face grave. "Ladies. Discussing the state of the nation, are we?" His smile didn't reach his eyes.

"Ellen was just saying what John thinks about Collins being set up," Sarah said.

O'Sullivan nodded slowly. "The boy's probably right. Collins was too smart not to know what he was walking into. But sometimes the hardest choices are the ones that history judges you for, even when you're trying to save lives."

Her eyes burned. Everything felt too raw, too complicated. Here she was, heavily pregnant with John's child – their first baby due in March – while Ireland tore itself apart over a Treaty that nobody really wanted but might be the only path to peace.

"I should get back," Sarah said, sensing the heavy mood. "Da will be wondering where I've got to. He's meeting with some of the other publicans today about where they stand on all this."

After Sarah left, Ellen eased herself with a stretch, one hand supporting her back. Six months along and the child never seemed to sleep, heels or elbows grinding under her ribs. How was she going to manage when the child arrived? The cottage behind Tierney's was small, and with all this political upheaval...

"Ellen, child, you should be sitting more," O'Sullivan said, his voice kind. "In your condition, you shouldn't be on your feet so much."

"I'm managing well enough."

O'Sullivan studied her with knowing eyes. "My Mary used to get that same tired look when she was carrying Michael. Are you getting enough rest? John taking proper care of you?"

Ellen's cheeks warmed. "He does his best. It's just... everything feels so uncertain with all this Treaty business. I worry about what kind of world we're bringing this child into."

"The same world every mother has worried about since time began," O'Sullivan said. "But you're strong, Ellen, and so is the baby. March isn't so far away now."

Before Ellen could respond, the shop door burst open, the bell nearly flying off its hook.

Patrick stood in the doorway, his face flushed. "So this is where my sister's taken to hiding," he said, his voice carrying that dangerous edge that had become all too familiar since Ellen left his house.

His bluster was undermined by the slight sway in his stance. He'd clearly been drinking; she could smell it, sharp and sour.

"Patrick." Ellen straightened, forcing strength into her voice she didn't feel. "What do you want?"

"What do I want?" His laugh was bitter. "I want to know if you're proud of yourself, Ellen. Living with a man who's ready to sell Ireland down the river for the promise of dominion status."

Ellen flushed as he honed in on her doubts about the British offer. Full Independence had always been the goal, yet the proposal from London granted only limited self rule under the British Crown. But if it stopped the killings, wasn't it worth discussing rather than rejecting it?

O'Sullivan stepped forward, his cheeks flushing with anger. "That's enough, McGrath. You've no call to come into my shop and abuse my employee."

"Your employee?" Patrick's eyes blazed as they moved to Ellen's obviously pregnant form. "She's my sister, though she seems to have forgotten that. Living with a man who'd have us kissing the English king's boots."

"I said, that's enough!" O'Sullivan's voice cracked like a whip. "Get out of my shop before I throw you out myself."

"Patrick, please." Ellen stepped around O'Sullivan, her voice pleading. "Don't do this. We were family once."

"We were," Patrick agreed, his voice suddenly quiet and even more dangerous for it. "Before you chose *him* over your own blood. Before you threw in your lot with the traitors who'd accept crumbs from the English table."

Ellen felt the baby kick sharply, as if reacting to the tension in the room. She placed both hands protectively over her belly.

"John's not a traitor," Ellen said. "He's trying to prevent another war—"

"Another war?" Patrick laughed harshly. "There's going to be a war anyway, Ellen. Between Irishmen this time. Collins and his Free State crowd against those of us who remember what we were fighting for. And when it comes, you'll have to choose which side you're on."

Ellen felt the baby move restlessly, responding to her distress.

The thought of another war, of Irish fighting Irish, of her child being born into violence, made her feel sick. "I'm on the side of peace," she said, forcing her shoulders square. "I'm on the side of no more mothers burying their sons."

Patrick stared at her, something flickering in his green eyes that might have been disappointment or pity. "Then you're on the losing side, sister. Because peace bought with surrender isn't peace at all."

He turned toward the door, then paused. "When your precious John and his new masters in Dublin start shooting Republicans, remember that you chose this."

The door slammed behind him. The shop felt too quiet.

"He's drunk," O'Sullivan said. "And angry."

"But what if he's right?" Ellen whispered, her hands moving protectively over her rounded belly. "What if there really is going to be civil war? What kind of world will my baby be born into?"

O'Sullivan moved to the window to watch Patrick's unsteady progress down the street. "The same world every mother has brought children into since time began, child. An uncertain one. But with love and hope and the chance of something better." He turned back to her, his eyes kind. "Your baby will be born Irish, Ellen. Free Irish, whatever that ends up meaning. That's more than we had when we were born."

Ellen nodded, though doubt still gnawed at her. Outside, she could see neighbours gathering in small groups, their voices low and urgent. Mrs Cassidy's finger jabbed the air at her son; Tom Clancy stood with Father Murphy, head bowed. Treaty talk again, surely. Even the children seemed to sense the tension, playing more quietly than usual.

The door chimed again. This time it was John, home from his work with Frank Tierney's horses. His face lit up when he saw Ellen, though concern immediately creased his features as he noticed her obvious exhaustion.

"You look tired, love. You shouldn't be on your feet so much."

He moved to her side, hand finding her belly where the baby was kicking. "How's our little one today?"

"Active," Ellen said with a weary smile. "Very active. But, John, Patrick was here..."

"What did he say? Did he upset you? That's not good for the baby."

"Just the usual," Ellen said. "Calling you a traitor." John's face went white, then flushed dark. "He's upsetting you when you're pregnant?"

"John, please," Ellen caught his arm as he started toward the door. "Don't. It won't help anything, and I need you here. Both of us do." She placed his hand firmly on her belly where the baby was moving. "Feel that? Our child doesn't care about politics. Our baby just wants to be born healthy and loved."

John's arms came gently around her, careful of her condition. "You're right. Our child will be born into a free Ireland, Ellen. Maybe not the Ireland we dreamed of, but free nonetheless. And loved. So very loved."

Ellen leaned into his warmth, wanting to believe him. But Patrick's words echoed in her mind: *"When your precious John and his new masters in Dublin start shooting Republicans, remember that you chose this."*

She thought of the women of *Cumann na mBan*, many of whom had already declared against the Treaty. Women who had fought and bled for the Republic, who saw any compromise with the Crown as betrayal. Ellen understood their position, even sympathized with it. But she was tired of fighting, tired of death, tired of watching Ireland tear itself apart.

Maybe the Treaty wasn't perfect. Maybe it was, as Patrick claimed, crumbs from the English table. But it was also an end to the Black and Tans, an end to midnight raids and summary executions. It was a chance for her child to grow up in a world where being Irish wasn't a crime.

"I love you," she whispered against John's chest. "Whatever comes, I love you."

"And I love you. Both of you." His hand moved to rest gently on her stomach. "We'll face whatever comes together."

Outside, the December wind was picking up, rattling the shop windows like an omen. Ellen closed her eyes and tried to imagine a peaceful future for their child. She feared that Patrick might be right about one thing: there would be another war before there was peace. This time it would be brother against brother, neighbour against neighbour; even in Clonbarra, she could feel the village fraying, every conversation pulling at the stitches that held them together.

The baby kicked again, hard and insistent. Ellen made a vow: whatever came, be it war or whispers or even Patrick, she would keep this child safe. In just months, she would hold her child in her arms. Even if it meant choosing peace over purity, compromise over principle. Even if it meant standing against her own brother.

FORTY

MARCH 1922

The first labour pain struck Ellen as she was hanging washing behind the cottage, March wind whipping the damp sheets against her face. She gripped the line with both hands, breathing through the sharp contraction that seized her belly like an iron fist. Too early, she thought, desperately.

But as the pain ebbed and left her gasping, Ellen knew this was no false alarm. The restless stirring she'd felt all morning, the dull ache in her lower back that no position could ease – her body had been preparing for this moment while her mind fretted over the worsening tensions since the Treaty ratification.

The conversations she'd overheard at O'Sullivan's shop earlier that day had painted a grim picture. Anti-Treaty forces were already organizing, refusing to accept what they saw as a betrayal of the Republic. There were whispers of arms being hidden, of men choosing sides for a conflict that everyone feared but no one seemed able to prevent.

Another contraction, stronger this time. Ellen dropped the wet shirt she'd been pinning and made her way carefully toward the cottage door.

The political upheaval of the past months had left everyone on edge. The Dáil, the new Irish Parliament the Volunteers had risked their lives to form, had ratified the Treaty by the narrowest of margins – 64 votes to 57. The country was splitting down the middle, and Ellen could feel the tension in every conversation, every sideways glance, every family divided against itself.

"John!" she called as she reached the kitchen, one hand braced against the door frame. "John, I need you!"

He appeared from the back room where he'd been mending harness, his brown eyes immediately alert to the strain in her voice. "Ellen, what's wrong? Is it—" His gaze dropped to where she cradled her swollen belly, understanding dawning on his face.

"The baby's coming." Another contraction building. She doubled over.

John was beside her in an instant, his strong arms supporting her as the pain crested and broke. "How long have you been having pains? Why didn't you tell me?"

"They just started. Sharp ones, anyway." Ellen straightened as the contraction passed, tasting copper fear on her tongue despite the cool March air. The cottage smelled of turf smoke and yesterday's bacon grease. "I thought it was just the baby moving, but..."

"We need to get Mrs Murphy. And Dr Casey." John's voice was steady, but Ellen could see the fear flickering in his brown eyes. First babies. Early ones. Risks that neither of them wanted to contemplate.

"Mrs Murphy first," Ellen agreed. The village midwife had delivered half the babies in Clonbarra and would know better than anyone what to do. "But, John, with everything happening... what if she won't come? Some people are taking sides already."

John's jaw tightened. Treaty debates splitting families, neighbours, entire communities. Those who supported Collins and the Free State on one side, and Republicans who rejected any compromise with the Crown on the other. People like Ellen and John caught in the middle – exhausted by war, hoping for peace even at a price.

"She'll come," John said. "Whatever Mrs Murphy thinks of the Treaty, she won't let politics keep her from a birthing."

Another contraction seized Ellen. Stronger. She dropped to her knees on the cottage floor, rough flagstones cold against her legs.

John knelt beside her, his hand gentle on her back as she breathed through the pain. When it passed, she looked up at him with eyes bright with unshed tears.

"I'm frightened, John. Not just of the birth, but... what kind of world are we bringing this baby into, tell me that? The country's tearing itself apart, families divided, and now there's talk of fighting between Irishmen..."

"Shh." John helped her to her feet, his voice soothing despite his own worry. "Our baby will be born into a free Ireland, Ellen. Not perfect, maybe, but free. That's more than we had, isn't it?"

"I have to get Mrs Murphy," he said, moments later, helping Ellen up and settling her carefully into the chair by the fire. "Will you be alright for a few minutes?"

Ellen nodded, though another contraction was already building. "Hurry. Please."

As the cottage door closed behind him, Ellen found herself alone with her fears and her pain. She thought of Isabella Russell – brave, passionate Isabella who had spied for Irish freedom and died for it. Ellen had already decided on "Bridget" for a daughter, but now she realized she wanted the baby to have Isabella's name as well. A tribute to a friend who had sacrificed everything for the cause they all believed in.

The contraction peaked. Stronger than any before it. Ellen gripped the arms of the chair until her knuckles went white, rough wood biting into her palms. Through the window, normal life was continuing – Tom Clancy leading a horse to the smithy, Mrs Cassidy hanging out her washing, children playing in the mud of the lane. Despite the political turmoil threatening to consume them all. And this felt different. More personal somehow. The enemy wasn't foreign soldiers in unfamiliar uniforms, but neighbours and family members. People they'd grown up with and trusted.

By the time John returned with Mrs Murphy in tow, Ellen's contractions were coming every few minutes. The midwife took one look at her and began rolling up her sleeves with the brisk efficiency of a woman who had seen hundreds of babies into the world.

"Right then, Ellen, love. Let's get you to bed and see what this little one's about, so we will." Mrs Murphy's voice carried the authority of experience, her greying hair pinned back severely and her capable hands already reaching for the medical bag she'd brought. The sharp scent of carbolic soap clung to her clothes. "How far apart are the pains?"

"Five or four minutes," Ellen gasped as another contraction gripped her. "They're getting stronger."

"That's the way of it, love. Your body knows what to do, even if it's a bit early." Mrs Murphy turned to John, who was hovering anxiously by the bedside. "I'll need hot water, clean linens, and perhaps you'd best send word to Dr Casey. Just in case, mind."

John nodded and disappeared into the kitchen. Ellen could hear him building up the fire. Clatter of kettle against iron hook. Familiar domestic sounds somehow comforting even as her body betrayed her with wave after wave of pain.

"Mrs Murphy," Ellen said, during a brief respite between contractions. "Is it true what they're saying? About civil war?"

The midwife's kindly face grew grave as she arranged her supplies on the small table beside the bed. Scissors glinted in the lamplight. "There's been talk, certainly. Angry words and bitter feelings. But surely sense will prevail, won't it? We've had enough of war, so we have."

Ellen wanted to agree, but she thought of Patrick's fury when he'd heard about the Treaty ratification back in January. The cold rage on his face when he'd spoken of Collins and his "Free State masters." Something final in his voice. As if he'd already made his choice about which side he'd fight on when the shooting started.

Another contraction. Different now. Deeper. More urgent.

Ellen cried out despite her determination to stay quiet. Her body preparing for the final push.

"That's it, love," Mrs Murphy said, encouragingly. "The baby's eager to meet the world, so it is. It won't be much longer now."

John returned with hot water and clean linens, his face pale but determined. "Dr Casey's coming as soon as he finishes with old Mrs O'Brien. Should be here within the hour."

"We might not need him," Mrs Murphy said, examining Ellen with gentle hands. "This baby's in a hurry, and everything seems to be progressing well. Sometimes the early ones are the easiest – eager to see what all the fuss is about."

Ellen found herself smiling despite the pain. The idea of her child being curious about the world, impatient to join the ongoing drama of Irish life, somehow made everything feel more hopeful. Whatever political chaos awaited them, there would still be new life, new beginnings, new reasons to hope for peace.

The next hour passed in a blur of increasing pain and growing urgency. Ellen gripped John's hand through each contraction, drawing strength from his steady presence.

"I can see the head!" Mrs Murphy announced suddenly. "One more push, Ellen. Just one more and you'll have your baby, so you will."

Ellen bore down with everything she had, feeling her baby slip into the world with a rush of relief and exhaustion. The baby's cry filled the cottage. Strong. Healthy. Indignant at being forced from her warm nest into the cold March air.

"A girl," Mrs Murphy announced with satisfaction, quickly wrapping the baby in clean linens. "Perfect little girl, and early or not, she's got a fine pair of lungs on her."

John's eyes filled with tears as Mrs Murphy placed their daughter in Ellen's arms. The baby was smaller than Ellen had expected but she was clearly healthy. Tiny fists waving indignantly. Eyes squeezed shut against the unfamiliar light.

"Bridget," Ellen whispered, looking down at her daughter's red, wrinkled face. "Bridget Isabella Power."

"Isabella?" John's voice was soft with understanding. "For Bella?"

Ellen nodded, unable to speak around the tears clogging her throat. Isabella Russell might be gone, but her memory would live on in this new life.

She wondered what Mam would have thought of Bridget, whether Seamus would have laughed at her fierce little cry. Both should have been there for this moment, fussing over the baby, arguing about who she looked like most.

"She's beautiful," John breathed, reaching out one finger to touch their daughter's tiny hand. Bridget's fingers immediately closed around his, gripping with surprising strength. "Look at that grip. She's going to be strong, just like her mother."

Mrs Murphy bustled about, cleaning up and making Ellen comfortable. Through the window, they could hear voices from the pub. Frank Tierney and his customers discussing the latest news from Dublin. Arguments growing more heated as the afternoon wore on. Words sharper now.

"What kind of world have we brought her into?" Ellen murmured, looking down at Bridget's peaceful face. The baby had fallen asleep, exhausted by her dramatic entrance.

"The only world we have," John said. "But she'll make it better, won't you, little one? All these children being born now – they'll grow up Irish and free. Maybe they'll be wiser than we've been."

Dr Casey arrived just as Mrs Murphy was finishing up, his medical bag in hand. But one look at Ellen and the baby told him his services weren't urgently needed.

"Fine work, Mrs Murphy," he said approvingly, after examining both mother and child. "Mother and baby both doing well. The little one's small but healthy."

"She's perfect," Ellen said, adjusting the blanket around Bridget's tiny form. "Whatever comes, whatever happens with all this political business, she's perfect."

Dr Casey's expression grew grave. "There's word from Dublin. The provisional government is taking firmer control. Collins is moving fast to establish the Free State." He paused, glancing between Ellen and John. "But there's also word that Anti-Treaty forces are consolidating under de Valera. The split is widening."

Ellen felt John's hand tighten on hers. They'd both hoped that the Treaty ratification back in January would end the divisions. But it seemed to be making them worse instead, communities fracturing along political lines that cut deeper than the old divisions between landlord and tenant, Protestant and Catholic.

"There's local news as well," Dr Casey continued, his voice dropping. "Edward Russell's back. Moved into Clonbarra House last week with his new English wife. Some colonel's daughter he met in London, by all accounts. She's already expecting."

Ellen felt a chill that had nothing to do with the March evening. Edward Russell – back in their village, back to the house where Isabella had grown up. The man who had arrested Seamus, who had watched her brother being dragged away to his death.

"His wife," Ellen said, cradling Bridget closer. "What's she like?"

Dr Casey shrugged. "Young thing. Very English, very proper. Doesn't seem to know much about her husband's... reputation here. Mrs Murphy delivered a basket of welcome goods from the Ladies' Committee, but the girl seemed nervous as a cat. Kept asking if it was safe to be living so far from London."

"What does that mean for us?" Ellen asked quietly, cradling Bridget closer. "For ordinary people just trying to live their lives? Especially with Edward Russell back in the big house."

Dr Casey shook his head sadly. "I don't know, Ellen. I truly don't. Russell's return... it's stirring up old resentments. People remember what happened to Seamus, to Isabella and Fintan. There's talk in the village." He met her eyes directly. "But whatever comes, you have each other. And now you have this little one to protect." He nodded, decisively, and wished them good night.

After the doctor and Mrs Murphy had gone, leaving Ellen and John alone with their daughter, they sat together in the quiet cottage as evening fell. "Do you think there really will be civil war?" Ellen asked eventually, watching Bridget sleep in her arms.

"I hope not. But I've seen the anger in men's eyes – on both sides. Collins believes the Treaty is the first step toward full independence. De Valera and his supporters see it as betrayal of everything we fought for. The gap between those positions..."

"... seems unbridgeable," Ellen finished sadly.

"Maybe. Or maybe sanity will prevail. Maybe they'll find a way to work together instead of tearing the country apart." John reached out to stroke Bridget's dark hair, so like Ellen's own. "She won't remember any of this, will she? The arguments, the divisions, the fear. By the time she's old enough to understand, maybe Ireland will have found its peace."

Ellen hoped he was right, but she couldn't shake the feeling that they were balanced on the edge of something terrible. The joy of Bridget's birth was already being shadowed by uncertainty about the future. About what kind of life they could build in a country that seemed determined to tear itself apart.

"I want her to be proud of being Irish," Ellen said. "Whatever Ireland becomes, whatever compromises we make or fights we must fight, I want her to know that her parents chose love over hate. Peace over war."

"She will," John promised, his arm tightening around Ellen's shoulders. "We'll make sure of it."

Ellen shifted carefully in bed, trying to find a comfortable position. Every muscle in her body ached, but Bridget was warm and perfect in her arms.

"Listen," John said.

Ellen tilted her head. Outside, she could hear Tom Clancy calling goodnight to someone. A door closing down the lane. The distant sound of a fiddle from the pub, playing something slow and sweet.

"It sounds so... normal," she whispered.

John moved a little, careful not to jostle them. "Maybe that's what we need to hold on to. The normal things. The good things."

Bridget stirred, making a small mewing sound. Ellen touched her daughter's cheek with one finger, marvelling at the softness of her skin.

"Do you think Edward Russell will cause trouble? Now that he's back?"

"I think Edward Russell has always caused trouble." John's voice was grim. "But we'll deal with whatever comes. We must."

Ellen looked down at Bridget's sleeping face. So peaceful, so unaware of the complicated world she'd been born into. "I want to tell her about Isabella someday. About who she was named for."

"We will. When she's old enough to understand." John reached out to stroke Bridget's dark hair again. "We'll tell her about all of them. The ones we lost, and why they died."

A log shifted in the fire, sending sparks up the chimney. Ellen could smell the turf smoke, could hear John's steady breathing beside her, could feel Bridget's tiny heartbeat against her chest. This moment – this was what mattered. Not the politics or the arguments or the fear of what might come.

"She's going to be stubborn. Look at that little chin."

John laughed quietly. "Gets it from her mother."

"And her father." Ellen smiled up at him. "Poor child doesn't stand a chance."

FORTY-ONE
NOW

"You need a break from all this," Conor said, surveying the chaos of documents spread across her cottage table. Empty coffee cups stood like sentinels among the papers, and Caitlin knew she looked as frazzled as she felt.

"I'm close to something. I can feel it." She pushed a strand of hair behind her ear, aware it had escaped her ponytail for the tenth time that morning.

"You've been saying that for a week." His voice was gentle but firm. "When's the last time you ate a proper meal? Or slept through the night?"

She opened her mouth to protest, then closed it. He wasn't wrong. The research had consumed her. She'd spent much of the last week online. Birth records, death certificates, newspaper archives that led nowhere. Harry Bennett had been avoiding the pub since their encounter, and even Delia seemed to have run out of stories.

"Come to Galway with me this weekend," Conor said. "Two days. We'll play tourist, eat too much, walk the promenade. Let your mind rest. Sometimes the answers come when you stop chasing them so hard."

"I can't just—"

"Yes, you can." He moved closer, his hands settling on her shoulders with familiar warmth. "The records will still be here Monday. But you're running yourself into the ground."

An hour later, Caitlin found herself packing an overnight bag, half convinced she'd lost her mind. Grammy's delighted texts didn't help:

> A WEEKEND AWAY?! With the physiotherapist?!
> Tell me EVERYTHING!

Conor picked Caitlin up on Saturday morning in his car, a thermos of coffee and fresh scones from the bakery already waiting. "Figured you'd skip breakfast," he said, handing her a scone still warm from the oven.

"You know me too well already." The words slipped out before she could catch them, but his pleased smile made her glad she hadn't.

The drive to Galway took them along the Wild Atlantic Way, the coastline spectacular in the morning light.

Standing at the edge of Europe, wind whipping her hair across her face, Caitlin felt something in her chest loosen. The Atlantic stretched endlessly before them, and for the first time in days, Ellen McGrath's mysteries seemed less urgent than the present moment.

"Terrifying, isn't it?" Conor said, his arm sliding around her waist as she peered over the edge.

"Beautiful," she corrected. "Beautiful and terrifying."

"Like most worthwhile things." He pressed a kiss to her temple, casual and sweet.

They reached Galway city by afternoon. Conor had booked rooms at a small hotel in the Latin Quarter – separate rooms, she noted with a mix of relief and something that might have been disappointment. The city buzzed with weekend energy: buskers on every corner, tourists mixing with locals, the smell of fish and chips competing with coffee and sea air.

"Right," Conor said, taking her hand as naturally as breathing. "First stop: proper Galway oysters. Then we'll walk the prom, maybe hit the Saturday market. Tonight there's trad music at Tig Cóilí if you're up for it."

"You've thought this through."

"I might have made a list." Colour pinked his cheeks. "Wanted to show you the best of it."

The oysters were briny and perfect, served with brown bread and butter at a tiny place overlooking the harbour. They walked the Salthill Promenade afterward, Conor pointing out the diving boards where locals swam year-round. "Mad eejits, every one of them."

At the market, he bought her a silver Claddagh ring from a local silversmith. "Tourist tradition," he said, but his eyes were serious as he explained the symbolism. "Crown for loyalty, hands for friendship, heart for love. How you wear it tells your status."

"How should I wear it?" The question came out barely above a whisper.

"Well, on the right hand with the heart pointing outward means you're single." He took her right hand, sliding the ring onto her finger with the heart pointing inward. "This way means someone holds your heart."

The weight of the moment settled between them. Caitlin looked at the ring, then up at him. "Conor—"

"No pressure," he said, quickly. "It's just... how I hope you might wear it. Eventually."

She turned the ring on her finger, feeling the smooth silver warm against her skin. "It's perfect."

That evening, they wandered Shop Street, stopping for fish and chips they ate while walking. Street musicians played everything from traditional reels to Ed Sheeran covers. Conor dropped coins in every hat, chatting with the performers in Irish.

"You know everyone," Caitlin observed.

"Galway's not that big. And musicians tend to know each other." He squeezed her hand. "I might have played a few street corners myself, back in the day."

"Now that I'd like to see."

"Careful what you wish for."

At Tig Cóilí, the music session was in full swing. They squeezed into a corner table, pints of Guinness appearing as if by magic. The crowd was younger than Tierney's, a mix of students and tourists and locals all drawn by the music.

"Dance?" Conor asked as a waltz began.

"Here? There's no room."

"There's always room for a waltz."

He led her into the small space between tables, other couples joining them.

They stayed until the music wound down after midnight. The walk back to the hotel was quiet, both of them content to let the night settle around them. At her door, Conor caught her hand.

"Thank you for coming with me," he said. "I know it wasn't easy to leave your research."

"You were right. I needed this." She looked down at the Claddagh ring, its heart pointing inward. "I needed... a lot of things I didn't know I needed." She hesitated for a second before saying, "I've changed my flight, taken advantage of the ninety days."

"That's made my evening." He kissed her then, deeply, with a hunger that matched her own. When they parted, both breathing hard, he pressed his forehead to hers.

"Breakfast tomorrow? The market does incredible crêpes."

"Breakfast," she agreed, though neither made any move to separate.

Finally, reluctantly, they said goodnight.

Inside her room, Caitlin touched her lips, still feeling the warmth of him. Her phone buzzed – Grammy, despite the time difference:

> The ring! I can see it in that last photo you sent! Heart pointing in! Oh darling, I'm so happy!

For once, Caitlin didn't roll her eyes at Grammy's matchmaking.

Sunday dawned clear and bright. They explored the cathedral, wandered the museum, took a boat trip to see the seals. Conor was patient when she stopped to photograph everything, amused when she tried to pronounce Irish place names, delighted when she laughed at his terrible jokes.

"I don't want to go back," she admitted as they drove home on Sunday evening, Galway disappearing behind them.

"We'll come again," he promised. "Often as you like."

"It's not just Galway." She watched the countryside flow past, searching for words. "It's... I forgot I could feel like this. Normal. Happy. Like someone who isn't broken."

He pulled over then, right there on the side of the road. "Listen to me," he said, taking her face in his hands. "You're not broken. Hurt, yes. Healing, definitely. But not broken. Never broken."

She kissed him for that, pouring gratitude and something deeper into the connection between them.

When they reached the cottage, her research still covered the table. But somehow it looked less daunting now. Less like an obsession and more like a puzzle she'd solve in time.

"Thank you," she said, as he helped her with her bag. "For the weekend. For knowing what I needed."

"Anytime." He touched the ring on her finger, smiled. "See you tomorrow? Beach walk before the tide comes in?"

"It's a date."

As his car disappeared down the lane, Caitlin stood in her doorway, watching stars emerge in the darkening sky. The weekend felt like a turning point – not just in her relationship with Conor, but in her relationship with herself. She was still searching for Ellen McGrath's truth, but maybe she was finding her own truth too.

Her phone rang. Grammy, of course.

"I need an update," her grandmother demanded. "Start with the ring and don't leave out a single detail."

For once, Caitlin was happy to oblige.

FORTY-TWO

JULY 1922

The baby fussed in Ellen's arms as she tried to balance the ledger, tiny fists waving with the same indignation Bridget had shown since birth. At four months old, she had opinions about everything: when to sleep, when to eat, and especially about being left with Mrs O'Brien while Ellen worked.

"Shh, love," Ellen murmured, bouncing her gently. "Mam has to finish these accounts."

Through the shop window, she could see Free State soldiers patrolling the main street. If this was safety, why did her stomach knot at Irish uniforms shouldering British rifles? John was somewhere among them, and still it looked wrong, like a suit that didn't fit.

The shop bell chimed. Sarah Tierney stepped inside, her face pale with worry. "Any word from John?" she asked, closing the door firmly behind her.

Ellen shook her head. "Nothing since last week. You'd think the Free State army would be better at getting messages through than the old IRA, wouldn't you?" She kept her voice light. "What about Brian? Any news from your father?"

Sarah's face tightened with worry. "Nothing from Brian either.

Da says they're probably together still: John and Brian both went with the same unit when they left. At least they can watch each other's backs." Sarah glanced around the empty shop before answering. "Da says the Free State troops are moving into Mayo proper. There's been fighting near Castlebar."

Proper fighting, not the little bursts Ellen had pretended not to hear about.

"Mrs Cassidy's boy was with the Anti-Treaty forces there. He's... he's not coming home."

Ellen felt Bridget's weight turn heavy in her arms, breakable as an egg. Another family destroyed. Another mother left to grieve.

Sarah's laugh was bitter. "Irish killing Irish. The British must be laughing themselves sick."

Before Ellen could respond, the shop door opened again. Edward Russell filled the doorway. Even without the uniform he carried himself like a man who expected people to take notice. Ellen's blood turned to ice. Edward Russell. In her shop. Her baby in her arms.

"Ladies." His voice carried that same cold politeness she remembered from childhood. "Miss McGrath, or should I say Mrs Power now?"

Ellen felt Sarah move closer, offering silent support. Bridget stirred, sensing her mother's tension. "Lord Russell." Ellen's voice came out steadier than she felt. "What can I do for you?"

Edward's pale eyes flicked to the baby, then around the shop with obvious disdain. "My wife has been craving chocolate. The pregnancy, you understand. I thought perhaps you might stock something suitable, though I suspect your... selection... is rather limited."

"I have some chocolate bars," Ellen said, gesturing to a small display near the counter. Her hands trembled as she reached for one. "Will this do?"

"It will have to, I suppose." Edward stepped closer to the counter, his gaze fixed on Bridget. "What a charming child. And what did you name her? I heard from the servants at the house that you chose something rather... sentimental."

Ellen's grip tightened on her daughter. "Bridget. Bridget Isabella."

"Isabella." Edward's smile was cold as winter. "How touching. You named your little tyke after my dead sister."

Ellen gasped. Sarah stepped forward, her face flushed with anger. "That's quite enough..."

"My wife, you see," Edward continued conversationally, "is expecting our first child. A son, God willing. A legitimate heir to Clonbarra House and all the Russell lands. A child with a name that opens doors. Not... obstacles." His pale eyes fixed on Bridget again.

"How is your wife settling in?" Ellen managed through gritted teeth, wrapping the chocolate with hands that shook.

"Quite well, thank you. She's thrilled about the baby, of course. A Russell heir at last." Edward's smile was predatory. "She finds it amusing that you named your... child... after Isabella."

"Bella was my friend," Ellen said through gritted teeth.

"Was she? How interesting." Edward leaned against the counter. "Because the people who killed her knew exactly where to find her, exactly when she'd be travelling that road. Almost as if they'd been... informed."

Time seemed to slow as Ellen realized what he was insinuating. Unbidden, her mind flashed to the warning Isabella had given her, about their being a mole in the village. And then, with a burst of horror that froze her blood, Ellen thought suddenly of a moment months before: Isabella falling silent mid-sentence when Patrick had entered the room. Had there been something wary in her eyes? Or was she just imagining things now, seeing ghosts in every gesture?

Ellen's hands stilled on the counter paper. "What are you suggesting?"

"I don't need to suggest." Edward's voice hardened. "My sister was murdered by Irish Republicans. The same Republicans who were guests in this very village. Who sat at local tables, shared local hospitality. Who perhaps even shared information with local... sympathizers."

Smoke. That's what it felt like in her chest, catching, stinging. Ellen forced herself to continue serving him, though her heart was hammering against her ribs. Seamus hadn't been caught up in it. Edward had used Isabella's death as an excuse to have Seamus killed.

"Your brother Patrick, for instance," Edward continued, his tone deliberately casual. "Quite the ardent Republican, wasn't he? Very well-connected with the IRA. And a local. One might even say he was in a position to know about Isabella's... activities."

"Patrick would never..." Ellen began, but Edward cut her off.

"Wouldn't he? A man who puts ideology before family?" Edward's smile was poisonous. "Such a person might easily convince himself that betraying one English spy was justified for the greater good."

Ellen felt the world tilt around her. "Isabella wasn't a spy for the English." She was so incensed that she didn't think before the next words left her mouth: "She supported Irish freedom!"

"Did she? Or was that simply what she told people?" Edward leaned closer. "You see, Ellen, my sister had many secrets. Some of them might surprise you. And some people knew those secrets. The question is, what did they do with that knowledge?"

Sensing her mother's distress, Bridget began to cry. Ellen bounced her automatically, her mind reeling. Was Edward implying that Isabella had been a double agent, and had been, in fact, working for the British? Or was he simply trying to cast doubt, to turn neighbours against each other?

Ellen placed the wrapped chocolate on the counter with deliberate control. "That'll be threepence."

Edward placed a shilling on the counter. "Keep the change. Consider it... charity. For the child's sake." His voice dripped with false concern.

"Get out," Sarah said, her voice low and dangerous.

"Certainly." Edward picked up his chocolate. "But, Mrs Power – or should I say Miss McGrath? – do remember what I said about being careful. About the company you keep. These are dangerous times for... irregular families."

He paused at the door, turning back with that cold smile. "Oh, and do give my regards to your brother Patrick. When you see him next, that is. I hear he's been keeping rather poor company lately."

The door closed behind him with a soft chime that sounded like a death knell. Ellen sank onto the stool behind the counter, her legs suddenly unable to support her.

Sarah knelt beside her. "Ellen, look at me. What he said about Isabella, about Patrick, you can't let him poison your mind like this."

Bridget began wailing in earnest, arching her back and screaming.

Sarah gently took Bridget from Ellen's trembling arms. "Come here to Auntie Sarah, little one." She studied the baby's face, her expression softening. "She has Seamus's eyes, so she does. That same bright spark when she's cross about something."

Tiredly, Ellen watched Sarah brush away a tear. "You see it too?"

"Course I do. God, I miss him. I miss the future we planned. Getting married, having a family." Sarah swallowed hard. "I miss Isabella too. I know I wasn't as close to her as you were. She hated Edward, didn't she? Said he was everything wrong with the Russells."

"She called him a poisonous toad once." Despite everything, Ellen almost smiled at the memory. "Made me swear not to tell anyone."

"Well, she was right. Look at him now, throwing around his cruel words." Sarah shifted Bridget to her shoulder, patting her back gently. "They'd both be so angry about what he said to you today. Seamus would have thrown him out bodily, and Isabella... she'd have found some way to make him regret every word."

Ellen stared at the coins Edward had left on the counter. "I don't know what to believe anymore. Everyone's lying to everyone else. How do we know what's true?"

"We know Edward Russell is a cruel man who enjoys hurting people," Sarah said. "We know he hated your family long before any of this political business started. Don't let him twist your thoughts about your own brother." Sarah handed a quieter Bridget back to her mam.

"But what if Patrick thought she was betraying Ireland?" Ellen's voice was barely a whisper. "What if he believed she was spying for the British? What if..." She couldn't finish the thought.

Bridget's cries were now hiccupping sobs. Ellen rocked her gently, trying to find comfort in her daughter's warm weight. But Edward's words echoed in her mind.

Ellen swallowed, and looked at her friend. "Sarah, if John doesn't come back, if something happens to him, will you help me with Bridget? Will you help me keep her safe?"

"Of course," Sarah replied fiercely. "But nothing's going to happen to John. Or to Brian. They're smart, and they're careful, and they're looking out for each other. They're coming home to us both."

Ellen nodded, though doubt gnawed at her like hunger. In this new Ireland they were building, nobody seemed safe. Not the Republicans fighting in the hills. Not the Free State soldiers trying to maintain order. Not the civilians caught between them. When the shooting stopped, there would be the counting – of the dead, the wounded, and the cost a civil war would leave behind.

What was truth now? What Edward said? What Patrick muttered in back rooms? What John couldn't write? Maybe trust was all anyone had left.

"I have to close early today." Standing carefully with Bridget still in her arms, she turned to Sarah. "Mrs O'Brien offered to mind the baby while I go to the church. I need to light a candle for John. For Brian. For all of them."

"I'll walk with you. These days, it's better not to be alone."

They locked the shop together and stepped into the summer heat. Down the street, Free State boys stopped neighbours and peered at papers, the glare of summer sunlight off their weapons forcing Ellen to squint.

FORTY-THREE
DECEMBER 1922

Ellen was feeding Bridget when she heard voices outside Tierney's pub. Not the usual evening chatter of farmers and merchants, but something harder. Angrier. She lifted the baby to her shoulder, patting her back gently as she moved to the window. Two figures stood in the lamplight by the pub entrance. Those shoulders, that stance – she'd know them anywhere. Her breath caught before her mind had even named him.

"John," she breathed. Bridget made a small sound of protest at being jostled, but Ellen barely noticed. She was already moving toward the door, her heart slamming so hard in her chest she thought he might hear it across the packed-earth yard that stretched between their cottage and the pub's back door.

Five months. Five months of no word, of fear gnawing at her every waking moment.

She pulled open the cottage door just as John looked up. Their eyes met across the small yard. For a second neither moved. Then he was striding toward her, his face gaunt with exhaustion and something darker.

"Ellen." His voice cracked on her name.

She wanted to throw herself into his arms, but Bridget was between them, and there was something in John's expression that made her hesitate. He looked older. Harder. His eyes were hooded now, more lined than she remembered, and it made her chest ache.

"You're home. You're safe." She muttered a quick prayer of thanks with a promise of a rosary later.

"Am I?" John's laugh held no humour. "Are any of us?"

Behind him, Sarah had emerged from the pub and was embracing a young man – Brian, it had to be her brother, Brian.

"Come inside," Ellen said. "Both of you. You look like you haven't eaten in days."

John reached out hesitantly to touch Bridget's head. "She's grown so much. God, Ellen, I've missed..." His voice broke entirely.

"I know." Ellen's throat was tight with unshed tears. "I know. Come in now."

Inside the small cottage, John sank into the chair by the fire like a man twice his age. Ellen settled Bridget in her basket and moved to the stove, her hands shaking as she prepared tea. Normal things. Domestic things. Maybe if she kept moving, kept doing, the distance between them would close.

She turned from the stove. "John. What happened?"

"Brian and I were sent home on leave. To wash, eat and rest for a bit."

She waited, sensing there was more, part of her knowing she didn't want to hear it.

He looked at her, and she flinched at the expression on his face. "We... we executed Liam Mellows." John's voice was flat. "Rory O'Connor. Dick Barrett. Joe McKelvey. Shot them in Mountjoy on the eighth of December."

"What do you mean, we? Liam was our friend, John. He came to our house, drank with Seamus and Patrick, argued with Da about Connolly's socialist ideas. You knew all those men."

"The orders came down from command. Reprisal executions, they called them."

Ellen's hands stilled on the teapot. "Reprisal for what?"

"Seán Hales was assassinated. Pro-Treaty TD."

Ellen frowned. "TD?"

"Member of the Dáil – the new parliament. He voted for the Treaty, same as most of them in Dublin. The Anti-Treaty IRA shot him for it and wounded Pádraic Ó Máille." John's laugh was bitter. "So our lot – the Free State – decided to execute four prisoners who had nothing to do with it. Just to send a message."

"But surely—"

"There's no 'surely' anymore, Ellen." John stood abruptly, pacing the small room like a caged animal. "Do you know what Mellows said before they shot him? He said he was dying for the Irish Republic. The same Republic we thought we were fighting for."

"John, you were fighting for the Free State. For peace. For—"

"For what? For the right to execute our own people? For the right to do the British's work for them?" He raked both hands through his dark hair. "God Almighty, Ellen, what have we become?"

The cottage door opened. Sarah entered with Brian. The resemblance to Frank made Ellen's throat tighten – same jaw, same brow – but the eyes... haunted, nothing like his father's.

"How are you, Ellen?" Brian's voice was hoarse. "Sarah's told me about the baby. She's beautiful."

"Thank you." Ellen poured tea for all of them, her movements automatic. "Will you sit and have a cup?"

Even as she spoke, she couldn't believe the words coming out of her mouth. How was tea meant to comfort men who had been made to kill their own countrymen – friends they'd once fought beside?

"We thought we were bringing order." Slumping back into his chair, John continued, "We thought we were ending the war. But it's not war anymore, Ellen. It's... something else. Something uglier."

Sarah moved to stand behind her brother's chair, resting her hands on his shoulders.

"Tell them about Mayo."

Brian's face darkened. "The Anti-Treaty forces took Ballina in

September. Overran the garrison, seized seventeen thousand pounds from the bank. We were sent to pursue them into the Ox Mountains." He paused, staring into his teacup. "Seven of our lads died at Glenamoy. Killed by other Irishmen. Seven boys I'd trained with, eaten with, shared cigarettes with. Cut down in an ambush."

"And then?" Ellen asked.

"Then we were ordered to burn farmhouses. Anyone suspected of helping the irregulars." Brian's voice shook. "Families turned out into the winter cold because their son might have passed information to the Anti-Treaty men."

Ellen felt sick. She turned to John. "You didn't—"

"We followed orders. We told ourselves it was necessary. That it would end the war faster. Save lives in the long run." He looked up at Ellen, his brown eyes full of pain. "Do you know what that makes us?"

The words hung in the air.

"It makes you human," Ellen said, after a moment. "It makes you men trying to do right in a world gone mad."

"Does it?" John smiled bitterly. "When Mellows was executed, half the lads cheered. Said he got what he deserved for betraying Ireland. The other half... the other half looked sick. Like they were seeing themselves in that prison yard."

Bridget stirred in her basket, making small mewing sounds. Ellen went to her automatically, lifting her daughter and settling back into her chair.

"What happens now?" Sarah asked.

"Now we try to pretend we're still the same people we were before," Brian said. "We try to pretend we didn't do the things we did. We try to build something decent on foundations of blood."

"The war can't last much longer," Ellen said desperately. "Surely people will see sense. Surely—"

"The war will last as long as there are men willing to die for their version of Ireland," John interrupted. "And there seem to be plenty of those."

Ellen rocked Bridget gently, humming under her breath. Such

a simple thing, comforting a baby. Such a normal, human thing. Why couldn't the rest of the world be this simple?

And then something rose slithering in her mind, breaking her fragile domestic care: "John, Edward Russell's back. Did you... did you hear anything while you were away? About Patrick? About what really happened to Isabella?"

Asking the question, the memory of another night clicked into her mind: Isabella's hurried goodbye, Patrick's sharp voice in the other room, the slammed door. At the time, she'd thought it was another row about tactics. But now...

"Russell came to the shop months back. He... he said things. About Patrick knowing too much about Isabella's movements. About him being in a position to... to inform on her." Ellen's voice dropped to barely a whisper. "I keep thinking about it. Wondering if it's true."

John's face turned white, then red with fury. "What? Patrick would never—" John began, but Brian cut him off.

"Patrick's with the irregulars now," Brian said. "We heard talk. He's operating somewhere in the Connemara hills with one of the flying columns."

Ellen's heart clenched. "Is he safe? Do you know if he's—"

"Safe?" Brian's laugh was bitter. "We're not burying our enemies now, Ellen. We're burying each other. None of them are safe. They're living like animals in the mountains, raiding and running, never knowing if the next farmhouse they approach will shelter them or betray them to us."

"I should have been here," John said through gritted teeth. "I should have been here to protect you."

"You were doing your duty," Ellen said. "For Ireland. For all of us."

"Was I? Or was I just too much of a coward to stay and face the real fight?" John stood again, his restless energy filling the small space. "Maybe Patrick was right. Maybe the real war is here, in places like this, against people like Edward Russell."

"Don't," Ellen said sharply. "Don't start thinking like that. That way lies madness."

"Maybe madness is all we have left," Brian said. "Maybe that's what this country has driven us to."

The fire crackled in the grate, shadows twitching along the walls as if even the cottage couldn't keep still. Outside, snow had begun to fall, dusting the windows with white. Winter had come early to Clonbarra.

FORTY-FOUR

NOW

The storm had been building all afternoon, dark clouds rolling in from the Atlantic like an advancing army. Caitlin had watched it approach from the cottage window, hoping it would pass harmlessly out to sea. Instead, it seemed to have settled directly over Ballycluan, as if the weather itself was conspiring to trap her with her thoughts.

Wind howled around the cottage corners with increasing ferocity, rattling the shutters and sending rain against the windows like thrown pebbles. The old stone walls felt solid enough, but the constant battering was getting to her nerves. Her manila folder sat on the table, filled with the information Grammy had given her, photographs from Delia, notes and other paperwork she may need to prove her case to Mrs Walsh at the convent.

She'd been pacing the small living room for over an hour, unable to settle to reading or research, her mind drawing continually back to Harry Bennett.

She hadn't been able to make contact with him, though she'd wanted to these last few days, and had asked around to see if anyone could help her. Someone had seen him packing up his car and heading away. The old man's reaction to Seán's name had been so visceral, so immediate. There was something that had drained the colour from his age-worn face and sent him shuffling away with warnings about leaving old rocks unturned. She wondered if he had been deliberately avoiding her since then and, if so, why.

As she paced, the power flickered once, twice, then died completely.

Darkness swallowed the cottage whole. The familiar shapes of furniture vanished, leaving her disoriented in what had moments before been a cosy refuge. Outside, the storm seemed to intensify, as if the darkness had given it permission to unleash its full fury.

The howling wind began to change, morphing in her mind into something else entirely. The wail of sirens. The screech of tyres on wet pavement. The rain hammering against the roof transformed, each droplet becoming the sharp crack of gunfire.

No. Not here. Not now.

But her mind was already spiralling backward to Charleston. The warehouse district on that rain-soaked night. Mark's voice in her earpiece, calm and reassuring: "This way. I've got eyes on the target."

She was back there suddenly, completely. The weight of her service weapon in her hand. Nemo's warm presence beside her, his training keeping him alert but controlled. The other officers moving through the shadows – Rhodes with his easy grin, Dunn with her meticulous attention to detail, Foster who'd been just six months from retirement.

All dead now. All because she'd trusted Mark Stanton.

Now, Caitlin fumbled for her phone, hands shaking as she activated its torch button. The small beam of light pushed back the darkness but couldn't touch the memories flooding through her. She needed candles, needed proper light to ground herself in the present.

The phone's light revealed the kitchen counter where she'd seen a collection of candles earlier. She stumbled toward them, her injured leg protesting the uneven gait her panic had caused. Her hands shook so badly she could barely grip the matches, and the first few broke before she managed to light one.

The flame caught, casting dancing shadows that only made everything worse. In the flickering light, the dark shapes seemed to move, to hide threats that her cop's instincts insisted were there.

A pounding at the door made her jump, her body automatically reaching for the weapon she no longer carried. Her heart slammed against her ribs as she froze, listening.

"Caitlin! It's Conor! Are you okay?"

Relief flooded through her so suddenly her knees nearly buckled. She hurried to the door, her hands clumsy with the unfamiliar locks.

Conor stood on the threshold, dripping from the short run up the path. His hair was plastered to his forehead, rainwater streaming off his jacket. Even with the car parked right outside, the downpour had soaked him in seconds.

"Power's out all over Ballycluan," he said, stepping inside and immediately closing the door against the driving rain. "I was concerned about you being out here alone in this."

He took in her appearance – the candle clutched in her trembling hand, her pale face stark in the flickering light, the way she stood as if braced for attack.

"Jesus, Caitlin. What's wrong? You look like you've seen a ghost."

And suddenly, she couldn't hold it back anymore. The careful walls she'd built around the truth crumbled like sand castles before a tide.

"His name was Mark Stanton. Detective Mark Stanton, Charleston PD. My partner for three years, my... my boyfriend for one of them." The words tasted bitter. "I thought I knew him. Thought I loved him. Thought he loved me."

Conor's hands stilled on his wet jacket. She watched something shift in his expression – not judgement, but the natural human recoil when confronted with violence so close to home. Then he seemed to collect himself, shrugging out of his jacket and guiding her to the sofa. He lit more candles while she talked, creating a circle of warm light that made confession feel possible.

"We got a tip about a major drug shipment coming through the warehouse district. Big enough to make careers, Mark said. Big enough to clean up that whole section of the city." Caitlin's voice grew distant, mechanical. "There were five of us on the team. Rhodes, Dunn, Foster, me and Nemo."

"Nemo?"

"My K-9 partner. A German shepherd, five years old. He had the best nose in the department." Her voice cracked slightly. "Best dog I ever knew."

The storm continued its assault on the cottage, but inside the circle of candlelight, the world had narrowed to just this moment, this confession she'd never made to anyone.

"Mark was team leader. He'd done the reconnaissance, planned the approach, coordinated with the DEA. We trusted him completely. Why wouldn't we? He was a good cop, had a stellar record, was being fast-tracked for promotion to lieutenant."

Conor settled beside her on the sofa, close enough to offer comfort but not so close as to crowd her. His presence was steady, patient, the kind of calm that invited honesty.

"The plan was solid. Simple. Surround the warehouse, wait for the handoff, then move in. But when we got there, it felt wrong. Nemo was agitated, kept looking around like he sensed something off. I should have listened to him."

"What happened?"

"Mark said he'd spotted movement on the east side, that we needed to reposition. His voice in my earpiece: 'This way. I've got eyes on the target.' I was so trusting. So *stupid*." Caitlin's hands clenched in her lap. "He led us straight into an ambush."

The memory unfolded in brutal detail. The sudden explosion of gunfire from multiple directions. The realization that they'd been expected, that someone had warned the dealers. Rhodes going down first, then Dunn. Foster trying to reach cover that wasn't there.

"I was pinned behind a shipping container with Nemo. Bullets everywhere, my team screaming for backup that wasn't coming because our radios were being jammed. And then I saw Mark."

She forced herself to continue. "He was with them. With the dealers. Standing calm as anything while my friends died, talking on a satellite phone, coordinating the whole thing."

Conor's intake of breath was sharp. He opened his mouth as if to say something, then closed it again, clearly struggling to process the magnitude of such betrayal.

"That's when I understood. This wasn't some operation gone wrong. This was execution. Mark had sold us out, probably been selling information for months, maybe years. And now he was cleaning house, eliminating the cops who might have gotten too close."

The worst part came next, the part that still woke her screaming.

"One of the shooters had flanked my position. I didn't see him until it was too late. He had a clear shot, and I was reloading. Nemo..." Her voice broke entirely. "Nemo saw him first. Launched himself right at the gunman just as he fired. The bullet that was meant for my head caught Nemo in the chest instead."

Tears streamed down her face now, months of held grief finally finding release. "He died in my arms. Kept trying to lick my face even as the blood... even as he..."

Conor's arm came around her shoulders, solid and warm. "I'm sorry. God, Caitlin, I'm so sorry."

"If I'd been paying attention, if I'd noticed the signs, they'd all still be alive. Rhodes had two kids. Dunn was getting married in the fall. Foster was six months from retirement, had a cabin picked out in the mountains. Nemo was just five years old. They died because I was too blind to see what Mark really was."

"No." Conor's voice was firm. "They died because Mark Stanton was a corrupt cop who betrayed his oath and his team. Not because you missed some invisible signs."

"But I should have known. I was sleeping with him, for God's sake. How do you miss that the person sharing your bed is planning to murder you and your friends?"

"Did you know what he was planning?"

"No, but—"

"Did you have any reason to suspect him? Any concrete evidence that he was dirty?"

"No, but I should have—"

"How?" Conor turned to face her fully, his voice cutting through her self-recrimination with startling directness. "Were you supposed to be psychic? To assume every fellow officer was a killer? How exactly were you meant to know?"

The questions hung in the candlelit air. For the first time since that terrible night Caitlin found herself considering them, instead of drowning in guilt and what-ifs.

"In the investigation afterward," she continued quietly, "they found evidence that Mark had been feeding information to the Ramirez cartel for over two years. Bank accounts in the Caymans, coded communications, the whole thing. Internal Affairs said there was no way anyone could have detected it – he was too careful, too smart."

"And you don't believe them—?"

"I want to believe them. But how do you trust your own judgement after something like that? How do you trust anyone?" She looked at him in the flickering candlelight. "How do I know you're not just another Mark Stanton, telling me what I want to hear?"

Instead of being offended, Conor nodded thoughtfully. "You don't. Not completely. Trust has to be earned back slowly, piece by piece. And it's okay to be cautious." His honesty was somehow more reassuring than any protestations of innocence would have been. "Is that why you came to Ireland? To get away from all of it?"

"Partly. I still have panic attacks sometimes – like tonight – but I haven't had one since I've been over here. I guess getting away from it has worked – being here must be doing me good. But mostly I came because Grammy asked me to. She wanted answers about her family before…" Caitlin's voice trailed off.

Outside, the storm was beginning to ease slightly, the wind's howl diminishing to a steadier rush. The rain still drummed against the windows, but with less violence.

"It's just so frustrating that I can't find anyone to talk to me. Particularly about Seán." Caitlin shook her head. "Why won't Harry? He obviously knows something."

"Maybe Harry's just an old man who's seen too much," Conor suggested. "Small towns have long memories. Could be your grammy's brother Seán was involved in something political, something that still stirs up strong feelings."

"You think I'm reading too much into it? Seeing mysteries where there aren't any?"

"I think you're someone who's been trained to look for patterns, to suspect the worst-case scenario. It's kept you alive, but it's also making it hard for you to just let things be what they are."

Caitlin considered this. "Grammy used to say I was too suspicious for my own good. Even as a kid."

"She sounds like a smart woman, your Grammy."

They sat in comfortable silence for a while, listening to the storm outside. The candles had burned down considerably, casting longer shadows but somehow making the cottage feel more like a refuge than a trap.

"Thank you," Caitlin said. "For listening. For not trying to fix everything or tell me it wasn't that bad."

"It was that bad." He held her gaze without wavering, his jaw set with quiet conviction. One hand rested on the sofa between them, not reaching for her, but there if she needed it. "What happened to you was horrible, and the fact that you survived it says how strong you are. But surviving doesn't mean you have to carry all the blame forever."

"How do you know so much about survival?"

"Because I've had to learn to forgive myself for things too. Different things, but the principle's the same. At some point, you have to choose between carrying the guilt forever or trying to build something new."

"Is that what you did? Built something new?"

"I'm still working on it." He stood up, moving to look out the window. "Storm's passing. I should probably head back to town before the roads flood completely."

"You could stay." The words were out before Caitlin could stop them. "I mean, if the roads are dangerous."

Conor turned back to her and, in the candlelight, his expression was gentle but careful. "Are you sure? After everything you just told me?"

She thought about it seriously. The old Caitlin would have said no, would have barricaded herself behind walls of suspicion and self-protection. But maybe Grammy was right. Maybe not everyone was Mark.

"I'm sure. At least, I think I am. And that's probably as close to trust as I can manage right now."

"Then I'll stay. I'll take the sofa. You can lock your door if that helps you rest easier."

She thought about this, and the idea did make her feel safer. Not because she didn't trust him, but because he understood why she might need those barriers, and he wasn't offended by them.

After they had settled for the night – Conor with blankets on the sofa, Caitlin in the bedroom with the door closed but not locked – she realized something had shifted. The story was finally out, shared with someone who hadn't tried to minimize it or fix her or tell her to get over it.

She moved to the bedroom window, listening to the storm ease as it moved on toward the mainland. Only gentle rain and the ocean's rhythm remained.

Through the glass, she could see that Conor had yet to blow out the candles: the cottage was surrounded by a circle of candlelight they'd created together – a small sanctuary against the darkness.

FORTY-FIVE

MAY 1923

The ceasefire came not with celebration but with an exhausted sigh that pressed against Ellen's chest. She stared at the words in the *Tribune* while Bridget babbled at her feet, knocking wooden blocks together. "Dumping of arms," the paper called it – an order from Frank Aiken, the IRA's Chief of Staff, to end the fight without surrender.

"It's over. It's *over*," she repeated to herself. John had gone to help Frank Tierney move barrels in the pub cellar. "The war is over, *a stór*."

Bridget looked up at her mother's voice, clapped her hands, and went back to her blocks. For her, this moment was no different from any other – just Mam sitting in the chair by the window, sunlight streaming across the stone floor, the smell of bread rising in the kitchen.

But Ellen felt the weight of it. No more raids. No more ambushes. No more young men dying for their version of Ireland. The guns were silent at last.

She folded the newspaper carefully and set it aside. Outside, Clonbarra looked the same as it had for months: Free State soldiers still patrolled, though less frequently now. Shop windows still bore the cracks from stones thrown during the worst of the fighting. But there was something different in the air. A loosening. People walked less hurriedly, looked over their shoulders less often.

A motorcar rattled past on the village road, its engine growl carrying on the wind. Ellen froze. For the briefest instant, she was back outside O'Sullivan's the morning Isabella stepped down, cheeks flushed, Fintan's hand lingering on hers. The memory hit like a blow, sharp and unexpected, and she bit her lip to stop the sob.

If Isabella had lived, would she still have laughed so boldly at danger? What would she have made of Irish fighting Irish?

The cottage door creaked open. John stepped inside, and the sight of his tight jaw made her stomach drop. Even with peace declared, he carried the war in with him.

"You've heard?" Ellen asked.

"Yes." He slumped into the chair across from her. "It's done. Officially, anyway."

"You don't sound pleased."

John's gaze stayed fixed on Bridget stacking her blocks, but his eyes were shadowed. "I keep thinking about the lads who'll never see this day. Families torn apart. For what? So we could learn to hate each other instead of the British?"

"I was thinking of what Isabella would have made of it. But she'd have told us we have to make the best of things." Ellen reached across the space between their chairs and took his hand. "For this," she said, nodding toward Bridget. "So she can grow up Irish and free, even if it's not the Ireland any of us dreamed of."

"Aye, maybe." John squeezed her fingers. "Brian says there's talk of an amnesty. Men coming down from the mountains, putting away their guns for good."

"And Patrick?"

John's face darkened. "No word. But, Ellen... when he does come back, if he comes back, he won't be the same man who left. None of them will be."

A knock at the door interrupted them. Sarah entered without waiting for an answer, her face flushed with excitement and worry in equal measure. "They're saying Patrick's been seen. Tom Clancy spotted him near the old quarry road this morning. He looked... rough, Tom said. Thin and wild."

Ellen's heart leaped and sank simultaneously. "Coming home?"

"Hard to say. You know how Patrick is about pride." Sarah glanced between Ellen and John. "Edward Russell's been asking questions in the village. About Patrick specifically. About where he might surface when the war ends."

John's jaw tightened. "What kind of questions?"

"The kind that make people nervous," Sarah said, grimly. "He's not letting old grudges die with the ceasefire."

Days later, Ellen was collecting eggs from the henhouse at the back of Tierney's pub. The morning air still held a chill, though the sun was climbing above the thatched roofs of the village. The henhouse stood at the far edge of the yard that stretched to the pub's back door, its boards dark with last night's rain.

Looking up, she saw a gaunt figure walking down the lane that ran along the side of the pub, its surface churned to mud by cart wheels and boots. The man was tall, broad-shouldered, but moving with the careful gait of a man who'd learned to expect ambush around every corner. She knew that walk.

"Patrick."

He looked up at her voice, and Ellen's breath caught. Sarah had been right – he looked rough. His dark hair was longer than she'd ever seen it, his face thin with hunger and sleepless nights. His clothes hung loose on his frame, and there was something feral in his green eyes.

For an instant she glimpsed the boy who once baited her fishing hook, who held her hand at Da's grave. The image shattered, leaving only this hard-eyed stranger before her.

"Ellen." His voice was hoarse, as if he'd forgotten how to speak to family.

She wanted to run to him, to embrace him despite all the harsh words between them. But the look in his eyes rooted her where she stood. This wasn't the Patrick who had left Clonbarra to fight for the Republic. This was someone harder, dangerous.

"You look well," he said, though his eyes were fixed on Bridget, who had toddled out of the cottage, and was staring at this stranger with frank curiosity. Behind her, the cottage's whitewashed walls gleamed in the morning light, smoke rising from the chimney to join the haze from other hearths throughout Clonbarra.

"She's got Mam's eyes, hasn't she? And a bit of Seamus about the chin."

"She's grown. She's walking now. Talking a bit. And she loves animals, just like Seamus did – follows the chickens around the yard, tries to pet every dog she sees."

Patrick's face softened for just a moment. "Does she now?" He moved closer. "The war's over."

"I heard. Will you... will you stay now? Come home properly? Go back to farming Da's – I mean, your tenancy?"

Pain flickered across Patrick's face. "Home," he repeated, as if the word had lost all meaning. "Aye, perhaps. If there's still a place for me."

"Of course there is. You're my brother, Patrick. You're family."

"Am I?" His smile was bitter. "After everything I've done? Everything I've become?"

Before Ellen could answer, another figure stepped out of O'Sullivan's shop across the lane and walked toward them. Edward Russell, immaculate as always despite the spring mud, walking with the confident stride of a man who owned everything he surveyed.

Patrick saw him. Went very still. Ellen felt the air between them crackle with old hatred, fresh and sharp as broken glass.

"Well, well," Edward called as he approached. "Patrick McGrath. I wondered when you'd crawl out of whatever hole you've been hiding in."

"Russell." Patrick's voice was flat, but Ellen could see his hands clenching into fists.

Edward stopped a few yards away, his pale eyes bright with malice. "Enjoying the peace, are we? Must be strange, having nothing left to fight for. No more glorious cause to justify your... activities."

"The cause isn't dead," Patrick said. "Just... sleeping."

"Is it? How touching." Edward's smile was cold. "Tell me, do *you* sleep well these days? Or do you dream about the people you betrayed?"

Ellen stepped forward, Bridget in her arms. "That's enough. The war's over. Leave him be."

"Oh, but I'm not talking about the war," Edward said, his gaze never leaving Patrick's face "I'm talking about my poor, misguided sister."

Patrick paled. "What are you saying?"

"I'm saying you took the bait beautifully," Edward said conversationally. "I'd known for weeks what she was doing. One of my officers passed her a harmless report about a munitions convoy near Clifden. When the ambush came exactly where I said it would, her guilt was certain. But I didn't accuse her. Oh no. I let the story take a different path. I let word slip that she'd been feeding the British information – that the IRA gunmen she drank tea with were dying because of her loose tongue. You were so eager to protect your cause that you didn't stop to ask who started the whispers."

The words hit Patrick like physical blows. Ellen watched in horror as understanding dawned in her brother's eyes.

"You... you *lied*? Isabella was never—"

"A spy?" Edward laughed. "Good God, no. My sister was many things – foolish, idealistic, romantically involved with Irish rebels – but she was no double agent. She really did support your precious cause." His voice dropped. "And you killed her for it."

The silence stretched between them. Ellen could hear her own heartbeat, could hear Bridget's soft breathing against her shoulder. Somewhere in the distance, a dog barked. It couldn't be true.

Patrick couldn't have done this. But deep down she knew. Isabella was gone because of him, and Seamus because of what followed.

Patrick swayed on his feet. "No. No, that's not... I never meant..."

"Didn't you?" Edward's voice was gentle now, almost kind. "You passed the information along, didn't you? Told your Republican friends that there was a British spy operating in the area. Told them exactly where she'd be and when. What did you think would happen, tell me that?"

"You bastard," Patrick breathed. "You murdering bastard."

"I never laid a hand on Isabella," Edward said. "I didn't need to. I had you to do it for me. Pity Seamus got the blame," he added softly. "Collateral damage, I suppose." Patrick lunged forward with a roar of rage and anguish. Ellen screamed. Edward stepped back, his hand moving to something at his side. A pistol, Ellen realized with horror.

But before either man could strike, John had burst through the pub's back door. He must have heard the shouting while helping Frank set up for the day as he was still wearing his work apron. He placed himself between them.

Sarah was close behind, also coming from the pub, and she moved to Ellen's side, her hand pressed to her mouth.

"Patrick, no!" John's voice was sharp with command. "The war's over! You can't—"

"Get out of my way, John," Patrick snarled, his face twisted with grief and fury. "This isn't about the war. This is about Isabella. This is about justice."

"This is about murder," John said. "And I won't let you become a murderer. Not for him. Not for anyone."

Patrick's hand moved to his jacket. The glint of metal. A gun. He'd kept one despite the agreement to the dumping of arms.

"He used me," Patrick said, his voice breaking. "He used me to kill an innocent girl. Isabella died because of me, because of lies he fed me about her being a spy."

"I know," John said, his voice gentle now. "I know, and I'm

sorry. But killing him won't bring her back. It'll only make you the thing he says you are."

"Maybe that's what I deserve to be."

"It's not what Isabella would want," John said. "You know it's not."

For a moment, Patrick wavered. Ellen held her breath, praying that John's words would reach whatever was left of her brother's humanity.

Then Edward spoke again. "How sweet," he drawled. "The rebels comforting each other. Tell me, McGrath – when you close your eyes at night, do you see her face? Do you see Isabella's terror when your Republican friends came for her?"

Patrick's control snapped entirely. The gun came up, aimed straight at Edward's chest.

"Patrick, don't!" John threw himself forward just as Patrick's finger tightened on the trigger.

The shot cracked the air wide open. Birds tore screaming from the trees. Bridget's wail pierced through the ringing in Ellen's ears.

John staggered backward, his hand pressed to his chest. Blood seeped between his fingers. Dark and wet against his white shirt.

"John!" The scream ripped from her throat, leaving her chest burning.

He looked at her, surprise written across his face.

No, this can't be happening. Not John. Not here. Not now. I can't lose him.

Then his knees buckled. He hit the ground hard, his breathing shallow and rapid.

Ellen shoved Bridget into Sarah's arms and dropped beside John. Blood pulsed hot between her fingers as she pressed down hard, but it kept coming, slicking her hands, slipping away no matter how she fought to hold it in.

"No, no, no," she begged. "John, stay with me. Stay with me, love."

His eyes locked on hers, clear for a fleeting heartbeat. "Ellen," he rasped. "Take care of... take care of..."

Her breath caught, willing the words not to end there. "Don't you dare," she choked out. "Don't leave Bridget."

But his eyes were already growing distant. The blood between her fingers was slowing. The man she loved, the father of her child, the only good thing to come out of all this war and hatred, was dying in her arms because her brother couldn't let go of his rage.

"You killed him!" Looking up at Patrick, she screamed at him. "You *killed* him."

Patrick stood frozen, the smoking gun still in his hand, his face a mask of horror. "I didn't mean... I was aiming for Russell. John got in the way."

"But you fired!" The words burst out, rising to a shriek. "You fired the gun! You pulled the trigger! You killed him!" Her whole body shook with it, her throat raw, hands still dripping red.

Edward Russell had backed away during the chaos, his pale face gleaming with satisfaction despite the blood on his hands. "Murder," he said. "Plain and simple murder. The war may be over, but some of us remember."

"Get away from here," Sarah snarled at him. "Get away before I find a gun of my own."

Edward tipped his hat mockingly. "I'll be sure to report this incident to the proper authorities. I'm sure they'll be very interested in how the ceasefire is being observed."

He walked away whistling, leaving behind him a family destroyed, a good man dead, and a peace that would never feel clean again.

Sarah held the crying child close, rocking her with trembling hands as Ellen screamed and screamed.

FORTY-SIX

NOW

The rental car's engine ticked as it cooled in the empty car park beside what had once been Tierney's pub. Caitlin sat for a moment, her hands gripping the steering wheel, staring at the building that now housed a petrol garage and shop.

"This is it?" Conor asked from the passenger seat, his voice carrying a note of disappointment. "This is where your great-grandmother lived?"

Caitlin pulled the manila folder from the backseat. "This was Tierney's pub. An uncle of Delia's husband, or grand-uncle, I think. A different branch of the family. According to the plans, O'Sullivan's shop where Ellen worked was somewhere over there." Caitlin pointed to a row of small, modern houses.

She opened the folder carefully, withdrawing a sepia-toned photograph dated 1921. In it, a group of women stood outside Tierney's pub, their shawls and long skirts marking them as belonging to another era entirely. One woman held a banner reading "NO CONSCRIPTION." Once again, Caitlin squinted at the faces – but the photo was just a little too blurred to be sure if one might be Ellen.

"Look at this one," she said, passing Conor a more recent

photograph from the 1960s. "You can see how the village was laid out then."

The black and white image showed a proper Irish village. Thatched cottages lined a main street, with shop fronts visible: O'Sullivan's Provisions, Murphy's Goods, and Tierney's pub sign swinging in the breeze. Children played in the road, horses and carts stood beside more modern vehicles. A church spire rose in the background with an open field beside it, and smoke curled from chimneys in the traditional pattern that spoke of families gathered around turf fires. Narrow lanes branched off between buildings, leading to unseen cottages and farms beyond.

Conor compared it to the scene before them. Where the photograph showed a bustling village centre, they now faced a mostly empty stretch of road. The cottages that had once flanked it were gone. In their place stood modern bungalows with satellite dishes and manicured gardens that spoke of weekend residents rather than farming families.

"It's like someone took the soul out of the place," Conor said.

They climbed out of the car and walked slowly down what had been Clonbarra's main street, Caitlin consulting the photographs like a treasure map. "O'Sullivan's shop should have been here," she said, stopping in front of a modern convenience store with a Coca-Cola sign and lottery advertisements in the window.

An elderly man emerged from the store, setting out a rack of newspapers. He glanced curiously at the two visitors studying their old photographs.

"You're looking for something in particular?" he asked, his accent carrying the musical lilt of rural Galway.

"We're trying to find where my family lived," Caitlin explained. "My great-grandmother was Ellen McGrath, later Ellen Power. She lived here in the early 1920s."

The man's face lit up with interest. "McGrath, you say? And Power? Well now, those are names with history in these parts." He gestured toward the photographs in Caitlin's hands. "What have you got there?"

Caitlin showed him the village photographs, and the man nodded approvingly. "That's Clonbarra alright, though it looks different now, doesn't it? I'm Michael Murphy. That's my shop you're standing in front of. My grandfather used to tell stories about the old days."

"Do you know anything about the McGrath family?" Conor asked.

Michael's expression grew more serious. "They were caught up in the troubles of those years – the War of Independence, then the Civil War after. Political family, you might say. And there was tragedy enough: the whole lot scattered or dead before peace ever came."

They followed Michael as he walked toward the church, pointing out landmarks as they went. "Now that church there, that's original. Father Murphy who served in your great-grandmother's time, he's buried in the graveyard behind it. The church itself hasn't changed much, though they've modernized the interior."

The grey stone church sat on a small hill overlooking the village, its simple lines speaking of rural Irish Catholicism. The graveyard beside it was older still, with Celtic crosses marking graves that dated back centuries. Newer headstones in dark granite stood alongside limestone markers whose inscriptions had been softened by decades of rain.

"The McGrath family plot is over there," Michael said, pointing toward a section near the back wall. "Though I don't think all of them made it back here for burial."

They found the graves easily enough. A small family plot with simple headstones. "Paddy and Mary McGrath." "Seamus McGrath, 1899–1921." "Patrick McGrath, 1896–1951."

But no Ellen.

They came across a grave for John Power, 1899–1923. Caitlin put her hand on the stone, her throat tightening. "Grammy's father," she whispered. "He died so young, just twenty-four."

Caitlin and Conor exchanged a look, but their guide continued talking.

"The old cottage where the McGrath family lived is gone," Michael continued, leading them back away from the village centre over a small incline and through a crossroads. "Nobody lived in it after the war. Fell into ruin in the 1930s, finally demolished in the 1970s when they put in the new housing estate." He pointed toward a cluster of modern homes with red tile roofs. "But if you want to see where it stood, there's still the foundation stones in the field behind those houses."

They walked through the estate, past trimmed lawns and children's bicycles, until they reached a stone wall at the back. Beyond it lay an overgrown field.

"That one there." Michael pointed to foundations about fifty yards away. "That would have been the McGrath place. You can still see where the garden was if you know what to look for." He nodded. "Right, must get on. I'll leave you to it. But if you'd like a drink or anything, please call back into the shop." He tipped his cap and walked back toward his store.

Caitlin climbed over the wall, her trainers slipping on the damp stone. The field smelled of wild grass and sheep, with the faint sweetness of gorse blooming along the hedgerows. She walked carefully toward the foundations, Conor following behind.

The stones that had once formed the walls of Ellen's home were gone now, but the outline was clear enough. Caitlin knelt and touched the limestone, trying to imagine her great-grandmother here: cooking over a turf fire, caring for her brothers, watching for news of the war that was tearing Ireland apart. She twisted the Claddagh ring on her finger, thinking of all the love stories that had begun and ended in this place.

"It's smaller than I expected," Caitlin said, pacing out the dimensions. "The whole house couldn't have been more than three rooms."

"Times were different then," Conor replied, looking around him. "People expected less. Look at that massive tree." He pointed to a huge oak behind where the cottage would have stood. "It looks old enough to have been here in their time."

Caitlin didn't let him finish; she was already striding toward the tree. She needed a little bit of space to swallow her tears. Sadness clung here like morning mist.

Conor seemed to sense her need for quiet. She sat in a spot overlooking the village while he examined the tree.

A few minutes later, he had to speak: "Caitlin, look at this."

She caught the emotion in his voice. Getting up and brushing dirt from her hands, she moved closer to where he stood by the ancient oak.

There in the bark, worn but still clearly visible, were carved initials: JP + E McG with a carving of a lark underneath. The letters were deep, cut with care. Time had darkened them, and the bark had grown and stretched around the marks, but they remained legible. A declaration of love that had survived a century of Irish weather.

She traced the initials with her fingers, her fingertips finding the grooves, rough against the softened bark – the touch of two young hands reaching through a hundred years. The tears welled up and flowed down her cheeks. "They really were in love, weren't they?"

He pulled her into his arms and held her while she cried. Not just for the young lovers, but for Grammy, who never got to meet her parents or to live in the country they had fought so hard to save.

FORTY-SEVEN
JUNE 1923

The smell of smoke lingered in the air for days after Clonbarra House burned and Edward Russell died. Ellen could taste it on her tongue as she walked past the blackened ruins, Bridget's hand gripping hers tightly. The child had been clingy since that terrible afternoon, as if she sensed that their world had cracked beyond repair.

"Look, Mam," Bridget pointed with her free hand at the charred timbers. "All broken."

"Yes, love. All broken."

The west wing of the great house where Isabella had grown up, where Edward Russell had plotted his cruel revenge, was nothing now but collapsing stone walls and ash. Patrick had vanished the same night it burned, leaving behind only rumours. Justice, if that's what it was, had come too late for her family, friends and most of all, John.

Some said they'd seen Patrick heading toward the coast. Others claimed he'd gone back to the mountains. Ellen didn't know which she hoped for more – that he was safe, or that she'd never see him again.

"Ellen?"

She turned to see Dr Casey approaching, his expression grave.

Behind him was Father O'Reilly, the new priest who'd arrived after Father Murphy died. Sarah Tierney walked beside them, her face pale with worry.

"How are you feeling today?" he asked quietly.

Her hand drifted to her belly, still flat but no longer hers alone. "The same. Sick as a dog every morning."

Dr Casey nodded, his eyes kind but worried. "It's early days yet. These things often settle down after the first few months."

But Ellen knew this pregnancy was different from Bridget's. There was a darkness to it. A wrongness that seemed to echo the violence of its conception – not the act itself, but the horror that had surrounded it. She'd been carrying this child for weeks before John died. Had felt the first stirrings of new life even as she'd watched his blood seep into the ground.

Father O'Reilly stepped forward, his face stern. "Mrs Power. Or should I say Miss McGrath?"

Dread settled in Ellen's chest at the hostility in the priest's face. "Father?"

"I've been reviewing the parish records," he said coldly. "Father Murphy left them in quite a state. I can find no entry for your marriage."

"Father Murphy married us," Ellen said, her voice rising. "Sarah was there. Frank Tierney witnessed it. Tell him, Sarah!"

Sarah stepped forward quickly. "It's true, Father. I saw them married with my own eyes. July of '21, just after the Truce. Father Murphy performed the ceremony at dawn. My father was there too – Frank Tierney, John's uncle. He witnessed it alongside me."

"With banns?" Father O'Reilly's voice was sharp.

"No, but—"

"Registered in the parish records?"

Sarah faltered. "Father Murphy said he would—"

"There is no record." Father O'Reilly's tone was final. "And I have it on good authority from the late Mr Russell that this woman was never properly married. That the man she claims was her husband took advantage of her, and her brother killed him for it."

"That's a lie!" Ellen's voice cracked. "My brother was trying to kill Edward. John stepped in front of the bullet – he was trying to stop the violence. He died saving Edward Russell's life, and Edward—" Her voice broke. "Edward repaid him by lying about us."

"You will not speak ill of the dead in my presence." Father O'Reilly's eyes were cold. "Mr Russell was a gentleman who shared his concerns with me before his tragic death. He told me of the violence in your family, the shame you brought upon them. Your brother is a murderer who killed both men. Why should I believe anything from such a family?"

"Patrick killed John by accident," Ellen said desperately. "John saved Edward's life. And Edward knew the truth – he knew we were married – but he poisoned your mind against us anyway."

"Mr Russell told me your brother murdered Mr Power in a rage over the dishonour you brought to your family," Father O'Reilly said coldly. "That seems far more credible than your story of accidents and noble sacrifices."

"But Father Murphy baptized Bridget," Ellen said desperately, pulling Bridget closer. "He put both our names in the register – mine and John's. He knew we were married. He performed the ceremony!"

Father O'Reilly's expression didn't soften. "Father Murphy made many... irregular decisions in his final years. A baptismal entry with both names proves nothing except that you claimed to be married. Without a marriage record, without banns, I can only assume Father Murphy was deceived, or that he bent the rules out of misplaced compassion."

"He wasn't deceived!" Sarah's voice rose. "I was there at the wedding. My father was there. We both witnessed it!"

"That's enough. You dare question the authority of a priest? The word of witnesses means nothing without proper documentation. The Church has rules for a reason, Miss Tierney. Your father may believe he witnessed a marriage, but without Father Murphy's registration, without banns, there is no marriage in the eyes of the Church or the law. This woman has one illegitimate child already and is now carrying another."

"Bridget isn't illegitimate!" Ellen's voice cracked. "Look at the baptismal record – both parents listed. Father Murphy knew—"

"Father Murphy is dead and cannot explain his choices," Father O'Reilly cut her off. "What I have is Mr Russell's testimony that you were never married, the absence of any marriage record, and a baptismal entry that proves only that Father Murphy was too trusting."

"This is wrong," Sarah said, her voice shaking. "You're condemning an innocent woman."

"I'm trying to save her soul." Father O'Reilly turned to Dr Casey. "Doctor, you can see the situation. Two children born out of wedlock, no husband, a brother who's a murderer on the run. The mother and baby home in Galway can provide for her needs and ensure her children are well cared for."

Dr Casey looked at Ellen, a kind but helpless expression on his face. "Ellen, perhaps it would be best. Just until the baby comes. You'll have proper care, and Bridget—"

"No." Ellen grabbed Bridget closer. "You can't take her from me."

"The children will be cared for. This is for your own good, Miss McGrath. And theirs."

"I was married," Ellen said, but her voice was barely a whisper now. "I was married."

Sarah was crying openly. "This isn't right. This isn't justice."

"This is mercy," Father O'Reilly said. "The arrangements have been made. You'll leave tomorrow."

Instead of walking straight home, Ellen took Bridget to their tree. As they walked she contemplated her choices. She had none. Not really. She didn't have enough money to run and if she involved the Tierneys or Mr O'Sullivan, they would face the wrath of the priest. He could threaten them with excommunication.

Sitting under the old oak, she laid her hand on the rough bark where once she, Isabella and John had played. She could almost hear Isabella's voice teasing her, daring her to climb higher, laughing until her sides ached. The silence pressed harder for her absence. Ellen bowed her head. Too many voices gone now, leaving only memories to keep her company.

That evening, Ellen sat in the cottage that had been her home with John, packing their few belongings into a battered suitcase. Bridget played with her wooden blocks on the floor, building towers and knocking them down with the focused intensity that only small children possessed.

"Where going, Mam?" Bridget asked, without looking up from her blocks.

"On a journey, love. To see some nice ladies who'll help us for a while."

"Da coming?"

The question hit Ellen hard. Bridget still asked for John every morning, still looked toward the door when she heard footsteps outside. How did you explain death to a child who'd just learned to string words together?

"No, love. Da can't come with us. But he's watching over us. From heaven with Granny and Granddad and Uncle Seamus."

Bridget considered this with the seriousness of a philosopher. "Da coming later?"

"Maybe, love. Maybe later."

It was a lie, but it was kinder than the truth. There would be time enough for Bridget to understand loss when she was older. For now, let her have hope.

Ellen folded John's spare shirt and placed it carefully in the suitcase. It still smelled faintly of him. Soap and tobacco and his own particular scent. She'd planned to leave it behind, but found she couldn't. Not yet.

A knock at the door made her look up.

Sarah stood in the doorway, her face pale in the lamplight. "It's true then? You're really leaving?"

Ellen nodded, not trusting her voice.

Sarah stepped inside, closing the door softly behind her. "Ellen, you don't have to do this. People will forget, given time. They'll remember that you lost John too, that you're grieving just like everyone else."

"Will they?" Ellen's laugh was bitter. "Will they forget that my brother killed the best man in Clonbarra? Will they forget that my family brought nothing but death and trouble to this place?"

"Your family brought *you*," Sarah said. "And Seamus, who could help an animal with only a touch, and who was also one of the best men to ever live. And your father, who never spoke a harsh word to anyone in his life. Don't let Patrick's sins define all of you."

"You heard the priest. I don't have a choice."

FORTY-EIGHT
NOW

The tour bus lurched to a stop outside the once-imposing gates of Clonbarra House. Now, the wrought iron sagged at odd angles, black paint sloughing in curls to reveal rust the colour of dried blood. One gate stood permanently ajar, propped open by a chunk of limestone that had probably fallen from its crumbling pillar years ago.

Caitlin wished Conor could have come with her, but he couldn't leave his patients. "I'll make it up to you," he'd promised that morning, kissing her goodbye. "We'll go together next weekend, take our time."

And something had told her this first visit needed to be hers alone.

"Right then," called the tour guide, a middle-aged woman whose enthusiasm seemed proportionate to the modest fee they'd all paid. "Welcome to Clonbarra House, one of County Galway's finest examples of Anglo-Irish Georgian architecture.

"The house you see today isn't the original. The first was built in 1847 by the first Lord Russell but was destroyed by fire shortly after the end of the Civil War in 1923. Lord Edward Russell died in that fire; his wife and baby daughter survived. His heir – a cousin – rebuilt part of it in the 1930s, smaller and simpler but on the same footprint, and it served as the family seat until..." She paused, consulting her notes. "Well, until it didn't."

A few tourists chuckled politely. Caitlin counted twelve of them – mostly German and American couples with expensive cameras and comfortable walking shoes. She kept to the back of the group as they disembarked the bus and passed through the gateway, her eyes already scanning beyond the formal tour route.

The house itself was decline disguised as restoration. The east wing had been converted into what appeared to be a café and gift shop, complete with a hand-painted sign advertising "Traditional Irish Tea & Scones." The main facade retained its classical proportions, but its limestone was stained black with decades of Irish rain. Several upper windows were boarded over with plywood, the sheets warped and split. The west wing was entirely boarded up, warning signs sprouting like weeds.

"The Russell family," the guide continued as they approached the main entrance, "were prominent landlords in this area for over a century. They owned nearly two thousand acres at their peak, and employed dozens of local families." She paused by a small plaque mounted beside the door. "Of course, like many Anglo-Irish families, they faced considerable challenges during the revolutionary period..."

Caitlin tuned out the sanitized version. Her attention drifted to the gardens stretching away from the house's south side. What had once been formal terraces had surrendered to decades of enthusiastic self-seeding. Rhododendrons, originally planted as exotic specimens, had grown into impenetrable thickets. Box hedges had become shaggy labyrinths that snagged at her coat hem. Through the tangle, she glimpsed stone – benches, urns, what might once have been a fountain. The past pressing through the present like bones through skin.

"The interior features some remarkable plasterwork," the guide was saying as the group filed through the entrance hall. "Notice the ceiling roses, believed to be the work of Italian craftsmen..."

Caitlin lingered, pretending to examine a faded photograph on the wall. The Russell family, circa 1923, posed stiffly on the front steps. Lord Edward Russell stood at the centre, his military bearing evident even in formal wear. Beside him, a young woman with pale features and nervous eyes – his wife, according to the small placard beneath, holding a baby. The photograph had been taken after the troubles. After Isabella's death.

But something about the composition felt hollow, as if the family were trying to project a normalcy that had never existed.

"The gardens behind the West Wing are closed to visitors, I'm afraid," the guide said, appearing at Caitlin's elbow with the practised manner of someone used to managing wandering tourists. "Insurance liability, you understand."

"Of course." Caitlin smiled apologetically. "Just admiring the family portrait."

"Yes, well. That would be the last generation to live here properly. Tragic end to the family line, really." The woman's voice carried the rehearsed sadness of someone who told this story twice daily. "Shall we join the others in the morning room?"

Caitlin nodded and dutifully followed, but her mind was already calculating. Forty-five minutes, the guide had said. Plenty of time for someone to slip away unnoticed.

The interior told its story in divided rooms and subdivided spaces. Georgian proportions remained. But adaptation had carved up grandeur into something smaller, more practical. What had once been a grand drawing room now housed a display of "Traditional Irish Crafts". The morning room offered "Local History Highlights": eight centuries in twelve bullet points. The 1920s rated one line: "Revolutionary period brought changes to traditional landowner–tenant relationships."

Caitlin's jaw tightened. *Changes*. As if people hadn't died. As if families hadn't been destroyed.

As the group moved toward what the guide described as "the restored library", Caitlin made her move. She simply stepped sideways into an alcove beside a tall window, counting on the other tourists' focus to mask her absence. Through the dusty glass, she could see the gardens more clearly now.

Her exit came easier than expected. A service corridor led to what had once been the servants' quarters, and from there to a door marked "Staff Only". She eased the latch; it stuck, then gave with a loud clack that made her freeze. No footsteps.

She slipped through onto a flagstone terrace. The afternoon sun felt warm after the house's chill, the air carrying the green smell of vigorous plant growth and roses climbing wild, their sweetness almost overwhelming.

The gardens were secrets keeping themselves. Overgrown paths led to hidden clearings where planned and accidental beauty had learned to coexist. She followed what might once have been gravel but was now mostly moss, winding between towering stands of bamboo and beneath the drooping branches of a massive copper beech.

"You're not supposed to be here."

The voice came from her left. Caitlin turned to find an elderly man watching her with shrewd eyes. He was tall but stooped, wearing clothes that had seen better decades – a tweed jacket with patches on the elbows, corduroy trousers stained with years of honest dirt. In his gnarled hands, he held secateurs that gleamed with the care of someone who knew his tools.

"I'm sorry," Caitlin said, raising her hands. "I was just curious about the gardens. They're beautiful."

"Tourists always are curious. But they always want to see the house, not the grounds." His accent carried the soft consonants of rural Galway. Pale blue eyes in a tanned, lined face narrowed as he studied her. "You're looking for something." Not a question.

Caitlin found herself impressed by his directness. "How did you know?"

"Forty-one years I've been working these grounds. You learn to read people." He tucked the secateurs into his jacket pocket. "Tourists look around like they're taking pictures with their eyes, trying to capture everything. You're looking for something specific." He paused. Waited. "Question is, what?"

Caitlin hesitated, then decided on honesty. The old man's manner suggested he had little patience for evasion. "I'm researching a family connection. My ancestors knew the Russells – specifically Miss Isabella."

The change in his expression was subtle but unmistakable. "Isabella Russell?" He laughed – a dry sound like autumn leaves rustling. "Now there's a name I haven't heard spoken aloud in some time."

"Did you know her?"

"I'm old, girl, but not that old. She died in 1921. I wasn't born until 1942." He gestured for her to follow. "But my grandfather worked here. He knew her well enough."

"What did he say about her?"

The groundskeeper studied her for a long moment, weighing some internal decision. "Come on, then. If you're going to be asking about Isabella Russell, you might as well see where she spent her time."

He led her deeper into the gardens, along paths that existed more as suggestions than actual routes. The vegetation pressed close – massive rhododendrons that had grown into green cathedrals, their branches intertwining overhead to create tunnels of dappled light. Ancient roses had climbed into the trees, creating cascades of pink and white blooms.

"My grandfather always said the gardens were Miss Isabella's domain. Her father and brother cared nothing for them – saw them as just another expense to maintain. But she loved them. Spent hours here."

They emerged into a small clearing. A stone bench sat positioned to take advantage of what must once have been a carefully planned view. Now the vista was partially obscured by self-seeded trees, but Caitlin could still make out the gentle slope leading down to a stream, and beyond that, the rolling fields of rural Galway.

"This was her place," the groundskeeper said, settling onto the bench with the careful movements of someone whose joints had accumulated decades of hard use. "Where she'd come to think. And later, to meet her young man."

"Fintan Murphy?"

He looked surprised, pale eyes sharpening. "You know more than I thought. Most people who come asking about the Russells have never heard of Fintan Murphy."

Caitlin sat beside him, feeling the sun-warmed stone through her jacket. Around them, the garden hummed with bees working the climbing roses. "I know they were murdered. That the IRA was blamed."

The old man made a sound that might have been a laugh or a snort of disgust. "That's the story Lord Edward put about. More convenient than the truth."

"Which was?"

For a moment, he didn't answer. His hands rested on his knees – callused, slightly bent, but still strong after decades of physical work. When he spoke, his voice carried the weight of someone sharing a secret kept too long.

"Edward Russell was a cruel man. Always had been, even as a child, according to my grandfather. The kind who'd pull the wings off flies just to watch them crawl." He paused, gaze fixed on some middle distance. "Couldn't bear the shame of his sister loving an Irishman. A Catholic Irishman at that, and a member of the IRA."

"So he had them killed?"

"The story my grandfather told was that Edward discovered his sister and chauffeur were spies. Instead of having them arrested, he made sure word got back to the IRA that they were British spies. Everyone was on edge during the War of Independence so it was easy enough to convince people an Anglo-Irish landlord's daughter was working for British intelligence."

Caitlin's chest tightened. Isabella Russell. Murdered by her own *brother*. Her mouth went dry; the folder edges bit into her palm before she realized she was clenching. "Is there any proof?"

"I believe my grandfather, who was as honest a man as ever drew breath. He said Patrick admitted to it. And I believe what happened to Edward Russell afterward tells its own story."

"What happened?"

The old man turned to look at her directly. She saw something like satisfaction in his pale eyes. "Edward Russell died in June 1923. Burned to death when Clonbarra House caught fire. They said it was an accident – overturned lamp in his study, something like that." He paused. Let that sink in. "But the timing was interesting."

"How so?"

"The Civil War was over, but John Power was shot dead in the village by Patrick McGrath. Edward was a witness."

Caitlin gasped. "You're telling me Patrick killed John? His sister's husband?"

The old man's eyebrows rose. "You really do know more than I thought. Yes, Patrick McGrath. Edward Russell got what was coming to him." Matter-of-fact. As if discussing the weather. "Whether it was Patrick McGrath or someone else, or just the hand of God finally evening the scales – that's not for me to say. But I will say this: my grandfather always claimed Edward Russell was terrified in those final weeks. Jumped at shadows, hired extra guards, had the locks changed on all the doors."

They sat in silence. Bees droned in the roses. Somewhere behind them, the tour group's voices drifted from the house. Caitlin tried to process what she'd learned. Patrick McGrath hadn't just been a Republican fighter. He was a murderer. He'd shot Grammy's father and may have killed a local landlord too.

"There's more," the old man said. "My grandfather told me about the McGrath family."

Caitlin's heart beat faster. Was this it? A breakthrough in her research at last? "What about them?"

"The sister, Ellen, her name was. She left Clonbarra right after all the trouble ended. Had a little girl and was pregnant again, according to the stories, and nowhere to go. My grandfather always felt bad about that. Said she was a good girl who got caught up in her family's politics."

Caitlin's heart began to race. This was closer than she'd ever come to finding a direct connection. "Do you know where she went?"

"The nuns. That's where girls in her situation usually ended up. There was a convent in Galway that took them in – St Brigid's." He stood up from the bench with slow care. "You'd better get back to your tour group before they notice you're missing. The guide gets upset when she loses tourists – insurance liability and all that."

"Wait." Caitlin rose as well. "Thank you so much. I don't even know your name."

"Tommy Clancy." He extended a work-roughened hand. "My grandfather was Tom Clancy – worked for the Russells for forty-odd years, man and boy."

"Caitlin O'Shea. From South Carolina."

"You've come a long way to dig up old bones." His smile was enigmatic. "Question is, what are you planning to do with what you've found?"

It was a good question. When she'd started this research, simple curiosity had motivated her. But now, standing in the grounds of the Russell estate with all these stories pressing down on her, she felt the responsibility of being perhaps the only person left who could piece together the truth for Grammy. "I don't know yet. But I think Ellen's story deserves to be told, don't you? She lost everything. Her brothers, her husband, her home. And then she just... disappeared."

"Not disappeared." Tommy's voice was quiet. Final. "Died. The nuns at St Brigid's kept records, even if they didn't share them freely. Ellen McGrath died there, giving birth to her second child."

Caitlin's breath caught. Would she find her great-grandmother's grave at the convent?

As she rejoined the tour group – who had indeed noticed her absence but seemed content with her mumbled explanation about "getting turned around in the corridors" – Caitlin found herself looking at the estate with new eyes. This wasn't just a tourist attraction or a curiosity. This was a place where real people had lived and loved and died. Where decisions had been made that echoed down through generations. Where Ellen McGrath had lost everything before disappearing into the silence of a convent cemetery.

The tour bus pulled away from Clonbarra House as the afternoon light began to slant toward evening, carrying Caitlin back toward Galway city. But her thoughts remained in those overgrown gardens, where an old man's memories had opened new paths into the past.

Tomorrow, she would finally visit St Brigid's Convent, she decided. If the records existed, she'd find them – push the boundaries of whatever "procedures" they had in place. Grammy deserved her mother's real story.

FORTY-NINE

Conor drove her to the convent. "I know you can drive yourself and you are fully capable, but you may find out some upsetting information. I'd like to be here. Just in case you need a tissue." He produced a box of them, making her laugh. "Or a friendly face."

"All this happened years ago. I'll be fine."

"If that's the case, we can use the day for me to play tourist guide and show you all the sights of Galway city. We missed a few on the weekend. It's a magical place. Not as special as Ballycluan obviously, but it's full of history."

Caitlin smiled her thanks, but her stomach churned with what the records might reveal. She'd dressed carefully for the occasion, adopting a more office-like appearance. Black trousers instead of jeans, with a smart blazer that felt like armour against whatever truths waited inside those walls.

The drive from Ballycluan to Galway had taken them through countryside that grew gradually more populated, stone walls giving way to housing estates and roundabouts. As they approached the city, the Corrib sparkled in the morning light, and Galway's medieval walls rose like ancient guardians protecting secrets within.

St Brigid's Convent sat on the outskirts of the city proper, down a narrow lane lined with horse chestnuts trees. Victorian Gothic, it was all pointed arches and dark limestone. Lancet windows seemed to watch their approach. A bell tower rose from the centre, its copper roof green with verdigris, and ivy climbed the walls with the patient persistence of decades.

The gardens surrounding the convent were immaculate. Box hedges carved geometric patterns. Late-blooming roses filled the beds, their petals scattered on gravelled paths. A statue of St Brigid stood in the centre of a circular lawn, her stone hands raised in blessing, her face smoothed by Irish rain. Everything was ordered, peaceful, beautiful in its restraint. But Caitlin felt it immediately: a heaviness that seemed to seep from the very stones. Despite the careful gardens and fresh paint on the window frames, there was something in the air that spoke of sorrow held too long, of tears shed in silence.

"Would you like me to come in with you?" Conor asked, his eyes studying her face with the professional concern of someone trained to read physical distress.

Every bit of her wanted to say yes. To have his solid presence beside her when she learned whatever truths these walls contained. The word "yes" formed on her lips, then died. She shook her head. "I can do it. Thank you."

He picked up his newspaper from the dashboard. "I'll be waiting. If you change your mind, let me know."

The main entrance was reached through a heavy oak door set beneath a Gothic arch. Carved saints looked down from niches in the stonework: martyrs and virgins, their expressions were serene in their eternal stone suffering. A brass nameplate beside the door read "St Brigid's Convent – Founded 1847" in elegant script that spoke of better times, more prosperous days.

Caitlin pulled the bell rope. A deep tone echoed somewhere in the building's depths. The sound hung in the air, as if the stones themselves didn't want to let it go.

The door opened to reveal a woman in her forties wearing civilian clothes: a navy skirt suit teamed with a cream blouse, sensible shoes, greying hair pulled back in a simple ponytail. Her smile was warm but professional, the expression of someone accustomed to greeting visitors who came seeking difficult truths.

"You must be Miss O'Shea. I'm Mrs Walsh, the convent administrator. We spoke on the telephone. I do apologize for the delays in getting you answers for your grandmother. How is she faring?"

Surprised to meet Mrs Walsh in person and to find her so pleasant, Caitlin managed to find her voice. "She's keeping well, thank you. Very impatient to find out what she can about her family."

"I can only imagine. If I had my way, things would move quicker. Come in, dear, Mother Angela is expecting you."

The entrance hall was surprisingly bright, with morning sunlight streaming through tall windows that faced the garden. Polished terrazzo floors reflected the light in subtle patterns. Religious paintings lined the walls: scenes from the life of Christ, portraits of various saints, and what appeared to be a history of the convent itself captured in oils that had darkened with age.

"Please, take a seat," Mrs Walsh said, gesturing toward a row of wooden chairs that looked like they'd been salvaged from a church. "Mother Angela will be with you in just a moment."

The waiting area felt like a museum of institutional life. Display cases held artefacts from the convent's history: photographs of young nuns in habits that covered them from head to toe, prayer books with pages yellowed by decades of handling, and small plaques commemorating various benefactors whose donations had kept the place running through leaner times.

One photograph caught Caitlin's attention. Dated 1923. A group of women in white aprons working in what appeared to be a laundry. Their faces were serious, worn by labour and circumstances. Some looked impossibly young, girls really, barely out of childhood. The caption read simply: "Residents at Work."

Residents. Not women. Not mothers. Residents, as if they were visiting rather than imprisoned by circumstance and social stigma.

Her hands clenched involuntarily. She forced them to relax, but her palms were damp.

"Miss O'Shea?"

Caitlin turned to find an elderly nun approaching, her habit modern and simple: a grey dress with a white collar, a small cross at her throat. Her face was kind, lined with wrinkles that spoke more of laughter than severity, and her eyes held the gentle authority of someone who had spent decades caring for others.

"I'm Mother Angela. Welcome to St Brigid's." Her voice carried the musical cadence of County Clare, soft consonants that made even formal words sound like a lullaby. "I hope you had a good journey. You brought the sun with you. Our gardens love the rain, but it does the soul good to get a bit of sun on our bones, doesn't it?"

Caitlin could barely find her voice. The nun was being kind. Genuinely kind. That didn't marry with the stories she'd been told, the images conjured by words like "Magdalene laundries" and "fallen women".

"We'll have coffee in here," Mother Angela continued, leading her through a doorway into what was clearly a formal parlour. "Or would you prefer tea?"

"Coffee is lovely, thank you."

The parlour was a study in quiet elegance. Well-worn furniture. Overstuffed chairs in muted florals. Small tables bearing reading lamps and books. Dark wood panelling reached halfway up the walls, topped by cream-coloured plaster. A fireplace dominated one end of the room, its mantel decorated with photographs of current and former residents of the convent: not the stark institutional shots from the corridor, but candid images of women smiling, working in gardens, holding babies.

Large windows overlooked the convent's private garden. Unlike the formal beds at the front, this space felt more intimate: vegetable plots were interspersed with flower borders, and Caitlin could see women in casual clothes tending to plants, their faces peaceful in the morning light.

"Did you drive yourself over?" Mother Angela asked, settling into the chair across from Caitlin.

"No, a friend did."

"Does this friend want to come in? We're happy to extend hospitality to anyone who's travelled so far."

"No, he said he'd wait in the car. But thank you."

Mother Angela smiled and rang a small silver bell that sat on the table beside her chair. The sound was delicate, nothing like the deep bronze toll of the entrance bell. Within moments, Mrs Walsh appeared with a tea service: not the institutional china Caitlin had expected, but delicate porcelain decorated with tiny roses.

"Coffee for our guest, please, Margaret. And I think we might have some of that cake Sister Clare made this morning? If there is any left?"

"Indeed there is, Mother. And I'll bring a selection of her biscuits, too."

"Please do. I have a feeling Miss O'Shea has come a long way for answers, and we should fortify ourselves properly."

As Mrs Walsh retreated, Mother Angela turned her full attention to Caitlin. "I dug into our records as per your request. It was such a painful time in our history, as I guess you're coming to realize." She paused, her fingers toying with the simple wooden rosary at her waist. "Dreadful things were done in the name of peace and, dare I say it, God's love. Our convent wasn't as charitable as it could have been."

The nun's gaze fixed on something beyond the window. When she looked back at Caitlin, her eyes held the weight of institutional memory, of sins committed by predecessors she had never known but whose legacy she had inherited. "Women like your great-grandmother, who should have been treated with respect and kindness, often received less than humane consideration. I can only apologize."

"You aren't old enough to have been alive back then," Caitlin blurted out, then blushed at her own directness.

Mother Angela's laugh was genuine, transforming her lined

face. "Thank you, dear, some days I feel much older. But still, it was all done in our name and that of our holy Church." She shook her head sadly. "The sins of the institution become the responsibility of all who serve within it, regardless of when we arrived."

Mrs Walsh returned with a tray that looked like more country house than convent: delicate cake slices arranged on a tiered stand; a plate of large, buttery-looking biscuits sprinkled with sugar; a small jug of cream; and sugar cubes in a silver bowl that caught the morning light.

"Oh, look, we're being spoiled," Mother Angela said, her tone brightening deliberately. "This coffee cake is second to none. Will you have a piece? Sure you will, won't you?"

Despite her nerves, Caitlin found herself accepting the offered plate. The cake was dense and fragrant, studded with walnuts and laced with cinnamon. It tasted of comfort, of kitchens where someone cared enough to bake with real ingredients and patience.

As she ate, she noticed on a small desk near the window a pile of manila folders stacked neatly, their tabs bearing names written in careful script.

One folder sat apart from the others. Thicker. Its edges worn with handling. Ellen McGrath was written across the tab in faded ink.

Her chest tightened. There it was. The reason she'd come. Her hand trembled slightly as she set down her coffee cup.

"And how are you finding Ireland?"

Caitlin's nerves began to dissipate under the nun's kind remarks, but her anticipation grew. Whatever truth lay in that folder, whatever records had survived nearly a century, she was finally about to learn what had happened to her great-grandmother in this place of stone walls and careful gardens.

FIFTY

Mother Angela followed her gaze to the desk, then rose with careful movements. "I suppose we should begin," she said, retrieving the folder. "These are Ellen's records. What I'm about to show you... shaped how the Sisters here understood your great-grandmother. It coloured everything that followed." She held Caitlin's gaze. "I've read this letter, and others like it, many times. It never gets easier. They were dark times."

Caitlin braced herself. "All right."

"Ellen McGrath arrived here on July the fifth, 1923. She was twenty-two years old, with a daughter named Bridget who was sixteen months old."

The nun slid a sheet of thin, brittle paper from the folder. "This letter was placed in Ellen's file shortly before her arrival. It is from Father O'Reilly, who took over the parish in Clonbarra after Father Murphy's death in April 1923."

"So he never actually knew Ellen."

"No," the nun said. "But his account carried significant authority." She held the page delicately.

"'Miss Ellen McGrath presents herself as a married woman. However, upon reviewing my predecessor's records, I find no entry of such a marriage.'"

Caitlin's jaw tightened. The ease with which he dismissed her grandmother's truth still startled her, even a century on.

Mother Angela glanced at her, then continued. "'Miss McGrath asserts that she and the deceased Mr John Power were united in holy matrimony, and she has induced her acquaintances to echo this falsehood. I have reason to suspect she has instructed these companions in her deception.'"

"He thought she coached them?"

"That is what the Sisters here were told. Father O'Reilly's word would have been taken as reliable." She lowered her eyes to the page. "And here... another voice enters." Her tone hardened as she echoed his severity.

"'I have the sworn testimony of Mr Edward Russell, landlord and respected gentleman of this parish, that no such marriage occurred. Mr Russell affirms the girl was never wed and that her brother, a violent and unstable man, murdered Mr Power in a fit of rage over her immoral behaviour. The whole family was involved in resistance and murder. Mr Power also served time in prison. With the girl now carrying a second child, conceived outside wedlock, I agree with Mr Russell: the infant already born would benefit from better influence than having this woman as their mother.'"

Caitlin flinched. "He used her pregnancy against her."

"Yes," Mother Angela said. "It painted her as doubly immoral. And for the Sisters here... that would have carried enormous weight."

Caitlin stared at the letter, pulse thudding. Edward Russell's lies had been taken as gospel simply because he held power.

Mother Angela turned the page. "'Father Murphy's baptismal entry for the child, listing both parents, is noted, but given his known laxity in enforcing Canon Law and tendency toward excessive compassion, this cannot be taken as proof of marriage.'"

Caitlin pressed a hand to her chest. "Would he not have assumed that if the priest recorded the baptism with the father's name, he must have married them? A priest wouldn't do that just because he was kind?"

Mother Angela hesitated. "One would think so. But Father O'Reilly chose to see it differently." She dipped her head to the paper.

"'Given the absence of banns, the lack of lawful registration, the questionable loyalty of the witnesses, and the girl's continued insistence, despite her condition, that she is a lawful wife, it is my firm judgment that she has knowingly misled the community. I trust the Sisters will guide her to repentance and protect her child from further scandal.'"

Silence settled between them.

Mother Angela lowered the page. "This letter arrived just before Ellen did. The Superioress and the Sisters were primed to see her as deceitful, immoral... even dangerous."

Caitlin swallowed. "So before she ever walked through the door, they'd already decided who she was."

"Yes."

"And Bridget?"

A shadow crossed the nun's face. "The Sisters believed the child needed moral protection. They were separated, and Ellen, pregnant and grieving, was told her daughter would be placed for adoption." She drew in a steadying breath. "It would have been devastating. For both."

Heat pricked behind Caitlin's eyes. "I want the rest of the file," she said. "Every note, every decision that followed that letter."

"You shall have it," Mother Angela said. Then, more quietly: "But Miss O'Shea... these documents tell you nothing about who Ellen truly was. Only how she was judged."

She passed the letter across. Caitlin read it through herself, her eyes filling with angry tears at the injustice. Edward Russell had taken everything from her family. She folded it carefully before handing it back. Mother Angela returned it to the folder.

Mother Angela took out another page, her expression growing more troubled. "Ellen was classified as 'difficult' and 'resistant to correction'. The records suggest she was often in what we would now recognize as a state of profound grief, but at the time..."

"They thought she was faking it."

"Malingering, yes. There was little understanding then of what we now call trauma. Ellen had lost her parents, her brothers, her husband. Then she was stripped of her marriage and her children. The assessment here describes her as 'prone to melancholy' and 'unwilling to embrace the redemptive nature of honest work.'"

Mother Angela looked ashamed. She turned another page, and Caitlin caught sight of a photograph tucked between the documents. A young woman holding a toddler, both of them looking directly at the camera.

Without thinking, she reached out her hand for it, and the elderly nun passed it to her, silently.

The woman's eyes held a depth of sadness that seemed to reach across a century.

"That's her," Caitlin whispered. Her gaze shifted to the child in Ellen's arms: soft curls, round cheeks, that stubborn little chin she'd known all her life. Grammy, before America. Before she'd been torn from her real family.

"Yes. Taken when she first arrived." Mother Angela took back the photograph carefully, studying it. "Bridget was placed in the children's dormitory with the orphans. Ellen was assigned to the laundry. She was... she was caught several times trying to visit her daughter outside of the designated visiting hours."

Designated visiting hours? Her own daughter? Stunned, all Caitlin could ask was: "What happened when they caught her?"

"Punishment. Confinement to her dormitory. Reduced meals. The philosophy then was that such behaviour needed to be corrected firmly." Mother Angela opened her eyes, meeting Caitlin's gaze. "I cannot tell you how deeply we regret the harshness of those times."

The afternoon light had shifted, casting longer shadows across the room. Caitlin's coffee had grown cold, forgotten in her hands as the weight of Ellen's suffering settled over her.

"There's more. In March of 1924, Ellen gave birth to a son. She named him Seán, the Irish for John, after her late husband. The delivery was... difficult. Very difficult. There was no medical assistance. The convent didn't call for doctors for these poor unfortunates. Ellen was weak for weeks afterward, and the child was small, premature."

"The baby survived though, didn't he?"

"The child did, yes. Ellen..." Mother Angela turned to the final pages in the folder. "Ellen died six weeks after the birth. The official cause was listed as complications from childbirth, but the nursing notes suggest she had simply... given up. She stopped eating, stopped speaking. We would recognize it now as severe postpartum depression, complicated by her existing trauma. But then..."

"They thought she was being difficult."

"Yes." The word was barely a whisper.

Caitlin set down her coffee cup with trembling hands. "What happened to the children?"

"That's where the story becomes more hopeful, I'm glad to say. In July of 1924, a woman named Sarah O'Riordan came to the convent. You may have come across her in your research as Sarah Tierney?"

Startled, Caitlin could only nod. Then when her voice caught up with her brain, she said, "Ellen's brother, Seamus – he was murdered by the Black and Tans – was engaged to Sarah Tierney."

"It says here she'd grown up with Ellen and claimed a family connection. It's not recorded what the relationship was." Mother Angela peered at the notes.

"She wanted both children?"

The nun pursed her lips as she read. "Sarah did, yes. But her husband was more reluctant. He felt they could manage one child, but two... The records show they had several discussions with the mother superior at the time."

"And?"

"Ultimately, they took Seán. In return for a large donation.

Sarah argued that he needed immediate care, that she could provide for him properly. As for Bridget..."

She turned to a different section of the file, revealing correspondence written on official letterhead. "The child was described in these records as 'difficult to manage' and 'prone to tantrums'. Looking back now, knowing what we know about child psychology, she was clearly traumatized by the loss of her parents and the separation from her familiar surroundings. But the assessment was that she needed 'firmer guidance than a local family might provide.'"

Caitlin's heart sank. "So they sent her away."

"To America, yes. There was a Catholic couple in Charleston, South Carolina. The Brennans. They specifically requested an Irish child, believing it would be a charitable act to provide opportunities in America that might not be available here. The records show Bridget sailed from Cobh in September of 1926. She was five years old."

The room fell silent except for the ticking of a clock somewhere in the convent's depths. Caitlin stared at the photograph of Ellen and baby Bridget, trying to process the magnitude of what she'd learned. Grammy had never been abandoned by a mother who didn't love her. She'd been torn away from a mother who had fought desperately to stay close to her, who had died of grief and trauma in this very building.

"Seán," Caitlin said. "What happened to him? Did Sarah O'Riordan raise him?"

Mother Angela nodded. "She did. Changed his surname to O'Riordan, of course. Raised him as her own son, although they renamed him Kevin Seán. I think the husband wanted to call him after his father or something. The records show she came back once, in 1927, asking if there were any other relatives. She'd heard rumours about Bridget's adoption and wanted to maintain some connection, but..." She shrugged sadly. "International adoptions were considered final in those days. There was no mechanism for maintaining family ties across such distances."

Caitlin thought of Grammy lying in her hospital bed in

Charleston, clutching those DNA results that had revealed the existence of a brother she'd never known existed. Kevin Seán O'Riordan. The connection that had started this entire journey.

"Do you know if he had children? Seán – Kevin, I mean?"

"The records here end with his adoption, I'm afraid. But Miss O'Shea, Caitlin..." Mother Angela leaned forward, her eyes kind but serious. "You mentioned DNA testing. If your grandmother's DNA is on those websites, she may match with descendants of Kevin Seán O'Riordan, if he had children. You may have family in Ireland you haven't discovered yet."

But then why didn't Gavin, Grammy's long-lost cousin, locate them? Even with that thought, though, the possibility hung in the air like a promise and a question mark all at once. Grammy's brother had lived, had been raised by loving parents, had possibly had children and grandchildren who were still alive somewhere in Ireland.

But Bridget had been shipped across an ocean, cut off from everyone and everything she'd known, labelled as "difficult" when she was just a traumatized child missing her parents.

"The couple who adopted her," Caitlin said. "The Brennans. Do you know anything about them?"

Mother Angela consulted the correspondence again. "Wealthy, by the standards of the time. He was involved in shipping, she was active in church charities. They'd lost several children in infancy and were eager to provide a home for an orphan. The letters suggest they were people who genuinely wanted to give Bridget opportunities. According to this final letter from Mrs Brennan, written about six months after the adoption, Bridget insisted on keeping her Irish name. Apparently she was quite determined about it, even at five years old. 'The child has a will of iron,' Mrs Brennan wrote. 'She knows exactly who she is.'"

Despite everything, Caitlin found herself smiling. That sounded exactly like Grammy. That iron will, that certainty about her own identity, had been there from the very beginning.

The nun broke the silence. "Were they kind? Was your grandmother happy?"

Caitlin hated dashing the hope in the nun's eyes. She took care choosing her words. "They weren't unkind. I think Grammy might have been too scarred by her experiences, even though she was so young. Grammy said it was my grandfather who first taught her to believe she was worthy of love."

"Not the first – her real mother proved that." The nun wiped a tear from her cheek. "When I think of all the harm we did, what was done to those poor creatures."

Caitlin stood and took the nun's hand in hers. She would have hugged her if she hadn't been sitting down. "You've been very kind to me. You can't blame yourself for the past." *Yet I do.* Caitlin pushed aside the voice in her head. "Thank you," Caitlin said, her voice thick with emotion. "For keeping these records. For sharing them with me. For... for treating this with the respect it deserves."

"I think you should keep the photographs and give them to your grandmother." Mother Angela closed the folder gently. "Ellen McGrath deserves to be remembered properly. She was a young woman caught in impossible circumstances, who loved her children more than her own life. The least we can do is tell her story truthfully." She stood, moving to a window that overlooked the convent's cemetery. "She's buried here, you know. In our grounds. There's a headstone now, though there wasn't always. Kevin Seán O'Riordan paid for it. Would you like to see it?"

Caitlin nodded, not trusting her voice. Outside, the afternoon light was beginning to slant toward evening, casting long shadows across the peaceful gardens where Ellen McGrath had found her final rest nearly a century ago.

Seán had known enough to honour their mother – so why hadn't he looked for Bridget?

"Do you know if Seán asked to find Grammy – I mean, Bridget?" She knew she should call him Kevin but she'd been looking for Seán for so long his name stuck.

Mother Angela came away from the window to open the folder

again, her lips pursed in a thin line. "The mother superior in charge of the convent back in the sixties decided it was best to leave things alone. She thought it would only upset the Brennans if she made the details public."

"Upset the *Brennans*? But Bridget and Seán were brother and sister! What right did they have to keep them apart?" Realizing she was raising her voice to the woman who had only tried to help her, Caitlin apologized.

"No apology needed. I share your sentiments. Unfortunately, even those of us who take a vow of Christianity aren't always Christian in our actions."

The nun rang the bell again. "Mrs Walsh, could you copy the contents of this file for Miss O'Shea. I want her to have the photographs, too. We are going to the graveyard but will be back in a while."

Mrs Walsh nodded, but then spoke: "Mother, why don't you let one of us take the young lady? You should be resting." She gave Mother Angela a look that said this wasn't the first time she'd tried to slow the nun down.

"Don't fuss, Mrs Walsh. I can rest when I'm dead. I'll enjoy the sunshine. Perhaps Miss O'Shea can lend me her arm."

Caitlin couldn't help thinking the woman in front of her would have put up an altogether different fight to keep Ellen with her children had she been around at that time.

FIFTY-ONE

The path to the cemetery wound through the back gardens, past vegetable plots. Mother Angela moved slowly but steadily, her hand resting lightly on Caitlin's arm. The sun cast long shadows across the grass, and somewhere a blackbird sang its territorial song.

"We've tried to make it peaceful here," the nun said as they approached a stone archway. "A place of rest, finally."

The cemetery spread before them in neat sections. To the right, marble headstones stood in orderly rows. Nuns who had served the convent, their names and dates carved deep into polished stone. A few priests had monuments too, Celtic crosses reaching toward heaven.

But it was the left side that drew Caitlin's attention and made her breath catch.

Wooden crosses. Dozens of them. Some faded to silver-grey, others newer but already showing signs of Irish weather. No names on most. Just dates, and sometimes not even those. "Unknown Woman died 1919", "Baby Girl 1921" "Mother and Infant 1924."

Row after row of the forgotten.

"We're working to identify them," Mother Angela's tone spoke volumes. "Going through records, trying to match dates with admissions. But so many were never properly documented. They came here in shame and left in silence."

Caitlin's throat tightened. All these women. All these children. Lost to history because society had deemed them unworthy of remembrance.

"Ellen's grave is this way," Mother Angela guided her past the wooden crosses to a small section near the back wall. Here, a few proper headstones stood among the simpler markers.

The stone was modest but dignified. Grey granite with simple lettering:

Ellen McGrath Power
1901–1924
Mother of Bridget and Seán Finally at Peace

Shocked, Caitlin gasped. There were fresh flowers at its base – purple asters and white roses.

"I'm sorry, I didn't think." The nun flushed. "I should have known you would assume family left those flowers. When I knew you were coming, I put them there. It seemed right that she should have flowers when her great-granddaughter came to visit."

Caitlin squeezed the old woman's arm in thanks, unable to speak. She knelt beside the grave, her fingers tracing the carved letters of Ellen's name. This woman she'd never known but whose blood ran in her veins. Who had loved her children so fiercely that separation had killed her.

"I will go back and give you some time. I'll let your friend know you are here." She moved away with surprising grace for her age, leaving Caitlin alone with her great-grandmother's grave and the weight of all the untold stories.

The cemetery was quiet except for the wind in the trees and that persistent blackbird. Caitlin thought of Grammy in her hospital bed, never knowing her mother was buried here. Never knowing she'd been loved, not abandoned.

"She never forgot you," Caitlin whispered to the stone. "Your daughter. She remembered you singing to her. She remembered you loved her."

The tears came then. For Ellen, dying of grief at twenty-three. For Grammy, spending ninety-one years thinking she'd been unwanted. For Seán, growing up knowing his history but unable to find his sister. For all the wooden crosses marking women whose names were lost but whose pain had been real.

She sobbed, shoulders shaking with the weight of generational grief. All the trauma, all the separation, all the unnecessary cruelty done in the name of morality.

Strong arms wrapped around her from behind. Conor. He didn't speak, just held her as she cried for all of them – the living and the dead, the named and the nameless.

"I'm sorry," she gasped between sobs. "I thought I could handle it. It was all so long ago."

"Grief doesn't have an expiration date," he said. "Especially grief for injustice."

She turned in his arms, burying her face against his chest. Safe. Solid. Present.

When the storm of tears finally passed, he produced a handkerchief from his pocket. "Mother Angela gave me Ellen's file for you – said you might need this too." He gestured to the handkerchief. "Apparently I don't look like the kind of man who carries clean handkerchiefs."

Despite everything, Caitlin found herself laughing – a watery sound, but genuine.

"But I do. In addition to boxes of tissues. My mam trained me well. Never leave the house without a clean handkerchief and decent socks. You never know when you'll need either."

She wiped her eyes, then looked back at Ellen's grave. The flowers Mother Angela had placed there moved gently in the breeze, their light colours soft against the grey stone

"I'd like to take some photographs for Grammy. But..." she lifted her trembling hand.

He took the phone from her. "I'll take them. Do you want to stand beside the grave?"

Caitlin shook her head, blowing her nose, tears threatening again.

"Ready to go home?" Conor asked.

Home. Not back to the cottage. Home. Something in the way he said it made her chest tighten in an entirely different way.

"Yes," she said. "But I want to come back another day. I want to bring flowers for the unmarked graves. For all of them."

"Of course." He helped her to her feet, keeping one arm around her shoulders as they walked back toward the archway.

As they passed under the stone archway, Caitlin looked back once more. The marble monuments caught the late morning sun, but it was the wooden crosses that held her gaze. All those women who had been shamed and hidden away.

But not forgotten. Not anymore.

"Thank you," she said as they reached his car.

"For what?"

"For being here. For just... being with me."

He squeezed her hand. "Always."

FIFTY-TWO

The drive back from the convent had been quiet, Caitlin still processing everything Mother Angela had revealed. Ellen's story, Bridget's adoption, Seán's existence. It all swirled in her mind like pieces of a puzzle finally clicking into place.

Conor had suggested stopping at Tierney's pub on the way back to the cottage. "Delia will want to know," he'd said. "She's invested in your search."

Now, stepping into the familiar warmth of the pub, Caitlin felt the weight of the day settling into her bones. The lunch crowd had thinned out, leaving only a handful of regulars nursing pints in the late afternoon light.

Caitlin caught sight of Harry Bennett sitting at the bar, staring into his glass with the focused attention of a man trying to forget something. *Typical, of all the days he finally shows up, I'm too upset to question him.* The sadness of today was pressing in on her and all she wanted to do was go home. To Annie Murphy's cottage.

Delia looked up from wiping down the bar, her face immediately creasing with concern. "Caitlin, love. You look done in. Sit yourself down. Conor, get her settled while I pour you both something."

"Just water for me," Caitlin said, sinking into a chair at a table near the window. The familiar sounds of the pub, the clink of glasses, the low murmur of conversation, the creak of old wood, felt surreal after the institutional quiet of the convent.

A few minutes later, Delia brought over a glass of water and a pot of tea. "Now then, tell me," she asked, as she poured. "Did you find what you were looking for?"

Caitlin wrapped her hands around the warm teacup, drawing comfort from its heat. "I found more than I expected. Ellen didn't abandon her children. She died at the convent, six weeks after giving birth to her son."

"Ah, the poor woman." Delia's eyes filled with sympathy. "And the children?"

"That's where it gets complicated." Caitlin took a breath. "My grandmother, Bridget, was sent to America when she was five. But her baby brother, Seán, was adopted locally. By a woman named Sarah O'Riordan, née Tierney."

Delia stilled. "Sarah? *Our* Sarah? From Clonbarra?"

"Yes. She claimed a family connection. She wanted both children but her husband only wanted one."

"I never knew Sarah adopted a child. To be honest, we lost contact a long time ago." Delia sat down, her expression thoughtful. "Sarah's father Frank was a cousin to Jack Tierney, my father-in-law. I think Jack and Frank got on well enough but... who knows what happened, the families got on with their own lives. Sarah married a Donegal man from what Jack's wife told me. Sarah died young from TB, I think."

"Kevin Seán O'Riordan," Caitlin said, the name carrying new weight now that she knew his story.

The sound of a chair scraping against the floor made them all turn. Harry Bennett had stood abruptly, his face pale beneath his weathered tan. Without a word, he turned and walked out, leaving his pint half-finished on the table.

Delia shook her head. "That man gets grumpier by the day. What's got into him now?"

But Caitlin barely heard her. The emotional weight of the day

– Ellen's suffering, Grammy's lost brother, the tragedy of a family torn apart – suddenly overwhelmed her. She felt tears threatening, her throat tightening with grief for people she'd never met but whose blood ran in her veins.

Conor's hand found her shoulder, warm and steady. "You've had a long day. Let me take you home. I'll cook once I've tamed that old Aga. You can rest or call your grandmother. Whatever you decide."

The decision made itself. Caitlin pulled out her phone, fingers trembling as she typed:

> I found her

A bubble popped up almost at once.

> Thank you, darling.

> I'll call you, tonight.

Caitlin stared at the phone. Hopefully by then, she'd be able to retell the story without breaking down. *When I can breathe again.* She slipped the phone away, already steadier for knowing the call was coming.

She managed a weak smile for Delia. "Thank you for the tea, for your help, for listening."

"Any time, love." Delia's voice was gentle. "This is heavy stuff you're carrying. But at least now you know the truth. That's something."

As they left the pub, Caitlin caught a glimpse of Harry's retreating figure down the street. His abrupt departure nagged at her, but she couldn't think about anything else just then. She wanted to go home and cry. To grieve for Ellen, for Grammy, for Seán, for all the lost connections and severed bonds.

Conor reached the car first. "Let's get you home."

Home. The cottage by the sea that had become her refuge.

. . .

The cottage was quiet except for the tick of the kitchen clock and the distant sound of waves. Conor had tactfully retreated to the kitchen after getting her settled on the sofa with a blanket and a fresh cup of coffee. She could hear him moving about, the clatter of pans and running water providing a domestic soundtrack to her racing thoughts.

Caitlin stared at her phone. The earlier text exchange with Grammy glowed on the screen. She'd rehearsed this conversation a dozen times on the drive back from the convent, but now all her carefully planned words had evaporated. How did you tell someone their entire life story was different from the one they'd been told? How did you resurrect a mother from the grave of abandonment?

Before she could lose her nerve, she pressed Grammy's contact. The phone rang once, twice—

"Caitlin, darling." Grammy's voice, thin but alert, carried across the line from South Carolina. "I've been staring at this phone like a teenager waiting for a boy to call. Tell me what you found."

"Grammy..." Caitlin's voice cracked. She cleared her throat, tried again. "I found where Ellen is buried. St Brigid's Convent in Galway."

A sharp intake of breath. "The convent...?"

"I met with Mother Angela. She showed me Ellen's file, Grammy. And I visited her grave." Caitlin closed her eyes, picturing the modest granite stone. "The headstone reads 'Ellen McGrath Power, Mother of Bridget and Seán, Finally at Peace.'"

"Finally at peace," Grammy repeated softly. "What else did the file say?"

"She didn't just die in childbirth. Grammy, she... she died of grief. The records say she never recovered after they took you away. When Seán was born, she begged them not to take him too, but..." Caitlin's throat tightened. "She stopped eating. Mother Angela says the trauma was just too much for her. She had what we know as postpartum depression, but the nuns back then..."

Silence stretched across the ocean. Then a sound – half sob, half gasp.

"She fought for us?" Grammy's voice was barely a whisper.

"Every day. The nun said Ellen was punished for sneaking off to see you outside of the allotted times. She fought them, Grammy." Caitlin wiped her eyes. "She never stopped loving you."

"Those nuns told me she didn't want me. That I was wicked, that she was a sinner who abandoned me." Anger crept into Grammy's voice now. "All lies."

"I know. Mother Angela apologized for what the convent did back then. She said it was wrong, all of it." Caitlin paused. "Grammy, there's more. About Seán."

"Tell me."

"He was adopted by a woman named Sarah O'Riordan. She was connected to families here in Ballycluan – the village where I'm staying. But she was also once engaged to your uncle, Seamus. The locals remember her. She wanted to adopt both of you, but her husband would only agree to one child."

"Someone wanted us both?" The wonder in Grammy's voice broke Caitlin's heart.

"Yes. And, Grammy… I think Seán might have lived here. Or at least visited. There's an old man at the pub who reacts strangely whenever I mention his name. I'm going to keep investigating."

"My baby brother." Grammy's voice strengthened. "He could have children, grandchildren. I might have more family."

"That's what I'm going to find out." Caitlin shifted on the sofa. "Grammy, I also learned about Ellen's life before the convent. She wasn't just some fallen woman like the nuns made you believe. She was part of a close family, parents and brothers who loved her – Patrick and Seamus McGrath. They all got caught up in the War of Independence."

"The documents Gavin sent mentioned her brothers, but not much detail."

Caitlin hesitated. This was the hardest part. "Seamus was murdered by the Black and Tans. But Patrick survived the war.

Grammy... there's something difficult I need to tell you about what happened after."

"What do you mean?"

"Patrick killed your father. It happened after the Civil War ended." The words felt heavy in her mouth. "I don't know all the details yet, but it seems the Civil War split families apart. Brothers against brothers."

Stunned silence. Then, barely audible: "Ellen's own brother killed her husband?"

"Yes. Can you imagine what that did to her? Losing Seamus in the war, then having Patrick kill John? And there was more – Ellen had a dear friend, Isabella Russell, from the local big house. She was murdered along with her Irish lover. The whole area was torn apart by the violence."

"My God." Grammy's voice was hollow. "No wonder she ended up at the convent. Her brother killed her husband. How does someone survive that?"

"She didn't, really. She had you and baby Seán, but no family left to help her. No money. Patrick might as well have been dead to her after what he did." Caitlin wiped her eyes. "She lost everyone – one brother dead, the other a killer, her husband killed by her own blood, her best friend murdered. And then the convent took her children."

Grammy made a sound of pure anguish. "No wonder she couldn't go on. To lose so much..."

"But she loved you until the end. The records are clear about that. You were never unwanted, never a burden. You were loved more than you can imagine."

"All these years," Grammy whispered. "All these years I thought... Oh, Mam." The childhood word slipped out. "I remember her singing. Those Irish songs I've been humming my whole life."

"The nun put fresh flowers on her grave for our visit," Caitlin said softly. "Purple asters and white roses. It's peaceful there, Grammy. A stone wall, old trees. You can hear birds singing."

"Will you go back? Take flowers from me?"

"Of course. I'll tell her everything. How strong you are, how you raised me." Caitlin's voice caught. "I already told her you remember. That you never forgot her songs."

"Did you... did you take any pictures?" Grammy's voice was hesitant, hopeful.

"I did." Caitlin pulled up the photos on her phone. "I'm sending one to you now. Can you see it?"

She heard the soft ping on Grammy's end, then silence. A long moment passed.

"Oh." The single syllable carried ninety-one years of longing. "She has a proper stone. With her name. With our names."

"Ellen McGrath Power, Mother of Bridget and Seán, Finally at Peace," Caitlin recited from memory. "You're named on it, Grammy. You were never forgotten."

"She claimed us." Grammy's voice broke. "Even in death, she claimed us as hers."

They sat with that truth, connected across the miles by technology Ellen could never have imagined, sharing an image of a grave that proved a mother's love had been carved in stone.

Caitlin wiped her face with her sleeve. From the kitchen came the sound of Conor quietly closing a cabinet, giving her privacy while staying near.

Grammy's voice turned hard. "Those *nuns*. Those righteous, Christian women who thought they knew better. Who decided a mother's love wasn't enough if there wasn't money or a man's name attached to it."

"Grammy—"

"No, let me be angry, Caitlin. I've spent ninety-one years thinking I was unwanted. Let me be angry for her. For all of us."

Heartbreakingly, Caitlin could hear the soft sound of her grandmother crying. Finally, Grammy spoke again, quieter now.

"And Seán. You'll keep looking?"

"Yes."

"He'd be in his eighties if he's alive. My baby brother." Wonder crept into Grammy's voice. "I might have family. Real family."

"You have family either way," Caitlin said, firmly. "You have me. And now you know Ellen loved you. That has to count for something."

"It counts for everything." Grammy's voice was fierce. "Everything, darling girl. You've given me my mother back. Given me the truth. That's worth more than all the years of not knowing."

They talked for another few minutes – Grammy asking about the convent, about Ireland, about the village where Ellen had lived. Finally, reluctantly, Caitlin yawned.

"You should rest. It's late there."

"I love you, Grammy."

"I love you too, darling. My brave girl. Ellen would have been so proud to know you."

After they hung up, Caitlin sat in the gathering darkness, phone still warm in her hand. Conor appeared in the doorway, backlit by the kitchen light, his tall frame creating a solid silhouette against the brightness. She watched him step forward, those steady physiotherapist's hands loose at his sides, blue-green eyes searching her face in the dim light with genuine concern. "How did she take it?"

She couldn't find the words. He lowered himself beside her, offering his quiet, steady warmth and presence as she leaned into him.

FIFTY-THREE

The next morning, a knock, crisp and sudden, broke the quiet. Caitlin had been sorting through Ellen's documents, trying to piece together a timeline for Grammy, when the sound made her jump. Through the window, she was surprised to see Harry Bennett standing on her doorstep.

Gone was the jovial pub regular. This was a different man entirely. His shoulders were squared, his ruddy face set in grim lines. He carried a manila folder under one arm.

Caitlin opened the door, her cop instincts immediately alert. "Mr Bennett."

"Miss O'Shea." He shifted his weight, uncomfortable. "Sorry to disturb you at home. Wondered if we might have a word?"

Something in his tone made her step aside. "Of course. Come in."

He entered slowly, taking in the cottage with a policeman's automatic assessment. His gaze lingered on the documents spread across her table – Ellen's photos, the convent records, genealogy charts.

"Can I get you something? Tea? Something stronger?"

"Nothing, thanks." He remained standing, turning the folder over in his hands. "I owe you an apology. And an explanation."

Caitlin gestured to a chair, taking one herself. "About yesterday at the pub?"

Harry's laugh was bitter. "About your great-uncle." He finally sat, placing the folder carefully on the table between them. "I've been carrying this around for days, trying to decide whether to come. Delia said you deserved to know. Said keeping secrets hadn't done anyone any good."

"Know what?"

Harry opened the folder, revealing yellowed newspaper clippings and official documents. A photograph sat on top. A young man in a Garda uniform, serious-faced but with kind eyes. The resemblance to Grammy was unmistakable.

"Kevin O'Riordan. You know him as Seán Power." Harry's voice was rough. "He was a Garda. A cop, like yourself. One of the finest officers I ever served with. He'd been on the force since 1947. I was assigned to work with him in 1963 when I finished training. Ten years we were partners. He taught me everything. How to read a situation, how to talk to people, how to be a good Garda."

Caitlin stared at the photograph. Her grandmother's brother, in uniform. Not a lost orphan at all, but a colleague. "You worked with him?"

"I was his partner." Harry's hands clenched on the table. "And I got him killed."

Caitlin waited, her throat tight. She knew that tone – the sound of old guilt that never healed.

Harry pulled out a newspaper clipping. The headline screamed: **GARDA KILLED IN BANK ROBBERY – IRA SUSPECTED.**

"It was January the fifteenth, 1973." Harry's voice was barely audible. "Allied Irish Bank on Main Street in Sligo. Kevin and I were on foot patrol, just a routine morning beat. We walked past the bank and saw the door slightly open, which was odd for that time of day."

He stopped, staring at the clipping. Caitlin could see his hands trembling slightly.

"I wanted to call for backup. That was procedure. But Kevin... he heard something inside. A woman crying. He said we couldn't wait while civilians were in danger."

The cottage was silent except for the wind outside and the distant sound of waves.

"They came out shooting." Harry's words were flat now, emotionless in the way of someone who'd told a story too many times. "Five of them, two armed with pistols. We took cover behind the patrol car. We weren't armed, of course."

His voice cracked. "Kevin saw a woman with a child, trapped between the bank entrance and the gunmen. He broke cover to get them to safety. I should have provided a distraction. Should have done something. But I froze."

Caitlin closed her eyes, already knowing how this story ended.

"The bullet caught him in the chest. No vest. We didn't wear them routinely then." Harry's voice broke completely. "I held him while we waited for the ambulance. He kept apologizing. Can you imagine? Dying because he saved a mother and child, and he was apologizing to me for not following procedure."

Tears ran down Harry's weathered face unchecked. "He died before the ambulance arrived. Bled out in my arms on that cold pavement while those bastards got away."

"It wasn't your fault," Caitlin whispered. "You were following training. He made a choice—"

"The right choice." Harry's voice was fierce. "He made the right choice, and I made the coward's choice. That's what I've lived with for decades. The woman and child lived because of Kevin O'Riordan. They lived because he was a better man than me."

Caitlin forced her voice past the lump in her throat. "I-I had to leave the police force over something similar. Three people, friends, good cops, died because of choices I made. It's easy to look back after the fact and decide you made the wrong move. But when you're pinned down and everything goes sideways, sometimes survival is the only choice left. I know what that haunting feels like. It's the hardest thing to carry."

He looked into her eyes, his expression almost begging to believe her.

"Harry, sometimes bad things happen to good people. It's not your fault, just like it wasn't mine. The fault lies with those who took the shot."

Caitlin stood and fetched some tissues. She squeezed his shoulder before handing him a couple and taking a few herself.

After a few moments, Harry pushed another document across the table. "This was in his desk at work. Never sent."

Caitlin picked up the faded envelope. It was addressed to Sister Catherine, St Brigid's Convent, Galway.

"He was trying to find his sister," Harry said. "We found drafts of other letters. He'd been researching, trying to trace what happened to her. But back then, the convents wouldn't release information. Sealed records, they said. Best for everyone."

The letter was brief:

Dear Sister Catherine,

I write once again seeking information about my sister, Bridget Power, who I believe was sent to America from your convent in 1924. I know you have told me such records are sealed, but I beg you to reconsider. I am all the family she has left in Ireland, and she is all I have of my birth mother. Surely God's mercy extends to reuniting a brother and sister separated by circumstances beyond their control?
I await your response with hope.

Your servant, Kevin Seán O'Riordan (on your records as Seán Power)

"He never got to send it," Harry said. "Wrote it the week before he died."

Caitlin pressed the letter to her chest, feeling the weight of another tragedy. Seán had died never knowing Bridget was alive in

Charleston. Grammy had lived her whole life never knowing she had a brother who'd searched for her.

"Why didn't you tell me this when I mentioned him at the pub?" she asked.

Harry's shoulders sagged. "Because I'm a coward. Same coward who froze that day in Sligo. Because talking about Kevin means admitting I failed him. Because I've spent years trying to drink away the memory of my best friend bleeding out while I stood there useless."

He met her eyes directly. "And because you look like him. Same eyes. Same way of holding yourself. When you said his name Seán at the pub, when I realized who you were... it brought it all back." He looked away, "I went to stay with my brother rather than face you. But I couldn't stay away. You deserve to know."

He gestured to the folder. "That's everything I saved. Newspaper clippings, commendations, photos from his passing-out parade."

"Did Sarah know he was trying to find Bridget?"

"She encouraged it. Used to say her greatest regret was not fighting harder to take both children back in 1924." Harry stood slowly, like his bones ached. "She died young of TB, but she told Kevin all about his real family."

"And Seán's – Kevin's family? Did he have a wife and children?"

Harry's expression softened slightly. "Mary. Good woman. She remarried a few years after, moved to Cork. Two boys, Shane and Patrick. They'd be in their sixties now. Lost touch after the move, but..." He pulled out a final piece of paper. "This is Mary's sister's address in Galway. She might know where to find them."

He moved toward the door, then paused. "Your great-uncle was the finest man I ever knew. The best copper, the best friend, the best human being. I've lived with failing him every day since. But knowing his sister's family has finally come home... maybe that's something. Maybe Kevin's story doesn't have to end in that street in Sligo."

After Harry left, Caitlin sat surrounded by the pieces of Kevin O'Riordan's life. Photographs of him in uniform, standing proud. Articles honouring his sacrifice. Commendations for bravery. The letter he never got to send. The contact details for his family.

She thought of Grammy in her hospital bed, believing she'd been abandoned and forgotten. All these years, her brother had been searching for her. Had died a hero, trying to protect strangers the same way he'd tried to find and protect his sister.

The tragedy of it all was overwhelming. Two siblings, an ocean apart, each believing they were alone in the world. Seán spending decades trying to breach the convent's silence. Grammy thinking she had no family who wanted her.

Both of them wrong.

But there was something else too. Love had endured across oceans, across decades. Seán had never stopped looking. Grammy had never stopped hoping. And now, finally, the circle was closing.

Caitlin picked up her phone to call Grammy. She had another story to tell now. One of heroism and heartbreak, but also of a brother's love that had never wavered, even unto death.

And, Kevin O'Riordan's sons might still be alive. Grammy had nephews. Family she'd never known existed.

The search wasn't over. It was just beginning. When Conor came around later, she'd give him the update. With his local knowledge and her investigative skills, they'd track down her relations. They had to.

EPILOGUE

FIVE MONTHS LATER

The Atlantic stretched before Caitlin, unchanged yet somehow different. Her leg protested only faintly as she navigated the familiar path along the water's edge, each step steadier than the last. Finn raced ahead, his bark carrying on the salt wind as he charged at gulls that lifted lazily into the grey morning sky.

Her phone vibrated against her hip. Delia's message glowed on the screen:

> Still on for brunch? Paddy's made those scones you love.

Caitlin typed back, smiling.

> On my way.

Their weekly gatherings at Tierney's had evolved from tentative meetings into something that felt like family gatherings. Even Harry showed up these days. Sober, sharp-eyed, his encyclopaedic knowledge of cold cases earning him a consultant's pass. He'd been helpful to Caitlin with the paperwork required to become an Irish citizen on the basis that her grandmother was born in Ireland.

The cottage door opened behind her. Her cottage. The thought still amazed her sometimes – this small miracle bought with compensation money she'd never wanted to earn. Conor emerged carrying two steaming mugs, his hair tousled by the morning breeze.

She launched Finn's stick in a high arc down the beach.

"Good arm."

Six months ago, that throw would have been impossible. "Good physiotherapist," she countered, accepting the coffee gratefully. The warmth seeped through her fingers.

"The one I found you, or my grandmother's seaweed poultices?" Conor's eyes crinkled with mischief.

"Your physio friend is brilliant. Your foul-smelling salves..." She wrinkled her nose. "Let's just say I'm grateful you don't have a good sense of smell."

"They worked, didn't they?" He looked absurdly pleased with himself. "Four generations of wisdom can't be wrong."

"I smelled like low tide for weeks. Finn wouldn't come near me."

"But you can throw a stick now." He ducked as she swatted at him, laughing. "Traditional methods have their place."

He pulled her into a long, deep kiss.

"Your grandmother called again?"

"This morning." Caitlin's voice softened. "She's definitely coming for Christmas. And she's bringing someone."

Conor's eyebrows lifted. "Who?"

"Josephine. Seán's granddaughter." The words still felt surreal. "Harry tracked her down through the old records. She reached out to Grammy, asked permission to visit. They've been corresponding."

"After ninety-one years," Conor murmured.

"Grammy cried when she told me about their first meeting. Josephine works in food production, travels to Charleston sometimes for business. They talked for hours." Caitlin's throat tightened. "Can you imagine? Finally meeting family you thought was lost forever?"

"It must have been difficult. Learning how her brother died, the violence done in the name of ideals he never knew."

Caitlin nodded slowly. Ireland's wounds ran deep – the push for independence, the lingering divisions in the north, the Good Friday Agreement that had brought uneasy peace but not resolution. And now new troubles: drug gangs poisoning communities, old hatreds waiting for the smallest spark to reignite.

"You're miles away," Conor said gently.

She blinked. "Sorry. Just thinking about all the stories we've uncovered. The families we've found."

Her work with Mother Angela and Mrs Walsh had expanded beyond her grandmother's search. Together they'd begun the painstaking process of identifying the unmarked graves at the convent, giving names back to the nameless. Each small victory felt like lifting a stone from her chest.

The work gave her days shape and meaning. Her Charleston rental and settlement check meant she didn't have to worry about bills while she traced lost connections and fought for recognition. It hadn't been enough to just put flowers on the unmarked convent graves. Those patches of grass with no stone, no name, no acknowledgment wouldn't stay that way. Not on her watch. Some days, the weight of all those erased lives nearly crushed her. But for every hard day, there was another where she matched a name to an unmarked plot, a photo to a family, a child to their history. She wasn't just healing others' wounds anymore. With each grave marked and each file recovered, she was slowly, carefully, healing her own.

"We'll need a bigger table for Christmas," Conor said, his arm sliding around her waist.

She turned to face him, this steady presence who'd anchored her through the storms. "Maybe a bigger house. Eventually."

The word hung between them like a promise. Inside the cottage, Ellen McGrath's photograph kept watch from the mantel, flanked by Seán's letter and a growing collection of recovered family photos. No longer artefacts of tragedy, but pieces of a story that led, somehow, to now.

Her phone buzzed again. Time for the brunch at Tierney's.

"Ready?" Conor asked.

Caitlin gazed out at the Atlantic – the same ocean that touched Charleston's shores, that Ellen had watched with hope and heartbreak, that had carried Bridget away and decades later brought Caitlin home.

"Ready."

They walked toward the village, Finn trotting contentedly beside them, his treasure forgotten in the shallows. Caitlin's limp had faded to barely a memory. The ghosts, Mark, her team who'd died, her own failures, still visited sometimes in the small hours. But they no longer owned her days.

Later, standing at the cottage window while Conor made dinner, Caitlin watched the tide retreat across the sand. Grammy's voice from their morning call still echoed: fierce, loving, unbreakable. Alive and coming home, or perhaps to Caitlin's new home, which amounted to the same thing.

She pressed her palm to the cool glass. This view no longer felt like the edge of the world but its centre. The stone-walled fields, the wood smoke, the crying gulls, all of it had worked its way into her bones during her healing.

A year ago she'd been counting pills on a Charleston couch, drowning in silence and shame. Now she stood here with scars that had become stories, with a man who saw past the damage to the woman still standing, with a horizon wide enough to hold whatever came next.

The past could not be erased. Ellen's choices, John's years in prison, Seamus's sacrifice, all of it was woven into the story she now carried. But alongside the grief, something unexpected had taken root. Hope.

She opened the window, letting the sharp sea air flood the

room. "Brave girl," Grammy always called her. For the first time in months, Caitlin believed it.

Soon, Christmas lights would string through the village streets. Fires would glow in every hearth. And for once, she would not be passing through.

She belonged here.

A LETTER FROM THE AUTHOR

Thank you so much for reading *The Irish Orphan's Secret*. If you want to join other readers in hearing all about my new releases and bonus content, you can sign up for my newsletter.

www.stormpublishing.co/rachel-wesson

If you enjoyed this book and could spare a few moments to leave a review, that would be hugely appreciated. Even a short review can make all the difference in encouraging a reader to discover my books for the first time. Thank you so much!

Irish history has always fascinated me. The more I read, the more I realize nothing is ever straightforward. Unlike the global conflicts of the World Wars, where the dividing lines were often drawn more clearly, Ireland's past is tangled with contradictions, divided loyalties, and stories where neighbours could be both allies and enemies.

The idea for this book began, as so many of my stories do, with my own family. While researching my roots, I stumbled across the Loughnane brothers – two young men from County Galway, brutally murdered during the War of Independence. As I traced names and connections through parish records and faded family stories, I began to wonder if they might, in fact, have been relations of mine. That possibility lit a spark in me. What would it have been like to live in a time when every choice carried risk, when silence could be as dangerous as action, and when even family ties could not protect you from suspicion?

It is from that seed of curiosity that this story grew. It is not a retelling of the Loughnane brothers' fate, but rather an exploration of the world they lived in – where courage, betrayal, sacrifice and hope sat side by side. Ireland's history is full of such stories, layered and complex, where truth is rarely simple and memory is often contested.

Even today, those rifts run through families. I remember my maternal grandparents sitting at either side of the fire, arguing – she with Michael Collins, he with Dev – and the battle was still alive in our house well into the 1970s. That taught me early on that history isn't just something you read in books; it lingers in our homes, our conversations, our silences.

While researching, I also found myself drawn once more into one of the most painful chapters of our past – the mother and baby homes and Magdalene laundries. I first explored these institutions while writing *Stolen from Her Mother*, but in researching this new book I uncovered even more heartbreaking truths about the lives of the women who endured them. So many births were never registered, deaths went unrecorded, and when they were, they were often entered under incomplete or incorrect names. Families searching for loved ones still face long waits for access to records, layers of bureaucracy, and far too many unanswered questions. Despite inquiries and renewed public awareness, much remains hidden. It is a part of our shared history that continues to echo – a reminder of how easily silence can conceal suffering, and how vital it is to remember.

Just this month, four survivors of these homes and similar "Christian" institutions are on hunger strike in Dublin. They are demanding the Irish Government give them the same rights other old age pensioners get i.e. pensions, health cards etc..

Thank you for reading my books, for sharing in these journeys through Ireland's past, and for keeping these stories alive. Every message, review and recommendation means more than I can ever say. You remind me that storytelling connects us – that by remembering, by listening, by caring, we honour those whose voices were once lost.

Best wishes,

Rachel

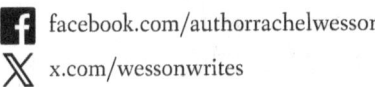

https://rachelwesson.com

facebook.com/authorrachelwesson
x.com/wessonwrites

ACKNOWLEDGMENTS

My deepest thanks to my editor, Vicky, whose guidance, clarity and unfailing support strengthened this book from the very first page. I am truly grateful for your expertise and your patience.

To the incredible team at Storm, thank you for everything you do behind the scenes. Your professionalism, creativity and kindness make the publishing journey a joy.

To my fellow authors who encouraged, advised and cheered me on at every stumbling point. Your generosity means more than you know.

To my family, for their love, endurance and understanding through deadlines, rewrites and long writing days.

And finally, to the readers. Thank you for opening your hearts to these stories, for every message and review, and for every quiet moment spent with my books. You are the reason any of this is possible.

Thank you, all of you, for walking this path with me.

Finally, this book is dedicated to the women and children of the Magdalene laundries and all similar institutions. May your stories continue to be told, and may we never again look away.

www.ingramcontent.com/pod-product-compliance
Lightning Source LLC
LaVergne TN
LVHW031536060526
838200LV00056B/4517